I JUST WANT MY PANTS BACK

I JUST WANT MY PANTS BACK

A NOVEL

David J. Rosen

BROADWAY BOOKS
NEW YORK

PUBLISHED BY BROADWAY BOOKS

Copyright © 2007 by David J. Rosen

All Rights Reserved

Published in the United States by Broadway Books, an
imprint of The Doubleday Broadway Publishing Group, a
division of Random House, Inc., New York.
www.broadwaybooks.com

BROADWAY BOOKS and its logo, a letter B bisected on the
diagonal, are trademarks of Random House, Inc.

LIBRARY OF CONGRESS CATALOGING-IN-PUBLICATION DATA
Rosen, David J.
I just want my pants back / David J. Rosen. — 1st ed.
p. cm.
1. Jewish men—Fiction. 2. New York (N.Y.)—Fiction. I. Title.

PS3618.O8314I18 2007
813'.6—dc22
2007000293

ISBN: 978-0-7679-2794-9

PRINTED IN THE UNITED STATES OF AMERICA

FOR RACHEL, DAMN IT.

All of man's problems stem from his inability to sit in a quiet room alone.

—BLAISE PASCAL

I JUST WANT MY PANTS BACK

I was a bored and hungry mammal. I lived in a small apartment on Perry Street that had a working fireplace, but only if you could find logs the size of cupcakes, as my hearth had the dimensions of an Easy-Bake Oven. I sat on my fire escape and watched happy couples come and go, finishing the rhyme in my head, "talking of Michelangelo." But they were never really discussing Michelangelo. Marc Jacobs, who had opened a store on the corner, was a more likely subject. I wasn't bitter. I didn't want a girlfriend, not really, at least not right away. But I could have used a functional vagina. It had been a while since I'd had access to one of those, and my penis kept reminding me how accommodating they could be.

Sunday was winding down, and the streetlights flickered to life. It was early April and the day had held hope that spring had finally arrived, but as the sun set a cool breeze informed us we weren't quite there yet. I zipped up my sweatshirt and wished once again that I smoked. It just seemed like something that might be nice to do, romantic. I stared at Hunan Pan across the street; soon I would call them as I always did, and they would bring me my supper. It was getting a little embarrassing, though.

"Hello, this Hunan Pan."

"Hi, can I get an order for delivery?"

"You ninety-nine Perry, number Three-A?"

"Um, yeah."

"Steamed vegetable dumplings and moo-shu chicken with extra pancake?"

"No, um, the dumplings and moo-shu beef."

"You sure?"

Sigh. "Fine. Give me the chicken."

"Okay. Fifteen minute, Mr. Snuka."

They may have known my voice, but they'd never know my name. I wasn't Mr. Snuka, aka Jimmy "Superfly" Snuka, the wrestler from the eighties. I was Jason Strider, a Jewish guy with sideburns. Ever since I moved to New York three years ago, I had used pseudonyms when ordering in. Raphael's, my second most frequent takeout, knew me as Sir Peter O'Toole.

I slipped back through the window into my apartment and began weighing options for the evening. Common sense held that I should eat my dinner, watch *The Simpsons* like the rest of my demographic, and get a reasonable night of sleep before work the next day.

But my penis, my damn penis. He just wouldn't shut up. And I had to admit, his argument wasn't without merit, or logic. His basic premise: "Any girl out tonight might be just as desperate as you." I offered that I had been out a lot this week; the last two nights hadn't ended until way into the morning, and even now a slight hangover hummed behind my eyes. But Lil' Petey, as I called him, was persuasive. The problem with being a boy is the constant struggle between listening to your brain and listening to your dick. The problem with being me was that somehow my dick had acquired the argumentative skills of a debate team captain. Or perhaps I was just weak.

I took a quick shower and had just barely gotten a towel

around me as the buzzer rang, announcing the arrival of my supper. I opened the door a crack and handed a small Hispanic man a few crumpled bills in exchange for his one crumpled bag. I quickly pulled on jeans and, over a long-sleeved T-shirt, a short-sleeved one that read "Henry Rollins Is No Fun." Then I began to eat straight from the cardboard boxes. Yum, the taste of déjà vu. Once finished, I went back into the bathroom and fussed with my hair a bit; it was the same shortish, messyish style that I had sported in one iteration or another since the bad Steve Perry bi-level back in junior high. I looked at the circles under my eyes. Darker and deeper every day. They were the reason I had, about six months ago, forgone my contacts and started wearing glasses, thick black frames I might've stolen from Elvis Costello, if we had similar prescriptions. Plus, the first night I had gone out with my glasses on, I had made out with a ridiculously hot girl. Call me superstitious.

I fished through the papers on my coffee table and found the flyer that a random woman with a disturbing number of facial piercings had given me on the subway. The LiZee Band, Sunday at 8:30, at the Umbrella Room. The band was named for the girl herself. She had dyed black hair and wore an ill-fitting business suit; it was a look that said, "It's because I have to, okay?" She'd approached me and every other young person on the F train, given us flyers, and invited us to see her band. The Umbrella Room was literally five blocks from my house. And eight-thirty was nice and early. It seemed worth the risk. Lil' Petey 1, Jason 0.

It was almost eight, so I cannonballed the ass-end of a joint with the remaining third of a two-liter Diet Coke and let them race each other to see which could get to my brain first. For me, Diet Coke and marijuana went together like ice-cold milk and an Oreo cookie. Like Jacoby and Meyers. Like sha-nah-nah-nah yippity-dip-da-do. I hit the lights, locked my door, and let gravity take me down the stairs like a slightly bent Slinky. Once I was outside, the cool night air felt great against my skin. I searched my mind for an adjective better than "great." I had been an English major, after all; I had been taught to avoid mundane adjectives. Refreshing, soothing, bracing . . . nope, "great" really did best describe the feeling.

I turned up Hudson and looked across the street at the people hanging out in front of the White Horse Tavern. The White Horse was where Dylan Thomas supposedly mumbled, "I've had eighteen straight whiskies, I think that's the record . . ." before keeling over and dying a few days later. It's an unproven story, but that didn't stop busloads of tourists in matching sweat suits from rolling up every Thursday through Saturday. Tonight, however, it looked as if just a few folks from the neighborhood were hanging out by the door, enjoying the evening. One was Patty, the fiftysomething bohemian woman who lived across the hall from me. Gray-haired, a bit of a mutterer, she wore sandals all year round: rain, snow, locusts—sandals. I never used to see her much, but lately we'd been bumping into each other in the building more often. I imagined her to be some sort of lesbian poet who chain-smoked cigarillos and once let Allen Ginsberg sleep in her bathtub because he was "tired and also filthy, just filthy." The one thing I did know from peeking at her rent bill (our landlord taped them to our doors like your mother might tape a note to "clean your room") was that she paid only $210 a month for the same apartment I paid a grand for. And a thousand bucks was considered a deal. So I kept an ear open every time she left her apartment, lest she fall down the stairs and I could inherit the New York dream. I was joking, but she had once given me a card with her "lawyer's" number on it, just in case anything should happen to her. Then she gave me an orange she wasn't going to eat.

"Hey, Patty!" I yelled across the street.

She waved. "Hi, neighbor."

I waved back but quickened my step. I was stoned and easily distracted and didn't want to fly off on a tangent. High, I often went too far for too little. No, I was on a mission. I was going to see this LiZee group. They might just become my new favorite band. Maybe I would buy a T-shirt and start a blog.

Going to a bar alone is no big deal for some people, but for me it was always a bit of an awkward experience. Somehow it always felt as if everyone were looking at me. "Did he come by himself?" "Did he get stood up by a girl?" "Poor guy might be suicidal, let's step away in case he tries to off himself and we get hit with flesh shrapnel; this is a new shirt." It wasn't something I did often, but I liked the adventure of it, although I had to deal with the slight anxiety as well. The pot both helped and hurt. It motivated me out of the house and led me to believe I might be the funniest person ever to roam the planet, but once inside the bar it sometimes gave me the inner confidence of a man whose fly was stuck open.

This was a side effect of partying that my friends and I called "The Fear." Mild paranoia was just a touch of The Fear, hardly worth bothering with; a full dose really came the morning after, a bottomless pit of regret and shame fueled by drugs, alcohol, lack of sleep, and the insidious feeling that you had somehow just fucked up monumentally. I had learned to live with The Fear, but we were not very good roommates and I believed he was using my toothbrush.

Luckily, when I arrived at the Umbrella, the LiZee band was already onstage tuning up, so I felt like just another guy who had come to check them out. The Umbrella was a tiny bar with a tiny stage; it was pretty dingy, with an, um, umbrella motif. There was one black one nailed to the brick wall behind the bar.

I made my way toward it and praised Vishnu that there was an open stool. I climbed aboard and ordered a Bud; it seemed like a Bud moment.

The band continued to sound-check. The guitarist, a balding, rotund dude whose tight T-shirt revealed a muffin-top of flab over the waist of his jeans, stood next to the bassist, a shockingly thin poster-boy for meth awareness. Together they looked like before and after, plus side effects. Their random plucking morphed into actual playing and suddenly LiZee started singing. She was no longer confined to her business suit; now she wore a white shirt and ripped pink tights. She was rubbing against the monitors provocatively, shrieking passionately, going for a sort of Karen O vibe. Even the most tone-deaf could hear she was missing. The only thing that kept me from leaving after song two was inertia. They had some damn comfortable bar stools at the Umbrella.

A girl squeezed between me and the guy on the next stool, who I was sure was related to someone in the band named Jimmy. Or else maybe he just liked to yell, "You rip, Jimmy!" The girl had plastic glasses similar to mine but tortoiseshell; her hair was in pigtails. She held her money up but was overlooked. Petey stirred.

"Want me to get the bartender?" I asked her over the music.

She smiled. "Thanks, could you ask her for a Jameson's, please?" She handed me a ten.

I took her money. "Uh-huh, no problem." Just a single drink, she was probably here alone. My crotch was gloating already. I made eye contact with the bartender, who shot back the "I see you but wait your fucking turn" look. An awkward moment passed. "She saw me, but I think she's making a martini for someone first," I said to the girl.

"That's cool. So how do you know this band?" She had a

smattering of freckles, and she did a sweet squinty thing when she pushed her glasses up her nose. She was so cute it hurt.

"I don't, actually." I told her the train story. "I was sitting home bored and I figured what the hell." I was hoping I had good breath, as she was fairly close to me. I dug in my pocket for a mint. Nothing.

"I don't know them either," she said. "I was walking past and I saw them setting up so I came in to watch. What do you think?" She twirled her hair, just like girls do on TV.

"Um . . . what do *you* think?" I responded, just as the bartender leaned in. "Jameson's please," I said, smiling at her.

"Rocks?" She sneered. She could hardly tolerate me. I fucking hated bartenders like that. Why the anger? You're at work and a band is playing, life is not so awful. I looked at my pigtailed friend.

"Neat please," she said. The bartender fixed it and I paid, giving the change to Pigtails. "I'm Jane," she said to me, holding up her drink.

"Jason." I clinked her glass with the Bud, which was getting low. "Nice to meet you."

"You too." She sipped and smiled.

The band played for another half hour but the last thing we did was listen. Jane started telling me about a "gorgeous" Swiss Mountain Dog she had seen on the way to the bar that had made her really want a puppy, and I responded with a story about Daisy, my dog growing up, that didn't really go anywhere except prove that when younger I'd given my dog a pretty queer name. Luckily, the pointless anecdote didn't put her off. She flashed me a grin, perfect teeth wet with whiskey.

"So, what do you do, Jason?"

The smile hung there, full of promise. I decided not to disappoint it with the truth.

We left before the last E chord died, and walked down Hudson. "So no way, you're really an orthodontist? I always thought of them as older," said Jane, now wearing a cabbie hat and strolling alongside me. She lived in Brooklyn and we were walking sort of toward a subway. We were near my apartment, but I was feeling a little too chicken to close the deal.

"Well, I'm not like a regular one, like in the 'burbs," I said, hands jammed in my pockets. "I'm a downtown, New York City orthodontist. My clientele are all artists and fashion people and their kids. Jeff Koons designed my office, know him?" She nodded. "Our dental chairs look like oversized red tongues, and all my dental hygienists wear big plushy costumes like Barney, but they're not dinosaurs, it's all dental-related—they're like molars and toothbrushes and plaque and stuff. Once Sting came in for a retainer and had me record the whole procedure on a DAT." I lowered my voice. "He's got a receding gumline, you know."

"Oh my God, Sting? That's hilarious." We walked on a bit more. "So what do you want to do now? Do you want to call it a night?"

"Um, I'm up for something. I could get another drink."

"I'm kind of hungry, actually; I didn't have dinner yet," she said, adjusting her hat. We stopped and looked around. There were no restaurants on the block.

"Well, we could go to my apartment, back there on Perry, and order in. And if you want, I have some weed there." I immediately regretted that choice of word, it sounded so AEΠ. But it didn't matter.

"That sounds perfect."

We sat on my small green couch. She finished off a slice while I twisted a joint. "Sandinista" by the Clash was in the stereo; not the sexiest choice, but it was what was already in there when I hit PLAY and I went with it. She excused herself to go to the bathroom, and I flicked the lighter and inhaled some smoke. Instantly I felt it, a small tingling in my ears and a bit of nervous energy. The toilet flushed and my mind began racing with the fresh THC and adrenaline. This was just too easy. What was up with this girl? What if she rifled through my wallet in the middle of the night and stole my Discover card? What if she had a penis? I made a mental note to check for an Adam's apple. I heard her gargling; she must've found my Duane Reade generic mint mouthwash. Christ, how embarrassing. I should've spent the extra forty cents for a name-brand variety.

The door opened and she sat down next to me. I handed her the joint and took a sip of her water. We started a halting conversation about God knows what, both of us waiting for the inevitable to happen. I put my hand on her leg and took the joint gently from her fingertips. Joe Strummer sang "Italian mobster shoots a lobster, seafood restaurant gets outta hand..." I started saying something about how the Clash were really influenced by Jamaican dub and then, I don't know who started it, but after seconds of leaning closer and closer to each other, we started kissing deeply.

The first trading of tongues officially ended my months of rejection, and I resisted the urge to hop up and perform a victory dance—an Icky shuffle or some spirited clogging. After what felt like the right amount of time, I gently reached up her skirt and made with the artful rubbing of the naughty pieces. It was fun sometimes to go vagina before going boobs, kept 'em guessing. Not that I didn't get to those, stat. One nipple was pierced with a hoop, but I didn't let that throw me; a few years back I had learned the hard way that the most important thing with those was simply not to yank them.

Jane unbuckled my belt and released Petey, who stood at attention. The same thought ran through my mind that ran through my mind every single time I hooked up: "I can't believe this girl is actually going to touch it!" Yes, every single time, it was like David beating Goliath or the apparition of Mary on a tortilla chip. A bona fide miracle.

After some grappling and half-naked clumsiness, we started toward the bedroom but never made it. As she leaned against my wobbly refrigerator and I fucked her from behind, I could hear the meager contents—an almost empty jar of Welch's grape jelly, some ancient rolls of film, and an economy-sized Heinz ketchup—fall and rattle around. She looked back at me mid-stroke and snarled, "I want you to fuck me in your fridge!" She ripped open the door and lay her chest across the wire shelf, her face wedged back near the light and a partially crushed box of baking soda that had been there since the dawn of man. "C'mon, do it!" she yelled, her voice muffled. "Fuck me!"

I thrusted and thrusted, pushing her deeper and deeper into my kitchen appliance. I was grinning like a lunatic. What a fantastic e-mail this was going to make tomorrow.

I awoke alone and surprisingly rested. Jane had taken off shortly after the sex; not only did she live in Brooklyn, but apparently she worked there too, so there was no sense really in her crashing at my house. I'd walked her outside and helped her to hail a cab. She gave me a peck good night, told me she had left her number upstairs, hopped in, and was off.

I sat up, rubbed my eyes, and allowed myself a celebratory smile, for lo, the long sexual drought was finally over. It had been four months. Tumbleweeds had begun blowing through my bedroom. A dry spell like that makes a man start to question his haircut, his clothes, if he has done anything to anger the gods. I had survived the slump the only way I knew how—positive thinking and excessive masturbation.

With girls, for me, it was always feast or famine. I was either 007 or the Elephant Man. Nothing nothing nothing, I'll never touch a girl again, then kapow! I'm kissing one girl and I have a date with a different girl later in the week. The fact that one female was interested in me seemed proof enough to others that I was worthy of fondling. Unfortunately, and more frequently, the reverse held true. So to have any hope of attracting prey, I had to keep blood in the water, like a shark fisherman. It was the Chum Theory; I hoped it would apply again now.

It was getting late. I hopped up, threw on my jeans, brushed my teeth—did only the things one deems necessary when rushing to get to work. Corners cut included showering, putting on underwear, and eating anything—other than a swallow of mint-flavored toothpaste. As I slipped on my sneakers, I saw that there was no scrap of paper with Jane's phone number in the most obvious place, on top of the coffee table. I looked around on the floor—nothing. Damn, she must've been doing the same thing as me: going out Sunday, simply looking for a little fun. How progressive. I pictured feminists everywhere slow-motion celebrating to "We Are the Champions."

"I feel so used," I joked aloud, smiling. Then the smile faded. Hey, what the fuck? How come that slut didn't want to marry me? Then I saw it. Her name, number, and e-mail scrawled in the middle of a heart she had drawn on a ripped envelope, hanging on the fridge door. "PS: You need groceries!" Clever girl. Clever, and filthy as all fuck.

I snatched it and was out the door, onto the beautiful old West Village streets. Almost every building had a historic look, stately brownstones that were painstakingly attended to. Except my building, 99 Perry. It was "painted" a pale shade of yellow, the color resembling a dirty towel that had been long forgotten, and was now covered in soot. The front door's lock was hit-or-miss, and the stairwells were creaky and peeling. It was one of the last rent-stabilized buildings in a wealthy neighborhood, and the landlord did as little as he could to keep it standing.

I hustled toward the subway. I was currently employed at a theatrical company, JB Casting. I answered the phone and manned the receptionist area. All of the actors were extra-polite to me, as if I might have pull and be able to help them get parts. It was a little sad, this job, and I had no real interest in it. As my parents might say, I was in the process of finding what I wanted to do with my life. And over the course of the last few months, I had had the epiphany that "casting director" and "receptionist" were two titles I could cross off my list.

I had graduated with honors from Cornell, but I was an English major who didn't do all the required reading and owed his diploma to the friendly folks at CliffsNotes. I had even framed the *New Testament CliffsNotes* that had gotten me through my Literature of Religion class. I hung the piece on my off-campus apartment's wall, titling it, "For Sinners Only."

After a couple of road trips down from Ithaca to see bands, I was sold on moving to the city. I had been a DJ at WBVR at school, and I figured I'd be able to find some kind of job in the music industry here, though I didn't know what. The career center had helped me get a few interviews at radio stations, but they were all in ad sales, which seemed a lot closer to telemarketing than Telecasters. Soon the rent and Hunan Pan bills were looming, so I just looked for any job to cover them until I figured out what I wanted. Truth was, I hadn't gotten around to doing a full investigation of the music world yet. I was still settling in, and frankly there were a hell of a lot more fun things to do here in the meantime. In the two and a half years since I'd arrived, I had worked three different jobs. Well, two, really; I had been a bartender at a bar that had changed names during my tenure, so I counted it as two different jobs. My friends from school mostly had found their niches by now. Even the ski bums were back from their year in Aspen serving muffins to Cher and had found entry-level jobs in PR, not that they'd even known what PR was. I traveled through Europe the summer after graduation. But when I came back, I didn't see the point in shaving every day and working long hours at something I wasn't sure I wanted to be doing.

The scary thing was that I was becoming aware that very few

people were doing what they wanted to be doing; they just got caught up in whatever they were doing long enough that it became who they were. Or as my dad put it, they had "picked and sticked." I had not. Which I'm sure ate at my folks, because they were textbook pickers and stickers. My parents still lived in the brick house where I grew up, just outside St. Louis, on a street full of brick houses. My mom had been a secretary for a local real estate attorney, Bob Hoefel, Esq., until political correctness came to town. She still worked for him, but now her title was "administrative assistant." My dad was just as loyal to his job. He worked at the same hardware store he'd been at since he was a junior at St. Louis University. Although now he was the owner. Strider's Hardware. The funny thing about that was, he wasn't remotely handy. He knew the stock like the back of his hand, he could pontificate on the subtleties that separated Benjamin Moore white dove semi-gloss from Benjamin Moore white dove eggshell, but for the love of God you didn't let the man climb a ladder to clean the gutters without a team of firemen holding out one of those "jumper" nets to catch him. His home-improvement mishaps had becoming a running joke between my mom and me.

It was pretty clear a career in home improvement wasn't his dream. But I felt like maybe dream jobs were a more contemporary desire. It seemed like in his day, a "good job" was all one looked for. Then you put a picture of your wife on your desk in the back office, pumped out a kid, managed a Little League team or two, got chubby from drinking beer and rooting for the perennially lousy Cardinals, and went into minor debt sending your wise-ass son to an Ivy League school, when he could've gone to Mizzou for close to nothing. (I felt guilty about that one. But Mizzou had scared the crap out of me—it was filled with giant corn-fed heifers of human beings—and like any eighteen-year-old, I felt the urgent need to get the hell out of Dodge.)

For some reason, my parents thought I might become a lawyer. I was never sure why they envisioned me as a legal eagle, but I supposed they saw how well Mr. Hoefel was doing. "It's a solid career," they had told me during winter break of senior year, holding out an LSAT prep book they had borrowed from the Richters next door. Cornell was pretty hard, and the last thing I wanted was more school after school. Hell, I didn't even know what lawyers did every day, except for what I had gathered watching reruns of *Matlock* while hung over. I kept picturing his desk covered with boring legal briefs and dandruff flakes.

Unfortunately New York was the kind of town where the first two questions out of people's mouths were, "What do you do?" followed by "How much is your rent?" Answering the whole truth to either of those usually wasn't the best way for me to go, if I was aiming to impress. So frequently I didn't. And although New Yorkers stayed single or married without kids well into their forties, with cutting-edge European moisturizers or smuggled infant stem cells keeping them young- and fresh-looking, beneath that veneer, they were relentlessly responsible adults. In fact, if adults were some kind of exotic animal species, New York City was their African veldt. People competed for jobs, parking, clothes, apartments, taxis, picnic spots, preschools, brunch reservations, dermatologists, dog-walkers, frozen yogurt, treadmills, Hamptons houses, seats at the movies, you name it. It made me dream about the promise of communism, but I just as soon dismissed it; there were no perfectly taut communist honeys. All those years of sausage and socialism really wreaked hell on a girl.

Hence my job at JB's, to which I was once again about to be

tardy. I got to the Twelfth Street 1 train entrance and tumbled down the stairs, pulling out my iPod and headphones as I did. I put it on shuffle, clicked PLAY, and hoped for a good subway set.

I arrived at the office at Thirty-second and Sixth at about ten-fifteen, or in layman's terms, an hour and fifteen minutes late. John Barry, the JB in JB Casting, was in his office with the door closed, so I figured I was fairly safe. It was a small office—just me, JB, another assistant like me named Melinda, and Sara, another agent. The space itself was a loft that consisted of a large reception area where actors would wait until they were called into a separate room, which contained a Polaroid camera and a video camera. There, one of us, usually Melinda, would film them doing whatever the small part required and then send a tape to the director, who would phone his choices in to John or Sara. It was pretty straightforward, and as far from glitzy Hollywood as one could get.

Melinda was on the phone at the reception desk when I walked in. I sat down beside her, went on the computer we shared, and opened up nytimes.com, my ritual; I figured it was worth seeing whether or not the world was coming to an end imminently before I started working.

Melinda hung up and pushed a few stray brown hairs behind her ear. She had a slightly round face that always sported a deadpan expression; she looked like a smart girl in Barnes & Noble, ready to say something sarcastic about your book choice.

"Good morning." She raised an eyebrow. "Doctor's appointment, right?"

Melinda had been at JB's for two years; she was an aspiring playwright, and like me, was only there for the money. Her salary went toward supporting her craft, whereas mine went toward supporting me. She was pretty funny too—if she didn't live with her girlfriend I might've thought about dating her. I had a feeling we'd probably stay friends after one or both of us eventually left JB's. Although I had thought that same thing about folks at the bartending jobs, and they had vanished into the ether.

"Actually, I got laid last night." I smiled at her and held up my hand, jokingly. "High five?"

"By a girl?"

"Yup." The phone started ringing.

"Well done." She motioned toward the phone. "Maybe that's her now."

Every day Melinda and I went to grab lunch, and every day I hoped and prayed and promised myself that I would find something to eat other than a turkey sandwich. Foiled again, I sat back down at the receptionist desk, opened up Instant Messenger, and took a bite. There was just nothing else to eat, it seemed. Well, at least today I had bought a different flavor of beverage than my normal Diet Coke—an old-school Dr. Brown's Black Cherry. Like the White Horse's patron saint, I was raging against the dying of the light.

On our walk, Melinda reminded me that that night was her last playwriting workshop. They were going to do a "table read" of her play, and then after, it was going to shape-shift into a party; "Jon" from her class had some sort of giant loft in the East Village, perfect for such an event. I was definitely going, I told her.

I logged into IM and wrote my friend Tina to see if she wanted to join, although odds were she already had plans. Tina was the sort of girl who epitomized the Reggie Jackson moniker, "the straw that stirs the drink." Somehow she knew everything and everyone, a one-stop shop for social life. Even in college, where we had met, she was that way. She simply loved to party the same way most people loved to breathe—regularly, deeply.

Now she was a web designer at an Internet ad agency; she made a lot of banner ads for pharmaceutical products, but every once in a while she'd get to build a really cool site for an independent film or something. About two years ago when she started there, we all thought Tina was going to be rich. The firm couldn't really afford to pay her much, so they gave her all these stock options that promised big money if they got bought out. But of course they didn't, and there went that. Her firm went from seventy to forty people in about two months. How she kept her job she could only attribute to one thing. Her boobs. She was proud of them; hell, we all were.

However, I had certainly never touched them. Tina and I had kissed once, early freshman year, but it didn't take. It wasn't completely yucky, like Frenching a sibling or accidentally getting slipped the tongue by an overly friendly dog, but something was off, it felt wrong. It was unspoken, but mutual. We were just to be close friends. In fact, we were often each other's wingman.

doodyball5:	arf
tinadoll:	flarfell
doodyball5:	hllllerghf
tinadoll:	liturgical. como estas?
doodyball5:	muy bien, finally got laid last night!
tinadoll:	you sure? u didn't wake up with your dick in a glass of ice tea again, did you?
doodyball5:	no, it was a real girl. she had tits and a vagina and everything
tinadoll:	everything? that code for hermaphrodite?
doodyball5:	shut up. it was pretty nuts, i fucked her "in" my fridge, seriously

tinadoll:	that happened to me once but the sex was bad so i ate a half a pizza
doodyball5:	geez hard to impress a slut like you. what happens later? melinda's having a reading/party
tinadoll:	i'm going to the movies at seven
doodyball5:	want to meet after at the party? gonna get there late anyway, have to cover a session
tinadoll:	nah. A girl needs a night in now and then
doodyball5:	ug
tinadoll:	gu
tinadoll:	what are u casting for?
doodyball5:	it's called "skinflint." whatev
tinadoll:	oh, stacey has something to tell you later
doodyball5:	yeah?
tinadoll:	?
doodyball5:	?
tinadoll:	sorry . . . it's a secret
doodyball5:	secrets are for losers. give it up
tinadoll:	my lips are sealed
tinadoll:	don't even say it, pervstein
doodyball5:	give me a hint, c'mon. am i in trouble?
tinadoll:	hmm, you might be. bye!
doodyball5:	just tell me

tinadoll has signed off.

doodyball5: ugh

Stacey and her fiancé Eric were old friends of mine and Tina's from school. It was cool that we all had ended up here; when I moved to the city I felt like I already had a built-in support system. In fact, Eric had helped me find the place at 99 Perry. A guy he knew from med school was moving out, and I attached myself to him like a barnacle to a ship. The guy recommended me to the landlord, who was a very religious Jew. I went to meet him in his basement office wearing a yarmulke, and when he asked if I had any questions, I queried him about the nearest shul. I'm probably going to burn in hell, but I got the apartment.

The afternoon crawled on at a glacial pace. Melinda left the office at five to help set up for her workshop. I was hoping the reading wouldn't be over by the time I got there, as I was on video duty for the *Skinflint* session. I hadn't even really read the specs yet; I was following a debate in the comments section on stereogum.com, a music blog, about the "greatest modern guitarists." Someone named Shreds81 was throwing a hissy fit about the "lack of respect for Slash, you fucking college weenies!" So I was pretty surprised when the first actor arrived and was only about three feet tall.

"Hi, I'm Leroy Hanson, I'm here for *Skinflint*," he said, shaking my hand with his tiny, pudgy palm. I did my best not to flinch but couldn't be sure that I didn't show surprise.

"Right this way, I'm Jason," I said, walking him back to the video room. I quickly read the specs.

For the LSD sequence, we need five *little people* who will wear fruit costumes (banana, strawberry, lime, lemon, pineapple) and dance in the background. We are looking for the *littlest people possible*, but it is IMPORTANT that they have long, skinny arms and legs, as these must stick out of holes in the costumes. SHORT, PUDGY, OR DISFIGURED LIMBS ARE NONSTARTERS. Please show CLOSE-UPS of limbs so we can make a judgment. Also, please have all actors dance. We will not see faces, so it does not matter if they are women or men.

I flicked on the lights and showed Leroy to a tape mark on the floor. I turned on the camera. "Okay, tell me your name, agent, whether or not you are in SAG, and um, your height, please." Leroy was a pro, and rattled them off. "Okay, I don't have any music, but can you show me some of your dance moves?"

Leroy looked straight into the camera. "What kind of dancing are you looking for? Disco? Waltz?"

"Good question." I hit PAUSE and re-read the specs, but it didn't say. "Umm, it doesn't say, but you'll be playing a piece of fruit, so dance like a piece of fruit would dance, I guess."

"How does a fucking piece of fruit dance?"

"Uh, I guess, well, just do a bunch of different stuff, that's probably safest." My God, Melinda was going to shit when she heard about this. She lived for awkward casting moments, and as I videotaped Leroy doing a surprisingly good "running man" with no sound but the whir of the camera, I couldn't think of anything more awkward. Oh, wait, yes I could. "Okay Leroy, now I just need to shoot some close-ups of your limbs."

By the time I had finished the session it was eight-thirty. I had videotaped about twenty little people dancing and was completely fascinated and horrified. Who knew there were so many little people in the city? And who knew so many of them could dance? One woman did a flip.

Before I left, I quickly composed a short e-mail to Jane. It wasn't every day you met a girl who invited you to fuck her in a kitchen appliance, and visions of my oven were dancing in my head. Besides, she had freed me from my celibate prison, so I wasn't about to play coy and wait a couple days to write to her. It would have been hubris to go the aloof route.

I was starting to get it down to a science, this first written contact. In fact, I had saved a few older e-mails that I had written to other girls, and I pretty much just needed to cherry-pick lines from those to make a nice opening message. It was bordering on lame, sure, but I was really only plagiarizing myself. I liked to think of it as recycling. It was good for the Earth. But this time I decided to be original; I thought up a subject (always the hardest part), "Freezer Burn?" and dashed it off.

> Hey Jane,
> It's Jason. Remember me? President and founding member of the LiZee fan club? Last eve was really fun. Shall we hang out again sometime soon? I know of many other average bands . . . Hope today was swell.
> Hugs. Not drugs.
> Jason
> PS: I don't often use the word "shall," but I'm trying to impress you.

I scanned it, added my cell-phone number to the bottom, and changed the "freezer burn" to "hiya" and the "hugs not drugs" to "bye" so I didn't seem too much like a spaz. You just knew any e-mail you sent to a girl was immediately forwarded to at least one of her friends or office pals and deconstructed like a Shakespearean sonnet in an Advanced Elizabethan Poetry class. Usually the line above the forwarded e-mail would simply say, "I don't know, is he weird?"

I said good night to the computer, put it to sleep, and then escaped the office to the street. A souvlaki vendor was frying up mystery meat and onions right outside the building; it was the savory smell of freedom. The Post-it that Melinda had given me said the reading was at Ninth Street and Second Avenue, so I hurried off toward the 6 train. As I walked, I fired off a quick text to Stacey, "Hear u are looking for me!" Tina had made me quite curious.

I emerged from the subway at Astor Place, starving. I grabbed a slice and crammed it into my eat hole as I headed toward Second Avenue. I got to the building, walked up three flights, and stepped into the loft. It was enormous, a wide-open space with large windows and very little furniture. As the door loudly creaked shut, twenty or so people sitting on folding chairs set up to resemble audience seating turned and looked at me. I smiled sheepishly and tiptoed over to an empty chair. Facing us, seated on one side of a table, were Melinda and four of her classmates.

One man was reading intensely: "It's easy for you to say! I can't even remember our address—our fucking address, Ruth! Did you know I keep it written down on a slip of paper in my wallet? And I have another one in my shoe, in case I lose my wallet!"

Melinda read, dryly, "Oh my God, what if you lose your shoes, though? Then what?"

The man sighed. "Very funny, sweetheart. See, I already forgot how funny you are."

From what I roughly knew, Melinda's play was about a famous composer whose Alzheimer's was rapidly becoming debilitating. As the disease progressed, the symphony he was working on became his saving grace—the musical notes were written down, so he didn't forget or get confused when he worked on it, the way he did in other aspects of his life. But as I watched, I started to realize where Melinda was taking the play; he was now beginning to forget how to read music. I'd walked in on the most tragic part.

I looked around the room. People were rapt, sitting on the edges of their seats. A few were audibly sniffling. Everybody was rooting for the play to be great, everybody was open, sincere. It was almost too good, the way movies depicted old artsy New York, this reading, this makeshift theater in someone's loft. I watched Melinda; she was so focused, furiously scribbling notes as people read their lines. Her lines, which she was showing to the world outside her workshop for the first time. She was oblivious to us, though, lost in her own creation. It was amazing to see her in her element, away from our little office world. God, what a joke compared to this. We were just tap-dancing at work, who cared, what difference did our efforts make? We were killing time for money. This was something else.

About twenty minutes later, Melinda looked up. "Curtain." Everyone began to applaud wildly and she smiled as she was hugged by the people who had read with her. I stood and whistled as loud as I could. I wanted to go over and congratulate her but it didn't seem like my turn yet. Then, boom, the lights dimmed and someone hit the stereo. The Strokes blared; for some reason their music always made me feel like I was in Urban Outfitters about to try on an overpriced T-shirt.

I took a deep breath and waded into the outer ring of the crowd around Melinda. I saw George first, a white guy with dreads who I knew through her. It was tough to pull off, the white-guy-with-dreads look; very few could do it. Only thing worse in that genre were the white girls on spring break in the Bahamas who got their hair beaded and then tragically forgot to put sunscreen where the hair was pulled apart.

"Hey, man, that was great, huh?" I asked George, shaking his hand.

"That, I think, is going to get bought." He held up a Pyrex pipe and changed the subject. "Can I interest you in getting high?"

And soon I was as stoned as a teen at the prom in 1978. I burned my throat a bit, so I left George and went to grab a beer out of the kitchen. It was crowded with folks smoking cigarettes and grabbing at some pita bread and cheese that was laid out on the stove. I reached into the fridge.

"Hey, can you hand me a Stella?"

I turned to see a girl with green eyes, a Joan-Jett-circa-"I Love Rock and Roll" haircut, and a polka-dot sweater. All curvy and shit. Like someone hand-packed her into her jeans. I passed her a beer. "Here you go."

"Thanks." She smiled at me. "So, what's your story? You friends with Jon?" She pulled a bottle opener/magnet off the fridge door, opened her beer, and then gave the opener to me. I fumbled with it a bit. I was higher than I wanted to be.

"No, I'm friends with the playwright, Melinda. Well, not friends exactly, we work together, I can't lie. Well, of course, I could lie—I'm actually quite an accomplished liar." I picked at the label on my beer as I rolled on. "But I made a list of New Year's resolutions, and right after 'Get buns and abs of steel' is 'Be more truthful.' My name is Jason." I stuck out my hand.

She shook it. "Carol." Surprisingly firm grip. A little manly. "Nice opening monologue."

"Thanks, I, uh, took drama in college." I tried a sip of the beer. Lukewarm. "I don't really know who Jon is, actually." I gestured to the apartment. "His place is awesome, though."

"He was the guy in the orange T-shirt who didn't have too many lines. I used to work with him at this ad agency. But now I'm a VP web producer at match.com." She smiled.

"Wow, congratulations."

"Yeah. It's a great place for me." She blinked, and touched my arm. "So what do you do with Melinda?"

I brought my beer to my lips, buying a second, contemplating my answer. It would be easy for me to latch onto Melinda's life, say we'd worked together on a play in the Fringe Festival or something. I'd certainly strayed farther from the truth before.

Last night, in fact. But for some reason I really didn't feel like playing that game, the one wherein we made ourselves sound better than we actually were. And since I had just gotten laid as an orthodontist, I felt a certain desire to abstain from it. "Melinda and I work at a film casting place; I'm an assistant there." I watched her for a reaction. "But there's only four people, so I'm this close to being CEO." I held up three fingers.

She took a prolonged swallow of beer. Fuck, they can never hide it. "A casting assistant, huh?" She glanced down, I think at my shoes, then back to my face. "So like, do you want to be a producer or something?"

She was already in Phase Two. My current credentials didn't sound that hot, so now she was sizing me up for "future potential." Like I was a young racehorse or a piece of real estate in a gentrifying neighborhood. This exact sequence had happened to me more times than I cared to recall. It started with "Oh, this guy looks sort of interesting," then went to "Oh, his job is kinda lame, though, but wait . . . maybe he has a plan," to, if it hadn't already ended with me immediately being dropped like a dirty diaper, "Wait, this one I can mold like a lump of clay into Perfect Boyfriend."

"Um, producer, I don't know," I shrugged, smiling. "Could be, I'm still sorting that out, to be honest. Or maybe an astronaut. I'm on the fence."

"Mmm-hmm. Tough choice." Carol took another taste of her beer. Her eyes darted around the room. "They're really different jobs."

I took her face in. Yeah, I didn't have a shot in hell of ever kissing this girl. No "assistant" did. She was probably racing her friends to be first to both procreate and be made partner. "I make more money than you, AND my baby was born first—in your face!" It was all camouflaged under the stylish haircut. A friend of hers walked past and they started chatting; she was about to sail away. On cue, the wind blew.

"Okay, well, I'm going to get back to my friends," she said, touching my shoulder, patronizingly. "It was nice to meet you." I watched her curvaceous body move as she negotiated her way out of the crowded kitchen. I guess you could say she had an hourglass figure. But time was running out.

I consoled myself with a mouthful of beer. Maybe I was high but I felt like everyone in the kitchen was looking at me, so I shuffled back out into the main room and found a spot to sulk. VP, Jesus. It killed me, that crap. All of a sudden these people who two minutes ago were proud to rule the bong thought they were Gordon Gecko or something. What was I to her, a retarded busboy at Stuckey's? I mean, I wasn't some poet, some Utopian dreamer; it wasn't like I wanted to live in 1967, abandon all material possessions, and give my children Native American names like Spirit Runner. I loved money and treasure as much as any pirate. These people who used their job titles just like maybe they had once used their major or their varsity letter or whatever to make themselves seem superior. Fuck 'em, I wasn't buying it. I leaned against the wall and drained my beer. I had made an excellent argument to myself, but there was no way around it. A girl turning you down, thinking that who you were wasn't good enough, hurt. It hurt every fucking time.

Especially painful was the first time it happened, at Seth Strasser's sixth-grade birthday party. We had just graduated from "Spin the Bottle" to "Run, Catch, and Kiss." All adolescent kissing games cruelly seemed to have the rules built right into their names, rendering moot any "I don't know how to play" excuses. The girls chased the boys under the June night sky, and Carol Kensington, a B-cupped beauty who was the inspiration behind many of my first locked-bathroom-door explorations, was closing in on me. I faked twisting an ankle, going down on the soft grass of Seth's front yard, all the easier to be caught and kissed. But Carol passed me over. Literally. She hurdled me in desperate pursuit of James Lerner, the "hottest guy in school." Well, until sophomore year, when it all went bad in an eruption of acne and an unfortunate attempt at a mustache. Carol's running leap was followed rapid-fire by Lisa Beeman's dainty hop and Mandy Tellman's misjudging the jump entirely and landing on my hand. They dashed off as I sat there, examining the grass stains on my good 501s. What made the whole thing worse was that only a minute before, Seth, wide-eyed and out of breath, had grabbed me in front of the garage and announced like a pubescent Paul Revere, "The girls are Frenching, the girls are Frenching!"

Wilco wafted through the speakers and I turned to see Melinda by the stereo. Nursing my minor wound, I straightened up, forced a smile, and headed over. "Author, author!" I yelled, giving her a hug. "That was phenomenal."

"Thank you so much for coming!" she said, hugging me back. "Oh, hey, sorry, I almost crushed you!" She bounced up and down on her toes. "Really, you liked it?"

I nodded. "Loved it. I've never been more impressed, Mel. I couldn't imagine doing something like that."

"Shut up, you could do it. You just make up stuff and type it."

"Sounds hard. Besides, I've been busy at JB's—you'll never guess what happened after you left!" I said, like an excited kindergartner.

Over a few drinks I proceeded to tell her the story of the dancing little people, which somehow devolved into us calling them tiny dancers, which somehow devolved into our combing through Jon's CD collection until we found *Elton John's Greatest Hits Volume II,* cranking up the stereo, and singing along to "Tiny Dancer" at the top of our lungs. It was kind of like that scene in *Almost Famous,* except they were rock gods on a tour bus and we were drunk idiots in an apartment. If I was someone else at the party, I would have hated us. But I was me. And I loved us. Hell, I was ready for an encore. Levon likes his money.

I didn't hang out much later after the sing-along. Melinda was the star and she had a lot of people to attend to. I was tired and a bit fucked up, and I didn't really know many people there. I saw the VP girl flirting with some tall dude in khakis and figured it was a sign to call it a night.

I headed home, stopping off on the way at my local bodega, Andy's Deli. It was funny that it was "Andy's," as every person who worked there was of some kind of Indian or Bangladeshi descent. I said hello to the night guy, a twentysomething Indian immigrant who went by the name "Bobby" and had pretty much only seen me when I was drunk. Once again, I did not disappoint.

"Bobby, good evening to you!" I said, reeling through the door and making my way toward the glass fridges in the back. He was behind the counter, looking through a magazine whose masthead read INTERNATIONAL ASS PARTY. He slapped it shut and slid it under the counter.

"Hi, Boss! Why no girl tonight, where is your girlfriend?" Bobby had this great wide smile; he was always happy, even though he had to work such crap hours. I didn't really know him and he didn't really know me, but I was pretty sure we were best friends forever. I probably wasn't the only late-night partier who thought that, though.

I grabbed a Canada Dry ginger ale out of the fridge and a Whatchamacallit from the counter. I didn't even know they were still making Whatchamacallits, but you had to admit: It may not have been a very good candy bar, but it had one hell of a name. And I decided to vote for it with my dollars.

"Just this, my friend?" asked Bobby, ringing me up.

"Yup. You know, I was just thinking. It's funny. I've only ever seen you here at work. You'd think we would have bumped into each other on the street by now." I handed him a fiver.

"Someday, someday! You are drunk, yes?"

"No. Never touch the stuff." A smile snuck out of my nose, swiveled into place, and gave me away.

He pointed at me and laughed. "Yes, yes you are! Most people who come in here after midnight are drunk. You are always nice, though. Some people are very bad. They smoke in store, they yell." He gave me back a couple of bucks.

"I'm sorry. People suck," I said, shrugging as if I had just imparted some grand piece of wisdom. I backed out of the deli. "Have a good night, Bobby, I'll see you tomorrow."

"Good night, Boss." Bobby smiled at me. "Do not vomit I hope!"

I made my way up my three flights. I wondered how Melinda knew she wanted to be a playwright; it seemed like it must have been all she ever wanted to do. I wondered if the VP had found someone worthy—perhaps even scored an SVP— and was now contemplating a merger. I unlocked my door, washed my face, brushed my teeth, took three Advil, got into bed with my ginger ale and candy bar, and turned off the lights to be alone with my shame.

I had just crumpled up the candy wrapper and thrown it onto the floor when I heard a text message come in. I was still sort of awake, so I shuffled over to the coffee table where I left the phone and checked it.

u up? janey

I scratched my head and smiled. The clock on the microwave read 12:47. Sure, I could be up.

Twenty minutes later I found myself in the women's bathroom of Tom's, some bar in Nolita, sharing a joint with Jane. She had been out for a while and had the slur to prove it. The second I walked in she dragged me by my hand to the ladies' room, whispering, "C'mon handsome, let's get high." I was a bit taken aback at first—she was quite aggressive. She still wore the glasses but her hair was out from the pigtails and she looked pretty damn sexy in a short bright-blue skirt and a white wife-beater tank top. Her nipples, like the built-in thermometers in Perdue Oven Stuffer Roasters, were declaring, "Chicken's ready!"

Jane handed me the joint after taking a long pull, and before I could put it to my lips she put her mouth next to mine and blew the smoke in. It was a sexy move and Petey instantly improved his posture.

"What's your name again?" she, I hoped, joked.

"Jason." I sucked on the joint. "Some call me Adonis."

She giggled. "So who are you really, Jason? C'mon, you're obviously not an orthodontist. What do you do in our city?"

"I kiss girls in bathrooms."

We started to make out for a second, then she pulled away and squinted at me. "No, really, what do you do?" We stood a few feet from each other, in front of the sink. Someone pounded at the door, and we ignored it.

"I work in casting, you know, for films and commercials and stuff."

"So, are you like a casting director?"

"Kinda." I scratched my nose. "Well, you know, I assist the director. And what about you? What exactly do you do?" I realized I had no idea.

"I'm a buyer for a toy company. I source stuff from China and the Far East that we think we could sell here." The knocking began again.

"Oh, that sounds fun."

"Kinda." She stubbed out the joint in the sink. "Well, now that that's resolved . . ." She moved in and kissed me sloppily. Her hand trailed down my stomach and grabbed Petey through my pants. Instantly I was as hard as a left turn in Midtown. I slipped my hand up her skirt. No underwear. Or pubic hair, for that matter. What a difference a day made.

"Not here," she said suddenly, straightening her skirt. "Too cheesy." Then she took my wet finger that had just been inside her and licked it sensuously. We opened the bathroom door and stepped out past a girl who glared at us.

Miss Manners and I hopped into a cab and pointed it west toward my apartment. She had my jeans unbuttoned and her tongue in my mouth. A radio sports reporter jabbered at us through the lone rear speaker—the Knicks had lost again. Jane suddenly jerked away. "Hang on, what time is it?" she asked, looking up through the partition to the radio. "Shit, it's almost two! I can't go to your place. I'm sorry, I have to get up early tomorrow for a really big presentation I'm giving."

"Don't worry, we'll be fast," I said, leaning in to continue the kissing. "You won't even remember it."

She avoided my lips. "No, I can't. I'm sorry, I totally spaced.

I have to be on the ball, it's a huge meeting! You know how those are."

Oh yeah, I hated those. The driver switched the station to some percussive Tito Puente number I couldn't put my finger on. "C'mon, we're almost there. You'll sleep over, there'll be pancakes and a full continental breakfast."

"I can't sleep over! I have no clothes." She thought for a moment. "Okay, what if I, uh, 'take care of you' before we get to your place? Then I can drop you and take this cab straight home."

Good sport that I was . . .

The mambo music pulsed as she went down on me with a fury. What a motivated little worker she was. I looked out the window at the bleary lights while she did her voodoo. I watched people in suits trudging home from late nights at the office, others I could see in all-night restaurant windows eating, laughing. A girl smoked a cigarette lazily, leaning against a parking meter. An old man with too-short pants lumbered along while his tiny dog pranced near his white-socked ankles. Something was happening in every nook and cranny of the city. Even the two of us in this cab, we were part of it. I looked down at Jane, her head pumping up and down, one hand up her skirt, fiddling about. I was quite enjoying my particular nook and cranny, I wouldn't trade it. I opened the window and let in the breeze, the sound of the streets overtaking Tito. We weren't that far from my apartment, only about two avenues and five blocks. I leaned back and closed my eyes against the wind.

Stopped at a light only a block from my house, I came. She skillfully milked every last drop from me: a mess-free operation. Clearly she had done this before. The driver pulled over as I quickly buttoned my jeans. I caught a glance of his tired eyes in the mirror and looked away.

"That was fucking hot." She smiled, and we hugged good night. I slid across the seat and out of the cab.

"Hey!" she said out the window. "I think you better at least split this ride with me, don't you think?" I laughed, and pulled out my wallet. I had two dollars.

I held them up to her. "Shit," I frowned. "Sorry."

Jane grabbed them and fumbled through her bag. "Fuck, I only have five myself." She handed all of our cash to the driver and got out of the car, grinning. "Looks like you got yourself a slumber party."

After a stop at the cash machine we quickly got ready for bed. Jane made me set the alarm for six, which I was fairly un-enthused about, because she had to go home first thing and put on her "meeting outfit." We rubbed each other all over but nei-ther of us was up for round two. I wasn't a real fan of round two; if you did it right, in my opinion, once was more than enough. We put our eyeglasses next to each other on the night-stand and spooned for warmth. Jane made a joke about me "owing her one" and gently tangled her leg between mine. I could hardly keep my eyes open. We lay still, and I started drift-ing off.

"Do you think I'm a slut because I texted you for sex?" Jane whispered in my ear.

I turned over so we were nose to nose. "Only in the best, most positive way."

She smiled. Her teeth were like Chiclets. I sort of wanted to touch them. She propped herself up on her arm. "So, there's good sluts and bad sluts?"

"Sluts are people too, sweetie. There's all kinds." I yawned, and covered my mouth. "Ooh—sorry."

Jane yawned back, and then lay down against me. "I'm glad you checked your phone, cowboy," she said, taking my hand.

"Me too," I said. "I was happy to hear from you."

She kissed me softly on the mouth. We whispered good night and I sank into the pillow.

The next thing I knew the clock radio was blaring. Apparently, it was raining men. I slapped the thing silly until it stopped. Jane was up like a shot and into the bathroom. I heard tinkling and the balling of toilet paper followed by a flush and the slurping of water from the tap. She reemerged.

"Hey," she whispered. "Can I borrow these pants?" I rolled over to see her wearing my favorite pair of Dickies, ones I'd had forever, made supersoft by thousands of washings. Despite the small white paint splotch I had gotten on the hem of the left leg (from sloppily painting the apartment—like father, like son), they were a key player in the very limited trouser rotation of new jeans, old jeans, old Dickies that I relied on. "Just to get home," Jane explained. "I don't want to wear my skirt right now, it feels too cold." She turned around and wiggled her ass at me.

"Sure," I croaked. I closed my eyes again. I heard some more getting-ready noises, and then warm lips pressed against my forehead and I opened one eye wide enough to see Jane and my pants quietly make their exit.

4

The week flew by, and to paraphrase Ray Davies, "I wished I was a different guy—different friends and a new set of clothes." Well, that wasn't really true; I had spent a good amount of time breaking in both and was quite content with them.

It was now Saturday morning. I lay with the pillow over my head, trying to block the sun out for at least another hour. I had just awoken from my recurring *Godfather* dream, wherein I made love to two hairless Sicilian girls who, after I finished pleasing them, plied me with decadent desserts. "Tiramisu, *signore*?" they'd giggle. "Profiterole?"

The ringing of my home phone shattered my sleep plans. Jesus, who called my home number anymore? Four agonizing rings later I got the answer as the machine picked up. *BEEP*. "Jason. It's Stacey. Are you there? Are you sleeping? Is someone sleeping with you? Yeah, didn't think so. Just kidding! I'm getting sick of the phone tag, so when you get up, call me. I really need to talk to you, call my cell."

It was closing in on eleven, so I got out of bed and let the poison drain out of my system. Then I curled up on the couch with the phone, dialed, and caught Stacey on her way to the gym. We decided to meet for brunch at twelve-thirty so I could hear the giant secret that had apparently taken Manhattan by storm.

Since she was exercising, I decided to do some myself. Hell, I was hoping to be seen naked again soon—Jane wasn't exactly a prude. Although I was thinking maybe we should grab dinner the next time we hung out, you know, something somewhat normal before the next sexplosion. I pulled off my shirt and did three sets of push-ups, three sets of sit-ups, and three sets of curls with the dumbbells I kept in my one itty-bitty closet. I had calculated my square footage at about three hundred, so I guess the closet wasn't as much tiny as it was proportional. I managed to work up a bit of a sweat lifting, so I showered, bringing a cold glass of water in with me for hydrating purposes.

At a quarter to noon I exited my apartment and ran into Patty, my neighbor from across the hall, who was coming back from the grocery store, her numerous white plastic bags a dead giveaway. She had a red bandanna tied around her head Aunt Jemina–style, and a weird-looking cigar/twig in her mouth. Or maybe it was some sort of sugarcane. Hard to tell. I helped her get her stuff inside her apartment.

This was a groundbreaking moment. I'd never seen the inside of her place; by her low rent I figured she must've lived there thirty years, and I was dying to see what it looked like. I stepped inside carrying two bags. Her door opened right into the kitchen. Disappointingly, the kitchen didn't reveal much— it was pretty much identical to mine, just flipped, and cleaner. She had a bunch of magnets on her fridge; one big one in the middle was an illustration of a cowboy on a bronco with the words WYOMING IS BUCKING AWESOME!

"Nice magnet," I said, putting the bags on the counter. "Have you been to Wyoming?"

"Been there?" She started to empty one of them. "I escaped from there. Don't get me wrong, it's great if you like cattle, or beef jerky or Republicans. But if you don't, just fly over and see it out the window." She put some bottles of tonic water on top of the fridge. "Anywho, so how's life, neighbor?"

"All's pretty good, I guess," I said, putting the last bag on the counter. "Just working, playing. You?"

"Oh me, who cares? I'm old and boring." She gathered up the empty bags and stuffed them in the cabinet under the sink. "But I expect more from you. Details, stories! These are the years you get all that stuff, don't you know that? Then you spend the rest of your life looking back at the so-called good ol' days."

"That's um, a little depressing, Patty," I said with an "I'm just kidding" smile. I could tell her some stories, all right, but they weren't the PG-13 kind you shared with your older neighbor. Maybe they'd bore her anyway, if she really lived the bon vivant life I pictured.

"Oh, you didn't know that about me?" she laughed. "I'm a huge buzzkill. I fear it might become my defining characteristic." She reached into the fridge. "Want some OJ? It's fresh, I just got it at the farmers' market."

I saw by the clock on her microwave that I was going to be late, and Stacey was punctual as hell. I edged toward the door. "I'm actually meeting a friend for lunch who has some big secret to tell me. I should probably get going."

Patty finished pouring herself some juice and took a sip. "Big secret, huh? I hope it's something good!" She started coughing. She put the glass on the counter and leaned against it as she hacked, doubling over with the strength of it. I could hear large wet things flying around inside her, like mattresses in a hurricane.

"Whoa, hey, you okay there?" I asked.

Her eyes were watery. "Oh yeah, phew." She smiled thinly, caught her breath, and turned away from me. "Wrong pipe."

met Stacey at a diner that was sort of halfway between our homes. She and Eric lived in Murray Hill, a neighborhood that was bland by NYC standards. I didn't like Murray Hill much. First off, bad name. Also, and maybe this was the bigger issue, people from Murray Hill—or people who seemed like they could be from Murray Hill (it had become a symbol to me more than an actual place)—tended to come down to my neighborhood en masse and take all the seats at the good restaurants. Thursday to Sunday, there was literally nowhere I could afford to eat that didn't have at least an hour's wait. These Murray Hillers and their ilk had subscriptions to *Time Out* and they were good at calling ahead and making plans. They could not be stopped.

We grabbed a table by the window, made fast work with the menus, and got our orders in; we were both starving. Only once our respective Diet Cokes arrived, and with them the assurance that the system worked, were we able to relax and begin talking.

Stacey had her brown hair pulled back in a post-workout ponytail, a few stray wisps hanging above her eyes. She unwrapped the scarf that hung loosely around her neck, revealing an NYU Law sweatshirt; she was in her third year there. Eric was a resident at Cornell Med, which was located in the city, uptown. They were on the cusp of being a power couple. Soon they could help me with any legal troubles I might have, and with any social diseases I might stumble upon. They were going to be Number One on the speed dial.

"You're so proud of your law school," I said teasingly, pointing to her sweatshirt.

"Yeah, that's why I wear it to the gym and sweat on it," she laughed. She brought her straw to her lips and took a long sip of her Diet Coke. "So do you want to talk about things and stuff, or do you want to get right to it?"

"I guess right to it," I said, glancing hopefully toward the kitchen. "With a five-minute break when the food arrives when there shall be no talking, only eating and digesting. Nothing is that new with me anyway, although thank God, the slump is over."

"Yay! So who is she, do you like her?"

"Her name is Jane. Sure, I like her fine, I guess, but it's a little early for all that, Stace. We've only"—I made air quotes—" 'gone out' twice. And actually, I wrote her Tuesday to see how this big meeting of hers went, and I haven't heard back yet."

Stacey wrinkled her brow. "Tuesday? Eh, I wouldn't worry about it, I'm sure she'll call soon. Anyway, I'm glad at least you have a 'good possibility.' " She knocked wood. "Oh hey, whatever happened with Scott?"

Scott Langford, fuck. He was a guy from Cornell who I was never really friends with, but we knew each other. He went to Columbia Journalism straight from college and was now an editor at *Fader* magazine. Stacey had run into him at some gallery and had thought he'd be a good person for me to contact. She even got his e-mail for me.

"I uh, I haven't gotten in touch with him yet, actually." I mock-cringed and held my hands in front of my face. "Don't hit me!"

"Jason! C'mon, that was like a month ago. You need to write him."

"I know, I know. I will."

She gave me her stern Stacey look. "Just do it today, when you get home."

"I will. For sure." I played with the white paper wrapper from my straw, twisting it around my finger. "But that's not why you called me here today, I take it."

"No." She leaned across the table, serious. "Okay, how long have we been friends, Jason—like seven years now, right?"

I nodded. We had met the first day of freshman year, which was sadly that long ago. I wondered what I'd been wearing. It's funny, it was probably a huge deal, my first-day-of-college out-fit choice, and yet I couldn't even remember it.

"It's crazy, right? I've known you longer than I've known Eric even. And he considers you as good a friend as I do, which I hope you know."

"That's nice. I feel the same way."

"Yeah, but if it came down to it, you're my friend first, right?" She smiled and winked. She was a big winker.

"Sure. I mean, by a couple of days." Behind Stacey's head I saw our waiter walking toward us with two plates of food. But then he continued past, damn it. The digestive juices in my stomach were bubbling like a witch's cauldron.

"Those days count," Stacey said, winking again. "Anyway, Eric really wanted to come today but he had a rotation. We both love you, you are so important to us, and um, we wanted to ask a big favor of you, for the wedding."

"Am I going to be the best man?" I asked. "That'd be pretty cool. I get to make the embarrassing toast! Yes!" Eric and I weren't crazy close, but I knew he didn't have a ton of guy friends.

"No, actually, Eric's brother Jeff and my brother are going to be co–best men."

"That's nice." I wrinkled my forehead, confused. "So, what can I do for you guys then? I can usher. I'm pretty good at ushing."

She took another sip of soda. "Okay, here goes. You intro-duced us. You get all the credit for that."

True, although it wasn't like I was a matchmaker or any-thing. Stacey had lived in my dorm, and Eric was in my geology class. It was supposed to be "rocks for jocks" but was one of the most difficult classes I had taken in college; in retrospect I'm sure the professor was fuming to himself, "Gut course, eh? I'll show you!" I'd sat next to Eric a few times and we'd become friendly. He was a junior when we were freshmen, but it was never an issue. He came over to my dorm one night to study for the midterm and Stacey popped in to say hi. He thought she was "intriguing," so the next time there was a party I made sure they were both there. Cut to fireworks and cherubs and lush string music.

"You brought us together, and we were thinking it would be really nice if you could bring us together again, officially. What I'm trying to say is, we'd be honored if you, Jason, would officiate at our wedding."

The waiter clanked our dishes on the table. "The spinach omelet is for the lady, and the bacon cheeseburger is for—"

"The rabbi," Stacey said.

After a few silent bites, Stacey explained that since neither of them was really religious, they didn't care if they had a real rabbi marry them. It wasn't like they knew any, and they didn't want to just hire some stranger. Apparently, it was fairly easy for someone like me to get the necessary paperwork to be able to perform the ceremony. The fact was that once they got the wedding license from the state they were legally married; the ceremony was just, well, ceremonial. Stacey, ever thorough, slid across the table a very thick packet of printouts she had culled from various sources. Some were testimonials from other amateur ministers who had had a "joyous" experience, others were essays from wedding sites that explained what made for a good wedding ceremony and what did not. Most important were the ones that explained exactly what I would need to do, which basically entailed going to an Internet site, filling out forms, and becoming something called a "Universal Life Minister." This title legally allowed me to sign the civil license and send it in to the state for official processing. And although it wasn't required, Stacey and Eric also wanted me to take a two-session class (that they'd pay for) at a temple where I'd learn how to structure a ceremony and incorporate some Jewish traditions within it.

As I leafed through the documents and she went on and on and on about how she saw the whole event playing out, I began to feel a little overwhelmed. I knew this was an honor and all, but like in the army, honor usually required great sacrifice, and I started to feel a little concerned about what I was getting myself into.

But of course I nodded along in all the right places and smiled and hugged her and quickly agreed to it. How couldn't I? I mean, was there some way I couldn't?

From the look on Stacey's face, not really.

It was Saturday night. It was on.

I stood with Tina in the corner of a bar on Avenue B and Seventh Street, cleverly called 7B. We each had a belly full of whiskey and a brain full of THC. Plus, to stay awake, we had been snorting Ritalin; I don't think it was curing our adult attention deficit disorder, though, as our conversational skills were now based on tangents, non sequiturs, and epithets. We were shattered and threatening to leave but had full drinks and were firmly planted with a good view of the bar. It was full of twentysomething downtowners in assorted stylish smocks. It was a little like looking into a mirror, but somehow we believed we were far more genuine than the others. You couldn't trust the others. They looked like us and they talked like us, but at night, they went home and slept in pods. You could just tell. Not us. We had beds.

Tina had been calling me Rebbe Goodgirl all night, after I told her the secret was out. I had been calling her a filthy whore, but it was falling flat. I was still feeling a bit weirded out by Stacey's request, and it was buzzing around the back of my brain like a fly trapped in a car. Stacey and I had been really tight at school, and I still counted her as one of my closest friends. Yet over the last few years, and even more so recently, we had begun to drift apart. Things were changing. Maybe it was because Eric was older, but Stacey was really into acting grown-up and hosting the kind of dinner parties where the cutlery matched and you sipped (never swigged) wine and played Pictionary and people were couples and the conversation veered to serious but boring topics like accountants and buying an apartment versus renting one. After a while everyone started to sound like Charlie Brown's teacher to me. I just felt like Stacey and Eric, and some of their new friends, were rushing to leave youth behind and become adults. They could not wait to take on the next phase of responsibility. "Give it to us!" they yelled. "We have broad shoulders!" It was just so goddamn dull. So the truth was, we didn't get together nearly as much as we used to. But I did love them, I really did. They just scared me sometimes.

Before the onslaught of toxins on the brain rendered me speechless, I voiced my doubts to Tina about the rabbi thing. She was quite supportive. She put her hand on my shoulder and said, sincerely, "You, sir, are fucked." Then she laughed, "I'm joking, but it's a huge responsibility, no question. It's her wedding, you have to be prepared and go into it knowing it's the most important day in her life. You cannot be the one to fuck it up. I'm so happy for them, but . . . the hell if I'd want to do it! I mean, you know Stacey, she's going to have like over three hundred people there, her grandparents are coming from Germany, she has like twelve bridesmaids, blah blah blah. And she's very, what's the word . . . particular."

"Oh, I'm feeling way less anxious about it now, thanks," I said. I scratched my head. "Why do you think she wanted me to do it?"

"Because of what she told you, you introduced them and all.

It sounds silly, but girls are really queer like that, trust me. And you're funny, and you'll make the ceremony fun, and she wants it to be really special, not just some other wedding. You'll be great. By the way, I have to listen to her talk about this all the fucking time, you're only just getting sucked in now. I've already heard her treatise on 'band versus DJ.' "

I groaned.

Finding out you were to stand as a rabbi in front of three hundred people, some from Europe, and fuse two friends together for life required somewhere around thirteen drinks—a true bar mitzvah–style drunk—and Tina and I had been doing our best to reach that magic number. The good people at 7B were obliging. It was your classic East Village joint, the kind of non-theme bar that was getting harder to find—local acts like the Bouncing Souls and the Liars on the jukebox, a couple of slimy pinball machines, tattooed bartenders whose bands were playing somewhere sometime soon—and if those reasons weren't enough to buy a pint, 7B was also the bar in *Crocodile Dundee,* the film in which Paul Hogan mouthed the famous words that defined a generation: "That's not a knife. THAT's a knife."

Tina was single too, although she had met some guy a week or two before who she had "a feeling" about. But as with Jane and me, she hadn't hung out with him sober and during daylight hours yet, and basically until that happened it could really go either way. The right drugs helped you tolerate the not-so-tolerable, and Tina always had the right drugs. Stacey once told us that one of the best parts of being in a relationship was that you could go home before you were too wasted or too exhausted. There was nothing to stay out late for, to have that one regrettable drink for. That was my favorite one, though, the uh-oh one, the crossover. The one that made you teeter between being fucking brilliant and dangerously out of line.

Stacey's pro-relationship comment was meant to sound nice and comforting, but it lacked the whole reason bars existed. Possibilities.

I told Tina all about my second encounter with shy, reserved Jane. She told me I could expect a cold sore in four to six days. She started texting someone about something and so I made my way to the men's room, bumping into more people than I should have. I was shivering with intoxicants. 7B's bathroom was a little cozy for more than one person, but as there was a line, people were crowding in two at a time, sometimes three, with the odd man out taking the sink. Classless. I eventually took my turn at the overflowing urinal with the "My unicorn could kick your unicorn's ass" graffiti written on the yellowing porcelain. Next to me was the filthiest toilet I had ever seen, one I could only describe as an absolute pit of despair. Someone had some serious digestive issues.

I got back to Tina and took my place next to her.

"Where were you, you fat piece of shit?" she asked, smiling dangerously.

"Spike Jonze is back there. He said he liked my sneakers but he hated my shirt. I think he wanted to kiss me, maybe. It was weird. I felt 'a vibe.'"

"And you let him get away with that? Where is he?"

"No, it's cool—I broke a mug across his jaw. He's fucked forever. He left bloody and crying."

She pulled the lemon from her drink and tossed it onto the floor. "That reminds me, I just figured out a new band name for myself, if I ever have a band." We both continued absentmindedly sipping our drinks and staring out at the people. I felt like they couldn't see us, like it was TV and it only worked one way.

"What is it?"

"Daddy's Stabbing Mommy."

"I don't get it."

"You know, like when a little kid walks in on his parents having sex and yells, 'Daddy's stabbing Mommy!' "

"You're retarded," I said, grinning.

She pointed at a stain on my shirt. "And you're a sad little rabbi with a dirty tallith." She turned her head and yawned loudly. "I think I need to go home. I'm going to have a massive bout of The Fear in the morning, I'm a fucking mess." She was. She looked like a smeared version of herself. Or maybe that was because I couldn't see straight. "Plus, Brett just texted me that he's downtown. I just might let him take me upstairs and give me a foot massage."

"We need to give that guy a nickname. Brett, that's just sort of . . . not descriptive."

"Okay, 'Jason.' He has a big dick, maybe you can come up with something from that," she said, laughing. "He does, though—seriously." She reached out and put her glass on the edge of someone's table. Then she put her hand up to them and waved. "Enjoy the veal, good night." She turned back to me. "Want to walk out with me?"

"Um, I think I'm gonna finish my drink. But it was fun, right? It was the best night ever?"

"Totally awesome, I can't wait to go home and write about it in my dream journal." Tina straightened herself out and threw on her jacket. "Don't stay out too late, Rabbi," she said, wagging a finger, then turned and began parting bodies on her way toward the door.

It only took four more swallows and a burning feeling in my eyes for me to realize it was high time to away to my bed. I checked my phone but there was nothing, zip. I fingered the buttons, considered texting Jane, but caught myself. I stumbled outside, gave some paper from my pocket to an exotic-smelling man with a yellow car, and soon I was home and asleep.

After the debacle at Seth Strasser's sixth-grade birthday party, it looked like it was going to be one long tongue-less summer for me. My hopes weren't high when I attended a pool party at Carol's house in mid-July. It was a classic hot summer day, and while other kids flirted awkwardly on the grass, I horsed around in the water, playing some game that was a combination of water polo and kill-the-guy-with-the-ball. Misty Blank swam over to me. Misty had an identical twin sister, Christy, but they went to private school so we didn't see them very often. That only made them all the more attractive to the boys; in our eyes the two blond sisters were both miniature Pam Andersons. I couldn't really tell them apart; I only knew it was Misty from the "MB" monogrammed on her one-piece.

"Hi, Jason."

"Hi."

She scratched her nose. "My sister likes you if you like her first."

"Really?"

"Yuh-huh. So?"

I shrugged. "I like her first, I guess."

She swam away. Ten minutes later I was out of the pool,

picking through some salty Ruffles and Lipton onion-soup dip when Christy, in a "CB"-initialed suit, flip-flopped over.

"Hi."

"Hi."

"Do you want to go for a walk in the woods?"

Barefoot, I followed her into the suburban-grade forest that marked the edge of Carol's lawn, the twigs biting into my tender feet. Despite the pain, I had enough of a grasp of manhood to know you didn't scream "Ow!" when you were oh-so-close. We were both still wet from the pool, and Christy's blond hair was dripping water down her back. We stopped by a tree. Christy leaned against it.

"Ever kiss anyone?" she asked me. She took a piece of gum out of her mouth and chucked it clumsily, the weird mechanics of a girl throw. It went six feet and hit the dirt.

"Uh-huh, sure."

It was cold there in the shade and I was shivering a bit. She put her closed lips up to mine. We stood stone still, lips stiff, hands hanging dumbly at our sides, like Siamese twins attached at the mouth. I opened my eyes and saw that hers were open too, so I quickly clamped mine shut again. I felt something on my lips. It was her tiny pink tongue, and it pried my mouth open and then it was inside. It was all warm and minty and it was official, I was French-kissing. More than anything sexual, I remember feeling relief. I had finally reached first base.

Back then, the girls really took the lead. But things seemed to have changed over the years. The girls just didn't seem to chase the boys all that much anymore. Or at least my girl Jane wasn't chasing me. It was now a week and a half since she had slept over, and I hadn't heard a peep from her. I had even texted her late Wednesday night after another bout of debauchery with Tina, "My turn—u up?" No response. I tried to rationalize that maybe she had gone to China or something for work, but in my head that annoying "Nah nah nah nah, hey, hey, hey—good-bye" song was playing. Repeatedly. It was just plain weird that she hadn't gotten back to me; I mean, I didn't remember completely blowing it. In fact, I thought it had gone sort of well.

It was nearing eleven on Friday and I was sitting at the receptionist's desk at JB's. The office was slow and so was the news online. I checked my e-mail every eighteen seconds, looking for something interesting, spam, anything. I watched the clock tick and tick. Melinda was running errands all morning, so I was stuck there all alone for the next couple of hours. I thought about my options. I could maybe start in on a rubber band ball; JB had one on his desk that was fairly impressive. Perhaps I could top it. Or I could make a paper-clip chain of ludicrous length—a paper-clip jump rope, even. God, I was bored. Maybe I could slip out and get high and eat a wheel of cheese. I just wished something would happen, anything. The worst feelings in the world were boredom and nausea. But at least when you were nauseated, you didn't have the feeling you were wasting your time.

I had nothing else to do, so I figured what the fuck and shot Jane another e-mail. She was on my brain, and my brain controlled the fingers that started jabbing at the keyboard. Hell, one more e-mail couldn't really make matters any worse at this point. And if I went zero for three, then I'd at least know it was officially kaput.

> Hey Jane,
> Woke up this morning and went to put on my Dickies and then I remembered—hey . . . you have them! Give me a shout and let's catch up, make a plan. I have other clothing items that will fit you fantastically . . .
> Mr. Giggles

I hit SEND and then began composing an e-mail to my folks. We were pretty bad at staying in touch; even in college I'd go weeks at a time without speaking to them. My mom liked to think of it as a genetic flaw in the family: We were all self-sufficient to the point of negligence. I caught them up on the news I thought they'd be most interested in: my imminent role as rabbi. They had actually met Stacey and Eric on a visit out to Cornell. "Your son is finally a rabbi, Mom, just like you always dreamed!" I joked. We weren't a very religious family, to say the least. Judaism was, for us, more Woody Allen, less Abraham and Esther. I had been bar mitzvahed and all that, but at the time it was really just about getting heaps of gifts and playing "Coke and Pepsi." We never, ever went to services; to me temple seemed like a building where men went to show off their new cars and women their new dresses and jewelry. Our cantor had even had an affair with a woman from the congregation. Now he owned a Mercury dealership on the way to the airport.

I shot off a few more e-mails to friends; maybe I could have lunch with someone or at least make plans for the weekend. It wasn't like I was changing the world at JB's—just the toner. Nights held a lot more interest.

I yawned and looked over at the office clock again. It had hardly moved. I forced myself to try to do something productive. I scrolled back in time until I spotted Stacey's e-mail with Scott Langford's info in it, and took a crack.

Scott—
Hi, it's Jason Strider from Cornell. Hope all is well with you.

I heard through the Cornell grapevine that you landed at *Fader*—major congrats on that! Don't worry, I'm not writing for a free subscription. (Although, if you can give them out easily . . .) But, I was wondering if you had any inkling how one could apply to be a music reviewer there?

I doubt you'd remember, but I DJ'd up at school. It was an eclectic show called "The Mostly Phenomenal and Fully Enjoyable Jason Strider Power Hour." I played everything from the obscure experimental, like Moondog, to the ironic, Menudo. Mostly though, I focused on all things Indie. Each week I'd review several new releases, in detail, on the air.

Anyway, I'd appreciate any guidance you can offer on the reviewer thing. Thanks so much, Scott.

Go Big Red!

Jason

I looked it over and did a spell-check. It seemed to make sense. I mumbled "Fuck it," and quickly clicked SEND. For a moment I had the sense of fulfillment one gets after completing a chore they've left undone for far too long, like doing the dishes or burying a body.

The moment passed. I leaned back in my chair and looked around. What else could I be doing right now? What would I be doing six months from now? I tried to see what my life would be like five or ten years down the road, but invariably it was impossible to see anything clearly. How did people do that? I had trouble picturing what I was going to eat for dinner.

I just didn't want to spend the bulk of my waking hours on this planet yawning and sighing and waiting for five o'clock, all for the little bits of green paper that eventually blew out of my life and into the hands of cabdrivers, bartenders, drug dealers, and bodega cashiers. But I hadn't found a reasonable alternative yet. And it wasn't working at some "real" but equally uninspiring job until ten every night so I could afford more expensive jeans and double desserts. Although lately I'd thought I heard Tina mumble when picking restaurants that a certain place might be too expensive. Too expensive for me, is what she meant. There just had to be some way I could beat the system.

The computer made the duck-quack sound informing me I had a new e-mail. Jane? Langford? Nope, it was Eric. Not only was he around for lunch, he wanted to buy me lunch. He hadn't yet seen me since I had been anointed his rabbi, and he wanted to thank me. Was I available?

Fuck yes, I was.

Eric and I finished up our lunch specials at the sushi place around the corner from my office and made our way back out to the street. The sun was beaming down and we basked in its warmth like sated lions; the soup, salad, and raw fish had filled us to the bursting point. Eric was really tall, I remembered now that we were standing. I always forgot his height, almost six foot five. He looked a little worn-out. He had spent lunch telling me some of the more disturbing tales of being a resident, which besides long hours and only one day off included having to touch horrible people on horrible parts of their bodies. "It's a bit like joining a fraternity and being hazed," he had explained. The things the ER doctors didn't want to do, the residents got. Which, in New York, according to Eric, often involved men who took too much Viagra and needed to have the blood siphoned from their unwaveringly erect penises with a hypodermic needle. Yeah, I just didn't like people enough to ever help them out with stuff like that. It went without saying that Eric was a far better person than I. He came from a family of surgeons—his mom, dad, and older brother. He would be one soon too; he just had to get through this penis-draining phase and on to the real work. He would; he was irritatingly patient.

Eric and I didn't hang out one-on-one all that often, but I

was always pleasantly surprised by how enjoyable it was when we did. He wasn't caught up in a lot of the pop-culture bullshit I was, and we tended to have conversations about real things, often politics or health topics I had read about in the *Times*. He also wasn't afraid to cry. I mean, he should've been more afraid, he was kind of a bawler. I had seen him tear up at least a half dozen times, most recently after he, Stacey, and I watched the old film *Heaven Can Wait* on cable. Over lunch I'd done my best Al Roker and predicted that his wedding day was going to be partly cloudy, with a passing shower of man tears.

As we stood there, faces pointed at the sun, I felt a tap on my shoulder. I turned my head to see a petite blond girl in a black sweater.

"Hey, Jason, how are you?" the blonde said, beaming. I knew that smile. Intimately.

"Holy shit—Annie!" We hugged. "I didn't know you were in New York."

"Yeah, I moved here about a year ago, I got a job at *People* magazine as a photo editor. I live up on the Upper West Side." She flipped her hair. She was dressed way more stylishly than the last time I had seen her. She actually did look like a photo editor. The trendy tight sweater, fancy jeans, some kind of stylish boots. "And you? What's your story?"

"I live in the West Village." She made a face, as if she were impressed. "Yeah, I was really lucky, and got this great place." I realized Eric was standing there awkwardly. "This is actually the guy who found me the place, Eric. He went to Cornell too, but he was a couple years ahead of us."

Eric reached out his hand and shook Annie's. "Hi, I'm old Eric."

"Hi, nice to meet you." Annie turned back to me. "I love the West Village, good for you," she said, grabbing my arm. "So what else? What are you doing for work?"

"Nothing too exciting, really. Right now I just work at this casting place around the corner." I shrugged.

"You don't sound that into it," she said, seeming genuinely surprised.

"Oh, you know, it's fine."

She fingered an earring, smiling. "When we broke up, I always had nightmares that the next time I saw you, you'd have models on your arm, a famous record producer or something," she said.

"Oh, well, I am hugely famous in Croatia. People have posters of me there." I laughed.

Eric excused himself and popped into a deli on the corner. Annie and I talked and caught up for five minutes and gave the brief versions of our deals, until he came back.

Annie looked at her watch. "Shoot, I better get going." We hugged again and said our good-byes. Then Eric and I continued around the corner.

"So what was up with that girl?" he asked. "You used to date her?"

"Yeah, it was after you graduated, spring of senior year. She's a year younger. I was working crazy hours at the fucking Sam Goody because I was saving up to go traveling, and she had a pretty easy semester. I'd close the store at ten, get home exhausted, and she'd force me to motivate. All I did that spring was re-stock CDs, smoke pot, and have sex."

Eric opened a pack of a gum and offered me a piece. "That doesn't suck. Annie, hmm. I feel like Stacey has mentioned her."

I took the stick and popped it into my mouth. "That was really weird seeing her again. She was like the only 'girlfriend' I ever had—even if it was just a few months. What kind of gum is this?"

"It's called bubble mint, it's some hybrid of bubble gum and mint gum."

"Hybrid, eh?" I grinned. "Okay, Doctor."

"Shut up." He blew a small bubble, pulled it back in his mouth, and cracked it. "Maybe you should have gotten her number."

"Nah. I mean, she was a crazymaker."

"What's that mean?"

"It just means we drove each other crazy all the time, in good ways and in bad. It's a chemical thing, I think. We had a lot, a lot, of screaming white-trash-type fights. We got thrown out of a bowling alley once because we were fighting over the right way to score spares, Jesus!" I laughed. "She also had a pretty bad eating disorder, which I didn't realize until later. She only ate baked potatoes and frozen yogurt. At the time I thought she was just 'quirky.' " I spat the gum into a trash can on the corner. "I'm not into it," I said, wiping my lip.

We began walking slowly in the general direction of my office. A river of people rushed around us like we were a rock in a stream, splitting and then re-gelling on the other side. It was sunny out, but the buildings were so tall in this part of town that we were always in shadow, no matter what side of the street we walked on.

"I still say you should've gotten her number. Just think, you could show her how much better in bed you've gotten." He slapped me on the shoulder with one of his big man-paws, and we hustled to beat the light and cross Sixth Avenue.

Eric dropped me off at the office and thanked me again for agreeing to shoulder the rabbinical duties. I took one last breath of spring air and then went upstairs, my posture immediately beginning to slouch as I passed through the entrance. It was still totally quiet. Melinda wasn't in yet and I had no new e-mails, certainly no reply from Jane. Damn it. I checked out nytimes.com, but there was nothing interesting; apparently it was the dullest day in American history. I leaned back in my chair and cleaned my glasses on my undershirt. Maybe Eric was right. Maybe I should've gotten Annie's number; even though she drove me nuts, I sort of thought I was really in love with her for a moment there. But it wasn't love. It was some kind of un-scratchable itch. It was crying three a.m. phone calls and screaming in an un-air-conditioned car at stoplights over directions and generally expending vast amounts of energy and passion playing devil's advocate on points I really didn't care about but couldn't leave alone. But maybe that was love, someone who could drive you crazy, someone you couldn't ignore even when you wanted to, who got under your skin. I mean I sure as hell wasn't sure as hell about what "love" was. Anyway, had I gotten Annie's number, I knew where it would eventually lead.

Beer. Intercourse. Tears.

Melinda never came back to the office, which meant I had to run the late-afternoon casting session. Toddlers for a Charmin commercial. After only about ten minutes I wanted to Krazy Glue the tip of my penis shut so that I'd never, ever impregnate anyone.

Kids were running around like they were on fire, crying, pulling each other's hair, spazzing out. Each one was trailed by a mother suckling another younger child, or perhaps, in their eyes, another "gold mine." These mothers were the worst, just the absolute worst. Their voices were so shrill they could pierce steel, the government should have considered employing them to sonically shoot down enemy missiles from the sky.

"What did I tell you, Charlemagne? Do you want to watch *Toy Story* later or not?"

"Brooklyn! Stop touching that girl!"

"Magellan, you do as that man says or I'm telling Daddy!"

All of the kids had ridiculous names like that, soap-opera-character names. There were Dakota and Blaze and Kash and

Sodapop ("We both really loved *The Outsiders!*") and D'Artagnan and Chynna and Pacifica and Charisma. Charisma—what the fuck, why not just name your kid Personality Plus? And, of course, all of the moms wanted me to know they were more than mere moms, they were also actresses. As they each approached me, their shrill commanding voices instantly softened, their thin frowns were replaced by flirty smiles and batting eyelashes. "Chynna shines when we are in scenes together. It really saves the directors a lot of time." A sudden blast of authority. "Chynna! Quiet! Mommy's talking!" Then back to flirty. "So" (hair-flip, stomach-in, boobs-out) "can I give you my head shot?"

The place smelled of forty kinds of fecal matter. There was a puddle in the corner and I was pretty sure it didn't come from a juice box. A rotund ten-year-old with bushy hair sat against the far wall, away from the action. He was chain-eating mini Snickers bars from a Halloween-sized bag, waiting for his mom and younger sibling. I got the sick feeling his folks kept him obese; he was a shoo-in for any "fat kid" role.

The only thing the toddlers had to do was smile to the camera and say "soft." Maybe one had actually done that, the rest just started babbling or playing with the only toy we had at JB's for sessions like these, a Fisher-Price xylophone. *Cling clang clang! Cling clang clang!* I was ready to shoot heroin directly into my eyes.

The day and the week finally came to a close, and I headed home. I stood among the zombies on a rumbling subway car that smelled of human rot. I looked around and saw the cause. A sleeping homeless man, filthy, sprawled in a seat, an open Styrofoam container filled with lo mein on his lap. The stench was awful, as if he were decomposing in front of us. He might have been, too. But no one complained. Or, for that matter, attempted to see if he needed help. We held our breath and waited for our stops, the homeless man finally snorting and coughing in his slumber, proving he was alive, probably spewing an invisible plague onto us all.

I emerged from the Germ Express and power-walked toward home. I got to my apartment, turned on an old Hank Williams album, and plopped down on my shitty green couch. Hank sang, "Yeah, my bucket's got a hole in it. My bucket's got a hole in it." It was the kind of music you could make love to, or curl up in the fetal position alone and cry to. I had a lot of records like that. Ones that made you feel like you were in a movie somehow when you listened to them, like every move you made had meaning.

Back in St. Louis, my house had been a short bike ride away from the local hip used-record store/head shop, Vintage Vinyl. It became the place where I spent the majority of my allowance and where I learned all about "rock and fucking roll, dude." It was intimidating to go in there; the music was blasting, it smelled like clove cigarettes, and there were a lot of Iron Maiden–type posters up replete with skulls and axes, all of which were frightening to a thirteen-year-old.

The first time I went in, after about ten minutes of wandering around not knowing what to look for, I placed Styx's *Cornerstone* on the counter. I knew nothing about the band—or any band for that matter. I picked it solely based on the NICE PRICE sticker, the cool Styx logo, and the simple fact that I had been in the S section, seeing if there were any "Striders." The cashier, wearing a skinny tie and a handful of pins on his shirt, snickered as he bagged it. I went back a week later, and as I walked past the register the same guy looked at me and sang, "Babe, I love you, ooooooooooh ooh babe." He clapped his hands together. "You didn't like that piece of shit, did you?" I shook my head. He asked me my name and I told him. "Okay, Jason," he came out from around the counter. "I'm Mike. Allow me to assist you." He led me over to rock/pop, humming something to himself. "Today's letter is the letter 'B.' No reason, I'm just feeling it. Let's see," he said, click-clacking through the discs. "The Buzzcocks' *Singles Going Steady*, and"—*click-clack*—"Bob Dylan's *Highway 61 Revisited*." I don't know why they kept Bob Dylan under B, but that was their system. Whether Mike turned me on to bands or I found them on my own, I discovered all kinds of great shit in that store. It was where I first bought albums by They Might Be Giants, Built to Spill, and the Dead Milkmen just because I liked their names, only to discover when I got home that I had scored, big time. Every so often you'd see members of local bands like Uncle Tupelo and Enormous Richard (despite Tina's efforts, Enormous Richard remained the best band name ever) in there, browsing. One time Mike was talking to this chunky guy who wore a cowboy hat and a neckerchief. It turned out to be Big Sandy, of Big Sandy and his Fly-Rite Boys. He was a Western-swing legend from California. We all got high, right in the store, back by the discount rack. On the bike ride home I swallowed about six bugs because I couldn't get the goofy, open-mouthed grin off my face.

I sat there for a few minutes, decompressing, listening to Hank, thinking of nothing. I studied the ceiling. I tried to focus on only the white of it without my peripheral vision letting anything else in. It was really hard to do. I tried but I couldn't hold it, so I gave in and let my eyes slowly wander around my apartment. It was dusty. The late-afternoon sun streamed through the window and lit swirling particles floating in the air. Something about it made me feel like I lived inside a giant nostril. There were clusters of stuff everywhere—black-and-white photographs on the mantel, piles of CDs on the floor, take-out menus on the countertop. One cabinet was open, and I could see an old package of green tea beckoning me in the back. Tea, why not? Antioxidants might come in handy.

I boiled the water and washed a mug. I had no sugar so I poured a few drops of lemon-lime Gatorade in, the theory being that lemon and tea went together. I took a sip. The theory was proven correct. I opened my window and climbed out to the fire escape, then sat blowing on the tea as I watched people on their way home from work. It was the end of another nice spring day, it seemed a shame we'd all wasted it.

"Hi, neighbor!"

I looked to my right and there was Patty, leaning out her window. "Good evening," I said nodding.

"Enjoying a beverage on your veranda I see," she said. "You're not going to jump, are you?"

"No, I love life," I said, taking a sip of tea.

"Good, because you wouldn't die from this height anyway. Just break your legs and embarrass yourself. But have you ever been up to the roof? A fall from there would probably be fatal."

"That's, uh, good to know. Just in case."

She took a deep breath and exhaled. "Ah, it's just beautiful out, huh?"

We stayed like that, me on the fire escape, her stretched out the window, for a few nice, peaceful moments. Then those passed, and we stayed for a few more quiet, awkward ones. She pushed her hair off her forehead and thought for a second. "Oh, hey, you totally piqued my curiosity the other day. So what was"—she deepened her voice dramatically—" 'the big secret'?"

"Oh, basically my friends want me to preside over their wedding ceremony. As like, a Universal Minister."

She clapped her hands together and chuckled. "Oh my God, that's funny. I mean, it's an honor, no?"

"It is, it is. And a big responsibility." I took another sip of my tea.

"Sure, it's their big day." Patty began to pull her head back inside. "Well, I'll leave you up here to contemplate the mysteries of life, I didn't mean to interrupt. Oh, by the way, do you know Robert Green, he lives in 2B?"

I thought for a second. "Oh, is he the guy who wears a cowboy hat sometimes?"

"Yeah. He's a drug dealer, you know."

"Really, that's weird. I mean, here in the West Village?"

"There are drug dealers everywhere, silly! Don't get excited, though; it's nothing we'd want. He used to sell pot and give us all a bit for free, to keep us quiet I suppose. He cleaned himself up for a while, probably as long as you've lived here. But now . . . he's selling crack. That's the worst, those guys get bloody desperate. That's the only reason I'm telling you, it's not like I'm a big gossip or anything. See those guys hanging out across the street? They're waiting for him to come home."

There were two scraggly-looking white dudes sitting on the steps of the brownstone across the street, smoking. I guess they did look like crack addicts, it was kind of hard to tell. Still, I found it hard to believe I had a crack dealer in my building.

"It's nothing to worry about, they won't do anything here, they don't want Robert busted. But you should know, just so you keep your eyes open." She coughed her smoker's cough. Again, you could hear the mattresses in her. "Ahem, sorry. Hey, speaking of drugs, you wouldn't happen to have any pot, would you?"

"Why, Patty, what ever gave you that idea?" I laughed at the unabashed question. "Has the hallway been reeking?"

"No! I mean, I've smelled it, but only a little. I just thought you might. If you could spare any, may I borrow a joint?" she asked, quite seriously.

"Of course, anytime. Oh, do you mean, right now?"

"No, no big rush. Now I have things to do, people to see. Boring things. But maybe I could stop over when I get back, or if you're going out, maybe you could slide a joint under my door? I'd really owe you one." She took a deep breath, like she was trying to eat the air, digest it. "God, these first warm days, they just sneak up on me. All of a sudden I walk outside wearing my winter coat and . . . it's spring." And with another swallow of air and a bony-armed wave, she slipped into the darkness of her apartment.

I carefully pulled my mug from where I had set it on a stair. I was done with this tea. I wasn't much of a hot-beverage guy, to be honest. I was the only person I knew who didn't drink coffee. Whenever I'd tell someone I didn't drink coffee I'd get a look like I'd just said, "Mmm, puppies, delicious!" in a PETA meeting. Glancing down to make sure I wasn't about to scald anyone fifteenth-century style, I slowly dumped the rest of the tea to the sidewalk. The pause while it fell, followed by the slap slap slap slap slap as it hit the pavement, was surprisingly fulfilling. I thought of David Letterman and his watermelons. Probably even funnier in person. I considered dropping the mug but thought better of it.

I stayed sitting there for a bit. The crack addicts gave up on Robert and walked off toward the river. I stared at the clouds hanging above the buildings across the street, looking for animal shapes. There was nothing I wanted to do but I felt like I ought to be doing something. I yawned and covered my mouth. So Jane had completely blown me off, huh? Fuck. Maybe I just wasn't sexually experimental enough for her, maybe she was looking for a guy with an extra ball or who liked to role-play "school-bus driver/little retarded girl." I was digging the idea of her, fine, I could admit that. I tried to think about where it might've gone wrong. I mean, she still had my pants; why would she have borrowed them if she knew she wasn't ever going to call me again? It didn't make sense.

Christ, what a whiner I was. I reminded myself that I was one lucky son-of-a-bitch living a pretty fucking cool life, and my complaints, compared to most people's in the world, were so minimal and stupid and small it was incredible I even bothered with them. I watched as a bird landed on the tip of a lamppost across the street. It fluttered its wings, teetered, fluttered again, and finally found its balance. "That's me," I told myself. "I'm just like that bird."

Then something deep inside me asserted itself. "What in the fuck are you talking about?" I muttered, then half-laughed aloud. Geez Louise. Maybe I had my period.

My phone buzzed in my pants pocket and I stood up.

"Hello?" I asked; the number was blocked. The sun was low in the sky now. I felt a little regal answering my phone outside, standing above the world, stretching. It was truly gorgeous out, what the hell was I griping about?

"Jason? It's Tina!" She was yelling and enunciating. "What are you doing?" I could hear loud music and laughter in the background.

She was calling from a pay phone, her cell was dead. Apparently some new restaurant had opened by her apartment on the Lower East Side and was giving out free drinks and free food for the next few hours. They had a big backyard and a rockabilly band was playing. Was I or was I not man enough to haul ass over there and get in on the good times?

I crawled inside, twisted two joints, and drained a Diet Coke for strength. I swallowed three Advil with a palmful of toothpaste water. I checked myself in the mirror, stepped into the hall, locked the door, and braced myself for the night. The good times were killing me.

I slipped one of the joints under Patty's door and was on the street in a flash. It was just as bucolic on the pavement as it had been above it. Trees were blooming and birds were chirping and the sun began to set. It felt like this was it, the official beginning of the good weather. Patty was right, it was like spring snuck up behind me and slapped me on the back of the neck saying, "I'm here!"

I walked toward the West Fourth Street subway and inevitable inebriation. I pulled out my iPod, earphoned up, and clicked PLAY. The Vaselines' "Son of a Gun" came on and I was happy to hear it. It was thick with distortion to start, angry as a Japanese monster, but then a catchy tune cut through and eviscerated the opening fuzz. I turned it up loud enough to drown out the rest of the Western world, loud enough to inspire tsk-tsking PSAs on tinnitus. My steps began unconsciously landing on the down-beat, my hands were slapping at my sides like they were a percussive instrument. As I crossed Seventh Avenue a sombrero perched atop a fire hydrant at the corner caught my eye. A dry cleaner pulled down the shiny new metal gate in front of his store; someone had already written "neckmeat" in black spray paint on it. There were male and female vocal parts to the song, and the Scottish girl singer had this bittersweet, nostalgic voice that made me smile and gave me a stomachache at the same time. I floated toward the train, safe in a musical bubble that none of the other New Yorkers screaming into their cell phones or setting off their car alarms could penetrate, not even a delivery guy riding his bike on the sidewalk who seemed determined to cripple me. The drums marched along at the perfect clip, and as I moved down Sixth I considered swinging from a lamppost like Gene fucking Kelly. I reached the subway entrance, fished out my MetroCard, and descended on beat into the underworld.

I got out of the subway at First and Houston and hoofed it down to Ludlow and Rivington. The Lower East Side had changed a lot just in the few years I had lived here. It went from being a slightly scary neighborhood whose only real nighttime draw was the odd rock-'n'-roll dive, to fancy new bars and cafés blooming on almost every street. And according to the alcohol-soaked rants of late-night bar prognosticators, this was only the beginning. The vintage clothing stores that gave way to the funky boutiques with new clothes would give way, eventually, to a Banana Republic. It was inevitable. The whole city would one day be a giant mall. Like everyone, I was against this sort of mallification, although I secretly looked forward to the escalators and free air-conditioning.

The restaurant Tina was at was called Old Devil. A couple made out in the entrance; I squeezed past them and into the fray that was the bar. I bumped into some guy in a cowboy hat and a T-shirt that read "Thou shalt not BlackBerry on the toilet." He leaned in close to me, his breath flammable, and imparted, "Life ain't nothing but bitches and money." He had something there.

I took a look around, scanning for Tina. It was a retro, rockabilly dream inside. Someone who must've owned very stiff dark-blue Levi's and a lot of pomade had dropped a big fat pile of cash to make the place look authentic—not in some Bennigan's version of the fifties, but in a real *The Wild Bunch* way. Stainless-steel walls, pies under glass, red-vinyl booths, even a gas-powered Wurlitzer jukebox pumping out Jerry Lee. I dug it. I was ready to scream "Go, daddy, go!"

Tina was nowhere in sight inside. Past the bar and through a small dining room, I saw a screen door to the backyard. I stepped through it. The sun had set, and the whole yard was lit up by Christmas lights strung on the surrounding buildings that walled it in. For New York, the yard was just enormous; it had a full-on oak tree in the middle, complete with a tire swing. On one side, a couple of guys were working a large Texas-style half-barrel smoker grill; burgers and dogs were sizzling atop its flame. Across from them a three-piece rockabilly band, with even the hard-to-fit-in-a-cab stand-up bass, were ripping it up, tearing through what I was pretty sure was "Chicken Flop," an old Hasil Adkins gem. The name of the band was on the drum, "Thee Hellcats." They must have been Olde-English-type honkytonkers, I reckoned.

I walked past some drunken swing dancers and found Tina leaning against a brick wall, a Pabst in one hand and a paper plate with half a burger in the other. A tiny bit of ketchup dotted the corner of her mouth.

"I know what you're thinking, Rebbe," she said, air-kissing me near the cheek. "I usually mock the ironic popularity of shitty Pabst with the hipsters, but it's free, and thus, I am drinking it." She took a long pull from the metal can.

"Actually, I was thinking, 'Wow, she's eating the bun of her burger'; I mean, that's a lot of carbs for a girl like you," I said. Tina was thin; she knew it.

"Comments like that are why I vomit myself to sleep," she

said, straightening up. "Follow me to *las cervezas*." As we serpentined through the people, she asked over her shoulder, "So, what ever happened with freezerface?"

"Nothing," I said. "Haven't heard from her in like two weeks. And she still has my pants, my good Dickies, she borrowed them the night she slept over. Any advice on getting those back?"

"Give up. Those are on eBay by now, Papi."

I grimaced. "But why? We're adults, she should return them. I mean, wouldn't you?"

"Many of my dishrags are the clothes of former lovers."

"Great."

Tina was drunk, and she was a dangerous drunk, like a boxer on rubbery legs who still somehow managed to counterpunch with ferocity. I followed her swagger over to a tub filled with ice and Pabst cans. I grabbed one, cracked it open, and spilled the cold liquid down my throat. I had some catching up to do.

Tina smacked her can into mine. "A toast," she said, "to your old Dickies. I wish them well."

"I might get them still. I was thinking of maybe giving her a call."

"Who, the girl you fucked in your freezer, who blew you in a cab the next night, who you haven't heard from since? Give me a break." She let out a small burp. "Those pants have twenty different kinds of DNA on them by now."

"Ugh," I said. I put the beer can to my lips and drank until my teeth were numb.

Three beers and a burger later, I felt whole again. The melancholy of the day was fully flushed out of my system. The Vicodin Tina gave me probably didn't hurt either. I mean it definitely didn't hurt, you know, being a painkiller and all. There were things to look at, and so I did. Girls had obviously tried on every shirt and skirt in their collections before deciding what to wear for this lovely evening, and bras thankfully seemed to be forgotten on the bed. Tina needed the bathroom and I was almost there myself, so we made our way inside. Along the way I fell in love with several girls, who—through a combination of my smudged glasses, the neon lights of the bar, and a magical mix of intoxicants—seemed to glow. Goddamn New York City girls. They had sass.

The line to the restrooms was somewhat long, as it tends to be in a bar passing out free Pabst. "Tell you what," I said to Tina. "Drinks are only free until ten, right? So you go first and I'll head to the bar, and then I'll go after."

"That's the most ingenious idea you've had since I met you," she said, and leaned against the wall at the back of the line.

I burrowed my way toward the bar, which was three deep with people. Miraculously, a sliver of daylight appeared, and I was in. I smiled at the beauty of it and began the game wherein I tried to catch the bartender's attention.

On my left, perched on stools, were two slinky little minxes, one blond, one brunette, both in jeans and those deconstructed T-shirts girls either buy or cut up themselves, the ones that show off soft shoulders and bra straps (or no bra straps) and fit just right. Girls really knew what they were doing. The little sassters were facing forward, I soon realized, trying to avoid the guy pressed behind them, a very drunk man with an un-ironic mustache in one of those button-up dress shirts that have no collar. He resembled Jeff Foxworthy. I felt like saying to him, "If two girls are ignoring you for this long and you're still harassing them, you might be a redneck. Or, possibly . . . an asshole."

I stood there, somewhat entertained, somewhat horrified, plenty drunk, possibly swaying, but for a full five minutes unable to get the bartender to acknowledge my existence.

"So come on, what's up with you two?" Foxworthy asked. "What, do you like girls?"

The girls shifted uncomfortably. "Yeah, that's it," one said.

"No? Well, do you like guys?" He leaned on the blonde's shoulder. She tried to shrug him off. "Tell me. Do you like girls, do you like guys . . . ?"

"Do you like robots?" I turned and said to them. Popped out before I could stop it. The grapes that go ripe in the sun loosen the screws at the back of the tongue. The Clash. *London Calling*, side three. "Get the vinyl," Mike had told me, "the lyrics are on the sleeve."

The girls' eyes lit up and they nodded and laughed. "Yes. We are in love with our robots, so leave us alone," said the girl with the brown hair, turning on her stool and giving me a smile with a "thank you" built into it. If I was ever to make a movie entitled, *Cute Postgraduate Girls Who Love Indie Rock and Are Certified to Teach Pilates*, she might star.

Foxworthy looked at me. "How 'bout you go fuck yourself?"

I should've had about a million witty retorts to that, it was so lame. But as this guy had, in the way that men have done throughout the centuries, instantly turned his spurned advances into hatred for another male, and stepped directly up into my piece, about all I could muster up was, "Sure. I'll go off and do that. I'll fuck myself real nice-like."

"You're a fucking wiseass," he breathed into my face. His eyes were glazed like a bad piece of pottery. That's when I knew it. I was going to get into a fight. I hadn't been in one since I was sixteen. Noah Lewis, in the smoking section behind the high school. He was bigger than me, a bit of a bully, but somehow I had knocked him down, and so remained undefeated to this day. That record was in jeopardy, as this guy looked a scootch more challenging. And my glasses were not a plus. I reached in my pocket for my keys, and balled them in my fist, like I had seen in some movie.

"How about backing the fuck up?" I said, as tough as I

could. I wanted to sound like a hard bastard, like they did in those British gangster movies. Like I just might glass the cunt. But I was an average lanky doofus, so it wasn't very believable. To be a badass, I needed some sort of a twitch or scar or at least a tattoo, something.

"Make me," he said, inching in closer. Goddamnit. I was feeling a lot more sober. I had the sudden idea that I should just step in and blast him in the face first, with my fist weighted with keys, before he could take a smack at me. Just cold-cock him before he could make a fucking move. I tightened my fist.

"Hey, asshole!" Tina had arrived out of nowhere, and was yelling at the top of her lungs at Foxworthy. So loud people started to look. He turned to face her. "Yeah, how about the next time you go to the bathroom, you don't pee all over the fucking seat! What the fuck is wrong with you, dickhead?"

"I wasn't even in the bathroom," he said, holding up his hands in innocence.

"Yeah you were, fuckwad!" Tina kept aggressively screaming. "I was right behind you on line and there was fucking man-piss everywhere. Ugh! You're a goddamn pig!" People gathered around us, curious. The tide had turned. I wasn't going to get in a fight after all.

"You got the wrong guy. Fuck you." He walked off, as onlookers pointed and chuckled.

Tina put her arm around my shoulders. "Who's got your back, Papi?" she smiled.

"I was so about to kick that guy's ass." I grinned with relief, relaxing my arms.

"I'm sure. I didn't want you to get arrested, though." She yawned. "Where're them drinks?"

Two shots of tequila, offered to us by the blonde and the brunette (I wasn't finished with them just yet; I didn't know what chivalry was worth these days, but I hoped with inflation it was at least up to heavy petting), were followed by several Pabsts, which we were now buying with American currency. Tina's new guy Brett arrived and we all went back outside with our drinks. Tina climbed into the tire swing and Brett gave her a gentle push. He was sporting a white belt and a complicated haircut. He was just Tina's type—sort of good-looking, kinda rock-'n'-roll, with a pocketful of pills. I took some Percoset and slipped them in my own pocket for a rainy day.

It was really a funny scene there, outside. Who were all these people in their hip clothes, where did they all come from? It was a perfect mix of hyper-cool whites and blacks and Latinos and Asians. I felt like I was in the middle of a Benetton ad or a bad Lenny Kravitz video. My God, the effort these people were making to be super-stylish, it seemed exhausting. Sometimes I loved that everyone knew what was going on minute to minute on the pop-culture countdown, and other times I was like, *enough* with all this presto-chango shit, find a style and go with it. I went with the lazy/myopic look. Jeans, Converse, old shrunken Izod, glasses. Occasionally a "Kiss me, I'm Irish!" pin. Consistent and sloppy. With a wink.

Tina had fallen off the swing; now she and Brett were sprawled out on the dirt below it, cackling. She was toying with Brett's hair, about two minutes away from either puking or making out with him. They were like Sid and Nancy, but with 401k's and pants from Barney's. I wiped my forehead with the cold of the Pabst can. Suddenly I was at this party alone. I looked at my cell. Nothing.

I made my way inside, figuring I could hang out with the minxes. Perhaps I might even collect my bounty from one. I allowed myself the momentary erotic daydream of them both paying up. I had never had a threesome, but it sounded like something for the memoir. Although it was probably a little nerve-racking. There were a lot of holes and things that a guy needed to tend to in a situation like that, a lot of sexual multitasking. You had to bring your A-game.

I moved into the light of the bar—well, the light compared with the dark of the backyard anyway—and my God, was I drunk. Fuck you I was. I confirmed this by knocking over a stool, but luckily no one really seemed to notice. The key was confidence. I screwed a smile onto my face, straightened my posture, and stepped forward, trying to seem cool, unflappable, like Bogart. I wasn't sure of Bogie's gait, though; all I could remember was the omnipresent fedora and the hill of beans and "the Germans wore gray, you wore blue." Man I was silly with it all. I saw the girls still in their same spots. I was probably too fucked up to be trying to touch anybody, including myself. But I wiped my forehead with the back of my hand to degrease it, and closed in.

"Ladies, may I join you?" I said like a proper prince, and pulled up a stool.

"Hi," said the blonde. She had a name, but who could remember it? It wasn't a sexist thing, I was just terrible with names, men or women. Dogs I did okay with. I was always preparing myself to say my own name and I forgot all about remembering theirs. I was going to order one of those late-night memory tapes someday soon. Then I'd have a system and would be pretty much unstoppable.

"Thanks again for before." She tucked a stray hair behind her ear.

"I'm almost, I'm sort of like a hero, right?" I said, smiling. "You guys need another a drink?"

I got us another round of fucking shitty Pabst, I have no idea why I hadn't switched off of it. I had no business having another drink anyway. No business. The brunette, whose name

I'd also forgotten, excused herself to the bathroom. I debated whether or not this was a move to let me and the blonde get chummier.

"Thanks for helping me and Sue before," she said.

Sue. One name regained. "Ah, it was nothing."

"So . . . ?" she said.

"So . . ." I said. "You don't really like robots, do you?"

"Yeah, I do," she laughed. "Robots are cool."

"Sure, until they become self-aware and start replicating. Then we're in big trouble."

"Well, we can always just unplug them, right?"

"Oh, if only it were that easy." I took a long pull on the Pabst. "The coming robot war, it's going to be hell." I grinned. She grinned back. I decided to go for it. I winked at her, charmingly goofy. "So, anyway, are you a little infatuated with me now? I mean, it's to be expected, I am a hero."

The blonde gave me a sad little look. "You are a hero," she said. "But . . . I have a boyfriend."

"Oh, uh, me too," I said, leaning back on my stool, trying to recover. "But I'm not all throwing him in your face."

Sue came back from the bathroom, interrupting at just the right moment, and pointed a finger at me. "You know what," she said grinning wildly, obviously a little a drunk herself. "I think it was you!" Her voice started to rise. "I think it was you who peed all over the bathroom, that's what I think!"

"That's bullshit," I said back, just as loud. I hopped off my stool. "I am deadly accurate, Missy. I'm like a laser."

About a half-hour later, after the three of us had swallowed even more poison, the blonde went home to Mr. Wrong. I chatted up Sue for a few more minutes. She was all taut and pretty and wasted, her lipstick smeared in the sexiest of ways. I wanted to challenge her to a WWE-style no-holds-barred wrestling match. I wanted to plant a flag on her pubis and proclaim to the four winds, "All this territory, including the hills to the north, belongs to me." But it wasn't going to happen. It turned out she had a boyfriend too, a boyfriend who showed up and bought us a round. He seemed like a good guy, the bastard.

I stepped outside, defeated. I raised my hand and felt my way into a yellow vehicle. The driver deciphered my slurred speech and headed toward my apartment. Out the window, a couple held hands at a bus stop. I checked my phone, my eyes struggling to focus. No voice mail, no late-night text from Jane, nothing. I snapped it shut and jammed the piece of shit into my pocket. What the fuck, Jane? Return a fucking message. Or at least give me my goddamned pants back. My poor Dickies, they were probably balled up on the floor of her apartment right now, surrounded by stray Prozacs and the cell-phone numbers to eight other dudes like me. And maybe a severed thumb. Shit, for all I knew she was a sexual predator with a thumb fetish. I really thought she was into me too, Jesus. Was I just blinded by vagina? I traced my upper lip with my tongue. Maybe I was going to get some kind of cold sore after all.

We slowed to a stop and the cab deposited me in front of Andy's Deli.

"Hey, Boss!" said Bobby as I came in. "How you been?"

"I feel like a hundred dollars." I burped and stumbled and grabbed a Gatorade from the fridge. "Can I get some Advil?" I asked. Did I have any left or didn't I? Better safe than sorry. It sure was bright in there. My retinas were *en fuego*.

"Oh, rough night for you, Jason, huh? How many you want—big bottle?" He held up a large size, and I nodded. "Okay. So no girl again tonight, man?"

"Why you always got to rub that in?" I slurred, fumbling through my wallet, eyes just slits. "I'm joking, Bobby, I'm a joker."

"Okay, okay. Good night, Boss. I pray for you!"

I climbed the stairs and unlocked the door. I stumbled over to my computer and after mistyping my password twice, opened my e-mail. Booze had convinced me my mission was just.

> Jane,
> Well hell, I'm getting that feeling that I'm probably not gonna hear from you. That's cool, I get it, no worries. I just want my pants back. I'd love to go out again, have a drink and get them, but if not, I still want them. You can mail them or messenger. or send via carrier pigeon, whichever:
> Jason Strider
> 99 Perry Street #3A
> NY NY 10014

I hit SEND with the middle finger and then flopped onto my bed as fast as I could. I lay there with my jeans and shoes on and closed my eyes for a moment. Shit. I had the bad feeling. The bed began making slow rotations, so I tried the trick where you put one foot on the floor and one hand on the wall to steady yourself. It didn't help. I was the tiny black ball and the bed was the roulette wheel. I felt a wave of hot unpleasantness wash over me. I hopped up, careened into the bathroom, dropped to my knees, and leaned on the toilet. I stared at the bottom of the bowl, where some weird yellowish film surrounded the hole, pieces of the film peeling off and floating. I gagged and considered my toothbrush resting on the sink. It was my expeditor in situations like this. I wasn't the kind of guy who wrestled with the dry heaves; if I was going to get sick, I got it over with Karen Carpenter–style. I took a deep breath and made the call.

Fuck it. I was going to fight.

I yanked my shirt off and lay down on the cool, but filthy, tile floor. I had this theory based on stuff Eric had told me that sometimes worked, and I was hoping it would work now. The mind becomes analytical in times of crisis. The vestigial nerves run the length of the body. They cause nausea, vertigo, et cetera. The coolness of the floor and the cold sweats combined to lower body temperature, and for me, sometimes, it got rid of the nausea. I lay there while sweat poured down my face in unfathomable amounts. It stank like beer a little bit. I wiped my brow, my hair was soaked. I tried to think happy thoughts. I even thought about baby kittens I had seen romping in a pet-store window, but soon the vision turned ugly and they were scooped up in a pillowcase by a dirty little boy and tossed into a creek. Where did that come from?

After a few minutes the sweats slowed, and I began to feel better. It was amazing how once the almost-moment of vomiting passed, you suddenly felt okay again. I sat up, bits of crap embedded in my back, pulled off my shoes and pants, and then got back into bed. I had dodged the bullet. Jesus shit, I hoped I wouldn't be a mess in the morning. Before I closed my eyes I looked at the clock; it was only two. I was going to be okay. I was. It was going to be all lollipops and rainbows from here on out. Now I just had to sleep, and maybe dream. That was it for my "to do" list. I needed to stop thinking. I put the pillow over my head and waited.

I awoke the next morning with more than a touch of The Fear. Besides some lingering queasiness, I had a pain in my head that turned the light from the window into a knitting needle to the eye. Had I almost gotten in a fight? And that e-mail, Jesus, nothing brighter than sending a late-night drunken message, moron. It couldn't be helped: The morning was going to be filled with feelings of longing and regret. Which is why if I was a real drinker, I would've gone right out for some kind of mimosa pick-me-up brunch. But instead I had the Gatorade and Advil I'd left on top of the toilet, still in the brown bag from the deli.

It was a gray Saturday morning, and I was glad to see it. I didn't need any glorious weather peer-pressuring me to get outside and enjoy the day. I wanted an egg-and-cheese on a roll and I wanted it now. I looked at the clock: ten-thirty. I wasn't the type who could fall back to sleep. That was a gift that some people had; they could go back to sleep after waking up, or they could fall asleep in the middle seat on a packed airplane or next to a native transporting live chickens on a bus racing along a cliff in the Andes.

I got dressed and went out to the diner around the corner, the Galaxy. The theme inside was just that. On the stained wooden walls were amateurish paintings of space scenes that looked a lot like a stoned sophomore's art-class watercolor of *Dark Side of the Moon*. I especially liked one over a booth in the back that showed an astronaut on what looked like an asteroid, sharing fries with an alien creature. It was painted directly on the wall, a fresco.

I went up to the counter to get my grease sandwich to go, but after I ordered I saw that I only had three dollars left in my wallet. That didn't help those feelings of shame subside. I promised the guy I'd be back and walked down the block toward a cash machine. How much fucking money could I have dropped last night? The drinks were mostly free, dinner was free, what happened? I tried to remember how much I had started with but had no fucking idea.

There was no line at the ATM, so I stepped right up and slipped my card into the slot. The nasty fingerprint-smeared screen told me I only had $145 left in my account. And payday wasn't until next Friday. Do-able, but not altogether comfortable. I guessed I wasn't getting that beach house with the stable of extremely flexible swimsuit models just yet. I got $40 and slunk out; I had to be among the bank's least valuable customers. I pictured the tellers sitting around watching the security tapes of me, laughing their asses off.

I got my sandwich and walked toward home. A shredded plastic bag blew past me and caught itself in a tree. The city was so disgustingly dirty sometimes. On a windy day like today I could feel bits of shit hitting me head-on; when I washed my face later the water would come off brown. I imagined my pores being packed with filth the way footprints on the beach were filled with blowing sand. And every few blocks, especially as the weather got warmer, the stink of urine would waft up. Human urine, dog urine, rat urine. I doubted there was a piece of pavement in Manhattan that had yet to be pissed on.

I got to my building and saw Patty on her way out the front door. She was wearing an Army jacket and had on an old hunter's cap with the earflaps down. And of course, on her feet, her signature sandals. The outfit was part Ted Nugent bow-hunter, part Deadhead magic-burrito maker.

"Hi, neighbor," she smiled. "The weather reverted on us, didn't it?"

"Yeah, it's a good day for TV I think," I said.

"Oh hey, thanks for the joint. I haven't tried it yet but it smelled very nice."

"No problem." I held up my bag. "Hey, I don't mean to rush off, but my egg sandwich is calling out to me."

"Go, go," she said, waving her arm. "Listen, are you going to be around later?"

"I think. I have no plans. Do you need a hand with something?"

"I might. We'll see." She turned to go. "I may knock on your door; if you don't want to see me, just pretend you're out." A gust of wind blew and she held on to her hat. "Oh, I can't stand this breeze. Do you know that in certain parts of southern Spain, the wind is so constant that it's been proven responsible for people becoming schizophrenic?" I shook my head. "It's true. The wind has powerful psychiatric qualities." She pulled sunglasses out of her pocket and put them on. Blueblocker specs with yellow lenses. She gestured toward the door. "Go eat before it gets cold. See ya."

I climbed the stairs, a bit weak and run-down. My tongue felt like it needed dredging and my sinuses were sort of achy. Could've been allergies, but I went into my apartment and, with the remaining Gatorade, swallowed a Vitamin C and beckoned my white blood cells to start fucking shit up.

I found my ass groove on the couch and fit myself into it like I was a Lego. Then I ate my egg sandwich, feeling somewhat anemic. The food wasn't filling me. I felt like calling someone but I wasn't sure who. Tina was probably on her couch, Brett providing comfort via a cold compress and an Atavan; Stacey and Eric were probably doing something that would make me feel worse, something productive like helping build affordable housing for the poor or learning how to salsa-dance.

I wished I had bought some chocolate, like a big ol' Cadbury Fruit and Nut or something. I had nothing sweet in the house but I didn't want to go back out. There was nothing for me out there, not today. I got up, woke up my computer, and checked my e-mail. There were two new ones. The first was from my credit-card company. They had a free gift for me. Right, and I had full payment for them. DELETE. The next one was from Langford at *Fader*.

> Jason,
> Hve no idea if we r looking. U can send me over 5 of your best published clips, or if u don't have since yours were broadcast, any unpublished reviews you've written that I can show my boss.
> Scott
> *Sent from my BlackBerry Wireless Device*

I re-read it and then went back to the couch. I lay down and put a pillow behind my head. I didn't have any published clips. I didn't have any unpublished ones either. Christ, I was fucking naïve. I turned on the tube and flipped around, looking for anything half-decent. I could write up some reviews, I supposed, just pick a few new albums and critique them. I mean not to-day, today would be a success if I simply didn't slip into a coma. It didn't seem like there was any rush anyway, he didn't really make it sound that hopeful. Odds were he probably only wrote me back because he felt he had to or something. I clicked again and again and then thank god, there it was, the thing that was going to eat up my Saturday: *Superman II*. I lay back on the cushions, eyelids heavy, as Terence Stamp began his reign of terror on Planet Houston. I waited patiently for my favorite line: "Come to me, Superman. Come. Kneel before Zod."

(A) knock on the door woke me up. "Who is it?" I yawned, rubbing my eyes. I had no idea what time it was, but *Superman II* was over, transformed into some kind of women's golf tournament.

"It's your neighbor," said my neighbor. Patty. I sat up, ambled over to the door, and opened it.

"Hi, oh, did I wake you up?" she asked.

"No, not really, I just sort of dozed off watching TV," I said. We stood in the doorway. I wasn't sure whether or not to invite her in.

"You've got sleep lines on your face. Did you fall asleep on corduroy?"

I felt my cheek. It did feel a bit corrugated. "Oh." I managed a chuckle. "It must be the texture of my couch, I guess. Hey, do you want to come in?"

"Great, thanks." She pushed by me and went into my small main room. "I like your place," she said, looking around. She sat on the couch, fished around in her pockets, and pulled out a cigarette. "Is it okay if I smoke?"

"Yeah yeah, no problem." I went into the fridge and pulled out a two-liter Diet Coke. "Want some?" I asked.

She shook her head and lit up. I poured myself a glass, grabbed a mug to act as an ashtray, and sat down on the other end of the couch. It was the only place to sit. I sipped the soda and started to shake off the sleepiness. "Sorry, I'm sort of out of it. So, what have you been up to? I've just been here all day. I mean right here, on this couch. I had a late one last night."

"Oh, yeah?" She blew a perfect smoke ring. I'm talking perfect. It hung above her head and rotated, slowly dissipating and softening until it disappeared into the ceiling. She ashed into the mug and looked around my apartment.

Patty smiled, and I smiled back. This was nice, something my parents might have done, had a neighbor over for a chitchat. Not that much different from the way it might happen in most suburbs of America, for better or worse. Well, actually, for better. I didn't get the suburbs. Working all day was bad enough, but braving a bus or train and then the subway and the streets and the overcrowded elevator just for the privilege? Two hours a day wasted. No, I'd never understand that.

Patty adjusted a pillow behind her back. "I was up very late myself. Almost until five. I'm trying to reorganize, you see. I've been going through all my possessions to just assess what I have, where I've been for the past year, where I'm going. It's the season of rebirth, you know." She exhaled another perfect smoke ring.

"How do you do that?" I said, pointing to it. "I always wanted to be able to blow those." I felt like a teenager outside the high school, talking to the bad kid.

"You don't smoke, though, do you, Jason?"

I shook my head. "Just the pot."

"Filthy habit," she said, consciously exhaling smoke away from me, out the side of her crooked mouth. "My clothes, my sheets, everything stinks. I used to have a dog, before you lived here. A little terrier mix, Jolly. Even she reeked of smoke. Believe me, you don't want to start. However . . ." She stubbed out her smoke, leaned back, and reached into her jeans pocket, pulling out the spliff I had slipped under her door yesterday. Was that yesterday? Christ, it felt like weeks ago. "I could try to show you with this little fellow."

"Oh, I don't know. I probably shouldn't," I protested, waving a hand. Getting high now wasn't a great idea, after only a few hours ago being on bended knee in the bathroom, pleading "*No mas!*" I looked at the microwave: 6:30. Hmm. But . . . if I got high now, I'd be exhausted early, and I'd definitely stay in tonight and not end up going out to some bar. It was some twisted kind of drug logic, but I was nodding along to it. Yes, it made perfect sense. Getting high was the healthy thing to do. "I probably shouldn't," I said again, grinning. "But fuck it."

"Good boy." She took the spliff between her fingers and straightened and tightened it. Then she flicked her lighter to the joint's end and inhaled, eyes slit, until it glowed. She took it away from her mouth and held the smoke in, finally opening her eyes wide, and blowing a wall of white. This was obviously not her first or four hundredth try at this. "Tasty," she said, examining the joint, then extending it to me.

I reached out and took it from her. "Now remember, I'm only doing this for educational purposes. So show me how to do the smoke ring." I took a toke, held it, and looked at Patty, expectantly.

She explained rapidly, "Okay, now, while you hold the smoke in your lungs, make an 'O' with your lips. Then let the smoke slowly pool in your mouth—but don't exhale—you have to open your epiglottis thing and just let it go there. Okay, when it's in your mouth, with one quick puff, blow all the smoke out through the 'O.' " She made the movement with her lips.

I tried to follow what she was saying but the smoke dribbled out, shapeless. "I have no idea what you are talking about," I half-laughed, half-coughed. I passed the joint back her way.

"You have to keep trying. You really have to will it." She took a deep drag and then blew a smoke hula-hoop. "Ooh, that's a good one," she said, watching it slowly expand, rotate, break apart. "It's one of those things where you have to picture yourself doing it successfully, mentally prepare yourself, and then one time, boom, it just all comes together." She shook her head. "Whoa, I'm feeling this already. Pot is so much stronger now than it used to be. When I first started getting high you'd smoke three or four joints on your own, can you believe it?" Like a game of Pong, the joint was volleyed back to me.

"Totally," I said, taking a pull. I tried the ring thing again. Bupkis. I waved my hand through the white cloud. "Even in the last few years I feel like it's gotten crazy strong. You have to be careful or next thing you know you think you're a pelican or something." Ping, back to Patty.

"Ha! Let me ask you this, neighbor," she said, putting the joint to her lips. It was about halfway gone. She took a short strong toke, blowing the smoke back out her nose, Continental style. "What kind of provisions do you have? Because I think we will soon be a bit hungry, don't you?" Pong.

"Not much. But we can call Hunan Pan." I gestured out the window toward the restaurant, then took a deep hit. I was going to be very fucking high. But it was mellow, a relaxing buzz. Patty was cool. The only thing that was weird was how normal it was, me and someone older, getting high. I gave up on the ring thing, leaned back on the couch, and blew the smoke toward the ceiling, like I was some kind of volcano. The headache I had had that morning was long gone. I ashed into the mug and gave the joint back to Patty. There were still a good few hits left.

"No, that's crazy. I have food. I'll cook," she said, and took another hit. "I think that's it for me," she exhaled. "I'm really stoned. Thank you, neighbor!" She handed me the joint, stood up, and did some kind of yoga stretch, her arms moving out in a circle and meeting over her head, and then she bent down to touch her toes.

I was really stoned as well. I took one last long toke and stubbed out the roach in the mug, figuring I'd retrieve it later for a possible bedtime hit. I watched Patty stretch, stoned to the tits. Ooh, I did not want to think about her tits, not cool. Man, was I high. My synapses were just firing at will. Thought, thought, thought, lots of sentences that never gelled into paragraphs, a non-sequitur freakout. I watched Patty and her yoga moves and I wanted to make a joke about "warrior three," and then I gawked at her bright flannel as if I were a hippie in a sixties cult movie saying, "The colors! The colors!" I giggled out loud. I was a good audience for myself when I was high. I was Dom DeLuise to my own Burt Reynolds. I took a sip of my Diet Coke and stood up. "What are you doing?" I asked Patty, who was still holding some yoga pose.

"Sometimes when you're high it feels amazing to stretch," she said, arms held straight over her head.

"Really?" I put the Diet Coke down and bent over to stretch my hammies. I wasn't very flexible, I couldn't even touch my toes. I hung over my feet, breathing slowly. I heard her laugh and I looked up.

"I just made that up," she said, giggling. "Sorry." She walked over to my stereo. "Music! How do I work this?"

I grabbed the remote off the coffee table and turned it on. The Ramones' *Rocket to Russia* began to play.

"Lobotomy! Lobotomy!"

"Too aggressive?" I asked, turning it down a bit.

"Oh no, I like the Ramones," she said, bouncing on her toes a little. "I used to know Joey a bit, you know."

"No shit, really?"

"Yeah. Well, I used to have a good friend, Shelly, who bartended at CB's." Patty moved back over to the couch and sat down. "I'd try to go there on Tuesdays and hang out with her, because the other nights she'd be too busy to spend any time with me. Tuesdays were the slowest nights, and that place could get rowdy. It was all kids in there; you have to remember, the drinking age was only eighteen back then, so there'd be a lot of drunk high school kids, and I was too old for that shit." She reached into her pants pocket, pulled out a cigarette, and held it between her teeth as she jammed both hands back into her pockets searching for a lighter. "The Ramones used to play on Tuesdays a lot before they got popular, I mean, nobody was really there except Shelly and me, and whatever other bands were waiting to play. Their whole shtick was really funny, you couldn't understand a word they were saying because they were so damn loud, but you could just tell they had something. When they were done playing sometimes they used to hang out; Shelly would slip them some free beers." She spotted the lighter on the table, lit the cigarette, and took a puff. She exhaled. "Joey was always very polite, very nice. Even after they became stars I'd still see him around town and he'd wave and say hi. It was a shame he died so young." She gestured at me with her cigarette. "Hey, how old were you then? This was seventy-five I think."

"I was zero," I said. I paced over to the window and looked outside. It was dark now. Another day gone. I looked back at Patty, who was playing with her fingers, cig dangling from her mouth. "You okay, Patty?" I asked.

"Yeah. It's just . . . sometimes, I don't know how I got so old." She looked up at me and smiled. "Time flies, right?"

I felt bad. "Totally, it totally flies," I babbled. "Like this whole week flew by, I can't even remember what I did. I went to work Monday morning and the next thing I knew it was Friday night, and I was at some bar drinking and saying, 'Hey man, I'm so glad it's Friday,' to a bunch of strangers. It's like I went to sleep one night and I woke up and the week was over."

Patty puffed on her cigarette. "I got news for you. You know how your week flew past? Well, when you get to be my age, that's how the years go. You wake up one morning and it's the next year." She inhaled, held, and then blew a smoke ring. It floated out at me on an angle. "I told you, I can be a bit of a buzz-kill," she laughed. Her laugh turned into a cough, the same kind I had heard the other day. A bronchitis cough. I felt like a wet stuffed animal was going to come flying out.

"Do you need the Heimlich?" I joked.

"No, no it's okay, allergies is all." She wheezed. "Spring is hard for me." She caught her breath, stubbed out her cigarette, and smoothed her hair. "Could you be a dear and get me a glass of water?"

I washed out a glass, filled it, and gave it to her. "Sheena Is a Punk Rocker" came on, my favorite Ramones song. So I said, "Hey, this is my favorite Ramones song. Did you ever see them play it?"

She finished a sip of the water. "Oh, yes, I must've. I might not have been paying attention, but probably. I don't really re-member. Another great part of getting older, Jason, is you for-get stuff."

"But just think, you forget all the really bad stuff too, so maybe it's a benefit," I said.

"That's true. But here's the thing. When you get older, one day you'll catch yourself looking in the mirror wondering, 'What have I been doing again?' I mean, maybe you're just try-ing to remember something, like right now I'm trying to re-member the Ramones, or maybe you're being deep, thinking back across the years, but it'll hit you. The game is for keeps. That's why you see a lot of gray-haired guys in Porsches, they had a moment and were like 'Hey, I don't want to miss out on this, I'm doing it now!' If you live in America and you're not some religious nut and you believe in free will and all, you have no one to blame or congratulate on how you lived except your-self. It's sort of a tough day, to be truthful. It was for me. I think even if you're president or really successful or whatever, it's still a tough one." She stared into the corner, where my computer was sitting on my tiny desk. "That for work?"

"Nah, it's left over from college, just for e-mailing and play-ing around online," I said.

"Oh. Wait, what is it you do for work again?"

I scratched at an itch on my neck. "I have this bullshit job at a casting company. It's very small, just four of us. We cast for like TV shows and commercials and stuff. I'm like the general assis-tant, you know, whatever they need, I basically do. It's temporary."

She laughed. "That sounds fun! Meet any stars?"

"Nah, it's not like that at all. It's really just for bit parts and extras. Like if a sci-fi movie needs a hundred female warriors, and they all need to be blond and over six feet tall, they'd call us. It's goofy."

"So, are you going to be a director or screenwriter or some-thing?"

I poured the last of the Diet Coke into my glass and put the bottle in the sink. "To tell you the truth, Patty, I have no idea. I found the job through this temp agency. It's, you know, fine. I don't need to shave or dress up, and it pays the bills. Eventually, I'd like to do something music-related." I thought about the e-mail I had just received from Langford. "I mean, I think."

Patty took off her flannel; a gray long-sleeve T-shirt was un-derneath. "That sounds like a good gig for now, then. No has-sles, enough money to live and get your footing. It's just a job. You'll have oodles of them."

I was somewhat shocked by the positive response. If I had said anything like that to one of my peers, nine out of ten would've just smiled and said, "Great," while inside they were thinking, "Loser." At least that's what their expressions would look like, as if they were trying to put on a brave face as I told them my cat had died. "Yeah, it's okay, I suppose. A little boring, but whatever."

Patty stood up. "I'm starving. Do you want to come over? I have all these vegetables from the farmers' market, and I have some rice, we could make a stir-fry."

"Sure, okay." I felt in my pocket for my keys and grabbed my wallet off the coffee table. "Should I run out and get some beers or something?"

Patty put her flannel back on. "First you can help me chop the veggies, then while I cook you can run out for some. Let's be efficient!"

We headed for the door. "Oh, the stereo," I remembered, and walked back across the room to turn it off. As I turned I saw Patty skipping out of my apartment and into the hall like a hyper five-year-old on too much soda. I hustled out behind her to get to chopping.

Patty arranged quite a cornucopia of vegetables on her countertop. There were some normal ones—carrots, snow peas, and such—and then there were some scary-looking root vegetables that I could not have named if I was on a game show and the prize for doing so was a car. Patty was using a cleaver to chop and was whistling some unknown tune. I washed the odd vegetables and peeled them over the sink, using a paper towel as a low-rent drain screen. I was getting into it; the repetitive motion and the revealing of bright, wet flesh underneath dirty peel was incredibly satisfying to my stoned self. It was a little quiet, so I asked, "Patty, can we put on a little cooking music?"

She held the cleaver in mid-chop and said, "Absolutely. Go in the living room, you'll see the stereo, just put on whatever. But something upbeat."

Oh my God oh my God and then it happened, I was out of the kitchen and in the living room, the never-before-seen inner sanctum, and I was both alone and high. Yes. It was the mirror image of my apartment in shape, but it was far more cluttered. There was a lifetime of "maybe I should hold on to this" in there. She had an old cracked brown leather sofa; on it were two throw pillows with crocheted images of dogs. Her coffee table was a steamer trunk with a giant ashtray on top, a stack of mail and a fan of books next to it. The walls, as much as I could see of them, were a pale yellow. They were covered with framed and unframed paintings, photographs, and illustrations. A giant one, it must have been five feet diagonally, was of the Jackson Pollock school and took up almost the whole wall above her fireplace. In front of it, on her mantel, was a garish gold trophy. On the third and top tier of this was a male statuette with his hands held above his head. Carefully balanced on his hands was a still-packaged Twinkie. It was the sight of this that assured me my generation did not invent irony, as much as we may have thought so. I checked out some of the photographs crowded onto the narrow floor-to-ceiling strip of wall in between her windows. There were shots of Patty with friends or maybe family from a while back. In one black-and-white shot, she was holding a cigarette and leaning against a brick wall in what looked like Chinatown. Her other hand, by her side, was giving the photographer the finger. She must've been my age, maybe a little younger. She was pretty; she reminded me of what some of the girls looked like when you saw photographs of Lou Reed in Max's Kansas City in old magazines. Her bangs hung in her eyes, a small smile was screwed on lopsided. In this shot at least, she had it, that look of cool and youth that never went out of style: She just didn't give a fuck.

I started to feel like maybe I was snooping a bit too long, so I moved to the stereo, which was like the one I had growing up, an all-in-one Fisher with a record player on top. Next to the stereo, on a tall bookcase, were stacks and stacks of vinyl, hundreds of old LPs. I was giddy just staring at it. I thumbed through a few on top and found a rare one in a simple all-white sleeve, maybe even a bootleg, a live recording of Bob Dylan and Johnny Cash. I put it on the turntable and lowered the needle. It crackled to life. A song called "Mountain Dew" started up. Dylan sang in his nasal, country voice, "My Uncle Mort, he's sawed off and short, he measure about four foot two . . ." When the chorus came, Johnny and Bob harmonized in an odd but beautiful way. "They call it that good ol' mountain dew, and those who refuse it are few." With the warmth of the analog sound and the needle pops I felt like maybe I had flicked a switch and sent myself back in time. I was considering turning on Patty's TV to see if the Vietnam War was still under way; the set definitely looked like it dated from that time period, and I was thinking maybe it was so old it could only tune in the seventies. Anchormen would smoke Lucky Strikes and Johnny Carson would make jokes about hippies while sporting an Indian headdress.

"Good choice," Patty yelled from the kitchen. "Dylan is my absolute favorite!" I hurried back toward the kitchen but something stopped me. I saw words in small writing low on the wall, just above the molding. I got on my knee and saw it was a tiny diagram with arrows. The one pointing toward my apartment said "Jason." One pointing down said "Robert," and another pointing up said "Rachel."

Patty had finished the chopping, so I headed out to grab some beers while she "seasoned" the wok. I went into the deli; Bobby wasn't there yet. I was disappointed for a moment because I was excited to see him when I was sober. But then I realized that even if I hadn't had a drink, technically being high as shit didn't really qualify as sober to most people. The guy working the register was absolutely blasting Madonna, which was just about the funniest thing I had ever seen, an empty bodega, lit bright by fluorescents, tended by a balding, middle-aged Indian humming along to "Holiday." I moved to the beat over to the beers, smiling, and tried to decide on one. I wanted to go with our Asian theme. The closest they had was Pacifico, and since the Pacific was on the way to Asia, that was that was that. I also grabbed a pint of Ben and Jerry's Phish Food. I could take or leave that band's jammy music, but they sure inspired a damn good ice cream. I brought the items to the counter, paid, and left the man and his Madonna in peace, hoping that maybe later, he might vogue.

When I got back to Patty's she was cooking with a fury. It smelled pretty good too. I snuck the ice cream into the freezer and cracked open a couple of beers for us. "So Patty," I said, watching her work the overfilled wok, "those are some great pictures of you in the other room. The one in Chinatown is awesome."

"You think?" she said without looking up, focused on moving the sizzling vegetables around. "Thanks. That was a while ago. I don't give people the finger nearly as much now," she laughed. "Hey, are you hungry? Because I think we might've been too high when estimating how much we needed."

"I'm still high . . ."

"Me too!" she slipped in.

". . . so I'm pretty hungry. Don't worry. Better to have too much than too little."

"That's my philosophy on food too." She stopped working the wooden spoon and looked up at me. "My arm is killing me. Time for you to take over. It's almost done."

I took the spoon and made with the stirring. The veggies crackled and smoked in the oil. "Hey, can I ask you something? Like, back when that picture was taken, what were you doing in life?"

Patty was pulling plates from her cupboard. "Then I was working at this store that made custom leather pants for rock people and folk singers. They were all the rage. People wore them every day, and once they started to stretch they'd come back and we'd readjust them. It was on Sixth Avenue, above a bagel place a couple of blocks from Washington Square. It was fun. The store was by appointment only so we didn't really work that much. It was cheaper in New York then, you didn't have to kill yourself."

I kept the vegetables moving. Some of the onions were starting to burn but the squash-looking bits still looked raw. I wanted to know more about Patty but I didn't want to be pushy. "So, how long did you do that for?"

"Oh God, just a couple years," she said, taking out cutlery. "Watch that—is something burning?" She stepped over and took a look into the wok. "Okay, just one more minute and that is done."

I turned down the heat and moved the wok off the burner. I dumped the contents into a bowl Patty had left on the side, sneaking a bite of broccoli. Not bad. "And like, what other jobs did you do after that?" I asked, sheepishly.

"My goodness, Jason, are you interviewing me for a position in your firm?" she asked. I was mortified until she laughed. "C'mon, let's eat and I'll give you the short version."

She cleaned off the steamer trunk and we sat down to eat. Stoned, we had completely forgotten to make the rice. So we ate the tasty vegetables and drank beer, and she briefly gave me her work history. After the leather-pants store, Patty had bartended for a few years at the White Horse, which explained why I saw her outside there every once in a while. After that she was a dog walker. "I controlled all of the NYU area. Me and this guy Paco, we had a little dog-walking service together—Hip Pups. We were like the dog mafia. It was the world's greatest job any season but winter. We made a lot of tips at Christmas, though; no one wanted to be cheap to the person taking care of their dog. Guilt money." Paco had died twelve years ago from what sounded like AIDS without her actually saying it, and she had sold "the territory" to some corporate dog-walking company. "They don't even screen who they hire. But they offered me a lot of cash, and it made me sad to do it without Paco." Since then, she still walked a few dogs in the neighborhood, "my babies," and bartended one Saturday a month at the White Horse.

We carried the dishes back into the kitchen. "So, Jason," Patty asked, putting her plate in the sink, "any serious girls in your life?"

"Nah," I said, handing her mine. "I did go out with this one girl a couple of times recently, but I haven't heard from her in a while."

"Bummer. How long has it been?"

"Two weeks."

"Ooh."

"Yeah, and the thing is, I know this is silly, but she has this pair of my pants I sort of really want back."

"That's awkward. It might be best to just remember them fondly."

"I know, I know. But what's she going to do with them, it's not like she's going to wear them. She could put them in the mail, or whatever."

"Yeah, but sometimes, Jason," said Patty turning on the tap, "you just have to go out and buy yourself a new pair of pants."

After she washed the dishes, I busted out the ice cream and we polished off the pint. Patty lit up a cigarette and had another one of those coughing fits. It was pretty nasty, and I didn't say anything at the time. But a half-hour later as we bid each other good night, both our eyes heavy with sleep, I couldn't help myself.

"Hey, um, my friend who's getting married is a resident at Cornell Med, and he could probably recommend someone who could check out those allergies, cheap, if you wanted." We stood in her doorway.

"Thanks, neighbor. I have a doctor, though. Don't worry." She gave me a hug. "Sweet dreams."

I went into my apartment. It was midnight. I washed and brushed and got under the covers feeling sated. I rolled over, got comfortable, and finally let my lids shut.

I was a little worried, though.

And then it was Monday. I sat at the reception desk and made a sesame bagel with butter last as long as it could. There wasn't much to look forward to after that. Melinda was in the back running a casting session for nuns for some movie, so there were actresses trying to look nunly sitting on the benches in the waiting area. Unfortunately the specs must have been for older nuns, real ruler-slappers; there were none I wanted to tempt toward the sins of the flesh.

I hopped on Instant Messenger to see what was happening with the kids. I hadn't caught up yet with Tina to see how her night with Brett had ended up, and I hadn't talked with Stacey in ages. Both were on my to-do list.

doodyball5: so . . . was it
tinadoll: yes princess?
doodyball5: proposed to over brunch?
tinadoll: nope . . . but it has a crush
tinadoll: just made out. im no slut
doodyball5: yes u r
tinadoll: that's true! he is sooo cute!
doodyball5: you guys can share gel and talk about jeans

tinadoll:	did u soil either of those two girls?
doodyball5:	nope
tinadoll:	pants?
doodyball5:	not yet
tinadoll:	im picturing a nice oven mitt
doodyball5:	i did do something tho . . .
tinadoll:	oh christ . . . you called the pants police?
doodyball5:	i drank and emailed
tinadoll:	have i taught u nothing!?
tinadoll:	how bad was it? did u tell her u love her?
doodyball5:	i just asked her to give me the damn pants back
tinadoll:	response?
doodyball5:	radio silence
tinadoll:	you should've went all-out crazy, threatened to kill yourself or something
tinadoll:	kidding. don't sweat it. if it makes u feel better, ive done far worse
doodyball5:	like the time you gave the entire east village crabs?
tinadoll:	you cant prove that
doodyball5:	heh. hey have you talked to stacey lately?
tinadoll:	no. let's start a chatroom. stacey and eric hold . . .

stace has entered the room.

tinadoll:	stacey!!!
doodyball5:	stace?
stace:	hi
doodyball5:	hello hello. what're you doing tonight?
stace:	i have my women's legal group and then i'm going to a party with ali's friend mallory

doodyball5: where? we're coming!

stace: a bar on 13 and A. some dorky internet party of some kind

doodyball5: well, wouldn't you like to hang out with me?

tinadoll: speaking of internet dorks . . .

doodyball5: will your party allow guests?

tinadoll: i'm not drinking tonight

doodyball5: lie

tinadoll: i have alcoholism

tinadoll: bad

e-diddy has entered the room.

tinadoll: yes!!!!

e-diddy: how's my doodyball? stacey? sweetie?

doodyball5: stacey is too busy for your love

tinadoll: speaking of . . . i just fell in love

e-diddy: w/?

tinadoll: a boy

e-diddy: yup, tell more

tinadoll: shit. i gotta go rock the house. see you all in hell

e-diddy: me too bye

e-diddy has left the room.
tinadoll has left the room.

doodyball5: whoa—is this party over?

stace: hi

doodyball5: oh hi miss bizzy

stace: that plus i cant type fast enough. all good?

doodyball5: status quo. u? been a while . . .

stace: I know! gonna have to catch up soon

doodyball5: over ketchup

doodyball5: btw . . . I wrote scott

stace: woohoo! and . . . ?

doodyball5: didn't sound too promising, but he said to send some writing samples

stace: that's something

doodyball5: yeah, now i just need writing samples

stace: you could do that fast, jason. send them soon and then keep checking in with him

doodyball5: that's the plan

stace: you have to be persistent

doodyball5: no doubt

stace: so . . . you know what happens this week, rt? your first rabbi class

doodyball5: i will pick out a good outfit

stace: i emailed you the info. weds 7 to 10

doodyball5: I am ready to rabbi

stace: k gotta go. next weekend dinner or drink or something?

doodyball5: yep

stace: call and tell me how class goes. bye

doodyball5: wait, don't go yet. im bored as bloody hell

stace has left the room.

doodyball5: balls

doodyball5 has left the room.

Melinda emerged from the back and pulled up a chair next to me at the desk.

"So, were the nuns fun?" I asked.

"So fun. They were all trying to act very serious and pious. Not one smile on that casting tape, that's for sure."

"Is it almost time for lunch? I'm getting the shakes," I said.

Melinda glanced at the schedule. "Yeah, I think we're cool. Let me just tell Sara that we're going out together so she'll answer the phone."

"You know, I've never actually talked to Sara."

"No!"

"Yeah, it's weird. I say hi, but I've never been caught in the elevator with her or chitchatted. Not once. I barely talk to JB either."

"Well, JB is totally antisocial, but Sara is nice. Someday you'll meet by the watercooler, if it's your destiny." Melinda put on some lip gloss and went over to Sara's office.

On the walk to lunch we caught up. It had been a while since we'd had a talk other than just mocking work. It turned out that Melinda's play had gotten some interest from a well-known off-Broadway producer.

"Why the fuck didn't you immediately tell me? That's sick!" I shouted.

"Because nothing's certain yet. These things take a long time and they are really flaky," she said as we crossed the avenue.

She hid it well, but she had to be bursting on the inside. To have someone legitimize her work must have been amazing. The producer had been at the reading/party a few weeks ago and apparently was really into the play.

"But if you sell it, I'll be all alone and I'll have no one to go buy lunch with. I'll be one of the lonely lunchers, feeding half my sandwich to pigeons from a bench. You should factor my mental health into your decision." We entered what we affectionately called "Stress Deli." It was a fine deli—a big one, really—but it got tremendously crowded during lunch. If you didn't know exactly what kind of sandwich you wanted as you got to the front of the counter, people would actually heckle you to hurry up. Worse, the women who worked the cash registers were little balls of Korean fury who would somehow divine what denomination of bill you were going to pull out of your wallet and would shove the change in your face before you could even get your hand into your pocket. At least once a week I'd end up with a massive bruise on my leg from some asshole with one of those twenty-five-pound briefcases who was in such a rush to grab some Dentyne Ice he'd ram me on his way through the store. But it was sorta the best place nearby, so we braved it.

All conversation was put on hold until we emerged with our sandwiches.

"That was like Iwo Jima," I said, shifting the bag from my right to my left hand.

"It sucks in there. But it's fast," said Melinda.

"Well, when you're famous and you come back to the office to visit we can always go there and remember the times we've had," I said, as we started walking. "Do you really think you might be leaving?"

"I don't know. I hope. We'll see. Anyway, business has been so bad at JB's, odds are I'll be laid off before I sell a play," she said.

I stopped for a second, leaned down, and tied my shoe. Looking up I said, "Really, are we doing bad? I had no idea."

"You had no idea? What do you do all day? Basically nothing, right? Which means we aren't overrun with business."

"How am I supposed to know?" I said, standing back up. "I feel like it's always been mellow there."

"That's sort of the problem, I think," she said as we continued walking. "It's not just a lull, it's kind of permanently slow. But we'll see. I wouldn't worry about it."

We cruised back to the office, and I told Melinda about the Jane situation. I was curious as to her opinion.

"Yeah, I don't think you'll be seeing those pants again," said Melinda as we reentered the office. "That's just the way it works. You took that risk when you lent them to her."

"Sheesh. I expected at least you'd be on my side. I figured lesbians would be a little more evolved in these matters."

"Oh, no, we're far worse. I still wear my ex's stuff, she was my size."

"Fuck, well, I guess they're gone."

Melinda stared at me. "Is it the pants, or do you really just want to see this girl again?"

"The pants. Honestly."

She shrugged, looking unconvinced. "Those must be some fucking pants."

I sat back down at the receptionist desk and commandeered the computer while Melinda leafed through an old *Us Weekly*. E-mail was opened and I saw that Jane hadn't responded to my tirade. I sighed. She wasn't ever going to. Okay, that was it. I was done. "*No mas*," I said to myself. I wasn't going to become a stalker. No, I was going to take the high road. Back to basic cable and beating off.

I closed e-mail and surfed onto *Pitchfork*, a hip music site I frequented, to read up on the latest and greatest. I figured I should take a good look at how they wrote their record reviews. I clicked on one after another, and each was longer and more in-depth than the last. They were filled with obscure details like bands' favorite BPMs, and highfalutin hypotheses like, "Of all the cyclical inclinations in the post-Vietnam rock-'n'-roll oeuvre, mod revivalism stands tall as the most oxymoronic." Jesus. As I read on, I unwrapped the butcher paper around my turkey sandwich and took a bite.

Goddamn motherfuckers forgot to put the cheese on.

The day ended and there I was, back at home, on the toilet. I had been sitting there quite a while.

I started thinking about the sixteen-hour drive I used to make twice a year during college, from Missouri to Ithaca and vice versa, alone in my bad little beige 1986 Honda Civic. After graduation, I made the epic drive one last time. The highway near Indiana seemed so straight and flat I probably could've fallen asleep and safely made it across the state. As I cracked open my fifteenth Diet Coke, an old Ford Mustang pulled up next to me. The driver shouted, "Buy American, asshole!" He sped past, his kids giving me the finger out the rear window.

The Honda had no disc player and the tape deck was busted. For a long stretch after the Mustang, all I could pick up was static. I was beat; I was like eleven hours in and starting to see visions. Desperate, I tried switching over to AM. And crackling through the speakers came a miracle, "You Are My Sunshine." I was instantly reenergized; I rolled down my window and sang along to the chorus at the top of my lungs, drumming my hand against the car door, delirious. "You are my sunshine, my only sunshine / you make me happyyyyy, when skies are gray." It was such a goofy, positive song. But then, speeding along, listening to all the verses for probably the first time, I realized that it really wasn't a love song at all. It was fucking dark. "You told me once, dear, you really loved me / no one else could come between / but now you've left me, and love another / you have shattered all my dreams." All sung to this smiley sing-along tune, which was disguising it. "Please don't take my sunshine away."

In the other room I heard the TV come back from commercial. I had left it on CNN. They were reporting that a coyote had been found and captured in Central Park. How the hell did a coyote get into Central Park? That sounded like a setup line for a cheap joke. "He took the 6 train." When you live alone, you can go to the bathroom with the door open. That way you don't miss the big coyote stories on TV.

I finished my business, went back toward the couch, and saw there was a message on the machine. It could've been there for days, I never checked it anymore. I hit PLAY.

"Hey Jason, it's Mom."

"And Dad!" I could hear him yell from somewhere in the back of the room.

"How's everything? We got your e-mail. A rabbi—that's very funny. We didn't realize a regular person could just marry people, but we'll take your word. Everything here is the same, it's finally starting to get warm. Work is slow, your dad and I have been going to see a lot of movies, no big news. Oh—the next time you come home we really want you to clean out some of the old stuff you have in your room; Dad is thinking of starting a project and making it into a home office. I've already alerted the paramedics, don't worry. We'll keep all your stuff in the closet and replace the bed with a pull-out couch for when you come visit. Which is going to be when, honey? Let's pick a date already. Okay, I don't want to use up your whole machine. Call us or write us. Love you!"

I had heard the threat of my room being turned into a "home office" for years now, and was pretty sure it was safe from renovation for several more to come. I made a mental note to call my folks this week and then picked up my phone and called the people who had taken on the responsibility of feeding me in lieu of my parents, Hunan Pan.

And then there I was, in a bar again. Moo-shu chicken followed by vodka, yep, my nights were damn predictable. After partial digestion, I had met Tina for a civilized drink. Just a quick one. She had to run to catch a band with Brett; I assumed I was invited but it turned out I wasn't. I don't know, she was a little weird about it.

"So," she said, smoothing down her hair, "what's happening with Mr. Fantastic?"

"You know, just being that guy. What about you? I mean, other than going to see bands without me, what's new?" I poked the lemon in my vodka soda with my straw.

"Oh my God, you are such a girl!"

"I'm a man, just look how hairy my arms are." I held one up to her face. It wasn't that hairy, actually.

Tina shoved it away. "Sheesh, I don't care, you can come. Brett has just been crazy busy, and I wanted some alone time with him." She stirred her drink. "You know, I'm still figuring out what I think. So far so good, though."

"I'm just messing with you. What's he so busy with?" I wasn't quite sure what Brett did every day. All I knew was that he was a couple years older than us and had finished up NYU film school around January.

"It's really exciting. It looks like he's going to direct this film. A real film, not like some student one. He's got funding and everything."

"Wow, impressive. How'd he manage that?" I was a little jealous.

"Honestly? Chutzpah. This guy who lives on his block, Donnie Sherman, had a novel come out last year called *Chase Me*. Ever hear of it?"

I shook my head.

"Supposedly it got good reviews. Brett liked it a lot, anyway. So around five or six months ago, he saw the guy at a café, walked over and introduced himself. Then he just put his dick on the table."

"The old dick-on-the-table, eh?"

"Works every time, from what I hear. He said, 'I'm a director. I'm sure you're talking to other people, but I loved your book and I really want to make a film of it. Can I buy you a drink?' Anyway, they hit it off. They wrote the screenplay together. Donnie knew a producer and he got them money somehow, and then Brett found a few other investors. Pretty nuts, huh?" She glanced around the bar, which was starting to fill up. "I haven't read the script yet; I'm scared if I don't like it I'll have to break up with him. But I think it might be a really good movie. They have a couple of great theater actors lined up, that girl from *Rent* is the lead. And Chris Makepeace is also going to be in it, you ever hear of him?"

I laughed. "Isn't that Rudy, Rudy the rabbit, from *Meatballs*? He was in *My Bodyguard*, too."

"He plays an aging former porn star who's just moved to Park Slope. Who knows, maybe it will be his *Pulp Fiction*." She polished off her drink. "Anyway, they're just really getting started casting and figuring shit out, and he's pretty obsessed with it, which makes sense. But that's why I wanted to see him alone tonight."

"Well, it sounds pretty fucking exciting. Seriously, it's huge. Tell him I say congrats."

Tina bought us a second round, two more vodka sodas. I brought mine to my lips and took a deep swig. "Ugh," I spat, "yuck, tonic!" I put the drink down and took a step back, stumbling right into a smoky little girl wearing a jean jacket and a scarf. "Oh, sorry!" I said, pulling it back together and offering a half bow.

"No, *qua*, it was my fault," she said with a French accent and a crooked smile.

I smiled in return and turned back toward Tina. Then my half-pickled brain caught up. French, huh? Tina raised her eyebrows and smiled. She put her hand up to my ear and whispered, "Body odor. I guarantee it."

Tina downed her drink, it was time for her to go. She went to the ladies' room to make sure she looked pretty for her man. I finished off my drink, despite the tonic, and looked around. It was early yet. It seemed like the French girl was checking me out, and she was only a few bodies away. I was just drunk and confident enough to make an approach. It was certainly worth me buying one more drink, in the interest of foreign relations. I reeled toward her.

"Hi," I said. "I'm Jason."

"Hello, I am Isabelle."

And soon I found myself ordering us two more drinks, a Bass for her and another vodka soda, this time with soda, please, for me. I was pretty buzzed; the last thing I needed was more alcohol, but unfortunately it was also the first thing I needed.

Suddenly we both had arms draped over our shoulders. "Hi!" said Tina, freshly made up and grinning ear to ear. "So, I'm off." She turned her head to Isabelle. "Hi. Bye." She turned to me, and glanced down at my Levi's. "And you, keep an eye on those slacks, 'kay, sport?" She pinched my cheek and moved on.

"What she say?" Isabelle asked, furrowing her brow.

I shrugged.

Isabelle and I talked for a bit and I learned that (1) yes, she was from France, here on vacation with her younger sister Esther who was back at the hotel, (2) her English was slightly less than so-so, and (3) she was sassy as all hell. A variation on a pageboy haircut, flirtatious eyes, the crooked smile, and that damn accent all arranged perfectly around a body a drunken Brit might call "fuckin' fit, mate." The clock struck two; where all the time went, who knew? We left the bar behind us and lit out into the early-morning chill. We walked and talked, where oh where could we possibly be going . . . oh, surprise! We were outside my building. Apparently, there was just enough chum left in the water.

The rest is exactly as I wrote it on my computer early the following morning, thinking it needed to be preserved for future generations, as Isabelle still slept in my bed:

ME: So, do you want to come upstairs?

FRENCH GIRL: Yes. Why not I think.

ME: Très bien. (*I raise eyebrows, "Aren't I clever? That's French."*)

INTERIOR, APT.

ME: Want a drink?

FG: You have beer?

ME: Yes. (*I open fridge and hand her a Stella.*) Here you go.

FG: Can I put on music? I love this Radiohead.

ME: Rock out.

FG: What?

ME: Oh, nothing. Turn it on, it's that button . . . no, the other . . . you got it. (*Music begins to play loudly.*)

FG: I love this music. "Carmel Police . . . mmm mmm mmm . . ." You want dance?

ME: Not just yet. (*I open another beer for myself.*)

FG: You have mariwahnah?

ME: Yeah—you want to get high?

FG: What?

ME: Smoke?

FG: Sure, why not. (*She dances and smiles, as tempting as Easter chocolate.*)

(*We get high and begin to dirty dance. We continue to talk while dancing.*)

ME: Sometimes when I get high I talk a lot, you might notice.

FG: What you say? (*She starts speaking rapidly in French.*) I think I cannot talk English right now. (*She kisses me.*)

ME: Mmm. Do you French people take classes for this when you're little, because I think, it's really a good idea. Fuck math.

(*Cut to bedroom. We are naked and things are happening.*)

ME: (*breathing hard*) I just want to say you are a good ambassador of your country.

FG: Ohh good. Mmmmph!

ME: Magnifique! Right?

FG: Mm! Mm!

(*We continue having sex, briefly pausing to switch positions with acrobatic grace.*)

FG: (*quite loud*) Oui! Oui! Oui!

ME: You mean "Yes, yes!"

FG: Qui lenipomonique! (*something French and unintelligible*)

ME: (*close to orgasm and punctuating each thrust with a shout*) U-S-A! U-S-A! U-S-A!

FG: Vive la France!

(*We lie side by side, satisfied.*)

FG: Mmmm, that nice, Jason.

ME: I guess you haven't learned the word "stupendous" yet.

FG: What that mean, "stuuup . . ."?

ME: It means like . . . it means "Welcome to America."

(*She lights a cigarette.*)

FG: You funny.

Somewhere back around New Year's I had promised myself I would try to write a sentence or two every day in a journal, which was really just a Word document on my dusty computer cleverly named journal.doc. I was big on it when I was traveling, and it was something I was trying to bring back, but so far it hadn't been brung. After having typed in my French connection yesterday, it seemed like now was the perfect opportunity to get the party started again.

It was after work on Wednesday. I was killing a little time at home before I had to head to the rabbi class, and I had been staring, frozen, at the journal document. The cursor blinked and blinked, but I couldn't think how to start. I was stumped. I knew it. It knew it. I punted and flicked the computer off.

There were few times lately when I felt I had to get something that happened written down, lest I forget it. My days had become routine, somewhat indistinguishable from one another. Lots of small funny things happened, sure, but nothing major. In school you had semesters and finals and spring breaks to delineate time; out here in "the real world," every day was sort of like the one before. I guess that's why people freaked out about birthdays: Those at least put a stake in the ground, somehow ended one chapter and opened a next. The last big chapters for me were quitting bartending and taking the JB's job, mostly because I went from working nights to working days; before that was graduating from college and coming to New York. These events were worthy of lines on paper, of contemplation over an afternoon beer alone or of reinterpreting song lyrics as specific advice written just for me, just for my life-altering moments.

I wrote constantly while I was traveling; I was one of those super-clichéd scruffy twenty-two-year-olds scribbling furiously on the train, one eye guarding my "rucksack." I was always seeing new things or waking up in new cities. Sometimes I'd get lost and caught in the rain and end up in an absolutely shady hostel listening to mice scamper and sleeping with my passport in my underwear. Other days would reveal secret parts of the Spanish countryside. One time an Italian schoolteacher in Prague kissed me in the back of a beer hall while her colleagues were sitting outside at a table, all because a guy I was traveling with had lied and told her my father had written *Twin Peaks*. Apparently, back in the day it was a huge hit in Rome. A graph line of my life then would have shown a lot of modulation. If I wrote every day now, all entries would be something like, "Woke up, went to work, drank soda, e-mailed, went out for drinks with X, and did/didn't have my bathing-suit area touched." The graph line had become far flatter. There were fewer highs and lows, and less need for written commentary. Just a lot of dittos.

Even during what were supposed to be the most fun times, in a bar, drink in hand, life was starting to feel repetitive. If every day was a rerun of the day before, then the nights were one long uninterrupted blur. And The Fear the following mornings seemed to be getting worse.

That lack of modulation weighed on my mind when I blew off work to go to brunch with Isabelle, the morning after our Franco-American summit. We ate some eggs at the Galaxy and then strolled around Chelsea, popping into the occasional gallery, before she went to meet up with her sister somewhere in Midtown. It was refreshing to move through the familiar streets with someone from out of town, someone seeing the city for the first time, wide-eyed, like I was during my own travels. She was amazed at the little things. A woman picking up her dog's poop in a bright pink bag, the man who sang opera as he sold small illustrations on the corner of Twenty-sixth Street. We kissed good-bye outside the entrance to the E train. First on the mouth, then both cheeks. She was flying out later that night. She gave me her e-mail and invited me to visit her in France sometime. As I walked away, I considered if that might ever happen, or more likely, if this was the last time I'd ever see this particular human being. Real good-byes eluded me; it was hard to grasp the finality, hard to escape whatever else I felt at the moment, the heat of the sun on my neck, my lips dry and chapped. I looked back and caught a glimpse of her head as she disappeared down the stairs. I thought about calling after her, I didn't know if she knew the right train. Instead, I took a breath and mentally wished her good luck and a good life. Then I slumped off toward work, thinking "dentist's appointment" would be the appropriate excuse for my tardiness.

Now it was time to away to the rabbi class. Temple Beth El, where it was being held, was on the Upper East Side, a bit of a trip from the West Village. I grabbed my iPod, took a swig from the two-liter Diet Coke in the fridge, and headed out of the apartment.

I hit PLAY, shut out the city, and walked toward the L train. After only three blocks, though, the damn battery died and I was back in cacophonous reality. I sighed, took off the head-phones, and pocketed the player. I grabbed a free *Village Voice* from a red plastic dispenser and made my way to the train.

Twenty-five minutes later I resurfaced on the Upper East

Side. I walked past a steady stream of chain stores—Baby Gap, Old Navy, Victoria's Secret, Baby Gap, Toys "Я" Us, Baby Gap. I looked down Lexington: This was fro-gurt country, there were frozen-yogurt outlets as far as the eye could see. Expensive knobby-tired baby carriages boxed me in as I moved along. It felt like a PG-13 version of the city. I checked my phone out of habit; I had a text message. Stacey, reminding me about tonight. Was she neurotic or was I that untrustworthy? I was pretty sure it was her personality flaw and not mine, so I texted her back. "Totally forgot! Drunk downtown. Shit!"

I arrived at the temple on Seventy-ninth Street, on time. I was a little nervous as I opened the door and walked down a long narrow hall in search of the rabbi's study, where the e-mail said we'd be meeting. The hall was decorated on both sides with framed paintings of various biblical scenes, along with black-and-white shots of Masada and the Wailing Wall. I sort of wished it was more like a Jewish Hall of Fame, or like an athletic stadium tunnel leading to the field of battle, and that there were framed 8x10's of Sandy Koufax, Sammy Davis, Jr., David Ben-Gurion, all our biggest stars, lining the walls. I could see a rabbi and a cantor walking down a hall like that, getting pumped to go out on the dais and give it their all. Someday, if they pushed themselves, their photos would be wedged onto that wall, perhaps in the coveted spot between David Copperfield and Leonard Nimoy. (Indeed, Mr. Spock was a Jew.)

The rabbi's study door was ajar, so I poked my head in. Two women and a guy about my age sat in folding chairs around a wooden table. Suddenly I wondered if I should have been dressed nicer than my jeans, faded Yoo-Hoo T-shirt, and hoodie. Or if I should have maybe brought a pen and a pad.

"Hi, is this the, uh, class for, um . . ." I wasn't sure what it was even called. "Learning how to preside over a wedding ceremony?"

"Yep," responded the guy. He had silver metal glasses and wavy blond hair, and he was wearing a light-blue shirt with a loosened maroon tie. "That's why we're all here. The rabbi hasn't arrived yet, though." He extended his hand. "I'm Mark."

"Hi, I'm Jason." We shook. "Jason," I said extending my hand toward the first woman, who looked to be around forty, with short gray hair and a belly that tested the buttons of her beige blazer.

"Nora," she replied. "Hi."

I leaned toward the other woman, who looked to be about my age. "Hi, I'm Jennifer," she said, smiling. She had blue eyes and thick curly dark hair, rabbi's-daughter's hair. And, I was embarrassed to notice in shul of all places, simply fantastic tits under her tight black V-neck sweater. Light, fluffy, perky, kiss-able. Mazel tov, my dear.

I took a seat and unzipped my sweatshirt. A man entered the room wearing a green sweater-vest over a white shirt and sporting a beard and a yarmulke. "Hi, everybody, I'm Rabbi Stan. Glad you all could make it."

We went around the table and introduced ourselves to Rabbi Stan. Every rabbi I had ever met, which wasn't a whole hell of a lot, went by his last name. Rabbi Pearlman. Rabbi Feldstein. Rabbi Bassen. Rabbi Stan, who looked to be in his late thirties, must have been some kind of New Age rabbi, the kind that let you call them by their first names and knew how to juggle.

"So, Jason, tell me what brings you to this class," Rabbi Stan said.

"Um, well, two good friends of mine are getting married, Stacey and Eric, and they asked me to preside at their wedding." Why else did he think I was here?

"To marry your friends, that will be wonderful. Do you know what type of ceremony you'll perform?"

"No, I'm pretty much a novice," I said, grinning. "I was hoping that I'd learn all about that here."

Rabbi Stan scratched his chin. It seemed like he might still be getting used to the beard; it was a bit patchy. "You will hopefully learn a lot here, but the ceremony design will be yours. Rabbinical teaching that is not."

I wasn't exactly sure what he was getting at, but that might've been because I was fixated on how he sometimes spoke backward, like a Jewish Yoda. Maybe he was trying to sound than his years older. "I'm sorry, what do you mean?" I asked.

"You'll decide how the ceremony will flow, you'll provide the words of love and guidance. You are not here to become a rabbi, you are only here to learn some of the Jewish tradition. After all, you will be a Universal Life Minister. You know the Internet site to go to, right?" We all nodded. "Our work here is only to offer guidance and advice for how you can structure your personalized ceremony. For you, not a rabbi like myself, were chosen by your friends to bring them together. But if you are here in my class, they want a bit of tradition, yes? Yes. You know, a great rabbi was once asked by a man to teach him the entire meaning of the Torah while he stood on one foot. The rabbi told him, "Do not do unto others what you would not have them do unto you. The rest is commentary." He smiled at us. "Piece of cake, don't worry!"

He asked the others why they were there. Mark was going to perform a small second marriage for his friend. Nora was going to be the rabbi for her sister's wedding. Jennifer of the teacup tits was, like me, going to be a rabbi for her friends from college.

Now that he knew our stories, Rabbi Stan rolled up his sleeves. "Today we are going to talk about Jewish law a tiny bit. But we will talk more about love. Love is a word we use a lot in society today. We use it too much, I think, it's lost the meat of its meaning. You love your dog. You love the Yankees, and ice cream, and vacations to the Poconos. I heard a girl in shul today say she loved her new sandals. Just loved them! But these aren't really loves, these are very strong likes. Things adored. Things perhaps treasured. But loved? Not in the old sense of the word."

As Rabbi Stan gesticulated I could see half moons of sweat forming under his arms. My eyelids were getting heavy, so I bit my tongue to help stay awake. It was the same trick I had used throughout high school and college. A little pain kept the eyes open.

Rabbi Stan continued. "'Would you dive in front of a bullet to protect those sandals?' I asked the girl in shul. 'No, of course not,' the girl told me. 'Then you are not in love with them,' I said. Now, I'm joking of course, but to marry two people you must have a grasp of the meaning of love. It seems at the very least that would be something you ought to know if you are to say, 'By the power invested in me I pronounce you man and wife.' Can I teach you love? No, it can't be taught. But I can tell you a few things about it.

"True love is more than anything a responsibility. It is the greatest responsibility, for lovers are the caretakers of each other's hearts, and lives. And to fulfill this responsibility requires great compromise and sacrifice. That is why the mother cleans the child's behind, even though it is quite unpleasant. You laugh, Jennifer, but have you changed a newborn?" Jennifer shook her head. "I'm kidding, but truly, you can't underestimate the importance of sacrifice. Willingness to do the things you don't want to do for the sake of someone else. It may not sound as exciting as lust and sex and God forbid getting a tattoo with a heart, but sacrifice and compromise are the Krazy Glue of love. It is what keeps a marriage together."

I began playing with a loose thread at the bottom hem of my shirt. Was a rabbi really the right person to be defining love? I mean, spiritual matters or morals maybe, but love? I would have liked to see his résumé. Not that I doubted him, or could think of a better person off the top of my head; I just wasn't sure this guy in the outfit from Sy Sym's had the "Love Ph.D." He was wearing a wedding ring, but was it his first marriage? How did he know she was the one, did he have an epiphany, was it a lightning bolt at first sight? Did that shit even exist? It felt like maybe Hollywood and Hallmark conspired to invent it. These were things I wanted to understand; sacrifice I had heard about. I kept pulling at the thread. I wondered whether, if I kept unraveling it, I'd eventually be sitting there topless. Or maybe just the torso part would disappear, and I'd still be wearing sleeves. It would be an interesting experiment. The rabbi cleared his throat and I was back in the classroom.

"Now, the other side of sacrifice and compromise is passion. Because in a marriage, you are willing to sacrifice and compromise on things that, in the end, aren't as important, so as to improve the ones you are most passionate about. For example, a man might take a lesser job so as to have more time with his family, et cetera." He held up his hands. "Or a woman, I do not mean to be sexist. Responsibility, sacrifice, compromise, and passion. The four horsemen of love, all perfect topics for a wedding ceremony. Okay, now, have any of you thought about your ceremonies?"

Nora had. "My sister and her fiancé are both English professors, so I was going to start with a reading of a poem, either a Shelley or a Donne, their favorites. Then I was going to tell the story of how they met, and then get into the vows, which I'm going to help them write." She crinkled her forehead. "How does that sound?"

Rabbi Stan took off his glasses and cleaned them with a

small piece of cloth he pulled from his pocket. "Well, Nora," he said, "I think the poetry is a nice personalized touch. But you must also think about how you will bring their friends and family into this emotional setting. Please do not think this cynical, but you must understand that a wedding is not a private ceremony. No, this is a stage show for two people to tell the world they love each other, to declare it to the four winds, and you shall be the master of ceremonies." Again he cleared his throat. "Think of this as the Super Bowl of their life. Never will they have more people gather to see them, rooting for not only a win, but also for a good game. So as they say, you will need some sizzle to help sell this steak. Because you can make it beautiful for the bride and groom, but if the rest of the congregation does not feel included, there will be coughing and talking and the worst thing you could have, which is grandparents audibly complaining. If you hear, 'What is she talking about?' from a senior, the ceremony is in trouble. It is the Jewish equivalent of a tomato thrown at a comedian. Trust me. I have been heckled by many of our elderly congregants when they don't like a sermon." He smiled.

"Has anyone else thought about their ceremonies?" We looked at one another. I sure as shit hadn't. I shifted awkwardly in my seat.

"That's fine," he said. "Let's take fifteen minutes and each of you brainstorm a bit what you think you might want to talk about. Then we will have a starting place for each of you." He passed out some paper, and I bummed a pen from Nora, who fished out a spare from the bottom of her bag. Rabbi Stan turned his back to us and went to the computer on his desk.

Everyone leaned forward and began scratching out wedding ideas. I wanted to think about Stacey and Eric, but sitting there, the rabbi's back to me, I had what alcoholics call a moment of clarity. In the not-too-distant future I was going to be standing on a stage in front of three hundred people wearing a suit. A suit I probably needed to buy, because I hadn't worn the one I owned—the "interview suit" my parents had bought me after college—in years, and it probably didn't fit. The word "oy" struck me as appropriate.

I attempted to think about what made Stacey and Eric special. They were incredibly dependable, rock-solid, the perfect candidates to hold your spare set of keys. Yeah, that sounded really romantic. What was I going to say? I hadn't given the whole thing too much meditation, but in the back of my head I had been thinking I might try to do a fun, sort of comic ceremony. But I could see now from the rabbi's whole love spiel that this was pretty serious. Still, it was hard to be sincere without also being dull. I tried to think of wedding scenes from books or movies, but all that was really coming to me was *The Graduate*. "Hello darkness, my old friend . . ." Great, now "The Sounds of Silence" was going to be stuck in my head. I began to doodle just so I wasn't sitting there with my pen in the air.

The fifteen minutes were up, and Rabbi Stan had each of us talk about the people we were going to marry, and then go through our first thoughts for the ceremony. When my turn came I talked about the only thing I scribbled that was even close, that most friends of Stacey and Eric's had only ever known them as a couple, since they had been dating so long. I thought it might have potential. After we each took our turn, the group gave pointers to and critiques of each person's idea. The comments I received were mostly, "You need to dig a little deeper," which, yeah, I knew. The class came to a close, and Rabbi Stan told us that we were to continue to work on our "ceremony starts." Next week he would spend some one-on-one time with each of us, helping us get to a place where we were comfortable enough to go the rest of the way on our own. I already felt like I needed a tutor. I wondered if there was a place you could buy wedding ceremonies like you could buy term papers.

We shuffled out of the temple and said our good-byes. Nora lived in Jersey and asked if any of us needed a ride to the Upper West Side. Mark lived there, so he hopped into her Lexus SUV and off they rode. Jennifer and I walked up Lexington; I toward the subway, she toward her apartment on Ninety-eighth Street. That worked out quite nicely for me. She was cute, American, and didn't strike me as a trouser thief. I was curious.

"So, what did you think of the class?" I asked.

"It was different from what I expected." She smiled. "I mean it was really casual. 'Rabbi Stan'? I'm Orthodox, so anything in temple for me is a lot more formal."

Orthodox? I looked at her. She was fairly stylish, I would have never guessed. Well, she was rocking that signature long jean skirt, but it wasn't ankle-length or anything. "Yeah, I've never met any first-name rabbis either," I said. We waited at the corner as the light was just changing in our favor. "So, I guess your friends aren't Orthodox, right?"

She laughed and pushed her curls out of her face. "Oh, no way. They are total hippies. The wedding is going to be in Rhinebeck on a horse farm, and they're roasting a pig! You know, a big one on a spit with an apple in its mouth? It's not going to be Jewish at all. I know that stuff anyway."

We walked some more and I decided to keep going past the first subway entrance at Eighty-sixth Street to the one at Ninety-sixth. We traded stories, bitched about the city a little. I told her about Stacey and Eric, and found out that Jennifer was in med school as well, not a resident yet but on her way. She asked me what I did, and I sort of panicked and told her I was an assistant producer. It wasn't a huge lie, just a one-word lie. I was an assistant, after all.

Jennifer also happened to have a great can, which I hadn't

noticed in the temple. Yep, overall the whole thing she had there was a tight little package. I considered asking her if she wanted to get a drink as we were walking past bar after bar, but the Orthodox thing threw me. So when we hit the next subway, I gave her a pat on the shoulder and said my good-bye.

"Hey, next week after our class, there's a med school party if you want to check it out. You can bring whoever you want, if you want to come," she said, the breeze blowing her sweater tight against her body. She was confident, I liked that. She wasn't posturing.

"Definitely. That sounds fun," I said, halfway down the stairs. "I'll bring Rabbi Stan."

She laughed, turned, and continued on her way. I cruised into the subway and through the turnstiles. I could hear the train arriving, so I raced down the pockmarked concrete stairs two at a time and slipped into the car just as the doors closed. Huffing, I flopped into an empty seat. The train hiccupped and then shuddered down the tracks, and I wondered if religious girls were good kissers.

It was almost midnight by the time I got downtown. I walked west on Eleventh Street, away from the hubbub of Union Square, where the train dropped me. I whistled "God Save the Queen" as I crossed Seventh Avenue. It was always amazing to me how once you crossed Seventh, the din of the city died down and, just like that, you were alone on a peaceful street lined with beautiful old townhouses. Uma Thurman lived somewhere on this block, and I looked into the oversized windows as I walked past, hoping for a glimpse of her or any other wealthy, naked woman who might care to put on a show for the have-lesses. Nothing doing, though. Empty rooms and fancy chandeliers were all that was on display. I kept moving through the light and shadows, looking this way and that, soaking it in. I was in no rush. I turned the corner and sidestepped two men kissing against a mailbox, taking up a good chunk of sidewalk. The air felt delicious and nutritious, even though I was a bit anxious about this wedding thing. I'd put some work into that soon, I told myself. Maybe this weekend.

I opened the door to that good old eyesore, 99 Perry, and went in. I walked over to the mailboxes; I hadn't checked mine earlier. They were located underneath and behind the staircase in a little area I liked to call the "Rats' Nest." I opened mine up, just coupons, a postcard for some band I didn't remember hearing, and a cell-phone bill. Suddenly I felt something on my back and I spun around.

"Oh, did I scare you?" asked a skinny, scraggly-ass white guy. He was wearing a blue T-shirt and ripped jeans, his short brown hair a mess. You could play connect-the-dots with his acne and probably draw *The Last Supper*. "Sorry, sir." He realized he was looming over me and backed up a step.

"Who are you?" I asked, trying to seem casual. It was cramped back there. Something felt weird and I didn't like it.

"I'm a friend of Robert's," he said. "I've been waiting for him, but it was cold out so I just came in. The front door wasn't locked."

It was true, the lock on the door sucked. I edged past him toward the stairs. This was definitely one of those guys I had seen out my apartment window that day with Patty. "Yeah, well if he's not here, you should probably wait outside, know what I mean? Robert doesn't like people waiting inside the building." I was bluffing but figured Robert would be with me on that.

"I know, but it's getting cold, man," he said, scratching his scalp vigorously. "I think he's up there, just sleeping is all. Could you knock on his door for me, sir? I'll wait down here, I don't want to intrude. I just think he may be sleeping." No, I didn't like this sketchy motherfucker who called me "sir" at all.

"No," I said firmly. "He must be out, the buzzer is really loud. C'mon, you gotta go. Robert will be pissed." I moved toward the stairs. I figured if I had to, I could outrun this junkie up to my apartment.

He took a small step toward me. His voice was pleading and getting louder. "Please, sir. Just knock on his door. Two-A. Pleaseeee! I really need to see him!"

"No, it's late, man. Go wait outside or I'm calling the cops.

Come on, don't make me be an asshole." I pulled my phone out of my pocket. The guy looked more than a little jittery. I had seen *Trainspotting* ten million times on cable; I wasn't taking any chances that this guy was Francis fucking Begbie.

His voice rose. He spit his words at me. "Why would you call the cops? I'm his friend, sir." He stared me dead in the eyes. I could feel a bit of perspiration beading up on my forehead. Why did everyone want to fight me lately?

I fingered the "9" button on my phone, then gestured with the phone toward the door. "He's not home, I'm telling you, man."

"Bullshit, *man*!" he erupted. "I know he's there, I can see in his window from outside. I saw him!"

The front door opened and in walked Patty. She looked up at me and then at the ragged crackhead. "Walter, what are you doing in here?" she said, staring at him.

"Nothing. I was cold and . . ."

"I told you never to come in here." Her voice was like a drill sergeant's. "Get out before I get the cops, and if the cops come . . . Robert. Will. Kill. You. Let's go. Out out out." She grabbed his arm and showed him to the door. "Wait outside, we don't care. In here, we care. Good-bye." And away he shuffled, like a teenager dressed down by a tough mom.

"You," I said, smiling as she turned back to face me, "are no joke. He wasn't going to listen to me, but you took care of him like that."

"Well, he knows I know Robert. But it's all in the tone of voice. It's the same with dogs. You have to talk to them like you're their master, that's the key. You don't ask them to sit—you tell them." She leaned against the banister. "What are you up to? Going in or out?"

"I was just on my way in," I said, still shaking off the scene. "How about you, calling it a night?"

."I was," said Patty. "But if you're up for it, I'd pop across the road for a quick one at the White Horse," she said, raising her eyebrows.

I was kind of wide-awake now. "Okay. But you have to escort me home after so Walter doesn't beat me up."

"Oh, hush," she said, walking to the door and holding it open for me.

*T*he White Horse was pretty crowded, so we grabbed two pints and found some space to stand in the corner near the jukebox. Patty held up her glass. "To the successful completion of our mission and the defeat of our enemies." I wasn't sure what that meant but I clinked her glass all the same and let the cold Harp numb my tongue. I flipped through the jukebox's offerings. Van Morrison was playing, furthering my belief that the White Horse did not have one of the more up-to-date jukeboxes in the city. Evidence: Huey Lewis was still present. I tried to picture the human who might put on "I Want a New Drug" without irony. It could only be one of the News.

Patty excused herself to go to the bathroom and I chipped away at my beer. I wondered if people might think I was out boozing with my mom. I kicked myself in the ass for the thought the second it zipped through my consciousness; I hated when I became a cynical bastard like that. There were a million of those in this city, it was a pretty unoriginal style. Not many people here could say a positive thing without adding a "but." They'd seen it all before, and even if they hadn't, they'd pretend they had. A spaceship could land and people would be like, "Oh, you're from Mars? That's so expected. I was hoping for Saturn." Any sincere thoughts were immediately roughed up and taken advantage of, like rubes stepping off the all-night bus from

Iowa. People laughed out loud a little less here, they were guarded. They didn't want to show they'd been surprised or something.

I looked around the bar. It seemed there was some kind of office softball team that must've come by after their game, as well as the usual mix of law students and neighborhood types. No one to wake Lil' Petey up. I did some small circles with my shoulders and rolled my neck around; I had a touch of a headache and the beer wasn't really helping matters yet.

I saw Patty squeezing her way back toward me through the crowd. She was carefully holding four shots in front of her as if they were hydrogen bombs she didn't dare drop lest civilization endeth.

"I didn't know it was going to be that kind of night," I said, genuinely surprised at the offering. I wasn't really thinking about getting shitfaced.

Patty smiled. "No one ever does until it happens." She balanced the shots on top of the jukebox. "This is sort of a sampler. I didn't know what you drank. I'm embarrassed, I should know what kind of poison my neighbor prefers. There's Jack, Bushmill's, Southern Comfort, and tequila. Your choice."

I picked up one of the brown ones I thought was the Jack, shaking off a twinge of foreboding. "You had to get four shots, huh?" I said, grinning.

"Tequila for me," she said, holding the glass up. "Please make the toast, neighbor."

I raised mine. "Okay, well, here's to you then, Patty. When you hear me retching later, please be kind and don't yell at me to shut up."

Mouths opened, hands tilted, and liquid was swallowed. I could feel the trail of fire go from the back of my tongue down through my pipes until it hit bottom and spread wildly in the dry grass of my stomach. I chased it with the bottom of my beer. "Blech," I said, eyes tearing.

Patty was already holding up her next shot. I lived next to the female Bukowski, it seemed. She handed me the SoCo. "C'mon, take your medicine," she laughed. "The faster you do it the less it hurts." She tipped her head back and sucked the shot from the glass like the cowboys in the Westerns do when they've rolled into a saloon after a long day on the trail.

I downed mine as well, although my form was closer to that of a freshman girl at a sorority mixer, eyes screwed closed and a look of disgust on my face. I wasn't an amateur when it came to shots, but sometimes when you haven't properly girded yourself, they can be a quite a shock to the system. Like jumping into a really cold pond.

I went to the bar with watery eyes and fetched us two more beers, wondering how long it was going to be until the two doses of evil got into my bloodstream and reached my brain. Any moment now, any moment now.

We drank those beers and then started on two more that a waitress friend of Patty's brought by on the house. Above the clamor of the bar, Patty was going on about what it had been like to live around here years ago, during the riots at the Stonewall. "Let me tell you something," she said, leaning toward me, "the gay guys weren't all muscled out like they are today. They were more effeminate back then. But they were still stylish as hell. And the cops, the cops were all these fat, out-of-shape guys in their polyester uniforms. Everyone down here was rooting for the gays. Less firepower but so much more panache." She poked me on the shoulder. "How you feeling, soldier? Am I losing you?"

"No, I was listening," I said, momentarily a bit unsteady. "Just getting my sea legs."

"Hey, do you want to go somewhere else?" She held her almost-full beer up to mine. "I mean, after these?"

"Sure. I mean, maybe." What time was it?

"Think about it. I know a fun spot. But first, the ladies' room." Patty strode off.

I was fading a little but game. Why not? All I had to do tomorrow was man the phones a bit, and remember to breathe. I could kill a lot of brain cells and still perform adequately, what a joke. Patty must've had an easy day in store as well. I had seen grown-ups drink before, but generally it was at weddings and things and they were wearing suits or pearls. Patty was wearing a long-sleeved T-shirt with STUYVESANT written in all caps on the front, with jeans and the sandals. If those sandals could talk. I guessed they'd probably say something like "Look out for that dog shit!" or something. Yeah, sandals didn't seem like they'd have much of a personality. Those high boots girls wore, now those you'd want to sit next to at a party. They knew the secrets of the back of the knee.

Patty returned and then I went to the bathroom. I carefully used my foot to lift the toilet seat. I did my thing and then used my foot again to flush. I was like Daniel Day-Lewis when it came to using public toilets without touching them with my hands. If only I could manipulate my foot to turn restroom doorknobs, I could live without any fear of bathroom germs. Maybe someday.

I found Patty in our spot near the jukebox. The crowd had thinned somewhat since we'd arrived. I still wondered what time it was, but then I thought maybe I'd better not find out. Grabbing my beer and bravely taking a big gulp, I asked Patty, "So, what were you thinking about next?"

"Well, neighbor, I'm thinking we should leave here, and go to this private bar I know on Sixth Avenue near Twentieth Street. I think you'll like it."

"What's its name?" I asked.

"I don't know, actually. I don't think it has a name. It's in an apartment." She proceeded to tell me it was an after-hours joint, a place that was open after the legal limit of four a.m. I had actually never been to one, but I knew Tina had had some fucked-up nights where she ended up at places like that. Patty explained that a lot of bartenders and waiters who worked the late-night shifts only got off at four, when no legal places were still open. These bars filled that need.

We drained our beers and walked outside. Patty immediately lit up a cigarette. I could almost see our apartment building from where we stood, and I was thinking of calling an audible. She took a long drag and let out a smoke ring. I watched as it curled up toward the streetlight and hung there, slowly dispersing and becoming part of the sky. It sucked that you could never see stars in the city, too much light leak. Patty yelled "Taxi!" and a cab pulled up beside us. She stamped on the butt and opened the door, and in we slid. She gave the driver an address and our heads snapped back with the G-force of acceleration.

I was feeling a bit like Jell-O as the cabdriver managed to hit every single pothole on his way up Hudson. Riding in the backs of cabs drunk sometimes made me a bit nauseated; all the grease and license stickers on the Plexiglas partition made it nearly impossible to look out the front windshield to see where you were going. I stared out the side window and watched stores and pavement and graffiti pass.

Patty let out a mighty cough as we crossed Fifteenth Street. One hand covered her mouth, the other braced against the partition, fingers flexed, white on the tips from the pressure. Her eyes were shut tight and a vein on the side of her forehead stuck out like a major thoroughfare on a map. She rolled down the window and spat. "Uggh," she grunted.

"You okay?" I asked, as the car rolled to a stop at a light.

"Yep. No big thing." Patty smoothed her hair. Her breathing returned to normal.

The cabdriver leaned his head back. He was a very dark-skinned black man, I guessed probably from Ghana—there were a lot of drivers from there, who knew why? He gave us the once-over, eyeballing us nastily; he was worried about having someone yak in the back of his cab. He shook his head and then punched the gas. He was a classic two-foot driver, one on the gas, one on the brake. I was sure that style had led to at least one vomit scene for him before, you'd think he would've figured it out.

We turned on Nineteenth and traversed the two avenues in silence. Patty stared out the window and I started to get tired again. But suddenly the taxi screeched to the curb and we were there. She pulled five dollars out from somewhere and we were standing on the empty avenue.

"You know," she said, looking around, "some cabdrivers are very nice. The others just hate humans, they deal with them all day and are sick of them. Those guys are just dogs eating garbage, in my book." She put her arm around me. "This way, neighbor."

We walked up to the buzzer of a low-rise building and Patty punched the third-floor button. After a pause, the door buzzed open and in we went to the fluorescent-lit lobby. Patty pushed the button for the elevator. Immediately the door opened. Inside was a big-in-every-way man wearing an oversized T-shirt and sunglasses and holding a walkie-talkie.

Patty smiled at him. "Hi, I'm a friend of Gus's. We're just going up to his place."

Gigantor didn't miss a beat. "Five each." I gave him a ten and the doors closed, the gears whirred, gravity was defied, and twenty seconds later we reached our destination. The Stones' "Country Honk" was playing as we stepped from the bright elevator directly into a dark room. It did look much like it was someone's apartment. We passed a few old sofas bordering a coffee table where some silhouettes sat laughing. It didn't seem very crowded; there were maybe thirty people in a room that could have easily held a hundred. Patty led me into the kitchen, where a bald man in a white T-shirt in his early fifties was filling the fridge with Bud bottles from a cardboard case. I guessed this was the bar.

Patty got a Bud and I got a Jack and Coke, hoping the Coke would wake me up a bit. At this point in a late, late night, trying to wake up was among the stupidest things I could choose to do. Also, a quarter-glass of cola was not going to undo any sort of damage. That would take drugs. And I could probably get drugs here. I shook the evil thought from my head, took a sip, waded through a few people, and sank into an easy chair against the wall. Patty pulled up a stool next to me and we drank, surveying the scene. People were generally older than I would've expected; only a few folks looked like they were in their twenties, the rest spanning that hard-to-pinpoint age of above thirty and under forty-five.

"A lot of the people here work at St. Vincent's Hospital; they get off their shifts and need a place to go. A lot of city workers on the eight-to-five shift as well," Patty said. "Sometimes there'll be sanitation workers; you'll smell those, and also a lot of the guys who deliver flowers to the flower district. It's early for most of them, though."

I straightened up and reached into my pocket, wondering exactly what time it was. My cell phone read 4:27. Pow, right in the liver. There was no turning back now. I took a big swig of my drink. I was on the moving walkway to Shametown. I promised myself that, before I shut my eyes later, I would drink an entire Gatorade. A friend had once told me that the best hangover prevention was Pedialyte, the medicine designed to keep infants from becoming dehydrated. I made a mental note to buy a case. Then I smelled something. Something warm and familiar. It wasn't fresh-baked bread.

Patty was exhaling a cloud of pot smoke from a Rasta-style cone-shaped joint. "I finally got some of my own," she smiled, passing it to me. "Do you want a little, or have you had enough?"

I took it and sucked in the sweet smoke. I tried not to think of her cold or allergies or whatever it was. "I want more than enough," I coughed with a bad British accent. Out came the smoke. "What movie?"

"I don't know," said Patty, taking the joint and putting it to her lips. "*Apocalypse Now*?"

"*Arthur*," I said. It was one of my favorites. Dudley Moore played a drunk amazingly well. My second-favorite movie with a drunk in it was *My Favorite Year*, starring my pseudonym, O'Toole.

Patty passed the joint back to me. "Dudley Moore, it was so sad what happened to him. Watching him degenerate like that, it made me cry. You know he was a fabulous piano player, but after he got sick he couldn't even do that. I saw him on *Sixty Minutes* before he passed, poor thing." She coughed and I heard the sea inside her shift.

I took a small pull on the bone and gave it back to Patty. "I'm done, thanks." My mind started speeding along and I found myself humming the sappy Christopher Cross tune from *Arthur*, "When you get stuck between the moon and New York Ci . . . ty . . . " I was thinking about Dudley, maybe he brought it on himself, maybe he flew too close to the sun by marrying Susan Anton, she was like a six-foot-two internationally credentialed piece of ass and he was like five-nothing and jowly. Then I felt bad. You shouldn't joke about others' misfortune. But others' misfortune was often the best thing to joke about.

Some comedians made entire careers out of it. Cartoons too. Look at *Tom and Jerry*. I fucking hated that Jerry. Asshole mouse. The best way to kill him, I thought, would be to feed him a fistful of Alka-Seltzers and a quart of tomato juice, then duct-tape closed all his orifices and wait for the big bang. Or was it his orifi? I took a sip of the Jack and Coke and breathed. My synapses were at DEFCON 5.

Patty was staring off over her shoulder, giggling. I figured she must have been as big a mess as me. I was a huge mess. I was a toilet. I was at the bottom of the landfill where all the toilets went, soiled and shivering but dancing gamely like a Rockette. "What are you giggling about, huh?"

Patty turned and pushed her hair behind her ears. "Oh, nothing. I just had déjà vu. I was thinking for a second that we were the same age. Because that's how I feel, especially when I'm tipsy, and when I look at you and see your little line-free face, I forget that I'm a lot older. This could be any night for me from twenty or thirty years ago, you know?" She smiled. "Anyway, I was thinking about this one guy I used to run with, Douglas, and how we used to always smoke pot in bars, kinda like this. Back then, I'd get so nervous and paranoid when I was high. I always thought some stranger on their way to the bathroom was going to narc on us. I was really silly about a lot of things, you know? Well, you don't know, but you will. But then again you kind of won't I guess, because I kind of don't. I'm still silly about so many things. Maybe it's because I never settled down or had kids, but I think my brain is in arrested development or something like that. Or maybe I'm just drunk." She laughed, took a long swallow of her Bud, and sank back into her seat. "But I'm happy with it all, you know? I did pretty good," she said quietly.

People had been arriving at the apartment, and little by little, it had filled up. I reached into my glass, took out an ice cube, and sucked on it, finally crunching it up between my molars. The time had come. "What do you think, Patty? Should we split before the sun rises?"

Patty stood up and stretched. "Yeah, let's go."

We got into the elevator with the big fellow and went back down to the lobby. It was that time when it's almost light but it's not but it is. We walked to the curb to hail a cab as a jogger bounded past. We looked at each other and cracked up.

It happened in the cab as we were speeding toward home. A bad wave of exhaustion and nausea. "Suddenly feeling grim," I said through tight teeth as I rolled down the window. Stupid fucking child-safety window only went down partway. Great, I was going to have to thread the needle. With vomit. But fuck them all, I didn't care if I puked in my shirt and had to wear it all day in the hot sun at a beach volleyball tournament.

"Keep it together, Jason," Patty said, rubbing my neck. "We are so close."

I bit my lip and focused out the window on the blur of the awakening city. The wind blew through my hair but I still felt like shit. We finally pulled up at the corner and I jumped out of the cab and started racewalking toward our building. Heel toe heel toe. Patty caught up with me a second later. "Let's get you upstairs, partner."

I never noticed it before, but the sun rose really quickly once it got itself started. Everything was turning yellow and the fucking birds were squawking. Patty opened the door and we hurried inside. Bad sweat drenched my brow. I took the stairs two at a time, keys already in hand. I wasn't going to make it. I reached our landing and made a desperate attempt at the lock, but it was too late. Krakatoa erupted deep within me and I covered the bottom of my door with what Jesse Jackson might've called a multicolored mosaic. Sucking for air, I tried to remember what I had eaten, my face inches above the mess. The smell hit me and I retched again. This was the worst, the fucking worst. I was on my knees waiting for the next wave. I wiped my mouth with my forearm, tears in my eyes, nose running. "I'm going to fucking die," I groaned. I let fly again. Less colors, more liquid.

Patty kneeled beside me and put her hand on my back. "No, you're not," she said.

I retched again, inverting my stomach like a reversible raincoat, but nothing came out. "Ugh, Christ! How do you know?" I cried, and spat into the puddle.

"Because it takes one to know one."

I looked over at her, a string of saliva hanging from my mouth.

"Lung cancer," she said.

I contemplated the tight little smile and the eyes that didn't wink to say, "Just kidding."

"I've got lung cancer," she repeated, her voice steady, her expression stone.

I turned back to the dirty floor. The taste of bile rolled over my tongue. Gravity took it from there.

12

After twenty-four hours of whispering "I promise I will never drink again," I was back at work Friday morning, on time. I felt mostly better but Wednesday night had been like a punch to the throat. I manned the receptionist desk, uncrumpled my brown bag, pulled out a bagel and OJ, and went online to see if any interesting e-mails had arrived during my sick day. Stacey had written, inviting me to dinner with her and Eric that night. I felt I could handle it, and so I replied in the affirmative. Besides, I had a few things I really should be asking them if I was to actually accomplish anything before my next rabbi class.

Tina had written letting me know there was an eighties-themed party that night as well. The thought of alcohol and girls dressed up like Olivia Newton-John circa *Xanadu* gave me the sweats, but I knew enough to know you never knew. That was the thing about promises; you could always say, "I made you, and I can break you." I hopped on IM.

> **doodyball5:** howdy
> **tinadoll:** super f-ing busy. sup?
> **doodyball5:** stop being such a power player. just responding

	to your e-mail. maybe a drink before your party?
tinadoll:	k
doodyball5:	because i cant pull off a late one. bad ugliness after rabbi class
tinadoll:	k
doodyball5:	jesus, you rot. call me when you have time for more than one letter
tinadoll:	k
tinadoll:	french girl?
doodyball5:	qui!
tinadoll:	b.o.?
doodyball5:	nothing I couldn't overcome
tinadoll:	my little soldier

Melinda wasn't in yet, the phone wasn't ringing, nothing was happening. I clicked from the *Times* over to *Pitchfork*, excited to mock her tardiness for a change. The site loaded and the record review section stared me in the face. "Ah yes, record reviews," I thought. Maybe now was the perfect time to finally write one myself.

I quickly opened up a Word document and saved it as "jason.reviews." I settled back in my chair and fingered the keys for a few moments, unsure of where to start. I didn't even know which record I wanted to critique. Sara walked out of her office and started to make photocopies in the far corner. I wasn't going to be able to focus on this at work. I quit out of Word and started Google Image–searching things like "grandma thong" to see if anything spectacular came up. Things did come up. Apparently, those who fancied old women liked their old women to also be "hairy." Now I knew. I was learning and growing.

Time passed, slowly but surely. JB came out of his office and holy crapola right up to me at the desk. It was an occurrence as rare as Halley's Comet.

"Hi, Jason. Have you seen Melinda today?" he asked, fingering the knot of his tie. JB wore jeans and a shirt and tie every day, without fail.

"Um, no, she hasn't come in yet, actually," I said. We had absolutely no rapport. "Maybe she's sick, usually she calls if she's going to be late." I paused, then decided to throw in for good measure, "There's a stomach virus going around, it really knocked me out of commission yesterday."

"Oh? Well, I hope she's okay. Let me know if you hear from her. Thanks, Jay." He crinkled his forehead. "Do you prefer Jason or Jay?" he asked. It was a question that would've been polite six months ago, when he had first hired me.

"Oh, um, either is fine." I cringed.

"Very good," said JB, and he walked back to his office.

I returned to the Internet, wondering if JB thought I was an oddball. It was getting near time for lunch, and I considered calling Melinda's cell phone. But I didn't have to; she walked through the door a moment later, taking her sunglasses off mid-step.

"Oh, hello," I said smugly, and opened my arms wide. "Don't worry, because I have it all under control."

She cracked a grin. "That's good. Because I just sold my fucking play!"

"What?! Awesome!"

"I know! I just came from my lawyer's. Can you believe I have a lawyer? I have a cramp from all the papers I had to sign." She was beaming.

"Wait a second. Like two days ago you were all like, 'I don't know, probably never happen, it's all preliminary' and shit," I said.

Melinda pulled a chair over and sat down. "I know, it was

close then, but I was feeling superstitious and I didn't want to jinx it. I haven't even told my parents or anything. Actually I'm going to call them and some other people, and then let's grab lunch and talk, 'kay?"

"Sure. Oh, hey, JB just came by looking for you, if you even give a shit anymore, Madam Playwright."

"Oh, I was supposed to help him on this thing. Oh, well." She got up and went back to the empty casting room to make her calls in peace.

I was happy for her but a little stunned. Wow, Melinda was out of here. Did you get rich when you sold a play? Nah, that couldn't be. But still, I was thinking it must be pretty good money; it had been bought by a well-known producer, not some after-school theater. Hell, if it succeeded, it might even go to Broadway. I could say I knew her when. "We were both receptionists at this casting place. I mean, well, I still am."

Melinda emerged and we went out to a diner around the corner. In between bites she told me the whole story. I chewed and listened and listened and chewed. She told me about her deal and how it worked, and the rewrites of certain scenes she had to do. She really liked all of the producer's suggestions, so she was excited to get started—which she needed to, stat.

"I better be invited to all the fabulous parties with all the fabulous people," I said, sipping my Diet Coke through the straw, focusing on getting the last drops hiding between the ice cubes.

"Of course!"

Melinda couldn't stop smiling and even picked up the bill. We headed back upstairs. She went into JB's office and closed the door. I went back to my seat at the desk. I sighed and checked my e-mail. Nothing. No one was on IM, either.

A few minutes later she emerged. She didn't even give two weeks' notice. She couldn't. Those rewrites had to start immediately. So she put the one or two things she had at the office in a box, kissed me on the cheek, and left. We each promised to make plans and soon. Then she was gone. That was it.

I ended up being stuck there until seven. I had to work the camera for a casting session for outlaw-biker types. I stood around for an hour videotaping hairy, fat guys, most of whom showed up in leather pants and/or leather vests. Each guy had one line to deliver, and almost all opted to deliver it shirtless: "Yeah, fuckin'-A right I fucked him." I was wondering if the role was for a gay porn film or a gangster flick. I couldn't tell from the film title, *Happy Father's Day*. That could have really gone in either direction. The place reeked of bad breath and musk by the time I left. People had so many different smells. And my job allowed me to experience them all. How magnificent.

After the last Hells Angel or Leatherman, I made my way over to meet Stacey and Eric for dinner at this Middle Eastern spot on Tenth Street that had great hummus and pitzas, aka pita pizzas. They already had a table when I arrived, and were sipping some wine and nibbling on olives.

"Hey, buddy," said Eric, shaking my hand.

"Look who's working late," said Stacey, giving me a hug.

I got myself a beer and, lickety-split, my whole temperance movement was kaput. We figured out our order and got it in to the waiter. Eric began telling us a story about how he had observed brain surgery earlier in the day.

"The amazing thing is that when you cut through the skull, it's not unlike being a carpenter. You really have to use your body. You could see the surgeon straining his muscles, flexing down on the saw. Even though it's mechanical, it still requires putting your shoulder to it." Eric brought his glass to his lips. "It was really intense."

"I'll bet," said Stacey. "I guess that's why it's considered the hardest thing you could do, hence the phrase, 'It's not brain surgery.'"

"Ha-ha," said Eric. He kissed his fiancée, then turned to me. "So how've you been, Jason, what's new in your life?"

"Not that much. Work kinda sucks, but that's not new."

"Hey, anything happening on the Langford front?" asked Stacey.

"Status quo." I popped an olive into my mouth and used my teeth to separate the meat from the stone. I was thinking about that surgeon. "Let me ask you this, Er," I said, taking the pit from my mouth and putting it into the designated pit dish in the center of the table. "What do you know about lung cancer?"

"Um, well, I know a little. What do you want to know?"

"Just an overview is all. Is it treatable?"

"Lung cancer is pretty aggressive, but like all cancer it depends on when it's caught, and different people respond differently to treatment." He scratched his eyebrow. "Why? What's up?"

"My neighbor Patty, I've probably mentioned her before, the eccentric older woman who lives next door to me . . ."

"The one you smoked pot with that time," said Stacey. Then she frowned. "Oh, gosh, no."

"Yeah, she told me she had lung cancer. She said she was dying. But this was after a really late night of drinking, I mean, she doesn't seem weak or sick." I took a pull on my beer. "But she does have this awful, disgusting cough."

"Well, it's impossible for me to tell, obviously," said Eric. "But what makes cancer patients weak more than anything is the chemo," said Eric. "Do you know if she's started that yet?"

"Wait," interrupted Stacey. "What do you mean she told you after a late night of drinking?"

I gave them the executive summary. Eric couldn't offer much more, but thought she at least sounded strong if she was pounding drinks. Stacey sort of tsk-tsked me on going out 'til dawn with my neighbor, then missing work hung over, but I let it go. I wasn't looking for a lecture, and defending myself would've brought one on. I was a little sorry I'd brought the whole thing up.

The food arrived and we all started shoving it in. Mouth half full of pitza, I changed the subject. "Let's talk wedding, shall we?"

"Let's," said Stacey.

"Okay," I said, "well, I've been hard at work on your ceremony, and before I tell you my preliminary thoughts, which, let me just say, won't be until after the rabbi helps me next week, I just wanted to ask you some really basic questions. Like, do you guys want to write your own vows, for starters?"

"I think the traditional ones are fine, don't you honey?" said Eric, taking another slice.

"I mean, yeah, they're 'fine,' but don't you think we should personalize them a little?" Stacey turned to me. "We haven't discussed it yet, obviously." Then back to Eric. "I don't think I want to repeat the same vows everyone else does, it just seems so impersonal." She took a sip of her wine. "What do you think?"

He looked back at her for a moment before speaking. "Okay, that's cool. So we'll write something up I guess."

"Okay, very good, now, let me ask you this," I said, reaching for more pitza.

"But," interrupted Eric, "I think it's nice to say the same vows as everyone else. And by everyone else, I mean the same vows our parents said, and our grandparents, you know? Tradition."

"Honey," said Stacey, wiping her mouth with her napkin. "I totally hear you, but I don't necessarily agree with the traditional vows. Take the part that says that I, as the bride, will 'honor and obey' you. That seems a little outdated to me, and I don't really want to say it."

"Jesus, it's not like you have to take them so literally," said Eric, spreading his arms. "But that's fine, let's just take that part out. Boom, done."

"But why wouldn't we just write our own? I think that would be nice," said Stacey.

"Because I think it's corny when people write their own," answered Eric, jamming a piece of crust into his mouth. "It's so pretentious." He put on a bad French accent. " 'Oh vee are so much more een love than anyone else has evair been. Vee have written zeese sacred words to describe our love to zee whole world.' "

"You're thinking of your cousins! That's just because they wrote those saccharine, lovey-dovey ones. Ours don't have to be like that. And the whole point of a wedding is to show your love to the world, anyway."

"That's a whole other story," Eric said, rolling his eyes at me. "Besides, when are we going to find the time to sit down and write vows? You know how crazy we've both been."

Stacey stared at him. "I think we can find the time to write our wedding vows."

Eric broke. He reached across the table and grabbed her hand. "Okay, okay, we'll write the stupid—" He smiled. "I mean *sacred* vows. 'Kay?"

Stacey pulled her hand away. "What the fuck did you mean by"—she deepened her voice to impersonate him—" 'that's a whole other story'?"

I got up from the table. "I'm going to leave you two lovebirds for a minute to visit the restroom."

I walked away briskly. Marriage looked awesome. I couldn't wait.

Inside the bathroom I splashed some water on my face and then texted Tina. I wasn't dying for a big night, but I hadn't seen her in a bit and I thought I should try to at least grab a drink. She had an actual relationship simmering and it was high time

I got some more details. Or I could just bag it and go home and knock on Patty's door. But Tina texted back instantaneously that she could meet me around the corner for a tipple. I wrote her that I'd call when the meal was over.

Back at the table the tension seemed to have subsided. Now they began to play the "What's our single friend up to?" game. I wanted to get back to the ceremony but I didn't want to reignite any arguments—maybe this was a thing best done over e-mail first, so they could discuss it privately before we got together. As we finished off the food, I answered their inquiries about "some girl who stole your pants?" and I told them about the French connection.

"So no one who's girlfriend material," said Stacey. She sounded dejected.

"I'm pretty single. But there's this cute girl in my rabbi class who invited me to a party. She's Orthodox, Stacey."

"What is that supposed to mean?" asked Stacey.

"I don't know, I just thought you might find it impressive," I said, shrugging.

"You know, having a girlfriend wouldn't be the worst thing in the world, Jason," she said. "It's fun, that's why most guys do it."

"Even Hitler had a girlfriend," I said, suppressing a burp.

Stacey frowned. "God, always such a wiseass."

"It's a song. The Mr. T Experience," I said with a wave of the hand.

Stacey brightened. "Ooh, I know. There's this girl in Eric's rotation. She's really cute."

"She's hot, bro," said Eric.

" 'Bro'?" I asked, grinning.

"No good?" asked Eric. I shook my head. "Whatever. Her name is Liza and she's pretty hot—a hot doctor. Just broke up with her long-distance boyfriend."

"I'm not much for the setups," I said, shrugging. It was true. I had been on a few. Desperately awkward. Even if the person was cool, you had the feeling like, here we are, two people so pathetically alone that friends have conspired to put us together. Plus, setups never put out; too many people in the know. "Maybe we'll end up at the same party sometime, and you can introduce me."

"She's not going to be single long, Jay," Stacey said, taking the bill from the waiter.

"I don't know, she probably won't jump into another relationship right away," said Eric, taking out his wallet. "I'm sure she'll date for a bit."

"You guys are like real estate agents—she's gonna be gone soon! No money down! Sheesh, just bring her out one night. And by the way, the Orthodox girl is in med school too—at Columbia."

"Now I'm impressed," said Stacey, smiling. "Listen, dinner's on us, for helping with the ceremony and all."

I feigned protest and thanked them and we went outside. They weren't up for meeting Tina, so we said our good-byes and shuffled off in opposite directions. Why did it feel like I had just had dinner with my parents?

*T*ina was sitting on a stool at a nasty little dive bar called Lucy's on Avenue A. Lucy was the owner, a Russian or Romanian woman, probably in her seventies; she still tended the bar.

I said hello and Tina said hello and we got two vodka sodas with lemon. She was wearing a gingham dress over cropped jeans, like a picnic blanket laid over a denim field. She reached over and tousled my hair.

"Time for a haircut, Tex," she said, grinning.

"Really? I was going to grow it long and then cut it asymmetrical, so it would look like I was always standing on a steep hill," I shot back, patting my hair back down. "Your boy have any product I can bum?"

"Don't make me kick you in the kidneys. Actually, he's looking a bit haggard himself. Making a movie is a shitload of work; I never really realized it until I saw all the crap that needs to get done."

"Duh. Don't you ever watch DVD behind-the-scenes stuff?"

"No, nerdlinger. Anyway, he's working like ten hours a day on the script and locations alone, and then he spends half the night trying to find the crew he needs. They've got some A-list people even though they have like a, I don't know, C-list budget. I guess people like the story. But they start shooting in September, and they're still looking for a stunt coordinator and a second camera crew. And he needs to begin locking in all the post-production people, the editor, the effects guys . . ."

"Hold up. There's special effects?" I was surprised, I didn't realize it was that big a film.

"It's not *Lord of the Rings*, but he said there's a couple things, yeah. And he still needs a music supervisor, you know, the person who finds the right songs. They're going to be a big part of the overall feel of the thing; Brett wants it to be like a *Harold and Maude* or *Rushmore*."

"*Harold and Maude* was all Cat Stevens, I'm pretty sure. I love that movie." I sang the main track, "If you want to sing out, sing out . . ."

Tina cut me off. "Don't sing out."

"Anyway, he's Yusef something now. And the guy from Devo picked all the songs in *Rushmore*, Mark Mothersbaugh." I took an ice cube into my mouth and rolled it around, considering it. "I have that soundtrack if Brett wants it," I said, crunching down on the ice.

"Me too. I think everyone our age has it, they basically handed it out freshman year. I doubt he's got Devo money, but I'll mention it." She held up her glass. "Anyway, enough about that. Good to see you, sir. What's new, what's exciting, what don't I know?"

"Cheers," I said, clinking her tumbler with mine. "Um, well, you're up to date on most stuff. You know about Isabelle, the French girl."

"Did you Chunnel her?" She giggled.

"Probably not. What's that?"

"You know, the Chunnel? It's when you go in England and come out in France." She let out a full cackle.

I detailed my vomitous night with Patty, leaving out the cancer part.

"Now your next-door neighbor knows how soft you are." She stabbed the lemon in her drink with the tiny red straw. "Anything less disgusting to report?"

"Well, as you well know," I sighed, "I'm now profoundly single, once again. My only possibility is this religious Jewish girl." I told her all about my Orthodox classmate.

"I don't think those kosher girls are too good about trimming it up, FYI," Tina said, slurping her drink. "I remember from gym in high school. Tikva Rubenstein—huge bush."

I relayed how Melinda had sold her play. "So now it's just me as the only somewhat normal person in the office. You'll probably be seeing a lot more of Doodyball on IM."

"That's so cool for her. So, are you going to get promoted to her position?"

I chuckled. "No. I don't think either of us exactly has a title, Tina. It's grunt work. I'll probably take some of her responsibilities, but I don't even know if they'll hire anyone else. I could probably do it all, it's just horseshit really."

"You should bust out of there too, then." Tina swiveled her stool to face me better. "I don't want to sound like your guidance counselor, but if you're not into that job—which, c'mon, you're not—then you should go find something you like. It's not like you're supporting a couple of kids."

This from a girl I had once seen pick a dime bag filled with white powder up off of dirty Houston Street and snort it without knowing what the fuck it was—and then call me a pussy for not joining her.

"Easier said than done, Oprah," I said, sticking out my tongue at her, then acquiescing. "I know, I know, I need a game plan. I'm working on it. Actually, Stacey hooked me up with Scott Langford."

"I heard about that. He works at *Fader*, right?"

"Yeah. I need to send over some album reviews for him to be able to do anything, though." I held the cold glass up to my forehead for a second, I had the slightest of headaches. It was really too soon for drinking again.

"Written any?"

"Not yet." I shrugged and smiled despite myself, and then pointed to Tina's empty glass. "Another one?"

"Nah, I want to get going to this party." Brett was meeting her there. "Did you want to come? I kind of want your opinion already. I really like him, I think. Is that weird?"

"Sooo weird. Shut up, that's great. I'd definitely like to get to know him better, but I don't think tonight is going to be the night. I'm still a wee bit shaky. And I don't want to cramp your style."

"You won't cramp my style. Not any more than usual, anyway. You sure?"

I was. I didn't have the knees for a big one. But I wanted to know more about this Brett. I mean, the guy was making a feature film. Was he a genius? Was he hilarious? Did he have any cute female friends who liked to wiggle it, just a little bit?

"He's funny. He's not funny like we're funny, of course. But he makes me laugh. He's a real go-getter, but not in an annoying way. I don't know, it's fun, it's comfortable, it hasn't been boring yet. He, like, makes me feel good about myself." She blushed. "Ugh, I sound like a Lifetime movie!"

"Nah, you sound like a girl with a crush is all," I said. I gritted my teeth and put away my quiver of sarcastic arrows. The truth was she looked happy. So I said it.

"I am, I guess," she said, tossing an ice cube at me. "How's this—you latch on to your little Golda Meir, and then we can double-date. Sound like a plan?"

"Sure, we'll get blintzes," I said.

"C'mon, seriously. It would be fun. We could have chicken fights, we could all move to Brooklyn together, split a brownstone. It'd be America's favorite new sitcom."

I scratched my neck. "Brooklyn, huh? First let me see if we get past date number one, then we'll talk real estate, 'kay?"

"Of course, of course, first things first, naturally."

We hung out for another ten minutes and then went our separate ways, her down and east, me, straight and west. As I got into a cab, I felt a twinge of remorse that maybe I should've made the effort to go meet Brett. But it was too late now, and besides, my pillow awaited. A good night's sleep had become pretty much the only productive thing I was doing with my time. I went home and fell into my bed like it was a warm pool. A Nestea plunge into slumber.

I woke up the following Wednesday thinking it had been exactly a week now since I had last seen Patty. I even knocked on her door Sunday and Monday, but she wasn't there. I told myself not to be a nervous Nellie. But it was eating at me.

It was early and I was still lying in bed. I began contemplating the bizarre dream I had just had. I was on the dais marrying Eric not to Stacey but to that crackhead, Walter. I kept looking at Eric for a clue, wondering what was going on. He slipped me a bit of paper that said, "If you don't marry us, his friend will kill Stacey." I glanced at Walter, who actually looked quite majestic in the wedding gown. Then all of a sudden an Apache helicopter landed and out came Bill Cosby and Jerry Berger, this fat kid I knew from sleep-away camp when I was thirteen. Jerry was still thirteen, and still had his two broken arms. We used to tease him because it was physically impossible for him to wipe his own ass. They approached the dais, and Cosby put his arm around Jerry. "I think you owe this young man an apology, Jason." Then Walter pulled out a knife and gutted Cosby, shrieking, "You are ruining my special day!"

My jaw ached. I must've been grinding my teeth. I got up and brushed them, still feeling a bit anxious. Then I dug into a pile of clothing on the floor of my closet, hoping to mine some buried piece of wardrobe gold. Stymied, I pulled out the same pair of jeans I had been wearing all week and threw them on my bed. The thighs were becoming somewhat charcoal-colored, but the only other pair I had, my "old jeans," were even filthier. Meanwhile, somewhere out in Brooklyn my perfectly good Dickies were probably on standby should Jane run out of paper towels.

I finished getting dressed, found my fully charged iPod, hit the street, and set off toward the office. The fresh air felt healthy so I snorted a noseful. I clicked PLAY; "Range Life" by Pavement came on and I began to match my stride to the loping rhythm. It was sort of a wistful, jangly number, I didn't really know what Malkmus was trying to say but I liked the way he said it, you felt it in your chest. The sun dappled the sidewalk through the trees; you could tell it was going to be hot later, but right now it was just right. I turned off Perry and started up Seventh. The music was well timed, the light changed and I crossed Eleventh Street without slowing a step. A dog walker with three dogs passed me, the back of his shirt read POOP INSPECTOR, STAY 200 FEET BACK. I neared the subway and Malkmus sang, "Don't worry, we're in no hurry." I took his advice and kept going past the entrance. It was definitely a walk-to-work day.

Malkmus gave way to Motörhead. It was way too nice out for Lemmy's heaviness, unless I was to happen upon a mid-morning knife fight. I rejected him with a click, and then switched off the shuffle mode, feeling very much like Luke Skywalker when he turned off his onboard computer and listened to Obi-Wan's entreaty to use The Force. I stood in a small crowd on the corner of Sixteenth Street, waiting for the light. To my right was a teenage girl wearing black-and-white-striped tights and carrying a purse that very well might've been a hollowed-out Tickle Me Elmo. She blew her nose in a tissue, her eyes were swollen. I searched for the right song, finally landing on "I've Just Destroyed the World." The longing, done-her-wrong Willie Nelson track played into my ears as I watched the girl sniffle. The light changed and she stomped away into the commuter swarm.

I kept moving north. I tried an instrumental, Django's "Japanese Sandman," but it was too up, too festive, it made me think of Christmas and escaping from the cold into a diner for a hot chocolate. No. I scrolled past some stuff I had been hearing a lot of lately, LCD Soundsystem and the Whites Stripes and Modest Mouse, until I found an old favorite by Will Oldham. His voice lilted and broke over a two-fisted piano refrain and my eyes moved with it, panning and synching with the song. I followed a couple of unhappy men in red jumpsuits as they pushed a wheeled trash can in the gutter. I looked left and saw a gaggle of middle-aged women in skirts and white sneakers scratch lottery tickets and sneak smokes outside an office building while passersby crisscrossed, off on their own missions. Meanwhile Will warbled, searchingly.

I turned east on Thirty-second toward my office. It was an awful garment-center block, always overcrowded, trucks double-parked everywhere, unloading. You had to fight your way down the narrow sidewalks. I scrolled past some mellow Belle and Sebastian, looking for the right piece of aggressiveness until I got to Q, clicked the Queers, and selected "Stupid Fucking Vegan." The track bounced and ripped and I basically red-rovered my way through a couple insistent on holding hands and slowing everyone down. I turned sideways and expertly squeezed between a wheeled clothing rack and a dude eating a hot pretzel with mustard for breakfast, managing not to touch either one. I was weaving through people like a damn Heisman winner. The song three-chorded toward the finish and so did I, I wanted to get to the office building before it was over. I raced along, stepping out into the street, avoiding pedestrian grid-lock. The last sloppy bass notes dribbled out and the song came to an end just as I revolved through the revolving door and stepped into the empty elevator. I turned off the player and removed the headphones, grinning. Nailed it.

The doors shut and it was suddenly quiet. The elevator idled, awaiting my command. I was a bit winded. I took a breath and then punched 12, the floor of my discontent.

A combination of e-mailing and a king-sized Raisinets got me through the day. I was finishing up now and getting ready for my rabbi class, which hopefully would be followed by a night of flirting and maybe even stroking a Jewish girl on her bathing suit places. Hope sprung eternal.

JB's hadn't really changed much in the few days since Melinda left. I led a casting session on Monday that she might have covered, for a "businessman." Every gung-ho actor who came in had greeted me with unflinching eye contact and a painful kung fu grip of a handshake. But other than that, I had been doing mostly the same old shit, answering the phone and making sure FedEx went out. A big yawn. I sent Melinda an e-mail to see how she was doing; in it I described in exhaustive detail what my lunches had been. It took me like an hour to compose. But like the lame Genesis song, there had been no reply at all. No reply at all.

The subway platform was as hot and humid as I imagined the Amazon to be during rainy season. The air was thick and still and it sucked the patience out of even the most reasonable human. I put on my headphones and flipped through a discarded *Post* I grabbed off a bench while I waited for the train uptown. The ink blackened my moist hands and I wished I had a wet nap or something. This was the perfect place to contract a nasty little disease; with these warm temperatures the whole of the subway system was like a giant Petri dish.

I was wearing a green button-up work shirt with the name "Danny Boy" stitched on the front. It was polyester and the miracle fabric wasn't breathing or absorbing sweat, so droplets ran down my sides. The firemen of my body had uncapped the hydrants of my glands and soon my belly button was a swimming pool, around which microscopic flagellates and *escherichia coli* lounged like they were starlets in Monte Carlo. Finally the train arrived in all its air-conditioned glory and I was even able to get a seat. Breathing in the man-made cool, I headed north, temple-bound. I reached into my messenger bag and pulled out my spiral notebook with the PAPAYA KING sticker on the cover. I turned to the first page, which had the wedding outline on it. I looked it over. About the best thing on the page was the "AC/DC" logo I had scrawled in the margin. Fuck, why did I have nothing? It wasn't like my days were jam-packed. My life was pretty simple, I had a bad job and two pairs of jeans. I found a pen and tried to think.

I got to class a few minutes late. The rabbi was already in mid-spiel, fanning himself with his fedora. I grabbed a seat at the small table and smiled at everyone, lingering on Jennifer, who smiled back. That felt nice. And she'd even brought her two perky friends with her, I was happy to note. 'Allo, chaps!

"Jason, welcome," said the rabbi, placing a hand on my shoulder. He was wearing another sweater-vest; this one was burgundy. "We were just discussing how today will work. Well, to be honest, it was not a discussion. I was saying that I'd like to meet with each of you privately for fifteen minutes, and then I'd like to spend the remainder of our time having each of you practice your ceremony in front of the class, who shall play the role of the congregation."

"Will that be enough time?" asked Nora, scratching her head with the back of her pen. "I mean, that only gives us like fifteen minutes each to practice what we'll say."

"Aah," said Rabbi Stan, clasping his hands. "Fifteen minutes is plenty! You are not speaking in front of the UN, you are speaking to an audience of friends and family who are wondering whether there will be hot hors d'oeuvres or not. They will be hungry and thirsty, they will want to get photographs of the bride and groom kissing—and that is it! On with the show, to the hora, to the toasts, that's what they look forward to. The whole ceremony will last more than fifteen minutes, but that includes vows and prayers. Remember, this is not your show—it's their show." He paused and ran his hand through his beard, sniffing his fingers as they passed his nose on the second stroke. It gave me the willies. "You open, you lead the congregation in a few prayers, you talk about love and what it means in terms of this couple, you marry them, you ask people to let the families leave before they step into the aisle, you go get a drink and a bite of something. That's a wedding." He held his hands out to the sides. "Now who wants to go first?"

I saw that everyone, except me of course, had several pages in front of them. Typewritten pages. "I'll, uh, go last," I said, smiling sheepishly.

"I'll go first, if no one minds," said Jennifer, looking around the table. She already had a red pen out, which contrasted nicely with her dark curls. She was prepared. I wondered what kind of underwear she had selected for this evening, and if she had spent a lot of time in the selection process. She was a nice contrast to the typical girls I slept with. Hmm, Orthodox Jennifer as my girlfriend, I guess it wasn't the craziest idea Tina ever had. Pretty close, though. The rabbi pulled up a chair beside her. I hoped she remembered we were to go out later.

Okay, I needed to concentrate. Less sex, more marriage. I looked at the outline once again. There wasn't much. And what I had added on the train sounded corny. Christ, I was a lazy bastard. I started to scrawl out some more thoughts, but I was having trouble coming up with any sort of thread that could lead to a grand finale. Endings, they were always such bitches. Beginnings weren't a picnic either.

Rabbi Stan made his way around the table. After Jennifer, he went to Mark, and then Nora. Nora was getting a little upset, I could tell, as the rabbi urged her to cut huge swaths of text. Every time I looked up I saw her, eyebrows knit, running Jennifer's red pen through another sentence or paragraph.

"Stop fucking off and focus," I told myself, instead of focusing. I was more than a little behind everyone else and I wanted to catch up. I pushed my pen around the page, hoping for a miracle. By the time the rabbi got to me, I had, well, something.

"Okay, let me see what you are thinking, Jason," he said, pulling up a chair and leaning over my notebook. He squinted at it. "I can't really read your handwriting, how about you talk me through it?" It was true, I had the penmanship of a chicken with Parkinson's.

I began to read what I had aloud. It was a story of how on their first date, Eric had taken Stacey to an all-you-can-eat Chinese buffet. I thought it was a funny story, and that it showed how Eric always knew Stacey wanted "everything she could get out of life," and planned on helping her to get it. The rabbi quickly stopped me. "Jason, this is very cute. Too cute, I believe. It feels maybe like a wedding on a sitcom, you know what I am saying? Who doesn't want everything out of life? If you want to use this anecdote, okay, but not just for the anecdote's sake. There must be some more revealing truth about your friends." He looked at his watch, then gestured to the page. "Take the next ten minutes and see what you can do."

I did what I could and then we all began to share our plans. Mark went first and kept his remarks really short, because, as he said, "This is a second marriage. I know they don't want me to make a huge deal out of it, just make it fun."

Nora went next. She started reciting a poem by Shelley:

The fountains mingle with the river,
And the rivers with the ocean;
The winds of heaven mix forever
With a sweet emotion;
Nothing in the world is single;
All things by a law divine
In another's being mingle—
Why not I with thine?
See, the mountains . . . ?

"Jennifer, does this touch you or bore you?" interrupted Rabbi Stan. "Be honest."

She squirmed in her seat. "Well, I don't know much about poetry."

"You are very polite," said the rabbi. "Allow me to translate." He put his head down and made a snoring noise.

"I think it's nice," said Nora defensively. "You have to imagine me outside reading this, on a sunny day."

The rabbi sighed. "Nora, you don't have to listen to me, I will not be offended. But consider a couplet instead of the whole poem. You will thank me, I promise."

Jennifer went next. She had her remarks on index cards. She was definitely the kind of person whose notes I used to photocopy in college. Her friends were getting married on September twenty-third, the first day of fall, on a farm. And her remarks were related, all about how farmers planted in the fall, and how this was really the perfect time for the bride and groom to begin a life together. To lay down roots. It wasn't bad. As she spoke, she didn't seem to know what to do with her hands. They were at her sides, and then she'd suddenly become aware they were at her sides and she'd gesticulate broadly. Then back they went again to her sides. Something about her presentation was deadly cute; she was confident and bashful all at the same time. A little dorky, sure. But it was disarming.

Rabbi Stan gave a quick clap when she was through. "Yes, very good!"

Then it was my turn. Perfect, right after the valedictorian. I tap-danced my way through, with a lot of hemming and haw-ing. I was a little kid giving a book report on a book he hadn't read. At one point I apologized for not being completely pre-pared, as "work had been just overwhelming last week." Noth-ing like lying in temple. I stumbled and bumbled through. It was painful.

Class wound down, and everyone began to pack up. Jennifer sidled up beside me.

"Hey. Your stuff sounded really good," I said, touching her on her shoulder.

"Thanks! Yours is, um, coming along," she said, biting her lip.

"I know, I know," I frowned. "I'm going to crank on it this weekend. Or hey, maybe I'll just steal your idea. Except my friends are getting married this summer, so that won't work, shoot." I gestured down the hall. "Hey, are we still going to the party? I could use a drink after that flop."

"Absolutely," she said. "Let's get our stuff and head on over." She pulled her hair behind her head with both hands, and I struggled to keep eye contact as her shirt pulled taut. Her stom-ach was so flat it reminded me of Kansas.

As we left, I walked over to the rabbi and thanked him. He gave me a stern, disapproving look. Comically stern, but still. "Don't worry, I'm going to get it there, I promise," I told him.

"I know you will, Jason. Because you must. But just in case, take this." He handed me his business card, onto which he had written his cell-phone number. So even rabbis had cards. With raised ink and rounded corners too. I slipped it into my wallet.

"Call me if you need more help, or if you have questions about the ceremony, or anything at all. Do not hesitate," he said, locking eyes with me. "I mean that." He shook my hand. "Just be sincere. The rest will follow." He pulled his hand back and finally broke into a smile. "Now, I won't see you after your ceremony, so this is pre-emptive: Mazel tov!" He clapped me on the shoulder. "Take care, Jason."

"Thanks, Rabbi."

I sucked down a big gulp of beer and looked around the room. Jennifer was off in the bathroom somewhere. I checked out the party space, a cafeteria at Columbia that had been transformed via balloons, streamers, two kegs, and several stray bottles of liquor. It was pretty crowded, and a few people were dancing in the middle of the room to something off what I thought was Eminem's first album. I didn't really know that much about hip-hop, somewhere around Tupac and Biggie I gave up on ever figuring it all out. Maybe it was that I didn't look good in baggy pants, who knows? The rhymes never seemed to touch me the way rock or country or folk did.

It had been like ten minutes and Jennifer was still nowhere in sight. I was starting to feel a little bored, and also a little dissed. I jammed my hands in my pockets and felt around. Ah, there it was, left front pocket, nuzzled up next to an ageless wonder of a Chapstick: a squished but functional joint. If I had learned anything in Cub Scouts, it was to always be prepared.

I slipped out to a bodega on the corner and bought a lighter. I chose the one featuring a photo of an Hispanic woman in a bikini eating a hot dog. It exuded class, and I was most certainly a gentleman. Quickly, I lit the joint and kept walking. It was never good to stand on a corner or in an alleyway with a joint, that was suspicious. No, you had to keep moving like you were just smoking a regular cigarette, a regular man about town simply enjoying his nicotine fix. I walked around the corner, sucking in furiously, moving as inconspicuously as I could toward an altered state.

On the way to the party, I had gotten to know Jennifer a bit more. She was from New Jersey originally and had gone to Wisconsin undergrad. She tried to go to shul regularly. She liked my glasses, and so obviously had good taste. When I had asked if there would be any drugs at this party, referring to the fact that it was a med student affair, she had looked more than a little taken aback. "You know, penicillin and stuff?" I said, making the joke clear, and putting the smile back on her face. I doubted she had a bong, let's leave it at that.

I licked my finger, extinguished the joint, pocketed it, and headed back to the party. Fuck, I thought, I should've bought mints at the deli. I wondered if I had smoked not enough, too much, or just right. Time would soon tell. I rooted for the Baby Bear outcome.

I looked around the room at the drunken physicians-to-be. They were like anyone else, I supposed, laughing and flirting. And yet someday I'd count on one of them to keep me alive. Odd. It wasn't like they were born to heal. Somewhere around sophomore year these folks were thinking, "I don't know, maybe I should go pre-med, but organic chemistry is supposed to be such a bitch." But they made the decision and powered through. To think that a job where you held someone's life in your hands came down to something as trite as a discussion over a cheeseburger at "The Rat" about what major to choose.

And then, over the sound of Wham! blasting through the cafeteria speakers, I heard the voice of Mick Jagger in my head.

"Oh here it comes . . . here it co-omes!" And just like that, the High, as if behind me on a hike, suddenly sprinted, caught up, clapped its arm around my shoulder, and shouted, "Howdy, old friend!" For some reason in the movie that my mind was currently screening, the High was played by a fresh-faced Randy Quaid in a cowboy hat and with a stick of straw in his teeth. I greeted him in return.

"I'm feeling really high," I said.

"Well, shucks. You smoked a lot mighty fast." Quaid wiped some sweat off his brow with the sleeve of his brown suede coat.

Suddenly I was starving. I shook Quaid out of my head and made my way over to a table that had some plastic bowls on it. Chex Mix. I dug in, hoping the med students had washed their hands. Crunching away, I wandered around and scanned for Jennifer.

I finally spied her way off in the corner talking to a tall, skinny guy with a Long Island look. Baseball hat, goatee, very light blue jeans, Timberlands. It seemed like they were having a bit of an argument; Jennifer was doing a lot of gesticulating. If I didn't know better I would have thought she was signing. Or throwing gang signs.

I was feeling pretty stoned, my eyes were having trouble focusing. It was crowded in there, I didn't know anyone, and I was on the verge of going to the ugly anxious place, so I heel-toed it back over to the booze table and quickly fixed myself a vodka soda. I took a sip, hoping it would take the edge off, then looked back to see that Jennifer was still flapping her arms at the guy. I kept looking at them jabbering away. I wasn't sure how to handle it. I finally decided to casually swing past them on my way to the little doctor's room and see what happened.

I slowly walked over by them and hovered for a second. Jennifer didn't even look at me, she just kept talking. I moved past them and went straight into the bathroom, feeling a little like a jackass, like an unwanted pursuer. My face was flushed. I was suddenly the teenage dork at the high school dance. The bathroom smelled like bad urinal mint. I sucked down a big mouthful of vodka and put the drink on the counter. I didn't really have to pee even, but I went over to the urinal and squeezed out a few drops, lest I be a guy in a bathroom with a drink, not peeing.

Washing my hands, I finally started to feel the vodka, and it felt good, calming. It took me down a notch. It was the voice of reason. Suddenly my posture was improving. I wasn't a jackass, no, not yet anyway. Yes, I definitely preferred vodka to regular potatoes, that was for certain. I smiled at myself in the mirror. I was okay by me. Then I winked. It was a pretty queer move.

Feeling stronger, I walked tall back out toward Jennifer and Long Island, determined only to use my peripheral vision as I passed. I figured if she didn't stop me, I was just going to keep walking straight to the train and head back downtown. Fuck it, the whole thing. I had my sea legs now. As I stepped past, though, Jennifer reached out and grabbed my hand.

"Hey, there you are. Let's go dance," she said, looking at Long Island, then tugging me toward the area where people were dancing. She kept pulling me right through it and back over to the alcohol. She filled up a red plastic cup with keg beer.

"So, um," I said, "what's the drama?"

"What are you talking about?" She took a long sip of beer.

"Oh, c'mon." I gestured back there, and grinned. "You've been gone for like a half hour. You can tell me."

She took the cup from her mouth. "Okay, okay, I went on like one date with that guy, and he was hassling me because I showed up to this party with you." She took another sip. "It's no big deal, really."

"Only one date, huh? He seems a little bent out of shape for that." I stretched out my arms. "Hey, I'm just a friend of yours from class, right?"

She blushed. "Right. I mean that's what I told him. Whatever." She took another big swallow from her cup. Lipstick showed from the rim, a slightly darker shade of red than the cup.

"Cheers," I said. "To Rabbi Stan."

"Cheers," she said. She took a sip and smiled at me, her blue eyes shining. She was really quite pretty.

It was then that I made my decision. I was going to get completely shitfaced. And I was going to get Jennifer completely shitfaced. "Can you handle two of us, Quaid?" I shouted, internally. No answer. "Quaaaaaid!" I yelled.

A pregnant moment of silence.

"Is a bullfrog waterproof?" Quaid boomed, somewhere off-screen.

I wasn't sure. But I turned to Jennifer and pointed to the vodka bottle on the table. "How about a shot of this?"

"Oh, I don't know," she said, waving her hand.

"All the cool kids are doing it," I said.

"I was never really a cool kid."

"Here's your chance at the big time, then."

"I can't pass that up, I guess."

"L'chaim," I said.

We both grimaced as the room-temperature vodka went from the bottoms of two plastic cups to the backs of our throats. The second shot wasn't any easier.

And then we were both dancing. I was not a good dancer, it wasn't one of my strengths, but I could do it in a pinch. Luckily the dancing took place during a block of the Jackson 5, and even a man as white as I, whose lineage seemed to go back to a land called Caucasia, could find the beat in that. Jennifer told me between songs that she hadn't gotten drunk in months; med school was just too overwhelming. The girl needed to blow off some steam. I did what I could to help. I got us both another beer. Every sip made the world a better place. For her. For me. For America.

I noticed that Long Island guy sort of lurking about. I was getting drunker and he must've been as well. Alcohol plus cuckolding begets violence. So I put my arm around Jennifer and suggested we go someplace else. And bang, we were on the street, in a cab, flying downtown with everything blurry and wonderful.

I don't know how I did it exactly. But soon we were on my front stoop sharing an oilcan of Fosters. We had gone into the deli, and while Jennifer was in the back looking at the beer choices, Bobby threw me a high-five. "All right, Boss, all right for you!" he whispered. Normally I don't allow the high-five, but this seemed like the reason it was invented. Jennifer emerged from the back with two oilcans, and I bought them without discussion. We sat down on the stoop, and she leaned in close to me, smelling like beer and something sweet. She kissed me softly on the lips.

"Hi, you," she whispered. Thus began what one could call "a make-out session." She was a really good kisser. And I liked to think I was holding my own.

Every so often I tried to softly convince Jennifer to come upstairs, but she was holding out pretty good. I started thinking maybe I should play it cool, maybe I should save that for our next date. Wasn't that how relationships normally began, slowly building up to sex over a few dates, instead of starting with a one-night stand? I mean Tina had probably been sandwiched between Brett and a hairless Tahitian boy on their first date, but they were the exception that proved the rule. It was kind of too late for such wise thoughts, though; Jennifer was going to come upstairs. I already had an ace up my sleeve, an ace I knew would be played shortly. And then it happened.

"I need to use a bathroom," she said, pulling back from a kiss.

"No problem," I said, standing up awkwardly due to Petey's half-salute. I pulled my ace out, the keys that led to the bathroom in my apartment, jingled them at her, and opened the door. Always fucking bet on the bladder. It cannot be denied.

We climbed the stairs. I glanced at Patty's door as I hunched to put the key in mine. I straightened up for a minute. How the fuck didn't I know what was going on with her? I felt a wave of nerves.

I turned the key and we entered my place. As Jennifer excused herself to the bathroom, I hustled. I went to throw on the first CD my fingers touched, but it ended up being *The Velvet Underground and Nico* and that was just not going to work unless we planned to tie off and shoot up first. So I shoved it aside and put in the second album my fingers touched, The Flaming Lips' *Yoshimi Battles the Pink Robots*, and then I uncapped two Stellas that had been resting in the crisper in my fridge. I saw some dirty clothes on the couch and tossed them into the cabinet beneath the kitchen sink. I looked the room over. It was acceptable, I supposed. I sat down on the couch and glanced at the clock. Three.

Jennifer reemerged. She walked over to the couch, sat on my lap, and started kissing me. The taste of mouthwash was strong. Damn it, I had to get name-brand mouthwash, this was getting ridiculous. We began making out again, like teenagers.

Once we started there was no stopping. I slowly made my way up her back, and went to unhook her bra. I tried with one hand but was unsuccessful. Damn my pathetic fingers, damn them! I brought in the left and with two hands the job was soon accomplished. She backed away from me for a moment, then pulled the bra out of the bottom of her shirt. We started kissing again and then, yes, I touched them! One I named Mt. Sinai.

The other I promised to name later, after I had researched the name of another famous Jewish mountain or large hill. They were all I had hoped for. I would gladly fight to defend them for my people. I kissed them as if they were the Holy Land.

We went into the bedroom, our shirts off now. Jennifer whispered in my ear, "You are really cute." She slipped her hands into my pants. "You know, I wanted to kiss you from the first minute I saw you in the shul." As she spoke the word "shul" her fingers lightly ran down my cock. We could recruit thousands to our religion with this technique, I thought.

I tugged off her pants. Her underwear was a black, lacy little number, hardly IDF standard issue. I awkwardly pulled my own jeans and boxers off, then quickly began kissing her again. Things were going quite well, I did not want any break in momentum. She was moaning. It was a good sign.

I slowly slipped her underwear over her hips and down her legs. Aah, Tina was wrong, the field was quite well manicured, my fears of kibbutz-level grooming unwarranted. This girl was fucking sexy, I could prove it in a court of law. I wanted to play Moses to her Red Sea. I wanted to be the afikoman to her hiding place. I wanted her to speak Farsi and I would be in the Mossad . . .

Suddenly she stopped and looked up. "Wait. I don't believe in sex before marriage," she breathed.

"Really?"

"Really," she said, sitting up. "But don't worry."

She put me on my back and began doing things with her mouth that you wouldn't think an Orthodox girl would have been so expert at. But it kind of made sense, given that she wasn't having sex and all. The girl was fucking thorough—I mean, she was like a cat cleaning its young.

"Will you do me a favor?" she said, pausing for a moment.

She slid her body around so her backside was near my head. "Put your finger in my ass."

"Sure," I coughed, "my pleasure." I gently slipped the tip of my index finger into the naughty place.

She began once more with the tongue work, then abruptly stopped and looked back at me. "Try your thumb."

I put my thumb in, and as she pressed back hard, it was soon deep inside the quivering cave. You just never really know how the day is going to end, do you? I looked away, suppressing a giggle. There stood Quaid, biting his fist. "You have your thumb in another human being's asshole." He tipped his hat. "Fine work."

Jennifer began to grind against my thumb, hard. It was really squeezed in there, and for a second, with her weight on it, I was scared it could break. She was moaning and yelping loudly, like . . . like a girl who enjoyed a thumb up the ass, profoundly. And then she suddenly pulled free of it and in one quick move was on top of me. I was inside her, it was happening.

"Hey," I breathed, surprised, "I thought . . ."

"No thinking," she whispered, eyes screwed shut, tentatively moving up and back. She slowly began to grind harder, then harder, then full-on, leaning forward and putting her fingers around my throat. She gripped it tightly, almost choking me. I felt my eyes bulging Marty Feldman–style. Then—flip-flop— she clumsily rolled over and pulled me on top of her. She wrapped her legs around me and began thrusting so spastically I understood what it must be like to fuck an epilectic. I remembered health class and considered looking for a stick to put in her mouth. I watched her writhe below me, all earnest and animal and just plain pretty, and I was back in the moment. I closed my eyes as we fell into a nice rhythm, and after several guttural noises we each reached fruition. I peeled off her and fell at her side, winded.

After a few seconds, Jennifer got up and went to the bathroom. I lay there for a moment, still feeling a twinge of pain in my thumb. I had the strange urge to smell it, which I repressed, but it was harder to repress than it should have been. She came out and tumbled back into bed. "I am so drunk," she said, curling into the pillow. "Oh my God, I can't believe we just did that."

"It was fun," I said, kissing her head. I took my turn in the bathroom, feeling fucking drunk as shit myself. I washed my thumb with soap and water. It looked a little pruney, like I had stayed in the pool too long. I stumbled into the main room, turned off the stereo, and stumbled back into bed.

We lay quietly for a few moments. Then I said, "Hey, you okay over there?"

"Yeah. I just . . . I just really shouldn't have done that."

"I'm sorry, I . . ."

"It's okay, Jason, it's fine. It's my issue. We really don't need to talk about it." She kissed my neck softly and closed the subject. As we both passed out, I gave in and smelled the thumb. Ivory soap.

And then, something felt wrong. Something woke me. Jennifer was sitting up in the bed. I pretended to sleep but I watched her out of a half-open eye. "Fuck, fuck, fuck," she mouthed. Her head dipped with each "fuck."

Then like that she was up and getting dressed. She followed the trail of clothes into the other room. My brain was fuzzy and so was my vision without glasses. The clock looked like it read 5:21. The sound went from the patter of bare feet on the wood floor to the clomp of heels. She walked past me in the bed, straight to the door, and fumbled with the bolt. She was just going to slip out. Not even say good-bye. I couldn't just let her leave. I had to say something.

"Hey," I whispered, pretending to wake up. "Are you going?"

Startled, she held the door open a crack, the light streaming in from the stairwell. She whispered without turning. "I have to go to an early study group." She was halfway out the door. "Bye," she whispered.

"Wait, um . . ." I whispered back. But it was too late. She was gone down the stairs. It sounded like she was running.

I lay there, puzzled, too much unwanted adrenaline now dripping into my too-tired bloodstream. My body chemistry was at the exact point where the balance was tipping from "still drunk" to "hello, hangover." Go to sleep, I told myself. Think about this later. Repress and deny, repress and deny. Eventually my thoughts slowed and my heart slowed and the vein throbbing in my forehead slackened. I was determined to get as much sleep as I could before I had to leave for work. I found a comfortable position and consciousness began to fade. I realized I didn't know Jennifer's number, her e-mail, anything. And she didn't know mine. The best I could do was call Rabbi Stan's cell phone. His polyphonic Hava Nagilah ringtone began to play in my skull. Christ, I was still a little high, wasn't I?

"Yessiree," said Quaid, tucking me in. He waved bye-bye and off I drifted.

U woke up and the clock read 10:45. Shit shit shit I was fucking late. I pulled on the boxers and dirty jeans that were strewn on the floor by the coffee table. I grabbed a shirt off the floor of the closet. I felt wobbly. I burped and tasted the bad taste. Oh my God. Oh my vengeful God.

I shook myself out of it, grabbed my wallet, flung the door open, and took the stairs two at a time, the subway my destination. I pictured Jennifer going down these same steps hours ago, and The Fear ratcheted up a notch. I sprinted out of the building and almost smacked into Patty on the sidewalk.

"What's the rush, stranger?" she said, a twinkle in her eye.

I was out of breath. "Hey. Wow, how are you? Good to see you." I was babbling. My head itched and I scratched it. She looked good, I thought, the same as ever, thank God. "So, oh yeah, I'm just running to work. I'm really late," I gestured to my watchless wrist.

"And I'm just on my way back from chemo. Fun stuff." She brushed a blowing hair from her eyes, smiled, and waved me on. "Go, go. Come by later tonight and we'll catch up."

"I will. Tonight. Definitely. So good to see you!" I yelled over my shoulder and double-timed it to the subway.

14

I got to JB's by 11:25, which frankly was a fucking miracle given the circumstances. I sat down at the front desk and tore into a chocolate doughnut with colored sprinkles that I had bought from a street vendor. To say I felt like dogshit would be an insult to dogshit.

I opened my IM and got Tina.

doodyball5:	the fear is here
tinadoll:	what?
doodyball5:	worst hangover ever
tinadoll:	how was yentl?
doodyball5:	that's why i'm writing
tinadoll:	please don't bore me
doodyball5:	she came back to my place
tinadoll:	she was drunk too, eh?
doodyball5:	yes, wasted. wiseass
tinadoll:	go on
doodyball5:	while we were fooling around . . .
tinadoll:	she puked all over you
doodyball5:	no.
tinadoll:	stop the suspense stephen fucking king

doodyball5: she said she didn't believe in premarital sex

tinadoll: that's a "con"

doodyball5: but 2 mins later . . . she slipped it in

tinadoll: !

tinadoll: wait—she did or you did?

doodyball5: she! i am a gentleman

tinadoll: naturally

doodyball5: but then at 5am, she snuck out—she left!

tinadoll: yikes. really?

doodyball5: yeah, it was weird. she totally bolted

tinadoll: um . . .

tinadoll: u didn't deflower her by any chance, did u spaz?

doodyball5: no!

tinadoll: u positive?

doodyball5: she didn't say she was a virgin or anything

tinadoll: no one ever does, dude

doodyball5: stop trying to freak me out. she wasn't a virgin

tinadoll: sure, maybe she just needed to run off to prepare shabbat dinner

doodyball5: you're making me feel worse. this isn't why i wrote u

tinadoll: you did nothing wrong. virgins are just super emotional

doodyball5: stop it, fucker! i feel bad enough. i sort of liked her

tinadoll: and now she is going to burn in hell for all eternity

JB walked over and I quickly quit out of IM. He was wearing a gray-striped shirt and, shocker—black pants instead of jeans. He paused at the front of the desk and looked sort of past me. "Hey, Jason, are you busy right now?" he asked, in a nasal monotone.

"No, not too bad," I said. "Just tidying up some files. Need a hand with something?"

"Yes, um, come on into my office for a second." He turned and started toward it, so I got up and followed him. I had never noticed how high an ass JB had. He could probably reach over his shoulder and take his wallet out of his back pocket. He waited for me to enter and then gestured to a chair, which I took. Then he closed the door.

On my first day at JB's, Melinda told me I could decorate the right side of our shared computer monitor; she had already plastered the left with Sleater-Kinney stickers. I hung up a newspaper clipping I had saved from the last few days of my European travel, which I had spent on my own, in Turkey. Everyone else had headed to Ios to get shitfaced, but I desperately wanted to go someplace off the beaten path, impressive, scary-sounding. I made a mistake when I got off the train alone in Istanbul, and I ended up bunking in hooker central. And the next day when I went into the vast spice market, I got stuck in a maze of bodies and cumin from which it literally took me hours to escape. It was just what I had wanted.

On my way to dinner one night, I picked up a copy of the English-language newspaper, the *Ankara Times*. I had learned by then that dining without reading material forced me to examine the food a little too closely; not an appetizing move when eating at the cheapest places. The big story of the day was about a diminutive world-champion Turkish weight lifter who, amazingly, stood only four foot eleven. The tiny folk hero had just been knocked out of a tournament and had subsequently announced his retirement to the nation, simply saying, "Good-bye, it's over."

I was already standing on the street outside JB's when I realized I had left the article upstairs. I held a Duane Reade bag filled with the only other possessions I kept at the office: A Duncan yo-yo, a calendar/address book, and a just-in-case deodorant. I couldn't believe I had just been fired. Or laid off. Or as JB had put it, "We're not really laying you off, we're just so slow right now there's no need for you. But as soon as work picks up, you'll hear from us." He was actually very nice about the whole thing, and I think, maybe, close to tears. My stomach was making weird noises the entire time, which both of us overlooked given the gravity of the situation. He promised to write me a letter of recommendation if I needed it and to let me know if he heard of any temp jobs or anything. Then he shook my hand and gave me my last check. Before I left my desk for the last time, I quickly sent Tina an e-mail telling her I really needed to see her for a drink tonight. I told her to meet me at eight at the Lakeside Lounge, and then I got the fuck out of there, unintentionally leaving the article's headline behind as my epitaph. BROKEN DREAMS FOR POCKET HERCULES.

I still felt hung over. But I looked both ways, crossed the street, and walked the thirty blocks home. I had to start saving money for more important endeavors.

I leaned back in my stool at the Lakeside and took a sip of the five-dollar Negra Modelo. I couldn't believe I was drinking again, after last night's debacle. But it was the traditional thing to do after getting canned, I rationalized. I had stopped by Patty's around seven but she wasn't in, so I left a note saying I'd swing back later and headed directly to the caring arms of the bar. Where else was I going to go? I poured more cold beer down my throat. I was doing the best I could to squash the "What now?" thoughts that were bubbling out of the nervous part of my central nervous system. That was best left for tomorrow. Tonight, I just wanted to be like a country song and drink to forget.

I looked at my cell phone. Eight-thirty. I hadn't heard from Tina after my e-mail, but then again, I had sent it from my work e-mail and I couldn't check that ever again. I banged out a text, asking if she was coming. She might just be on her way. In New York there were a million uncontrollable circumstances that could make you late and very few that would help you be punctual. I polished off the Negra Modelo and ordered another, which the bartender, a gangly woman in a straw cowboy hat, served instantaneously, as if my thirst had been foretold. Tina wasn't there, yet already I'd dropped twelve bucks, with tip. Ooof. I looked around. The bar was still pretty empty this early. Another couple sat in the corner, and there was a young guy in a baseball hat sitting on a stool at the end of the bar reading a book. That wasn't much for me to work with. Who else could I get to join me? There was no way in hell I was calling over to Stacey and Eric's house. Just the thought of what Stacey might say gave me hives.

At nine I called Tina's cell. No answer. I ordered and chugged my third beer. Eighteen dollars. I started getting the feeling she wasn't coming. I also got the feeling of being buzzed again. I ate a stale peanut out of a bowl. I eyed the muted ESPN highlights on the bar TV. I tried not to feel pathetic.

I called Tina—no answer again—so I left a message. The bar had filled up and I had just spent almost two hours drinking by myself. I walked outside and looked up and down the street, like maybe she'd just be pulling up.

I started walking toward the L train when I heard a huge crack of thunder. A beat later giant raindrops began pelting all the poor suckers like me on the street. Everyone scattered, ducking into doorways and delis. I ran all the way to the subway; by the time I got there I was completely soaked. My sneakers squished and my glasses fogged up. I jumped onto the train and plopped into a seat, shivering in the air-conditioning. The man across from me wore aviator sunglasses and was listening to an old Walkman, zipping and unzipping his fly to the beat, it seemed. He peered over the top of his glasses at me and smiled. Great.

I looked away and caught my reflection in the window as we sped through the dark tunnel. Awesome day. Fanfuckingtastic. Water was dripping down my face. I was really getting my ass kicked.

Finally we reached my stop. The rain continued outside and I gave in to it. I couldn't possibly get any wetter. I trudged the few blocks home. At every light I leaned my head back, opened my mouth, and tried to at least get a free drink.

I stepped inside my apartment, stripped down, and toweled myself off. The towel smelled like mold; I really needed to do a wash. I guessed I could do one the next day, seeing as I wouldn't be going to work. There was a bobby pin on the floor in the bathroom, it must've been Jennifer's. I picked it up and rolled it around in my fingers, wondering how she had spent her day. Probably scrubbing off the shame I had brought upon her.

Miraculously my wet cell phone was working and I saw I had a text from Tina. She and Brett had just gotten out of a movie; could we catch up tomorrow? I was fucking annoyed, although I had no right to be, since she didn't know why I wanted to go out, after all. But still, she should have been available, somehow she should have known. It wasn't fair, but fair could suck it.

I put on some dry clothes, a gray T-shirt and the only dry, non-suitish pants I had left, the super-dirty jeans. It wasn't like Mr. Laid-Off could go on a shopping spree to the Pants Emporium either. Goddamn that Jane, I hoped her vagina was being plagued by a yeast infection or locusts, something itchy and hard as fuck to kill. I flicked a bit of what seemed to be chocolate off my left thigh. I put my tongue to my finger. Yep, chocolate. I was like a hobo.

I went over to Patty's, hoping she was in. I tried to buck up and appear cheerful as I knocked the old "shave and a haircut" on her door.

A moment later it opened. "Well hi, neighbor, come on in," she said, giving way. Patty was in her pajamas, really pajama bottoms and an oversized three-quarter-sleeve baseball shirt. She looked like she might have been asleep, although I could hear the TV on. I shuffled inside and we went into her living room.

"So, how have you been?" I asked her, sitting on the far end of her sofa.

"I've been better," she smiled. She clicked off the TV with the remote and sat down. "Soooooo. I guess I sort of dropped a bomb on you last week. But you know, you already seemed to be feeling pretty rotten so I thought what the hell, why not give you the bad news then? Better than ruining a happy time, right?" She stood back up. "Hey, you want something to drink?"

We went into the kitchen to make some tea. She filled a kettle under the tap. "I'm feeling pretty tired these days, as you can imagine. What with the poison I'm ingesting to kill the other poison before it kills me. All this killing really knocks a girl out," she said, putting the kettle on the burner.

I pulled some mugs out of her cupboard and located the honey in the same one. We didn't have all that many cupboards in our tiny identical kitchens. I placed the stuff on the counter and sort of asked the big one. "So, like, how's that all working, the chemo?"

"Well, remember how I told you I was dying?" Patty said, wiping her hands on her PJ bottoms.

"Yeah."

"I am. But just in the way that all human beings are slowly aging and dying. In terms of the lung cancer, well, I might have overstated the case." She smiled. "My doctor thinks I should be able to lick this, no problem. They caught it late, but luckily it's not too aggressive. Sorry about the scare, but what can I say?" She twirled around rather nimbly and did a variation on jazz hands. "I do have a flair for the dramatic!"

I exhaled with relief. "Well, thank God you're okay. I was definitely nervous last week, especially because we didn't run into each other. But then, you know, the thought did cross my mind about knocking down the wall between our places so I could expand in. I was trying to be a glass-half-full kind of guy." I smiled, to make sure she didn't miss the joke.

The kettle whistled and Patty took it off the stove. "Now you sound like a real New Yorker, Jason." She poured the hot water into our mugs and dropped in the tea bags. I doctored mine with honey; she took hers straight. "But listen, little lamb, I'm not totally okay. I have to go through all this damn chemo and stuff. And it's going to make me really weak some days. So, if I need a hand getting groceries or something, do you think maybe you can help me out?"

"Of course," I said, blowing on my tea to cool it. "I'll give you my cell number and you can call me any time you need me. Seriously, any time." I meant it.

"Thanks," she said, touching my arm. "And I promise not to abuse it and call you if I'm just feeling lazy or hung over!" She took a sip of her tea and then wiped a drop of it off the counter with her thumb. "Getting old, Jason. It isn't for sissies."

We moved back into the living room and sat down in our respective seats. "Anyway, I'll definitely be around if you need me. I got laid off this morning." I tried to smile. It took a fair bit of effort.

"Ooh, that's too bad," Patty said.

"Yeah. It was kind of a surprise."

"Well," she said, shifting in her seat, "on the bright side, it's not like you loved that job, right?"

"No, but the money was helpful." I stood up. "I mean shit, I'm kinda screwed a little now, you know?"

"I know," said Patty softly.

"Sorry, sorry." I sat back down and blew my nose in the paper towel the teacup had been resting on. I was getting a little misty, for fuck's sake. "It'll all be okay. I'm just having a world-class-crappy twenty-four hours. Last night this girl I sort of liked slept over, and then at five in the morning she snuck out as if she suddenly realized I was Satan." I folded the paper towel in my hand. "Well, okay, okay, it's come to my attention that she may have been a virgin." I shook my head. "No, she wasn't, she wasn't, but somehow I traumatized her. And then this morning, bam, I got canned. Jesus fucking Christ."

Patty slid over next to me and gently rested her hand on my shoulder. "Maybe if you didn't blaspheme so much," she said, cracking a grin.

I blew my nose again and chuckled. "Sorry," I said, looking up to the sky.

"You should have just stayed home today." She raised her mug to her mouth, then put it back down in her lap without taking a sip. She closed her eyes for a moment, then opened them. "Oh, I just got a wave of exhaustion."

She shook her head, like a dog trying to get its bearings. "I was saying, you should have stayed home. You have to learn to read the signs, Jason. Things tend to come in streaks, you ever notice that? It just takes one solidly good or bad thing to get one rolling, and it keeps on going until, well, until it's done. That's where the whole 'find a penny, pick it up, all day long you'll have good luck' thing came from. Of course, there's good streaks and bad streaks, and they start with a good or bad sign." She patted my head. "And my dear, a virgin running from you is histori-cally not a good sign."

"Yeah," I said. "And she was an Orthodox Jew, which proba-bly makes it an even worse sign."

"Oh, yeah, you're fucked." She waved her hands. "I'm joking, I'm joking. Your streak might already be over, enough bad stuff has happened. Maybe it was a twenty-four-hour streak. Like a little virus."

I put the paper-towel tissue in my pocket. I suddenly felt like an idiot looking to Patty for compassion. "Yeah, I hope so. It's just a job, who cares, right?" She had cancer, for chrissakes, and look at me, whining. I made Narcissus look selfless.

"Right. Positive thinking. You know what also might help?" Her lips curled into a grin. "Medical marijuana."

"No shit! You have a prescription?"

"Nah, not really, but I do have some pot. Oh, wait, you had some of this the other night, actually. It's good, right?" She walked over to a dark wooden end table and pulled a bag out of the drawer. "Just a little, and then we'll both go get some sleep."

She rolled a nice fat joint and we smoked a bit of it. Just half. I was a little afraid I would have a massive bout of The Fear; the joblessness thing was just starting to seep into my conscious-ness. We said good night and I shuffled back across the hall. I was really glad Patty was okay. Beyond that it had been a shit-eating day and I just wanted to brush my fucking teeth. I worked the bathroom, hit the lights, and crawled under the covers. Maybe I'd find a kick-ass job now. Maybe Jennifer would somehow get my number and call tomorrow. Lying there, I def-initely felt buzzed. Maybe I could just stay plastered and ride out the whole bad streak. Maybe soon I'd find a penny on Perry Street.

A month and a half later I lay in bed, and I still had the fucking bad-luck virus. Turned out it wasn't a twenty-four-hour bug, but more like an Epstein-Barr kind of thing. I willed myself to sit up. I had grown to hate mornings; when you had nothing to do all day there wasn't any reason to hop up and get started. It wasn't all "Good day, sunshine!" and shit.

I was living on dollar slices and free Happy Hour food. I understood why the poor were fat. I was one of them, and soon I too would have a gut. Not that it would matter, really, as once again my bedroom had become a ghost town. I had never heard from Jennifer, and I was in no position to track her down now. That double-dating idea of Tina's was long gone. Hell, I couldn't remember the last time I so much as talked to a girl. It was as if we were two like magnets, girls and I; as I got closer they were repelled. They could smell the stink of failure on me.

I hadn't worked since that last day at JB's. It was pretty hard to believe. I was all over Craigslist and the *Times* employment listings, but I was having trouble even knowing what to look for. I'd take any sort of job at this point, but I was still hoping there might be something at least semi-interesting. I had found one exciting possibility, an opening for an assistant at a record label, Erasable Records. Hell, it was perfect for me—I knew a lot about music, and about being an assistant. I had a bitchin' phone manner, everyone said so. So I was pretty psyched when I scored an interview. I shaved, put on a skinny tie and a blazer, and tried to look very first-day-of-work, Ric Ocasek for them. But when I got to their loft with the poured-concrete floors and the framed gold albums, I found out that I had to take a typing test, which I subsequently failed. I typed with two fingers, I always had. I was slow but accurate, I tried to explain. No dice. Typing tests at a fucking record label? Not too rock-'n'-roll. I went home and sulked and illegally downloaded some music to spite them.

The first week out of work, honestly, was almost fun. I reveled in being flung from the workforce. I listened to a bunch of old albums and drank beer in the middle of the afternoon and occasionally hopped on IM to bug Tina.

doodyball5:	anybody home?
tinadoll:	just me, heather furburger
doodyball5:	hows the working world?
tinadoll:	exactly how you left it. stupid. any news, interviews?
doodyball5:	nope. just saw an army commercial tho, seemed intriguing
tinadoll:	you'd so be the squad "bitch"
doodyball5:	don't ask don't tell
tinadoll:	have to go, have a meeting with a moron about an idiot
doodyball5:	see if either needs anyone like me. preferably the idiot
tinadoll:	seriously! you never know

doodyball5:	sure, ill get us both canned
tinadoll:	im uncannable
doodyball5:	that sounds both dirty and like a challenge
tinadoll:	later

But pretty soon I was sick of my couch and being inside my tiny apartment. I didn't worry about the ceremony, I didn't work on writing any record reviews. I just didn't. Sitting there, atrophying, I was feeling like the dullest man in town. And one of the sweatiest. It had been ninety degrees and humid as hell and I didn't own an AC. Anarchy, motherfucker.

I was also pretty damn close to broke. I'd been living paycheck-to-paycheck, and then I stopped getting paychecks. The day I found out I didn't qualify for unemployment wasn't a banner one, either. I was going to have to figure out something quick, though, because I wanted to attempt to pay the rent—and by "attempt," I meant send in some kind of minimum payment.

That's when I did it. I had no choice, really. I sent the SOS e-mail out to the Midwest to ask my folks for a check. Fucking shameful. I didn't tell them that their son was unemployed. Instead, I just wrote that I needed a new bed, that mine was "like lying on a chain-link fence," and I didn't have enough cash to cover it. Two days later a FedEx envelope arrived with a check for seven hundred dollars and a note from my dad:

Hey kiddo,

Hopefully this is enough for a fancy New York City bed. Your mom and I miss you, hope everything is fine and dandy. What do you think about spending Labor Day with us in St. Louis? It will be horribly hot and sticky but

I checked the airfares and they're dirt-cheap. Probably
because it will be horribly hot and sticky! Let us know
and we'll get the ticket, our treat.

Love you,
Dad

I was pretty emotional at the time; AT&T commercials were
making me teary. So as I read my dad's note and fingered the
check, I was sniveling like a nine-year-old girl who just saw
Bambi's mom eat it. They were such fucking rocks, my parents.

But seven hundred dollars wasn't even close to what I
needed. I had sent a few hundred to the landlord the first
month and a few hundred the next month, and now I was operating on fumes. I was finding it surprisingly rough without
money. I mean, I thought I lived quite simply; I wasn't any kind
of shopaholic or gourmand. But the truth was, the city was almost impossible to move through without hemorrhaging cash.
Gum. A bottle of water. Beer. A subway ride. Fuck. I was never
more than ten paces from someone who wanted the few bits of
green paper I had left. And I was doing a lot of walking. Manhattan was such a terribly boring place to be broke, too. It
wasn't like you could chill and enjoy nature for free. Movies
were fucking $10. Most places wouldn't even let you use a bath-
room unless you bought something.

I was so desperate I had even begun looking for bartender
jobs, but everything seemed to be filled up by NYU grad students who stayed in town during the summer break. Patty tried
to get me in at the White Horse, but they had no need. She and
I had been hanging out a lot lately. Like me, she had pretty
much all day free. She was doing okay for someone with lung
cancer, which she said was in remission. "Like my bank balance," I'd joke. She did have some bad days when she was fright-

eningly weak, though. Days when she would call me and, in a small voice, ask if I could just pick up some toilet paper or orange juice, some little thing. Even then, she'd still tell me she was getting better every day in every way. My "How are you feeling?" inquiries had become a running joke, always met by the same answer.

"Like a rhinestone cowboy," she'd sing, smiling.

I stopped by daily. Popping in to Patty's had become part of my new little routine. Wake up around ten. Drink some deliciously free tap water for breakfast. Go online, see if the world was still intact. If yes, check the job listings. E-mail the one or two of them that seemed like decent possibilities. Go buy a $1.50 slice from Joe's for *almuerzo*. Swing by Patty's, bullshit bullshit bullshit, go for a walk together or play backgammon or listen to records or just hang out. Go back home before the day was over, call a temp agency. Masturbate on the couch to the cutest girl I'd seen that day. Nap. It wasn't like I was sitting around feeling sorry for myself, watching TV all day. I couldn't. I had put a hold on my cable service.

However, I had been smoking a lot of Patty's "medical marijuana." More than I should have. I told myself I was only allowed to get high at night, but on days with no new job leads, I had been slipping. It was something to do, and it was free. On the occasions when Patty didn't want to play, I'd break out the iPod and go for long stoned walks in neighborhoods I didn't know that well, like Chinatown and even Wall Street. It was amazing down there, I'd just find a place in the shade to sit or lean and I'd flip through songs, watching the well-dressed world scurry by, thousands and thousands of people. There were plenty of janitors and bike messengers and even tourists, but the vast majority was a whirlwind of gray suits and side parts and buttoned collars, and what stamina, I mean no one was wilting or ruffled, even in the heat. I started to tire of my music collection and walked into a CD store and spent money I didn't have on a couple of random discs. I used to do shit like that all the time, go into a store, gamble on a few things that looked promising, go home hopeful that I had found a gem and would soon be e-mailing friends with the subject line, "just found your favorite new band." I wondered why I had stopped doing that. I walked out of the store and into the heat. Maybe I liked the guy I used to be more than the one I was becoming.

But mostly Patty did want to hang out. One afternoon, stoned to the gills, she tried to get me to shave my head in solidarity with her. But I didn't think it would help with any potential interviews, or ladies. Plus, she had lost very little, if any, hair. She was just fucking with me, it seemed to be a new hobby for her. I didn't mind playing the sidekick one bit. Sometimes we'd walk around the neighborhood together; she'd need to go to the dry cleaners, drop off some mail, whatever. All the shopkeepers knew her. She introduced me to them as "Jason, my assistant." It was about the only reference she ever made to my employment situation and I appreciated it.

The truth was, Patty was pretty much the only one around for me to hang out with. Stacey, Eric, and Tina were always busy. Stacey and Eric were focused on the upcoming wedding, and Tina was living in Love Country. She and Brett were officially a couple and they spent all of their time together in what I imagined was a never-ending hug on the couch. Of course, I did see them occasionally. But whenever I did, it was inevitably all about fixing me. Two nights ago I had gone with Tina for burgers at Great Jones.

"Okay, now seriously, Jason, just hear me out. Maybe you should go back to school."

"I really don't want to get into this again, Tina. Don't make me throw my drink at you."

"I would kill you in a heartbeat," she said.

"With your breath," I countered.

"C'mon. Let's talk about journalism school for two secs."

"Let's not and say we did." I took a bite of my burger. It had American cheese on it, which was such a better choice than cheddar, because cheap American cheese melted neatly over a burger, like a tightly pulled sheet on an army private's cot. "Otherwise I am going to have to avoid you. Not that I see you much these days anyway," I added under my breath.

"I'm not trying to be a bummer, I just was thinking j-school could be a cool option," she persisted. "Look at Scott Langford."

"That doesn't even make any sense," I said, unable to hide my annoyance any longer. "First off, I'm broke. Second off, I'd be applying for next year—one year from now, so it solves nothing." I threw back some of my Bass.

"Well, how about just writing some of those reviews, then, and sending them to him?"

"I'm working on it."

Tina looked me over. "You, my friend, are so not working on it."

"I'm working on working on it. Fuck." I finished off the Bass. "Maybe I don't want to be a music writer."

"How would you even know that, if you haven't . . ." She saw the look on my face and stopped. She held up her hands. "Okay, okay, sorry."

"No, don't be." I forced a smile. "You're only trying to help the less fortunate."

"Shut up," she said, leaning in and stealing a couple of my fries. Well, not stealing, since she was going to pay for them. "What did you mean, by the way, you don't see me much?"

"I meant I miss being normal and not always talking about my job bullshit," I said, avoiding eye contact. "I'm glad you and Brett are hitting it off, and I know when people start dating they hang out by themselves a lot. But I still want to go out and have fun and debate whether the people around us are jerks or dorks."

"I miss that too," Tina said. "But friends talk about what's going on in each other's lives, and you being unemployed is bigger—just by a hair—than playing jerk-or-dork." She took another fry and chewed on it. "I didn't think I was soooo unavailable. I guess right now Brett's so busy being young Marty Scorsese that when we finally do get to hang out, we want to just chill and be together. You know, less drinking and pills, more DVDs. It's kinda nice. You'll see, as soon as you decide to get a girlfriend."

She excused herself to the bathroom. I sat there and chewed on a cold fry. "Decide to get a girlfriend." Oh, I just had to decide, how easy. The old Tina might have punched the new Tina right in the ovary for saying shit like that.

And then there was Stacey and Eric. A week ago they had bought me another in our series of dinners, ostensibly to go over wedding stuff. The wedding was coming up shortly, and I had the distinct feeling that they were starting to have second thoughts about the whole thing. The whole thing of Jason as rabbi, that is. I had been avoiding telling them exactly what I was going to say, since I hadn't even started writing it yet.

And obviously, I had no excuse. All I had was free time, but I just wasn't feeling the muse. As if I needed a muse—I just needed to sit my ass down and write it. It wasn't like I didn't want to do a good job, or even just get this thing off my back and done already, but for some reason I just couldn't get it up to get it finished. I had sat down and opened up my notebook a number of times—well, definitely twice—but before I could accomplish anything, I'd always find something to distract me. A stray M&M. A shiny piece of metal. Nothing ever got done.

Even though she could have no idea that her ceremony remained unwritten, Stacey was treating me differently. It had been simmering for a while, but now it seemed the soup was ready. The length of time I had been unemployed, and her notion that I was doing absolutely nothing to change that status, were unfathomable to her. Exhibit A: Langford. Plus, I hadn't been shaving a whole lot, only when I had the rare interview, and I looked a bit of a mess. Frankly, that's how I felt, so why hide it? The night of our most recent dinner together, she fed me snide remarks about my level of dishevel and I just kept claiming, "Hey, I'm growing peyes for you two." She kept eyeing me with a genuine expression of worry, like a shopkeeper eyes a group of rowdy teens, and it was pissing me off. I just knew that, when I excused myself to the bathroom, Stacey and Eric were discussing me, like, "I know, you're right. He'll ruin our wedding. But if we take this away from him, what will he have left?" She sent me text messages all the time with fortune-cookie-like aphorisms in them, such as "You make your own luck."

That night I was supposed to see Stacey again—Thai on Second Avenue—under the auspices of going over the wedding stuff again. It was only a few weeks away now. There was nothing really left to go over. I needed to stop being a pussy and write the damn thing, was all. She was using the get-together to practice being a Jewish mom, with me playing the role of guilt-absorbing child. I hoped we'd have fun. I didn't like being unhappy with my friends. I was trying to stay positive, but I was feeling such negative vibes. It was as if no one had anything else to gossip about.

Like sands through the hourglass, so were the days of my life. I was doing a lot of sitting around the house alone, thinking. I had started writing again in the computerized journal, my current entry entitled "Unemployed, Broke, and Horny." It was cathartic to bitch in long, unedited bursts. My apartment should have been spotless given that I wasn't doing anything, but since there were no girls in sight, and with visits with Patty always happening at Patty's, the ennui and inertia were winning. I was perfectly content to let the plastic cups and paper plates pile up near the dirty laundry and assorted detritus.

I finally motivated out of bed and moved over to the couch, where I disregarded the wedding notebook on the coffee table, open to a page that screamed DO THIS, ASSHOLE! in large black ballpoint scrawl, and leafed through a copy of *The Stranger* I'd had since college. I always loved the opening paragraph. "Maman died today. Or maybe it was yesterday." That fucking Mersault had learned to float through the pleasure and the pain with none of it touching him. I could see that in a positive light from my current position. I got distracted, reached over to the coffee table, and checked my cell out of habit. I had a new text from Stacey, trying to confirm tonight. I responded in the affirmative. Just after I sent the text, the phone rang. Weirdly, I saw on the caller ID that it was the main number from JB's.

"Hello," I answered.

"Hello, is Jason in?"

"This is Jason," I said.

"Jason. Hi, it's John." Pause. "From JB Casting."

It took me a second to realize that John was JB. "Oh, hi," I said, sitting up.

"Jason, how have you been? Are you working?" JB, Mr. Tact.

"I've been doing a few things, mostly trying to finish my novella."

"Oh, that's nice. Well, if you are free today, we had a last-minute casting call that needs dozens of roles filled. You'd be perfect, and it pays five hundred for the day. I thought maybe you might be interested."

Was I! "Sure. Five hundred for the day, huh? What is the, uh, role?" I imagined he must need people to fill an audience for a scene with a band or something; I wasn't sure what else I was good for. Background person at the library?

JB explained that Discover Card was doing a massive NYC promotion, and they needed lots of "young, friendly NYC folks" to help them pull it off. He gave the address of a place on Park and Thirty-third that I had to be at by eleven, and hung up. Five hundred bucks! I could kiss JB on the penis.

*T*hree hours later I stood on the back of a crowded bus, dressed as a giant, three-dimensional slice of chocolate layer cake with vanilla icing. I was a diabetic's nightmare. All the other "young, friendly NYC folks" wore similar huge, puffy foam outfits. We were all standing; you couldn't sit in bus seats in these ridiculous costumes. Every type of food was represented: a lobster, a big hot dog, a ham sandwich, a cookie, and in the largest costume of all, a thin black guy dressed as an entire roast chicken. Had it been fried, I think he could've sued for racism.

The Discover Card Company was sponsoring a special restaurant week in NYC. The bus was dropping us off on different corners in Midtown to hand out information on the special discounts available if you paid with the glorious Discover Card. They must have been grouping people as full meals, because the main-course chicken, a piece of broccoli played by a slightly plump Goth girl, and I, the dessert, were dropped off together on the northwest corner of Bryant Park and told to spread out a bit. I looked at Broccoli. You had to be seriously committed to be Goth in summer. Today it was supposed to hit the high eighties. Her thick black eye-makeup would soon be running down her stalk, that was for sure.

The sun was really intense. I found a spot in a bit of shade and held out my stupid flyers. My cake costume went from neck to knee, with white stockings for my legs. Thigh-highs. And, this was the worst, on my head I wore a chocolate beanie with a foot-tall pink-and-white plastic candle sticking out of it. The whole getup was not made of any sort of natural fiber or anything that remotely breathed, and even in the shade, I was cooking on the inside. If I were a wrestling coach, I would recommend this cake suit to my team so they could make weight.

There I stood. A moron. I was trying to be Zen, trying to picture the five hundred beans in my mind, but it wasn't working. Not with every business-casual asshole in Midtown walking past and mocking me. They were all just so funny in this part of town. Maybe after they finished making spreadsheets they hit the comedy clubs, because I was hearing all sorts of brilliant cracks like "Hey, got milk?!" and a tsk-tsking "I told you to get your MBA." And then there were the secretaries in shiny white Reeboks, giggling at me and saying in grating Queens accents, "Oooh, now that makes me want to diet!" Oh, ha-ha. I had angry little daydreams of the many different ways I might torture them; the most vile involved wrapping a sweet potato in barbed wire and shoving it right up their asses. I was one surly slice of cake. I wiped the sweat from my brow on my hand, and I wiped my hand on my gauzy vanilla frosting. My face was so slick with oily perspiration that my glasses kept sliding down the bridge of my nose. I waited for more abuse and adjusted my candle cap; the elastic on it was tight and really kept in the heat.

I was getting delirious. I needed to talk to someone simpatico, so I crossed the street to see the roast chicken, who was standing on the far corner. As I waddled through the intersection, a car honked at me, and a sanitation worker hanging off the back of a garbage truck gave a wolf whistle as if I were a sexy girl. Maybe the stockings flattered my calves.

Roast Chicken was grinning, trying to engage passersby. He looked like he was having fun. That did not seem scientifically possible. "Hey, man," I said, touching his wing, "how's it going? You sweating to death?"

He smiled. "Nah, I'm cool. Couple more hours and it's payday."

I noticed he was also wearing stockings, golden-brown ones. "Can I ask you a question? How is it that you aren't miserable right now? I'm dying." I wiped some more perspiration on my frosting.

"I'm just rolling with it, is all," he said. He looked around, then down at me. "And also, I'm really stoned," he said, grinning again. "Smoked chicken, heh. Beth got me high."

"Beth?"

He flapped toward Broccoli. "Yeah, Beth. We got high before we changed into these costumes. She has a little one-hitter."

Broccoli Beth, you crafty little vegetable. Hell, I didn't even know Goths liked pot. I thought they were only into . . . shit, I had no idea what kind of drugs they did. But they were the polar opposite of life-affirming hippies who had sort of claimed pot, so I would never have guessed she would've been packing. But I was glad I wasn't high. I needed something to dull the sense of reality, not enhance it. Now, a Vicodin, or an old-fashioned Valium, that might have helped. I cakewalked back to my spot, thinking I was really glad I had a diploma from an Ivy League institution. What a laugh.

The next two hours passed like a kidney stone. A mustached Hispanic man in a tank top walked right up to me and whispered that he would very much like to eat me. A little kid poked my frosting, made a farting sound, and laughed. A fat man's dog barked and nipped at me. A very cute girl in a wife-beater stopped, lowered her sunglasses, and looked me over. She was stunning, a tight little body and blond funky hair, kind of rock-

'n'-roll but not so much that it seemed like you could only meet her if you were in a band. She looked familiar.

Then I realized who it was. "Annie?" I said. I took a step toward her. She looked fucking fantastic. "Hey, it's Jason."

"Jason?" she said, as if trying to place me. She pointed at my costume. "What's going on?"

"Oh, you know, same old."

She squinted, then smiled awkwardly. We stood there in the heat like any young couple flirting on a summer day, she the stylish girl, me the slice of cake.

"So, uh, how've you been?" I asked.

"Why are you wearing that costume?" she said, her smile fading. She touched it with her finger.

"What costume? This is Gaultier." I shrugged as if to say, "Hey, it's funny." She gave me back a look that was . . . it was pity. Pure pity. Like she was looking at a homeless child in a gutter in Peru.

"Is this your job?" she asked, furrowing her brow.

"No, it's, well . . . it's obviously a long story," I said, exasperated. "Hey, let's make a plan and I'll tell you all about it. We should have exchanged numbers the last time we saw each other, that was dumb of us. Do you have, uh, a card?"

"Do you have a pocket?"

I looked down at my cake suit. "Good point."

She slid the sunglasses back up her nose. "You look ridiculous."

"Yeah, I know it. It's just a temp job."

"Normally, you're a hamburger, right?" She grinned. "Just kidding, just kidding." She patted my cake shoulder. "Listen, I actually have to run to this meeting. I'll see you around, Jason. Try not to melt out here."

Then she was gone. I was the shit she had wisely stepped

over. I bet she'd be on IM in ten minutes with someone from school: "You are not going to believe who I just saw ☺." I turned to watch her go and adjusted my itchy candle cap. A stream of perspiration escaped the elastic and drooled down my fore-head, stinging my eyes.

By the love of all that is holy, the bus returned on time. I pulled off the nasty hat and leaned on one of the seats as we went to pick up other assorted dinner items scattered about Midtown. This piece of cake needed an Indian Ocean–sized drink of anything but milk.

Ⓐfter changing back into my civvies at the loft, I was now in some dark bar called Fiddlesticks, buying a round of drinks for Goth Beth, Derek (formerly known as Roast Chicken), and a nameless girl who had been a pickle. The Midtown Irish pub was conveniently located near a check-cashing place that turned my day of shame into $303.36, after taxes and check-cashing fees. Following the capitalist food chain, the bartender was turning that money into the universal problem-solver, my friend and yours, alcohol.

I was already drunk. I was rehydrating by dehydrating. We had been there since about six, and it was nine-thirty. Derek had been trying to kiss Pickle for well over an hour, and slowly but surely his persistence was wearing away at her resolve. As I predicted to Beth that Pickle would be smooched before mid-night, my pocket vibrated. I pulled out the cell; I had a few new messages. It was too loud in the bar to hear, so I checked my missed calls. Five from Stacey. Oh, fuck.

Fuck fuck fuck! Dinner with Stacey. That was supposed to be at eight. Damn it. She was going to be perturbed, to put it mildly. I contemplated how to handle it. I did have a job today, okay, that was a positive. And now you could say I was network-ing. But I decided that calling her drunk and saying any of that would not be the best way for me to acquire forgiveness. I'd deal with it tomorrow, sober, with a protective shield of lies. Yes, that was the smart play. I congratulated myself on the choice by tak-ing a giant slurp of Beth's cranberry and vodka by mistake. "Eww," I spat. "Healthy juice mixed in with my alcohol!" Beth smiled. Hmmm, without all the Goth makeup and with booze coursing through my arteries, she looked downright acceptable.

As I picked up my own drink, a vodka soda, my phone buzzed again. It was Stacey, again. I took two quick long swal-lows, walked out to the street, sighed, and answered. She let me have it right from the get-go.

"Where the fuck are you, Jason?"

"Hi, Stacey," I said. "I'm so sorry. I had a job today, it came up at the last minute and it was just horrible, and I completely forgot about dinner. You won't believe what I had to do."

"That's bullshit. How could you forget? We confirmed it this morning. You couldn't call me?! Eric swapped rounds with one of his friends so he could have the night off and join us. We're sitting at a table for three."

The street was empty. I sat down on the curb and put my fingers to the bridge of my nose. "I'm really, really sorry, Stacey. I didn't mean to forget. I really did have a job today, and it . . . I'll tell you about it later but it was shitty and I forgot. I'm sorry."

"I don't care, Jason. What's with you lately? I mean, how can I trust you to do the wedding when you can't even remember dinner?"

I stood up. "Because dinner is just dinner, it's not a wedding, people eat it every night. C'mon, I mean, sheesh, I'm sorry. I mean maybe I'm a little drunk right now and I fucked up, but I'll remember your wedding."

"Whoa-whoa-whoa. You're drunk? Are you at a bar right now? Jesus, Jason . . ."

"Slow down. I got drunk after the shitty—"

"It's just the way you've been lately, Jason. You do everything half-assed, and the wedding—I'm sure you mock it with Tina and all—but it is obviously very important to Eric and me. You can't marry us in front of our families half-assed. And you know, the last time we saw you . . . I don't mean to be rude, but you need to hear this. You looked like crap, like you don't give a crap, you're just soooo bohemian or something. And that's not exactly how we thought you were going to take this responsibility. Maybe it was a bad idea."

Now I was pacing back and forth in front of the bar. "I am taking it seriously, okay? I just got laid off . . ."

"Six weeks ago."

"Hey, I'm unemployed, I'm allowed to look like shit and be in a shitty mood. I went to those classes, I'm not blowing off anything—how many times have we talked about it, how many dinners, how many phone calls? You don't trust me? That is so insulting, Stacey, I don't even know what to say. What am I going to do, show up wearing a swastika?!" I was yelling, and I was shaking.

"That's just how I feel right now, Jason," she said quietly, doing the calm thing now that I was mad. Oh, how I hated that! "I don't know what to say. You just seem a little out of it, or in a bad place or something, I don't know. You don't seem to want to talk about it, and maybe it's not the best time to do something like this, something for people other than yourself. I'm going to talk to Eric and we'll figure out what we're going to do."

"Oh, give me a break. What am I, some drugged-out high school kid on an after-school special? Don't sound so sorry for me, ugh!" I was squeezing the phone with all my might. Completely flummoxed, I blurted out, "You know, my fucking GPA was higher than yours."

Her voice was quaking a little. "I'm sorry you had a shitty day," she said. "Bye." She hung up.

"Fuck!" I yelled to the empty street. I snapped my phone shut and then reopened it. Then I shut it again and thought better of it and opened it again. Then I dialed Eric's cell-phone number as fast as I could.

"Oh, hi there, Jason," he said.

"Are you standing right there with Stacey?" I asked, heart pounding.

"No, no. She just ran into the bathroom crying." He put on a mock-happy tone. "Soooo, how are you?"

"I'm sorry. I'm really sorry, Eric, she just was nagging me and I had a really shitty day—a really shitty couple months too, and I'm drunk." I took a breath, and kept pacing. "Tell her I'm sorry. I'll call her tomorrow and apologize."

"I will. And you will."

"Are you pissed at me too?" I asked.

"Yeah, I mean, my fiancée's crying and you blew me off for dinner," he said. I thought I could hear him take a sip of something, I was imagining wine. Wine they bought to calm themselves because they were mad at me. "I'm not exactly thrilled with you right now, you could say."

I stopped pacing and stared down the street. A homeless guy was directing someone in an Audi wagon as they parallel-parked. "C'mon, Er. It was only dinner. Give me a chance. I will not screw up your wedding. I'm not a loser." The wagon hit the minivan behind it, setting off the car alarm. The homeless guy cackled. I put my finger in my ear.

"Well, you're acting a little bit like a loser right now, dude." He paused. "But you are doing the wedding. It's way too late to find a real rabbi now, those guys get booked like six months to a year in advance." He took another sip of whatever it was. "Just, do me a favor. Call Stacey tomorrow and apologize."

"Done. I will."

"And, just slow down a bit. Okay? Stacey's worried about you, and, well, so am I."

I told him I would. I didn't think I had been speeding off anywhere, though; frankly, it felt like I was going in reverse. But I played nice and said good-bye. Then I walked right back into the bar.

Yes, leaving would've been the right thing to do. The mature thing. The thought burped up after I did the shot Derek handed me. But I didn't feel like it, how about that? My hair was crunchy from sweating all day. I was chafing at the crotch. I didn't want to go home and think. I didn't want to lie on my couch again and be sad, brush my teeth and feel sad, and get in bed and jerk off sad. Christ, it was all so dull and pathetic and tiresome. So I got another drink after the shot and I bullshat with Beth. I gladly accepted a hit of Ecstasy from that pickle chick. She had a shitload in an Altoids tin. I swallowed it knowing full well it was an eight-hour ticket to God knows where.

I looked around at the laughing faces. Everyone was having fun, I must've been having fun. For like a half-hour I felt good, like I could lift five hundred pounds right up over my head. It was all gonna work out. It always did.

Then just like that, I felt the nausea. I hurried to the bathroom and locked the door. My tongue felt swollen. I was leaning over the toilet, retching, puking up pure liquid. I wondered how much money in alcohol I was spitting into the shitter. I coughed a final time, then balled up some toilet paper and wiped my mouth. I felt a little better. I washed my face with cold water and looked in the mirror. Jesus, my pupils! They took up my whole eyeballs—I couldn't even remember what color my irises were as I looked at the black saucers that had replaced them. I was like a fucking Japanese *anime* character. Oh boy, I thought. Oh boy, oh boy.

I went back out to the bar. The E was really starting to kick in. Who were these people? Everyone's sneakers were sparkling like they had special Christmas lights in them. Some shitty Chieftains song was playing and the fiddle in it was like a paper cut on my eye. I squeezed past a guy so close I could smell his breath, I could see his nostril hairs growing, they were getting longer and longer and they looked sharp like bayonets and I felt relieved when I finally got past him and found my way back to the table and sat my ass down. I gripped the sides of the chair with both hands.

Beth turned to me. "Where did you go?" she asked. Her face was like a puddle someone had thrown a pebble in, rippling gently.

"So tell me," I said, back to her, "what is it about death you Goths love so much?"

"What?" she said. "We don't love death."

"Yeah you do! You loooooove death. You want to marry it. Rock-'n'-roll is supposed to be about sex and drugs, but you Goths can't wait to die and be buried and rot. It's all misery and spiderwebs and blackness. Explain it to me." I crossed my legs. "I want to learn the ways of your kind."

"What? You're wasted!"

I took a sip of a drink, it might have been my drink, it was wet like I recalled my drink being. "And yet, I am speaking the true word. Verily, I might add."

"Give me a break, we like drugs and sex just as much as classic-rock people like you," she said, poking me in the chest.

I grabbed her finger, hard. "How dare you?! How dare you call me classic rock! Do I look like Sammy Hagar?"

She laughed, "No. Tom Petty."

I held her finger still. It was warm, I could feel the blood in it, circulating, doing its thing. I pulled her in and tried to kiss her.

"No, I don't think so," she said, pushing me back.

"C'mon, I have like every Cure album," I said, sliding away from her, giving up, taking another sip of whatever it was in front of me. I hummed into the glass, "The Lovecats . . . da da da da da da da da da da da . . ."

"Hey, Cakeboy, you want this shot of SoCo? I bought it for you," said Derek, clapping me on the back.

"I fucking hate SoCo," I said, and downed it. It tasted like cough syrup and dirt.

I don't know how much later it was, but all of a sudden that same Derek was manhandling me out of the bar and tossing me toward the gutter like I was a wet sack of trash. I was airborne and then I landed right on my coccyx, right on the corner of the curb. I let out a yelp and I saw stars and they were twinkling and then I wished I saw little birds like in cartoons and I might have just for a sec. I had walked up to that pickle chick and kissed her right on the mouth. Her tongue was cold and hard and wet, like a snail shell. Then Derek ripped me off her and here I was, Raggedy Andy.

I rolled over and looked up and Derek was standing almost on top of me. His ratty Converse were by my hair, the hem of his pants hung inches above my nose. The hem on one leg was flecked with white. White paint. Fuck a fucking farmer!

"My goddamn Dickies!" I yelled. I grabbed the cuff and inspected it. Paint splotches all around, they were definitely mine! Crackling through my head came fractured images of how they arrived here, how they got on the legs of the dude who just trashed me. I saw Jane fucking Derek, doing all kinds of filthy things to him and his big black dick. Yes, goddamnit—it was black, black as a chess piece. And big, the stereotype was true and everyone fucking knew it. I shared a high school gym locker with my friend Nate, he was black and I'd see his junk dangling, an elephant trunk searching for peanuts, making my Jew cock, my Lil' Petey, my next-door-neighbor-that'll-give-you-a-ride-to-the-airport-in-his-unexceptional-but-reliable-Camry average-sized dick look like an itty-bitty jalapeño pepper. I saw it all, first Jane worshipping Derek's monolith, and then her swaddling it gently in my Dickies.

I squinted up at Derek. "Where'd you get 'em?"

"What?" He looked down at me. He was smirking, the fucker.

"These pants." I yanked on the cuff. "These fucking pants. Where? They're mine."

"Yeah, okay. Fuck you." He put his foot on my chest and let a goober drop from his mouth. It splattered right on my neck.

"You fucking horrible piece of shit!" I let go of the Dickies and desperately wiped at the loogie with my hand. It was a snotty one, it felt like warm jelly, it was fucking miserable. Derek turned away and started back into the bar.

"Those are my fucking pants!" I yelled after him. "You cunting fuck!" I tried to get up, and an excruciating pain immediately shot through my coccyx. I lay back down to ease it and slapped my hand on the curb. "You have to be fucking kidding me!"

I heard people laughing and then the bar door closed and it was all muted. I rested my head on the concrete, my ass bone was just aching. I hoped I didn't break it. Not my sweet ass, not my pride and joy.

I don't know how long I lay there, resting, afraid I might need some kind of truss. Some assholes walked past and said something I was pretty sure wasn't complimentary. All I could see was their shoes, and they had that sparkle too. I decided that gray was a really good color for cement, it suited it. Cement sounded gray. Fucking Jane, fucking slut, fucking whore, fucking thief, fucking chicken fucker. Shit, maybe Derek didn't even get the pants from her, maybe she'd had a lesbian affair and that girl stole them from her and then Derek slept with the new girl and got the pants. Or maybe Derek and Jane were married and she cheated on him with me, maybe I cuckolded him, maybe I fucking won, it could've been. The pants permutations were astronomical. Neon mathematical equations flashed across the concrete.

I turned my head the other way, toward the street. In front of my face were a bunch of butts scattered in the gutter. I stretched out and scraped up a few of the bigger ones. I put one that had lipstick on the filter in my mouth and imagined who had been sucking on it, what she looked like, how it tasted on her lips. Then after a little while, I slowly stood up. It hurt but I could do it. I patted my pockets until I found my lighter. I had a long walk home. I was going to finally learn to smoke.

*T*he stairs at 99 Perry were extra-steep, and tonight they seemed steeper than ever. My coccyx flared on every one of them. I vowed to call the landlord the next day and lobby for an elevator, an escalator, a ski lift, a rope tow, or a Sherpa-like person to provide piggyback rides. I held on to the railing with one hand and held a bag with two black-and-white cookies and a Gatorade in the other, courtesy of Bobby. The red neon Bud sign he had installed in the window was the most beautiful thing I ever saw, I kept telling him. I really, really wanted to lick it. I knew it would be delicious if only he'd let me try. He gave me the cookies for free, the first time he had ever given me something for free. I was pretty sure I kissed him on the cheek afterward, the handsome devil. He kept telling me to keep my voice down.

I knocked on Patty's door, the shave-and-a-haircut. She opened up after the second rendition.

"Want a black-and-white cookie?" I said, reaching into the bag and fanning out the two cookies in front of her face.

"I don't think so," she said, standing in a flannel nightgown, frowning. "It's a little late for dessert."

"It's never too late for cookies, Patty! Santa has milk and cookies in the middle of the night," I said, leaning against the doorjamb.

"Shh," she said. "Come in here, it's the middle of the night." I shuffled inside and she closed the door. She looked me over. "What are you on? You stink of booze, and something," she said.

"Cake," I said, mouth already full with a bite of cookie. We went and sat in her main room. Between bites of cookie and swallows of Gatorade, I explained my sweaty working day.

Patty rubbed her eyes. Her voice was raspy. "You're lucky that was so awful because you woke me up, and I was feeling a little bit of anger toward you for that. If someone doesn't answer after one knock, don't keep knocking for ten minutes."

"I knocked twice," I protested.

"Nuh-uh," she said. "Trust me." She stretched her arms behind her head, yawning. "You look like a homeless person. What's up with your hair?"

"I was a piece of cake all day. It's a demanding job!" I eyed the second cookie. "You want to share?" I said, holding it up.

"All yours," she yawned. "And stop yelling."

I ripped it open. "Sucker," I said. I took two big bites, one of white, one of black, for maximum flavorfulness. "It's good to get a taste of the yin and the yang at the same time," I said, crumbs falling from my mouth.

Patty eyed me, arms crossed. "So what's up?"

"What do you mean?" I responded, before taking a slug of Gatorade.

"I mean, you didn't pop in to chitchat, did you?" She gestured to the clock behind me. It was after four. She adjusted herself, leaning heavily on a throw pillow. She looked tired. Her face seemed to sway and the skin was sagging off the bone. But everything was moving around on me, really.

"Kinda," I said. "I thought you'd be up and we could hang. Or maybe go get a drink at that Gus's place?" I pulled out some moist, balled-up bills from my pocket and smoothed one. "My treat!"

"Jesus, Jason," she said, "you sure you don't want to talk about something? I mean, please tell me you want to. Because it's late and as you are well aware, I do tend to get a bit tired these days for obvious reasons." She pushed some hair off her face and tucked it behind her ear. "And although I like to think I'm a pretty laid-back person, I think you know that no one is quite this laid-back. So spill it, or let me get back to bed."

I sat there for a second. "Seriously? I don't think I can be serious right now." I looked both ways, and stage-whispered, "I'm on drugs."

"Okay, hit the road then, Jack. I'm exhausted."

"Wait." I wiped the crumbs off my shirt. I swallowed and tried to pull it together. "No, um, I don't know. I'm having a tough time, I guess. The job thing, some other stuff. You know it all, Patty. It's been hitting me hard lately. My friends think I'm a bit of a fuck-up. But whatever, everything is fine, I think."

Patty leaned over and broke a piece off the cookie. White. She considered it, and then put it on the coffee table. "Well, Jason, I haven't known you all that long, but maybe you should listen to your friends. Maybe you've become something of a fuck-up."

I smiled at her but then realized she wasn't joking. Or done.

She continued. "I mean, I, for one, did not choose a life that was defined by what I did for a living, so I would never lecture you on that. But this is the cold hard facts of life, neighbor. You spend the bulk of your day doing something for money. Welcome to America. So start looking for what it's going to be. Who cares what it is? Find something that makes you happy, it's not a vision quest. And by that I mean, look harder than you are." She propped herself up on her elbow. Her skin looked translucent, like a jellyfish. I could see the muscles working in her jaw as she spoke. And I could see the sound waves emanating from her mouth, spreading in ever-larger concentric circles until they washed over me.

"And let me ask you this, I'm just going to say it. Why don't you ever date a girl? It's none of my business, but I don't think you have ever told me about one girl you've dated, like, a few times. Think about that. It's not normal. I'm not someone who's for normality necessarily, mind you, but still. It's something you might think about next time you're doing some self-examining—which should be soon, Jason."

"You're really harshing my mellow, Patty," I said, blinking, trying to grin.

She yawned, and scratched her pale cheek. "Humor is an excellent defense mechanism, neighbor. I know, I use it all the time. Especially these days." She picked up the broken piece of cookie she had left on the table and popped it into her mouth. "Ugh, it's stale." She swallowed and cleared her throat. "Look, we never got real deep about this, and shoot, I can't even tell if you're really hearing me right now anyway, but when you're in my 'situation,' you tend to look back across your life, and you get a good sense of where you got it right and where it could've gone righter. Maybe that's why I'm so worked up. I think the world of you, Jason. You know that. You could be a star. You could also end up a cynical New York asshole—you know, you see them on the train, a really intelligent, really bitter nothing who's forgotten how to smile." She shrugged. "I'm just saying. Maybe your friends have a point. I don't know, maybe they don't." She dropped her head down to her chest. "Maybe we're all full of shit." She stopped, and put both hands to the side of her head and rubbed her temples. "I'm exhausted. I have to get back in bed. Could you help me, please?"

I took her arm and helped her up and we walked, her leaning against me, over to her bed. She sat down slowly and then carefully lay back onto the pillow. I helped her swing her feet up onto the mattress. "It's so warm these nights that I never even use a blanket," she said, grunting. She reached for another pillow, I grabbed it and put it behind her head. "You know what it is, Jason? You're neither here nor there right now, you're just floating between ports. And it probably feels sorta nice to be between, right? Because you only have to think about yourself." She looked me in the eye. "Yes, neighbor, so you're a little lost. So what? You should be, you're young. Believe me, you'll miss it when you're found. Knowing the answers, or more of them anyway, is boring." She adjusted herself a little to get comfortable. "Hit the lights, okay?" she said softly, eyes closing.

"I'm sorry, Patty," I said. "I didn't . . ."

"Shh," she whispered, eyes still closed. "Save it for tomorrow. I love to wake up to flowers, you know."

The room was starting to tilt and spin on me. I backed up, hit the lights, and started out. "And, Jason," she called out to me, "forget being a fuck-up. Not everyone can wear it like Serge Gainsbourg."

I unlocked my door, stepped inside my shitty little apartment, and sat down on the couch. I wasn't tired. My heart was racing, it was thumping in my chest like an oversized subwoofer in a Toyota Tercel. Maybe it was the E. My eyes flicked around the room. I stood. I felt panicky. This was not the place for me. I rummaged through my silverware drawer. I knew I knew I knew I had some dope in there. I found a sizeable roach and a lighter and like that I was the fuck out the door and on the empty street and I was smoking and I was alive. That was something, wasn't it? It was still pitch-black out and I walked west to make the night last as long as it could.

It was too late for bars and too early for coffee shops. I walked a few blocks, smoking the joint, getting to know the concrete, until I was more or less smoking my thumb and fore-finger. I didn't feel much from it, but my brain might have al-ready been at full capacity. There was no traffic, so I strayed from the sidewalk into the street. I could see all the way to the river from there and I aimed my body toward it.

I was utterly alone. I didn't think there had ever been an-other time that I had seen absolutely no life in the city—no cars, no one sleeping under a stairwell, nothing. It was impossible to be alone here, you got used to doing private things in public. You had no choice. We all got to see everyone else's business and everyone got to see ours, so we were all even. Nobody had anything on anyone, at least not for long.

But now it was just me. The rest of the city was home dreaming about this or that or up worrying about something or taking a Xanax or a Tums or having a half-asleep pee or getting the shit fucked out of them or wishing they were getting the shit fucked out of them or whatever it was people did in apartments other than mine late at night or early in the morning. What a bunch of shit was flowing through my head. I crossed the highway and then the jogging path on the side of the Hudson and then walked all the way out to the end of the pier that jutted a hundred yards into the river. It was as far as I could go.

I leaned on the rail, looking across the water to Jersey. There was a strong breeze. The wind came off the water and I was the first person on the island of Manhattan it hit. It had traveled great distances to suddenly encounter me, the immovable object, which it flowed over and around and possibly through and then re-gelled on the other side off to somewhere else. What the significance of that was, I had no idea. I ran my hands through my crackly hair. I desperately wanted to think deep thoughts but they weren't coming. I wanted a fucking moment of clarity, an epiphany, something, I needed something. I screamed as loud as I could. I considered jumping into the water but that seemed stupid and dangerous. I didn't know what to do. It wasn't coming. Ordinary people don't turn on a dime. All I felt was sick and detached. I tried again, I tried to focus on Patty's words, on me, but everything was fuzzy. Even the water looked fuzzy. I took off my glasses, they were filthy. It was like I was practicing for cataracts. I spat on the lenses and cleaned them with my shirt the best I could.

And then I got tired. My jaw ached and the only real

thought I had was that I had to pee. I let my water join the river's and then I lay down, carefully, on the concrete pier. My ass bone was still tender as fuck. Maybe something would come to me in a dream.

woke up, the sun in my eyes, and I had it, I had my deep thought: Sleeping outside was a fucking retarded thing to do. My back was stiff, my head was throbbing, and my ass was a lump of pure pain. I got up and hobbled toward my house.

I stopped in some deli and saw that it was eight-thirty. I wondered how long I had slept out there. I bought a five-dollar bunch of tulips, bad ones dyed blue, the only ones they had, and a bottle of water. I was glad to see that I still had my wallet. The deli dude gave me my change and a look, so I gave him a look in return. I got back to 99 Perry and climbed the stairs. I looked at my door and I looked at Patty's and then I went over to hers. I shave-and-haircutted it.

No answer. I wasn't going to make the same mistake twice so I started to shuffle over toward my place when I heard something. I went back to her door.

"Patty? You up?" I asked, ear to the door.

"Come here," she said.

I tried the door. It was locked. "The door's locked, Patty."

"Jason." A pause. "I need help."

Everything happened in a blur from there. I ran down to the first floor and banged on the super's door for what seemed like a century and he went upstairs in his robe and tried fifteen different keys until he got Patty's door open. I went in and she was in bed, pale and crying, and I called an ambulance and they took her and they wouldn't let me in the back.

I sat on a plastic chair and breathed in the hospital smell and read a *Marie Claire* someone had left behind. Every once in a while a middle-aged nurse would walk by and ignore me. I thought nurses were supposed to be super-sexy; I mean, a nurse outfit was always the slutty Halloween costume choice for girls who wanted to get laid. Looking at the opaque-hosed, orthopedic-shoe-wearing nurses here, I wasn't sure how that outfit ever became known as erotic.

I had been waiting about three hours to get in and see Patty. I kept being told "in just a little while." One of the nurses had asked me if I was family, and it struck me that I had no idea if Patty even *had* family. I should have lied and said yes, I probably could have been in there by now. All they had told me was what I already knew, she was weak from cancer. I couldn't get anything more in-depth than that. So I waited in the plastic chair, trying in vain to find a comfortable position, wondering if I should get my bottom X-rayed. My phone still had one bar on the battery, so I squeezed out a few texts. First to Tina:

in hospital with patty. ick.

Then to Eric.

Finally I was directed down a hall into an elevator, up three floors, and then down another hall to Patty's room. It was tiny and there was another bed in there, but it wasn't occupied. She was lying under the covers with some tubes up her nose. The TV was on and I took that for good news. I figured they didn't let you watch *The Bold and the Beautiful* if things were too serious. But maybe it was the opposite, maybe they let you do what you wanted because you were too far gone. "You want bacon and ice cream and an opium suppository and some unfiltered Camels and a German Shiza DVD—sure, what more harm could they do?"

Patty's eyes opened as I pulled up a chair and sat next to her. "Hi, neighbor," I said, smiling. "How're you feeling?"

"You look like hell," she said in a scratchy voice just above a whisper. She blinked a few times, slowly.

"Yeah, and I think I smell too. You should be glad you have that oxygen supply—I still haven't showered."

She laughed weakly. "So. I owe you an apology, Jason."

"What? I owe you one. I did have flowers for you by the way, but I left them in your apartment." I hung my head. "Sorry about last night, and all."

"That's itty-bitty. I owe you a big apology. See, I told you a lie." She stopped to take a breath. "A whopper."

"About what?"

"Getting better. I'm not. I have lung cancer for chrissakes, Jason." She smiled, the corners of her eyes crinkling. Her skin looked like old, delicate parchment. "You know, you are terribly gullible." She adjusted herself ever so slightly, then reached out her hand. I took it. "Sorry about that, neighbor, I just wanted us to have some laughs. I didn't want to be remembered for being a buzzkill. I've been working on that, you see."

I swallowed even though my mouth was pretty dry. "So wait. I mean, like, what's the prognosis?"

"Death. Relatively soon." She coughed lightly. "Don't be upset. I've known for a long time. It's not going to be like tomorrow, don't freak out yet." She stopped and took another breath. "Do you still have that card I gave you, the lawyer?"

"Yeah."

"Call him. I gave him a list of everyone to contact. He knows what to do."

Her hair was all caught up in one of the tubes that went to her nose. I leaned in and gently untangled it, smoothing it back. "What can I do?" I asked. I hadn't the first clue.

"Want to stay with me for a little while? I may nap, but it'll be nice to see a friendly face when I wake up."

"Sure." I gestured to the soap opera on the TV, and tried to smile. "Only if we change the channel, though."

"Ugh, just turn it off."

I found the remote and took care of it. I grabbed another chair to rest my legs on, maybe I could get some sleep myself. I was so tired. It didn't make any sense. Patty had just told me she was going to die; she was going to die relatively soon. And all I could think was how much I wanted to shut my eyes. I didn't want to cry or scream or run down the hall, I just wanted to lie down, just for a little. All I really felt were crushing waves of exhaustion. I curled up on the chairs. It was so quiet in there.

"Jason."

"Yeah?"

"Is there anything you want me to tell God for you?"

I giggled. "Shut up."

"You sure? You don't want three wishes or something?"

"This is so weird, Patty. I feel like we're just hanging out. I can't get my head around it," I said.

"Hanging out is the best part." She coughed. We were both quiet for a bit. Patty's eyes closed, and then so did mine. I floated just above sleep.

"Want to hear something funny, neighbor?" Patty whispered.

"Yeah." I opened my eyes and looked over at her. Her eyes were still closed. She looked tiny under the covers. I watched her mouth move.

"My cemetery plot is in New Jersey. Can you believe that? I haven't been to Jersey in twenty years." She leaned her head to the side and yawned. Her hair fell across her face, obscuring it. "So long, New York," she whispered. "Howdy, East Orange."

We both fell asleep. A little later a nurse woke me up and kicked me out. Visiting hours were over. I'd have to come back tomorrow after nine.

Three days later I fought my way through Port Authority commuters and got on a Red and Tan bus. My suit jacket was folded on my lap. I put my headphones on and stared out the window. We made it through the tunnel and rolled into New Jersey.

19

My suit felt a little itchy and my heart was pounding. The setting sun grew warm against my back; I could feel myself sweating and wished I could just loosen my damn tie. I took a breath and tried to swallow the lump in my throat. Then I leaned into the microphone, and began. "Hello, my name is Jason Strider, and I've been a close friend of Stacey's and Eric's for many years."

I stood on a small dais built on the sand of the bay in Westhampton, facing the seated congregation of wedding guests. They were smiling and fanning themselves. Tiki torches lined the area. "For those of you who know Stacey and Eric well, you know that they've always done things their own way. So tonight, instead of a traditional rabbi, they asked me to officiate over their marriage. I do so now with great honor, and . . . with a certificate I received over the Internet." A reassuring group chuckle wafted toward me. I continued, "Let us open with the blessing over the wine."

I said the prayer and handed the silver chalice to Stacey, who sipped from it, and then passed it to Eric, who did the same. It was so quiet you could hear the bay lapping up against the pilings, and the occasional seagull caw. I began the ceremony proper and I started to feel more and more confident. I knew it by heart. I had rehearsed like a hundred times in front of my bathroom mirror. The only thing I hadn't practiced was actually holding the microphone. It was pretty hard to act casual with it; I imagined I looked a bit like a thirteen-year-old holding a cigarette awkwardly, pretending he knew how to smoke. I instantly had a newfound respect for Wink Martindale.

As I spoke, my eyes flitted between the bride and groom, and the audience behind them. Well, as much of the audience as I could see through the happy couple, their parents on either side, and the best men and bridesmaids who surrounded them. Some of the bridesmaids, mostly Stacey's family members, were pretty attractive, actually. They all wore fairly sheer "champagne" satin dresses held up by spaghetti straps, and almost all wore them quite well. Stacey had some good genetics, it turned out. I tried to avoid looking at them so as not to be distracted, especially since Tina was also a bridesmaid and I just knew if we locked eyes I'd be done, I'd fall straight into nervous hysterics.

I started by saying that even though I was so honored when Stacey and Eric first asked me to preside over their wedding, I was also incredibly intimidated. The truth was I was no expert on love, yet in a short time I was expected to stand in front of all of their friends and family and pontificate about the subject. "Time passed, the wedding was getting closer, and I was getting worried. What I was going to say? Finally, just two weeks ago, while the three of us had dinner together, it hit me. Now, as a side note, this was the one dinner I actually bought them, instead of the other way around. So, it was already a magical night." Eric flashed me a grin, his eyes already starting to well up. "But I digress."

I began to tell the story of how Stacey and Eric had gotten into a fight, about appetizers of all things. "Eric really wanted to have those mini–hot dogs at the wedding, the pigs in blankets. But Stacey didn't think those were really classy enough for such an important night. And as I sat there, picking at my french fries, I watched them work it out. It was like they were in their own little world. They went back and forth, really listening to each other's feelings. When one got loud the other would calm that one, and soon they were laughing about the silliness of the whole thing. It was a trivial little fight, a tiny blip in their lives. And yet for me, it was telling." A breeze started up; I patted the top of my head to make sure my yarmulke was secure.

"A very close friend of mine once told me that the most important things in life happen when you're just hanging out. What I think she meant was, well, you can have a good time with just about anyone on a roller coaster, or at the Super Bowl, or in Vegas. But it's really how you feel in the little moments that count. If you find someone who makes you laugh while you're standing on line at the DMV, or when you're sick with the flu, or who you can still have fun with while, say, having a heated debate about the pros and cons of wedding appetizers, well," I paused, "that's something."

It wasn't Shakespeare, what I had ended up with, but then again, this wasn't a play. It was the real thing and it was okay to be a little corny, a little clichéd. The most important part was that I meant what I said. I had learned that at Patty's funeral. It had been windy and gray that morning, traditional funeral weather. I could feel every little pebble on the concrete path scratching at the bottom of my rarely worn, hard-soled suit shoes as I walked in silence toward the grave site. The priest was a complete hack, but each of his oversentimental sentences about "this special life" set me trembling. They were nothing original. Hell, love wasn't anything original either. But eventually it stung each of us, nonetheless.

I thought of Rabbi Stan and quickly eyed the crowd to see if they were with me. They were. Stacey kept turning to Eric, suppressing nervous giggles. She looked pretty, she wasn't overly made-up, everything about her was simple, natural. She couldn't stop smiling. I could see every one of her teeth almost to the molars. Eric looked sharp too. His tux was all black, no silly sea-foam cummerbund or anything like that. A six-foot-five guy in a tux could come off a little goofy, but he was making it work.

I touched Stacey on the shoulder, and I looked back and forth at each of them. "And in a few short moments, after our two friends are officially wed and we begin the reception outside on the deck, let us all enjoy our own little moment hanging out with them . . . while eating some mini–hot dogs." A few people applauded and catcalled and Eric pumped a fist in the air.

It was time for the vows and the exchange of rings, so I handed it off to the bride and groom. Stacey began, and I stepped back and caught my breath. I started to think about Patty. I had seen Robert at her funeral; he stood across from me at the grave site. He tipped his cowboy hat in recognition as the priest spoke—well, shouted, so he could be heard above the rushing hum of the nearby turnpike. Robert was pretty upset that Patty's grave was so poorly positioned, so close to the busy highway. I tried to see the bright side: It was the road back to the city.

It took almost no time for Patty's apartment to be cleared out. Apparently she had some family in the Bay Area, and one of them, Aaron, a nice middle-aged hippie with John Lennon glasses and a graying ponytail, flew in, separated the wheat from the chaff, boxed up what he wanted, and left the rest. He asked me about Patty, as he didn't really know her. She was his second cousin; the lawyer had tracked him down. He let me have the Chinatown photo and a few Dylan albums. I didn't have a turntable but I wanted them all the same.

The landlord took over from there and sent in the Salvation Army, who bagged and tagged what was left behind, some for charity, some for trash. Then came the construction guys, who loudly clomped around and ripped out the kitchen and the bathroom and replaced them with cheap new appliances and fixtures and then slapped the whole place over with flat white paint. "Upgrades" like those somehow made it legal for the landlord to raise the rent. They left the door unlocked and I snuck in late one night and looked around the barren space; my footsteps made small echoes in the empty room. You would have never known a woman named Patty lived there. Every trace was gone, it was just some old patched-up piece-of-shit apartment. I slowly paced back and forth in the place. I figured Patty was the kind of person who might show me a sign, it didn't seem that silly to me then. But I didn't sense anything, just the overwhelming smell of fresh paint. The New York real estate market was a pretty goddamn good lesson in the fleeting and brutal nature of life. A couple of days later some girl moved in. I hadn't met her yet. She played the flute. I could hear it in the hall sometimes.

A breeze blew across the beach. I watched as Stacey slipped the ring onto Eric's finger. Past them I could see Tina, craning her neck, caught up in the moment, her camera dangling on a strap from her wrist.

I couldn't sleep much those first few days after Patty was gone. I don't know if I felt grief exactly, but I felt something, a nervous energy. I found myself staying in a lot. I started cooking dinner; I made an entire tray of lasagna one night that probably could have served twelve. In the early-morning hours, I finally bit the bullet, opened up a blank Word document, and focused on Stacey and Eric, banging away until I had done it, I had written the ceremony. Then I sent an e-mail to Tina for Brett's number, called him, and met him for a drink. He said "Hey" and I said "Hey" and then I figured well fuck, the faster you do it the less it hurts. I told him I wanted to be his music supervisor. I certainly wasn't A-list and I'd never done it before, but I knew music. I had DJ'd, I had helped "discover talent" at JB's, I'd work my ass off if he gave me a shot. I rambled on too long like that, it sort of poured out, until I eventually landed on my best selling point: I'd work dirt-cheap.

He nodded. "Jason, first off, I'm really sorry we haven't had the chance to hang out much, this movie is killing me." He said that Tina always talked about how funny I was, how much I knew about music, and how she was sure we'd get along great. But the thing was, he'd already hired someone. He told me it was a woman who used to be high up in A&R at Sony. She was new to it but had just finished several films that were in Sundance. Landing her was a coup. "However," he said, taking a long sip of beer and leaving me hanging for five hundred years on the hopeful adverb, until he swallowed and continued, "I also happen to know that she's looking for an assistant." He promised to put in a very good word. "I mean, I'm the director, right?" He grinned goofily, "I'm still getting used to saying that." We hung out a bit longer and then he had to run. I got in touch with the woman the next morning; we had a nice chat on the phone and were having breakfast on Tuesday. Tina said her fingers were crossed. Stacey said she'd give me a wake-up call from St. Barth, where they'd be honeymooning.

The sun was melting in the water now. Eric was facing Stacey, half-blubbering, half-speaking his vows. Their parents stood on either side of them, smiling nervously, tissues held in clenched hands. Next to them were the best men and the bridesmaids. They were all beaming, rapt.

Then I saw something.

The second bridesmaid in. Her gown had slipped, the thin strap was off the tan shoulder, leaving one whole breast exposed. The nipple was staring right at me, lit up, laser-locked. I was hypnotized. I was the only one in the whole place who could see it. Petey yawned in my pants, and began to wake up. Great, fucking great, I was going to be the rabbi with a boner.

Eric finished his vows and placed the wedding band on Stacey's finger. Boom, I was back on. I took the microphone from him, turned away from the tit and toward the bride and groom. It was almost magic time; in the audience people fumbled and readied their cameras. I cleared my throat and, goddamnit, persevered. "You have spoken vows of love, vows you each took the time to write yourselves. You have exchanged rings. You have consecrated yourselves to each other in front of family and friends. So now . . ." I started grinning and couldn't stop, "it is my duty, honor, and privilege, by the power invested in me by the holy World Wide Web, to pronounce you two . . . man and wife! You may kiss the bride!"

Eric lifted Stacey's veil and, without hesitation, kissed her passionately. The audience erupted in applause and cheers and flashes popped and I got the chills. Goosebumps. The whole deal. Eric's and Stacey's parents exchanged hugs. Bridesmaid Number Two must've shifted or something because when I looked back that way the breast had retreated behind the curtain. I caught Tina's eye and she grinned at me. One of the best men leaned in and put the cloth-wrapped glass on the ground near Eric's shiny shoes. Eric looked at Stacey, and then he stomped on it.

"Mazel tov!" we all roared.

It was official. They were married. They kissed again and laughed and then stepped forward and hugged me simultaneously.

"Thank you, I love you!" yelled Stacey in my ear, sniffling.

"Great job, man!" said Eric, mussing my hair, knocking off my yarmulke.

Then they turned and bounded off the dais, holding hands. I just stood there and watched them go. I was smiling from ear to ear. The crowd fell in behind them, everyone happy, everyone headed toward the bar.

I stayed behind, alone on the dais. It grew quiet. Attendants came out and started to extinguish the torches and fold the chairs. I started to amble in, then stopped for a second, and gave thanks. Nice restraint, Petey.

And so, yes, hell yes, I was soon intoxicated. Guilty as charged, Your Honor. I hadn't really drunk much since my night in the gutter and now I was feeling strong as an ox and swift as a puma. All night everybody wanted to run to the bar and get the good rabbi a drink, and it would have been rude of me to refuse. I was nothing if not gifted in the ways of etiquette.

It was after dinner. We had eaten, we had Hora-ed, and now the people, as they will do at that point in a wedding reception, were dancing. From the relative safety of the carpet, I watched as a crowd of shoeless girls surrounded Stacey on the dance floor, chanting, "Go, Sta-cey, go, Sta-cey," while the DJ blasted Herbie Hancock's "Rockit." It was quite the spectacle. Eric was pushed out onto the floor and the two of them danced in the middle of the fray like cute, overstimulated toddlers. Stacey tried to get me to join her by lassoing me with an invisible rope and pulling me, hand over hand, toward the dance floor. I quickly held up two fingers, mimed a pair of scissors, and cut the rope, laughing.

Tina and Brett were out there too, away from the fray, drunkenly slow-dancing. Tina was a wreck, a fantastic, sparkling, slit-eyed mess, swaying with the beat, hanging onto Brett for balance. She felt me staring at her, looked up, and smiled. Then with her eyes locked on mine, she slowly raised her hand off his back, smirked, and gave me the finger.

I wandered away, grabbed a Corona from the bar, and

weaved through a sea of formalwear until I made it to the deck. Then I kept going, out onto the sand, down toward the water. The music began to fade behind me. I wished I knew a sea chantey, I felt like belting one out. As I stumbled along, I reached inside my jacket pocket and whipped out a perfect little joint. From my pants, I pulled a lighter. I brought the two together. I had a feeling they'd become fast friends.

I found a spot, lay back on the sand, and stared up at the sky, thick with stars. The moon hung low and bright, not quite full but in the ballpark. I put the joint to my lips, took a huge hit and held it, held it, held it, slowly letting the smoke pool in my mouth. Then I made an "O" with my lips, mentally prepared myself for success, and exhaled.

ACKNOWLEDGMENTS

The author would like to buy the following people a pony:

Gerry Howard, my sagelike editor; Emilie Stewart, my agent and *consigliere*; Sandra Garcia, Noah Vadnai, Mallory Kasdan, Evan Benjamin, Tami Brown, and especially Rachel Kash, early readers and gentle critics; Chris Noel, Darin Strauss, Cheryl Van Ooyen, Mark Sarosi, and Penny Hardy for their shrewd suggestions; Fred and Karen Rosen for their love, encouragement, and genetics (height and eyesight notwithstanding); Becky Cole for her support; Rachel Rokicki, Anne Watters, Katie Halleron, and everyone at Broadway who helped make the magic happen; and my dog, Billy, for his patient bladder.

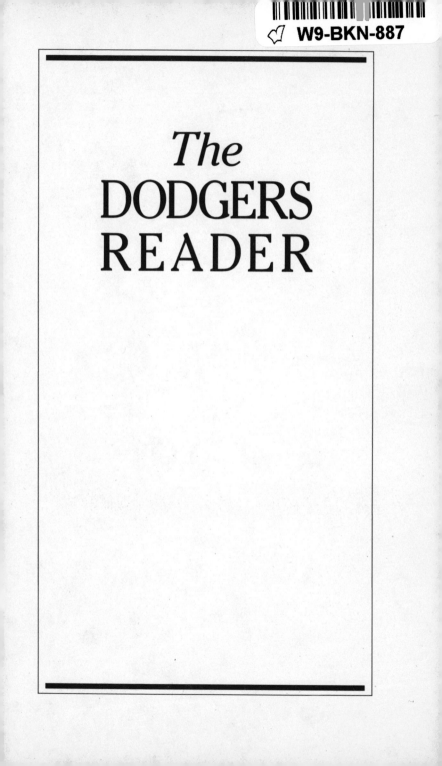
The DODGERS READER

The
DODGERS
READER

Edited by Dan Riley

HOUGHTON MIFFLIN COMPANY

Boston / New York / London 1992

For information about permission to reproduce selections from
this book, write to Permissions, Houghton Mifflin Company,
215 Park Avenue South, New York, New York 10003.

Library of Congress Cataloging-in-Publication Data
The Dodgers reader / edited by Dan Riley.
    p.   cm.
  Essays and articles published from 1947 to 1991 in various
periodicals and newspapers.
    ISBN 0-395-58778-6 (pbk.)
    1. Brooklyn Dodgers (Baseball team)—History.   2. Los Angeles
Dodgers (Baseball team)—History.   I. Riley, Dan.
GV875.B7D63   1992   91-42403
796.357'64'0974723—dc20 CIP

Printed in the United States of America

Book design by Robert Overholtzer

BBS 10 9 8 7 6 5 4 3 2 1

The editor wishes to acknowledge previously published material:
  "The Dodgers" from *New York City Baseball: 1947–1957* by Harvey
Frommer. Copyright © 1980 by Harvey Frommer.
  Excerpt from *Bums: An Oral History of the Brooklyn Dodgers* by
Peter Golenbock. Reprinted by permission of Putnam Publishing
Group. Copyright © 1984 by Peter Golenbock.
  "Was the Move Justified" from *The Dodgers Move West* by Neil J.
Sullivan. Copyright © 1987 by Neil J. Sullivan.
  "Take Them Out of the Ballgame" by Maryann Hudson. Copyright
© 1991 by the Los Angeles Times. Reprinted by permission.
  "1947: Brooklyn Dodgers 3, New York Yankees 2" by Dick Young.
Copyright © 1947 by New York News. Reprinted by permission.
  "1951: New York Giants 5, Brooklyn Dodgers 4" by Red Smith.
From *The Red Smith Reader* by Red Smith, edited by Dave Anderson.
Copyright © 1982 by Random House, Inc. Reprinted by permission of
Random House, Inc.
  Excerpt from *Walter Alston: A Year at a Time* by Walter Alston.
Copyright © 1976 by Walter Alston.

"My Blue Heaven" from *The Artful Dodger* by Tommy Lasorda and David Fisher. Copyright © 1985 by Tommy Lasorda. Reprinted by permission of William Morrow and Company, Inc., Publishers, New York.

The editor wishes to thank Mary Miyagishima for her tireless and cheerful effort in helping to prepare the manuscript for publication.

Contents

Introduction   ix

A SENSE OF PLACE

Harvey Frommer
  The Dodgers   6

Peter Golenbock
  From *Bums: An Oral History of the Brooklyn Dodgers*   38

Neil J. Sullivan
  Was the Move Justified?   70

Maryann Hudson
  Take Them Out of the Ballgame   93

DEFINING MOMENTS

Dick Young
  1947: Brooklyn Dodgers 3, New York Yankees 2   106

Red Smith
  1951: New York Giants 5, Brooklyn Dodgers 4   112

Walter Alston
  From *A Year at a Time*   115

Juan Marichal and Charles Einstein
From *A Pitcher's Story*   124

Jim Murray
It Could Happen Only in Hollywood   134

A CAST OF CHARACTERS

Jimmy Cannon
Jackie Robinson's Precious Gift   143

Leo Durocher with Ed Linn
Mr. Rickey   147

Fred C. Harris and Brendan C. Boyd
From *The Great American Baseball Card Flipping,
Trading and Bubble Gum Book*   158

Don Drysdale and Bob Verdi
Was I Mean? Well . . .   170

Thomas Boswell
Koufax: Passing the Art Along   185

Maury Wills and Mike Celizic
In Control   191

Bob Welch and George Vecsey
Out of Control   196

Steve Garvey and Skip Rozin
From *Garvey*   204

Jim Murray
They Won't Call Him Dr. Zero for Nothing   211

Mike Downey
Joker, Ace of Hearts Is Released   215

Tommy Lasorda and David Fisher
My Blue Heaven   218

Introduction

The Dodger Reader is the fourth in line in our series of team anthologies, following similar books on the Red Sox, the Yankees, and the Cubs.

Lots of changes in those four clubs over the years.

Name changes: the Cubs were originally called the White Sox; the Yankees originally the Highlanders; the Red Sox, astonishingly, were once the Speed Boys. The Los Angeles Dodgers, of course, were once the Brooklyn Dodgers. So make that name and place changes.

Changes in ownership, too: they've been bought and sold by, among others, banks, chewing gum companies, playboys, TV networks, third-string catchers, and third-string human beings.

Changes in tradition: they now play night baseball in Wrigley and losing baseball in Yankee Stadium.

And innumerable changes in personnel: Bill Skowron played for the Yankees and Dodgers. Tommy John played for the Yankees and Dodgers. Dennis Eckersley played for the Red Sox and Cubs. Bill Buckner played for the Dodgers, Cubs, and Red Sox. Don Zimmer, God bless him, played for the Dodgers, coached for the Yankees, and managed the Red Sox and Cubs. You can still drop a jaw or two at a cocktail party of casual baseball fans by mentioning that Babe Ruth, the very embodiment of the Yankees, once played for the archrival Red Sox or that Jackie Robinson, the sine qua non of the Dodgers, was shipped off to the hated Giants in his final year.

It all appears like so much random coming and going . . . a kaleidoscope of names, games, faces, and places. Shake it up and you've got the New York Cubs. Shake it again and you get the Los Angeles Red Sox. A ball club is a ball club is a ball club, said Gertrude Stein . . . or Yogi Berra . . . or somebody like that.

And yet . . .

Yet it is a conceit of this series of books that each of these teams, as well as others not yet examined, has forged a special identity that's now indelibly impressed upon the collective memory of twentieth-century baseball. Should the Cubbies hoist the world championship flag over Wrigley next October and manage to keep it there till 2001, their lasting image will remain that of the game's lovable losers. Should the Red Sox get to a World Series seventh game, ninth inning, none on, two out, and a three-run lead that they actually manage to hold, their lasting image will remain that of the game's premier heartbreakers. And despite their hardscrabble existence near the bottom of the American League East in recent years, the lasting memory of this century's Yankees will remain that of the Bronx Bombers, high and mighty pillagers of ballparks throughout the land.

And how about those Dodgers? What will be our lasting impression of them? Surely the number of transformations they've undergone in close to a century of existence would seem enough to defy our best efforts at casting their image in stone. What would it be? The inept but charming Bums? The evergreen Boys of Summer? Team Hollywood?

We invest the Yankees with awe because they represent what we wish to be — perennial winners. We invest the Cubs with affection because they represent what we hope we never become — perpetual losers. We invest the Red Sox with angst because they represent what we often seem

to be — Sisyphus, forever condemned to slog our rock up
the hill, only to have it roll back down before we reach the
top. But it's the Dodgers who reflect back exactly what we
are, not as individuals, but as a country. With apologies to
the PR departments of the Dallas Cowboys and Atlanta
Braves, the Dodgers come closer than either or any other to
truly being America's Team. Being of both East Coast and
West; being of both the old, homogeneous America and the
new, multicultural one; being of both noble experimentation
and self-aggrandizing opportunism, the Dodger character in
many ways symbolizes the national character. Up, first, from
the white, working-class neighborhoods of urban America,
struggling for identity and respectability; then emerging
strong at midcentury and turning a rich, multicolored face to
the world; then following the inevitable American move
West, El Dorado pursued more eagerly than any pennant;
and finally settling into a haze of hyped-up happiness. Victory
celebrated as affirmation that the Big Dodger in the Sky
really does like us; defeat breezily dismissed.

But whoa! Whoa. What is this? This is shortstops and
fungo bats we're talking here, not *Moby Dick*. How much
symbolism can we freight on a ball club? As much as it can
handle, I say. "If you build it, they will come," goes J. P.
Kinsella's most famous line. They will come because they
have no place else to go. We need these ball clubs as vessels
of our unifying myths, because in this increasingly litigious,
contentious, fragmented society of ours, they are among the
last institutions capable of enlisting an allegiance that rises
above socioeconomic, political, religious, and racial differences. Regardless of class, New York fans, from readers of
the *Post* to readers of the *Times*, can put on their Yankee
caps and draw strength from the team's incomparable string
of world championships. Regardless of politics, Cook County
Democrats and downstate Republicans can be bipartisan in
their empathy for the Cubs' incomparable string of non-
championship seasons. Red Sox Catholics and non-Catho-
lics — atheists, too — can unite in a common prayer for

deliverence from their very maddening purgatory. And LA fans, from the cops on the beat to the boyz 'n the hood, can cheer alike for old Dodger Blue.

Every major and minor league team has the rudiments of a team identity — the logo, the colors, the nickname. But as we get deeper into this series, there seem to be three essential elements necessary for a team to forge an identity strong enough to thrust the team into the cultural mythos.

First is a sense of place. The club has to be an integral part of a particular community over a long period of time. The Dodgers, of course, pushed the envelope on that one with their move to California. But unlike the Senators, who moved to Texas and couldn't resist a name change to Rangers or Rustlers, the Dodgers had the good sense to remain Dodgers. And unlike the Braves, who maintained their name but also their wanderlust, the Dodgers had the good sense to stay put once they reached their promised land. It's a credit to both the Dodger PR department — which never sleeps — and the jilted fans of Brooklyn — who never forget — that unlike almost every other nomadic team in sports, the story of the Dodgers of Brooklyn and the Dodgers of Los Angeles remains forever intertwined.

Second is a series of defining moments that are either acted out on the national stage or that command national attention. Unlike the Cubs, who command national attention by their dogged inability to assume the national stage, Dodger history is a clockwork of defining moments. To begin with, they lost two of the most famous ball games ever played — the Bobby Thomson home run game and Don Larsen's perfect World Series game. Then there was The Move itself, which opened up baseball, if not to a large degree the whole country, to the West. And, lest we forget in our current siege of racial antagonisms, moments don't get any more definitive than the one in which the Dodgers handed Jackie Robinson a uniform and said, Let's see what we can do about making the game and our society better for all of us.

Finally, there's character—both the capital *C* kind that we like to find in our heroes and the small *c* kind, as in *colorful*, that we like to find in all our amusements. Through good fortune and effort, the Dodgers have been able to fill more than their share of rosters with some of the game's most enduring characters—and not a few spots on those rosters with men of enduring character.

D.R.

A SENSE OF PLACE

I never had my heart ripped out, so I really don't know what it's like to have your ball club moved to another town. From what I can gather from old Brooklyn fans, though, especially those quoted in Peter Golenbock's *Bums,* it's a pretty painful experience. The hurt and the anger are something to behold, and perhaps a little bewildering too. After all, folks in Milwaukee once lost their Braves to Atlanta, and folks in Seattle once lost their Pilots to Milwaukee, and we hardly ever heard the level of bewailing and bemoaning we've heard from Brooklyn fans.

Roger Kahn, who built his own reputation on Brooklyn Dodger nostalgia, took a can of spray paint to Walter O'Malley's reputation in his *Boys of Summer.* Therein he accused O'Malley of pettiness for making reporters at Ebbetts Field use a pay phone, of baseball illiteracy for never having been heard to discuss curve balls or second basemen's hands, of contemptuousness for having described ballplayers as money hungry, and of course, of the de rigueur transgression of our time — racism. Describing an exchange with O'Malley after an article he'd written reporting a racial slur directed at Jim Gilliam, Kahn wrote:

> The phrase I had heard, "How would you like a nigger to take your job?" was, O'Malley insisted, the same as "another Jewish judge," cacophony piped by unchosen lawyers in courthouse smoke rooms. "It's rude, but doesn't mean much," O'Malley said, "and I'm surprised that you were taken in."
> My defense — "I'd write 'another Jewish judge,' too" —

drew a wintry response. "A Froebel boy [Froebel being Kahn and O'Malley's alma mater] should know how to evaluate things realistically," O'Malley said, and "Froebel boy" had never sounded so pejorative.

"One man's ceiling is another man's floor," wrote Paul Simon, a Yankee fan. And it's startling to note with what alacrity Kahn proves that point when, within a few paragraphs of his "Froebel boy" story, he sums up O'Malley this way: "Many baseball writers took him for a warm friend, without recognizing that, as with an underboiled potato, O'Malley's warmth was mostly external. The shock was all the stronger when he led the Dodgers out of Brooklyn and left some journalists to cover golf matches contested by wiry women." ("Golf matches contested by wiry women," of course, may indeed be the third gate of hell for a sports writer, although it's hard to imagine what heights of righteous indignation Mr. Kahn may have scaled had he ever overheard Walter O'Malley refer to boxing matches contested by wiry-haired blacks!)

The whole vendetta gets entirely out of hand when someone in our pages goes so far as to compare O'Malley to Hitler! For moving a baseball team? Why is that? Why's the emotion so deep? Is it because they're New Yorkers, and New Yorkers are naturally over the top about everything? Or is it because the Dodgers of Brooklyn truly were of the neighborhood, woven into the fabric of the place and, unlike the Braves of Milwaukee, not just passing through on their way from Boston to Atlanta?

Maybe it's a little of both, although there really can be no denying the authenticity of the feelings. They truly loved their Dodgers in Brooklyn — and they truly hated Walter O'Malley. In all the pages that follow, it's hard to find a kind word about O'Malley. Yet at the risk of sounding like a lackey for yellow dog capitalism, it's also pretty hard to argue with the logic of what he did. As a transplanted easterner myself, I can relate to the instinct to pull up roots, leave the loved ones weeping in the driveway, and head West in pursuit of one's fortune — no one had to offer me half of Los Angeles to do it either. So, though many of the pages ahead

may reek of vitriol against Walter O'Malley, I remain personally dispassionate about the man, preferring to view him in
the long tradition of club owners, like Frazee of the Red
Sox and Steinbrenner of the Yankees, whose unobstructed
attention to self, for better and often worse, has left their
permanent imprint on the clubs they owned while making
somewhat of a mockery of the concept of community trust.

In O'Malley's case, betrayal of that trust yielded enviable
riches. As Neil J. Sullivan contends in "Was the Move
Justified?" — about as objective a discourse as you'll find on
the subject — the Dodgers ended up in a ballpark that's
arguably the best in the land, playing before three million
paying customers a year. Whether or not Los Angeles fans
of the Dodgers are as emotionally wedded to the team as
their Brooklyn predecessors clearly were remains a question
of continuing debate. Los Angeles, of course, has always
been on the receiving end of these franchise moves — the
Rams from Cleveland, the Lakers from Minnesota, the
Raiders from Oakland, the lamentable Clippers from San
Diego, Gretzky, and thus the Kings, from Edmonton. So
Angelenos can afford to be a little — how should we put
this? — laid back about their team. As Maryann Hudson
documents it at the end of this section, they have a well-
deserved reputation for leaving games early, even if the
dramatic structure of the game is moving inexorably toward
a breathtaking conclusion.

This is not to imply that Dodger fans would not be upset
if, in that most unlikely of all events, the Dodgers were ever
to up and move — where? Tokyo? They would be upset. For
about a week. And then it would be back to life as we know
it. That's because Los Angeles, unlike Brooklyn, is a city
of the future — fluid, fluctuating, and full of disposable,
replaceable parts.

Hard to imagine the Dodgers ever being anything less than
a permanent fixture, though. Fortunately we don't have to
tax our imaginations. We have history. And so we begin *The
Dodger Reader* with a bit of history — Harvey Frommer's
chapter on the Dodgers from his book *New York City
Baseball*.

Harvey Frommer

The Dodgers

New York City Baseball

You couldn't say anything you wanted to about those Bums.
Because their fans loved that team.

— Junior Gilliam

On a cold and windy April 9, 1913, almost twelve thousand
paying customers entered the grand and ornate rotunda to
get through the turnstiles to watch the first regular season
game ever played at Ebbets Field. The park was built on
four and a half acres of the lowest slope of Crown Heights on
filled-in marshy swampland called "Pigtown" by neighborhood people. Built at a cost of $750,000, the park derived its
name from Charles H. Ebbets, who rose from his job selling
peanuts and scorecards to become president and principal
owner of the team. The Dodgers lost 1–0 to the Phillies; the
most spectacular fielding play was made by a Dodger outfielder. His name was Casey Stengel.

Over the years, the little park fused Flatbush with Go-
wanus, Red Hook, Greenpoint, and Brownsville. It hosted
Italians, Jews, Poles, Irish, blacks, the hoity-toity, clerks,
bankers, kings — all of whom had as much fun being there
with each other as they did viewing the baseball action.

It was an antique of a ball park that in its prime seated
32,000 — the least in the National League. A large sign
placed there by the New York City Fire Department said
that attendance of more than 33,000 was not permitted,

but there were many times the sign was ignored, especially when the Giants came to play. On August 30, 1947, for example, an Ebbets Field single-game attendance record was set when 37,512 jammed into the park to watch the Dodgers battle the Giants. On September 24, 1940, a night-game attendance record was set — 35,583. Some days hundreds stood in the aisles and on the rooftops of nearby apartment houses to see Brooklyn baseball. A closed-in place, a sandlot stadium located at the intersections of Bedford Avenue (beyond right field), Montgomery Street (in back of left field), Sullivan Place (behind first base), and McKeever Place (in back of third base and the left field stands), Ebbets Field was a people's park.

It was called the home of "Dem Bums," a nickname the Dodgers had picked up or earned, depending on one's perspective, when an excitable fan during the depression years used to scream out his anger at the inadequacies of the team. He would squeeze the chicken wire screening in back of home plate and bellow, "Ya bum, ya. Yez bums, yez!" Bums meant Brooklyn. Bums meant Dodgers. And Bums they were called in newspaper headlines and stories; cartoonists vied with each other to create the most appropriate caricature. Cartoonist Willard Mullin developed a national reputation for his interpretation of the Brooklyn Bum.

Ebbets Field was a park of intimate dimensions so that "when you had a box seat," according to Red Barber, "you were practically playing the infield." Former Dodger publicist Irving Rudd recalls, "You could see the tan in a player's face from a good seat, the cords in his neck." Sal Maglie, who pitched there both as a Giant and a Dodger, remembers Ebbets Field "as a place where you were never secure. A game was never settled until the final out because the place was so small."

Brooklyn Borough President Howard Golden muses: "Whether you sat in the box or reserved section, or you sat in the bleachers, you were part of the action. I remember sitting in the top row of the bleachers as a kid, happy to sit there with my lunch and to spend my dime for a soda. You'd go out and spend a weekend there. Part of our upbringing and education for a whole generation took place at Ebbets Field."

The 40-foot-high screen in right field was just 297 feet from home plate, a favorite target for left-handed pull hitters. The distance from the plate to left field was 343 feet to the wall (9 feet 10½ inches) that had to be cleared for a home run. Dead center field was 405 feet from home plate.

It was claimed that half the fans on any given day walked in off the street from their homes located in the residential neighborhoods that ringed the ball park, and that after a game they could all be home within twenty minutes.

For those who came by car, there was limited parking, just one small lot on Montgomery Street. However, the area around the park was the hub of much public transportation. The IRT subway stop was two and a half blocks away. The Prospect Park BMT subway station was a walk of a block and a half. Fans came to Ebbets Field on the Flatbush Avenue bus, the Reid Avenue bus, the Empire Boulevard bus, the Franklin Avenue trolley.

The arguments, odd happenings, and odder characters that congregated at Ebbets Field prompted Red Barber to refer to the ball park as "the rhubarb patch." Opposing players employed earthier expressions. It was a place of curiosities and a home for the curious.

"Whether we won or lost," recalls Wilhemena Brandt, who worked the Dodger switchboard from 1941 until the day they left Brooklyn, "every day was a busy, big day on the switchboard that was located right next to the visiting clubhouse at the corner of Bedford Avenue and Sullivan Place. Fans called up with every kind of question you could imagine, like the wives who wanted their husbands paged to make sure they were at the ball game like they said, or the lady who wanted to know when to put the roast on."

The circular entrance rotunda was a grand and aesthetic touch when the park first opened in 1913. In the '40s and '50s it proved to be an obstacle course. Fans went around in circles attempting to determine which entrance to use to enter the actual ball park. Pushing, shoving, name-calling, and fist fights were logical outgrowths of the frustration.

Some fans enjoyed picking on those athletes who could not fight back. The visitors' bull pen was a bench close by the reserved seats in the left field corner. A daily assortment of tomatoes, raw eggs, half-filled paper cups, hot dog buns, and other items were gleefully tossed at the visiting athletes by the "Flatbush faithful." The biggest barrage was usually fired at Giant players.

The noise level at the park produced earaches. It spilled out onto Bedford Avenue and into the surrounding neighborhood. It was possible five blocks away to tell if the Dodgers were doing well or not in a particular game by the rise and fall of the sounds.

Former Dodger general manager Buzzie Bavasi recalls, "You'd call the fans at the park by their first name. You'd turn the lights on for a night game and fifteen thousand would come out just to see why the lights were on."

Jim Thomson was in charge of stadium supervision and management. "You either got along with the fellow sitting next to you," he said, "or you fought him. There was no in-between. There was always a brawl of some kind at Ebbets Field."

Ebbets Field was part of the life of Dodger fans, a second home. Jackie Robinson and pitcher Russ Meyer "got into a brawl in Philadelphia," recalls Thomson. "The Phillies and Dodgers then came back to play at Ebbets Field. We had only sold about two thousand seats for the game. The next morning there were lines halfway around the block. The fans all wanted to see the continuation of the fight between Meyer and Robinson. That's what made Ebbets Field. The fan became part of the player's life."

The press box at Ebbets Field was located just about ten feet above the left field stands. And in this area resided journalism critics. "There was a guy," Jack Lang recalls, "who day after day used to holler insults up to us. He especially had it in for Herb Goren of the *New York Sun*. 'Hoibie, you were wrong again yesterday, you idiot,' he would yell."

Tex Rickard was the public address announcer in that

Coney Island of ball parks. "He had worked at Ebbets Field for fifteen dollars a day," said Lang, "for as long as anyone could remember." Rickard had a wonderful sense of perspective that perfectly fitted the context of Ebbets Field. His convoluted malapropisms made him another one of the prized characters of Dodger fans. "A little boy has been found lost," and "Will the fans along the railing in left field please remove their clothes," were just two of his more famous lines.

One day during a frenetic pennant race, some of the Dodgers, according to Jack Lang, noticed that the number of the Cub pitcher performing in a crucial game in Chicago had not been posted on the scoreboard. They asked Rickard, who sat on a little chair next to the Brooklyn bench, to find out the name of the Chicago pitcher. Rickard used the dugout phone to call Dodger publicist Frank Graham, Jr., in the press box. Graham informed Rickard that he did not know who was pitching but would call back with the information. A few minutes later, Lang said, Graham called back.

"Bob Rush," announced the voice of Graham.

"Hi, Bob Rush," responded Tex Rickard. "How you doin'?"

Disorientation was just one the traits that enabled Rickard to lay claim to his reputation as one of Ebbets Field's outlandish characters. He also had a faulty memory. One day a new catcher came in for the Dodgers. His name was Livingston.

With all the assurance in the world, in a deep and resonant voice, Tex Rickard announced to the Ebbets Field crowd: "Now catching for the Dodgers — Stanley Livingston."

Others who changed from mild-mannered civilians to eccentrics in the telephone booth that was Ebbets Field included the successful businessman who blew a whistle until he ran out of breath. Then as his second act he would switch to releasing previously inflated multicolored balloons. The most famous whistler was Eddie Batan. His "peep-peep, peep-peep" pleaded for the Dodgers to launch a rally. Another character was a primitive precursor of the "Cookie Monster." He was passionately involved with Dodger outfielder Harry "Cookie" Lavagetto. The fan would run up and down the aisles bellowing, "Cookie! Cookie! Cookie!" And there was Abe, the gambler. A large, serious man, he stationed himself in the stands behind third base, collecting and dispensing money for the bets he had made.

One of the prime tourist attractions at Ebbets Field was Hilda Chester. A rather large woman with a leaning toward flowered print dresses, she was a Brooklyn favorite and anathema to the opposition. Equipped with a large sign proclaiming "Hilda is here," and armed with a large cowbell in each hand, she would ring her bells, creating earaches and producing support for the Dodger cause. "She would shake that bell," recalls Horace Stoneham's wife, Valeda, "until you were just ready to jump. She was the Dodgers' biggest rooter."

"Hilda was a sensitive, caring lady," said Irving Rudd. "Once in a while some people didn't understand her and would talk to her as if she were some demented asylum inmate. She would tell them to talk nicely. She was a dame who just wanted to ring a cowbell. Once TV came in she became self-conscious."

The Dodger batboy of that time was another character. Nicknamed "The Brow" because of his furrowed forehead and the tricks he could perform with a pen, he personally autographed baseballs for fifty cents each. His customers would then sell the autographed baseballs with the "authentic Dodger signatures" to eager collectors. At World Series time tourists would cheerfully pay as much as fifteen dollars per ball. "The Brow" at work was an artist in his deft and swift imitations of the signatures of Dodger favorites. A "Duke Snider" leaned to the left, southpaw style. "Gil Hodges" was signed with flourish. The autograph of "Roy Campanella" was written in a cramped catcher's style, leaning to the right. "Pee Wee Reese" displayed excellent penmanship and the "P" and the "R" were created out of sweeping loops.

Former Dodger outfielder Carl Abrams remembered an autograph seeker who probably never heard of "The Brow." "For twenty straight games," Abrams said, "one kid got my autograph on a penny postcard. Finally I had to satisfy my curiosity. I asked him why he was doing it. 'I need thirty Cal Abrams so I can get one Carl Furillo,' the kid said."

Another group of characters were the members of a little musical band that Red Barber dubbed the "Dodger Sym-phoney," in his phrase, "a little rag-tag group that just made a lot of noise." They were all Italians, and they came from the same neighborhood in the northern section of Williams-burg, Brooklyn. The five original members included Brother Lou Soriano, Jerry Martin, who played the snare drum, Jo Jo Delio, a clanger of cymbals, Paddy Palma, whose specialty was the bass drum, and Phil Cacavalle, trumpet man.

"It was a real cockamamie band," says Jerry Martin. "None of us read music, but we made a lot of noise and all the Dodger fans used to fight to come sit near us. After a while, everybody wanted to get in the act and a lot of them did." Martin maintains that Shorty Laurice, a diminutive fig-ure who wore a stovepipe hat, was added to the Sym-phoney by Walter O'Malley. "That Laurice," Martin still gripes, "wasn't even from our neighborhood. He just sucked his way in." Laurice became the leader.

Chased all over the park by security personnel in the early years, eventually the little band, through the intervention of Jack Collins, Dodger business manager, was given seats 1–8 row 1, section 8, behind the Dodger dugout. "We had a lot of fights with people who came and tried to take our seats over the years," said Martin.

The efforts of the Sym-phoney were part-time; they played at night games and on weekends. "We all held down full-time jobs so we played when we could," said Jerry Martin. "Sometimes we'd travel with the team to Boston or Philadelphia. They paid us nothing. We paid our own way. They didn't even give us pretzels."

The brassy sounds and oddball routines of the Sym-phoney carried through the summer afternoons and evening through the park into the bleachers and out into Bedford Avenue. "They could hear us good — Ebbets Field was closed in, it was a bandbox," said Soriano. When they weren't in their seats behind the dugout, they wandered through the stands, pied pipers in street clothes. "We never needed police protection at Ebbets Field," Martin said. "Everybody loved us."

Only umpires and opposing players were irritated. When the little band disagreed with an umpire's call against one of the Dodgers, it musically protested to the tune of "Three Blind Mice." The big number of the Sym-phoney, however, was a song called "The Worm Crawls In." (Its real name was "The Army Duff.") The number earned the affectionate devotion of Brooklyn Dodger fans and the irritated antagonism of opposition ballplayers. Numerous choruses were played as an accompaniment to the self-conscious strides of an opposing ballplayer who was headed back to the bench after an unsuccessful turn at bat.

The climax to the tune and the cat-and-mouse game between band and player was the "bang" timed on the bass drum at the very instant the derriere of an opponent touched down to the dugout bench. "They'd go to the pump [water cooler] or walk around," Soriano said. "We wouldn't hit it. They'd think we forgot about them. We never forgot. We had patience. Big Johnny Mize gave us the most trouble. But he like the rest of them used to finally sit down and we'd go BANG!"

Once things went "bang" around the Dodger Sym-phoney. "I had brought my brother to the game," the excitable Soriano recalls. "He was a little odd. He was a Giant fan. Whitey Lockman hit a home run to put the Giants in the lead. My brother grabbed the cymbals and started jumping up and down and banging them together. He was dancing all around, he was so happy. The fans behind us got pissed off. 'What the hell you bringin' Giant fans wid' ya?' one of them yelled. I said, 'Don't mind him — he's my brother and he's crazy!'"

The biggest controversy the Sym-phoney was ever involved in took place when the musicians' union insisted that the Dodgers pay union scale for a standby band. "They thought the Sym-phoney was employed by us," Walter O'Malley recalled, "and they insisted they would strike Ebbets Field unless we agreed. We decided on a Music

Appreciation Day. Anyone with a musical instrument was admitted free. They came with cornets, drums, calliopes, old wash boards. There was some racket and a lot of fun. The *Daily News* the next day said that was the best way they ever saw to break a strike threat — treat it with a sense of humor."

Poignant, slapstick, satirical, dumb, good-natured, unintentional . . . humor pervaded Ebbets Field. An advertisement on the thirty-foot-high right field wall said: "THE DODGERS USE LIFEBUOY." One morning early arrivals saw the work of what they assumed to be a Giant fan who sneaked in while Brooklyn slept. Under the sign, the anonymous artist had scrawled in red letters: " . . . AND THEY STILL STINK!" In 1947, with Durocher suspended for the entire season by Commissioner Chandler, the "faithful" brought homemade signs to Ebbets Field: "OPEN THE DOOR CHANDLER," "WE MOURN OUR LOSS," "LET LEO OUT!" "CHANDLER FOR DOG CATCHER."

"HIT SIGN, WIN SUIT," was the most famous sign at Ebbets Field. Located at the base of the scoreboard, approximately four feet high and forty feet wide, the space was rented by Brooklyn clothier Abe Stark of 1514 Pitkin Avenue. With Furillo positioned at least half the time in front of the sign, which was situated almost four hundred feet from home plate, there were very few who were ever entitled to the free suit. The sign and the name on it became so popular that many claim Abe Stark's climb through Brooklyn politics to the borough presidency was helped by it.

Signs dominated Ebbets Field. Atop the scoreboard was the Schaefer Beer sign. The "h" lit up to indicate a hit and the "e" lit up to denote an error. Other commercial writing included: "Bulova — Official Timepiece — Brooklyn Dodgers"; "Once again you're clean — Gem Blades"; "Stadler's Winthrop Shoes"; and "Van Heusen Shirts."

It was claimed that Ebbets Field was a place where anything could happen and where everyone wanted to be. This was more fact than claim. In 1951, for example, the tiny ball park drew almost two million paying customers. Five times in the 1947–1957 era, the Dodgers led the league in home attendance. Ebbets Field was an attraction for visitors from all walks of life, from all over the world.

When Douglas MacArthur was relieved of his command in Korea by President Harry S Truman, one of the first places the controversial general visited was Ebbets Field. He delivered a speech that began, "I've been told that one has not lived unless one has been to Ebbets Field and has watched the Dodgers play baseball." Publicist Irving Rudd claims, "I slipped him the line."

Rudd arranged for famed commentator Ed Murrow to visit the ball park and mingle with the players in the clubhouse. Rudd remembers Dodger utility infielder Rocky Bridges shouting at Murrow as he left, "And good night and good luck," the broadcaster's famous closing line. Other celebrity visitors to Ebbets Field included former Governor of New York State Averell Harriman and columnist Walter Winchell.

Governor Harriman, a shy and dignified man, "asked a lot of intellectual questions and hardly spoke above a whisper," recalls Rudd.

Winchell visited Ebbets Field sporting a gray fedora and an expensive silk suit. In the '40s and '50s, Winchell was known and feared for his ability to create or destroy celebrities and for his Sunday radio show that began at 10:00 P.M. with these lines: "Good evening Mr. and Mrs. North and South America and all the ships at sea . . . Let's go to press." In 1948, Winchell was the highest-paid newscaster in America. ABC paid him five hundred twenty thousand dollars. His sponsor, Jergens Lotion, provided a sum almost as huge to the quick-talking gossip journalist. "Winchell mesmerized and boggled the Dodger players in the clubhouse," according to Rudd. "He had such power and fame that the players did not know how to act. He wound up devoting a whole column to his visit to Ebbets Field."

One August morning in 1952, Rudd was awakened by Dodger president Walter O'Malley and told to rush down to Ebbets Field. "The King of Iraq" (Faisal II), O'Malley said, "has come to the United Sates and has indicated he wants to visit our ball park." The seventeen-year-old king had been invited to the United States by President Truman. Rudd said, "Here was a king who knew nothing about baseball, but he had heard about the Dodgers and Ebbets Field. I got to the press gate about eleven and suddenly a whole bunch of cars pulled up. These big guys, State Department security men, got out and there's this nice-looking guy with a big hat. He was about five foot five, five foot six, and the same size as me. And here I am, a nice Jewish kid from Brooklyn saying 'How do you do, Your Majesty' — it was like you read in the books in school. There I was with a real live king!"

It was a weekday afternoon. Rudd was the only official member of the Dodgers present. "So I had no choice but to walk him on the playing field. Suddenly I'm pointing out the bases. I'm telling him about the outfield. Then a whole bunch of photographers and a newsreel crew starts shooting. They shout, 'Irv, point again. Take his arm. Do this. Do that.' I'm dying. I told a couple of the Ebbets Field employees, 'get Buzzie [Bavasi], get Fresco [Thompson] [Dodger vice presidents], get somebody!' and the cameras are poppin', and this 'n that."

Rudd peered over to the Dodger dugout thinking he could at least introduce the king to one of the Dodger coaches. "It's a little after noon," Rudd recalls, "usually the first guy up the steps with a bag of balls was coach Jake Pitler. On this day, up the steps comes Jackie Roosevelt Robinson — in the flesh. I said to myself, glory be, I'm saved.

"Your Majesty, I want you to meet a real fine gentleman. 'Hey, Jackie, Jackie, I'd like you to say hello to the King of Iraq.' Jackie and I used to kind of kid each other a lot and that must be why at that moment he gave me a withering look as if to say what the hell is he up to now. But I did convince Jackie I was on the level. Later the king was on Jackie's radio show."

Another special part of the Ebbets Field atmosphere was the nicknames. Part of the reason for the nicknames was the intimacy of the ball park. Part of it derived from the passionate emotional attachment of the fans to the players.

And part of it was the inability and/or unwillingness of Brooklynites to bother with the finer points of articulation and diction.

Fred "Dixie" Walker came to the Dodgers in 1939 from Detroit and played at Ebbets Field until 1947 when he was traded to the Pittsburgh Pirates for Billy Cox. ("Name eight Dodgers without Cox" was a popular joke of the time.) Of "Dixie" Walker, Frank Graham observed, "Dodger fans yelled to him when he was in the lineup and yelled for him when he wasn't." A big, smiling blond, he was dubbed "The People's Cherce."

Cal Abrams was "Abie." Abrams played for the Dodgers from 1949 to 1952. "I got cheated three times of a World Series share. In 1950, Sisler hit the home run to give the Phillies the pennant. In 1951, Thomson hit the home run to give the Giants the pennant. In 1952, the Dodgers won the pennant but they traded me early in the season to Cincinnati." Abrams came back to Ebbets Field with the Dodgers in 1951 after hitting .477 on a western trip and inspired the *Daily News* headline: "MANTLE, SMANTLE, WE'VE GOT ABIE." Abie lost his batting eye shortly afterward by hiring himself out as a Coney Island batting range instructor. Batting against a machine, he fouled up his fluid swing and eye-hand coordination.

Kirby Higbe, a portly pitcher, became Kirby "Higelbee." Carl Erskine was "Oisk." Roy Campanella was "Campy." Don Newcombe was "Newk" and Carl Furillo was "Skoonj" in tribute to his Italian love of scungili. Gene Hermanski was "Ski" and there was The Preacher and Robby and Shotgun and Sandy and Pistol Pete. . . .

One of the true favorites of Dodger fans was Harold Henry Reese, born July 23 in Ekron, Kentucky. Boyhood skill with marbles and his 5-foot 10-inch, 160-pound frame earned him the nickname "Pee Wee."

"I always felt that he held the Dodgers together," said Sid Frigand. "He was somewhat less than bigger than life among all those stars and he had that nice quality of steadiness."

A lifetime .269 hitter, the man they also called "The Little

Colonel" averaged almost a walk a game during his sixteen years as a Dodger. Others on the team hit peaks and valleys — Reese was the solid man, just getting the job done day after day, season after season.

He had very few enemies and his gentlemanly manner earned him a lot of friends. Once Dodger manager Charlie Dressen brought in Clyde King to relieve. When King finished his warm-up tosses, he explained to Pee Wee that he was not quite ready. "Go back to your shortstop position and stall around a bit, Pee Wee, I'll try to sneak in a few extra practice pitches."

Reese sauntered back to his position and called "time," complaining that he had gotten something in his eye. He went over to Billy Cox for aid. Reese's protestations were so convincing that King, instead of taking the extra warm-up pitches, headed over to third base to see if he could be of any assistance.

On July 22, 1955, one day after he had collected his two thousandth hit, the handsome Kentuckian was given a birthday party at Ebbets Field. "It was the first and only night up to that time where fans were asked not to kick in," notes Irving Rudd. "All they were asked to bring was a cigar, a cigarette, a lighter, candles — anything they could light up for Pee Wee."

Rudd remembers Dodger executive Buzzie Bavasi asking him how much he thought the Dodgers would draw that night. "I said, 'Maybe twenty thousand or so.' He said, 'Anything over eighteen thousand, I'll give you a buck a head.' I wished I had gotten it in writing. We pulled thirty-three thousand. We sold out at seven P.M.! We closed the gates that night. At the Prospect Avenue station of the BMT and the Franklin Avenue exit of the IRT you had to show your ticket as you left the subway or you were not allowed to get on the street. There were cops lined all the way down Franklin Avenue turning people away from the park."

Bloomingdale's and Wallach's donated clothing. Grossinger's gave Reese a lifetime pass to its hotel and a set of golf clubs. "Chock Full O'Nuts contributed two two-hundred-

fifty-pound cakes, each with thirty-six candles on them,"
said Rudd, "plus tons of coffee. Nathan's gave pounds and
pounds of hot dogs. All the old timers returned — even
Larry MacPhail was there." A congratulatory telegram from
Vice President Nixon and a cablegram from President Eisen-
hower were read to the festive crowd.

The poignancy of the passage of years was evident that
night. In 1940, Dodger fans bragged about the "Gold Dust
Twins" — Pee Wee Reese and Pistol Pete Reiser. A switch-
hitting outfielder, Reiser led the National League in batting
average and slugging percentage in 1941. He was an impas-
sioned defensive player and crashed against the concrete
walls of Ebbets Field going after fly balls. At the age of
twenty-two, he was all through as a superstar. "Reiser could
run, field, and throw," said Leo Durocher. "But that brick
wall would never stop him. He thought he could go right
through it. If he didn't run into the walls, there's no telling
what he could have been."

Fifteen years after Reese and Reiser broke in as Dodger
rookies, Reese was being feted at Ebbets Field and Reiser
was managing at Thomasville, Georgia, in the lowest minor
league.

Joint Masters of Ceremonies, Happy Felton and Dodger
announcer Vin Scully, introduced Reese. "When I came
to Brooklyn in 1940," he said, "I was a scared kid . . . to
tell you the truth, I'm twice as scared right now." The
lights were dimmed and with varying levels of competency
but with the same high ardor, the fans of the Dodger captain sang "Happy Birthday Pee Wee, Happy Birthday to
you. . . ."

Reese recalls the time. "With something that big going
on, there was the thought you'd fall flat on your ass. There
were so many people there. I remember Gene Conley was
the pitcher for the Braves. He was a six-foot, six-inch right-
hander. I didn't hit him too well. The first time up I got a two
base hit, and I knew I would be okay." Reese collected two
doubles and a single, and the Dodgers won the game, 8–4.

The zaniness that permeated Ebbets Field was there that

night. "My daughter," Reese remembers, "was taken out to a large fishbowl on the field. The fishbowl had a lot of keys in it. She would pick a key and then a car would be driven out to her. If the key fit I was to get the car . . . but the key didn't fit. She went out and picked another key and another car was brought out. I don't know how many times this was done. Looking back it was funny.

"She kept picking keys and they kept driving out another car. Finally someone decided to bring out one car and have her pick keys until the one key that fit the car was found."

It was not only the Reeses, Walkers, Higbes, Robinsons, and Sniders that Brooklyn fans related to. Ebbets Field was a place where some players from the opposing teams were respected and responded to almost as well as those on the Dodgers. Brooklyn-born players who had defected to the "enemy" side fell into this category. Tommy Holmes says, "Brooklyn was my home and my second favorite team." A star for the Boston Braves, he was a special favorite of the crowd at Ebbets Field. "They always treated me very well," he recalls, "except one day I did especially well against the Dodgers and four fans followed me home to Bay Ridge, shouting 'traitor, traitor, traitor.'" Sid Gordon, a New York Giant, then a member of the Braves, was another home-grown favorite.

Bill Nicholson, a free-swinging outfielder for the Chicago Cubs and then the Philadelphia Phillies, had excellent rapport with the fans at Ebbets Field. They used to love to see him swing, especially when his bat failed to make contact with the ball — ten thousand, twenty thousand voices would shout, "swish, swish!" Bill Nicholson became "Swish" Nicholson all over the league.

St. Louis Cardinal star Stan Musial was first referred to at Ebbets Field as "Musical," for his name posed pronunciation problems. Though he racked up the Dodgers with his frozen rope hits, the Ebbets Field fans respected his ability. "The Man," a name connoting admiration, became Musial's nickname not only at Ebbets Field where it originated but throughout baseball.

Ebbets Field was Brooklyn's pride — a loud, lively, human symbol of the Dodgers. Hall-of-Famer Monte Irvin remembers the noise: "You could hear those Dodger fans, almost every word. They'd yell at us [the Giants], 'You're gonna get buried today. You'll never get back to New York alive. If you try and win today, we'll be waiting for you outside the ball park.' They tried to intimidate us. They hated the opposition but they sure loved Brooklyn."

Jack Carney remembers the atmosphere: "I was in a little alcove and worked off a wooden platform and a metal chair with the WOR-TV dugout camera. It was a front-row seat to history. The Dodgers weren't gettin' paid too much, but they knew they were accomplishing somethin' in baseball. The fans knew what they had. There was true spirit at Ebbets Field, not phoney adulation. And everybody there had a lot of fun."

Jim Gilliam remembered the fans: "They were the best. They knew the game for they had it for so long. They knew when a guy was in a slump. They knew when a guy was trying. You could come to Ebbets Field and watch a game but you couldn't say anything you wanted to about the Bums because their fans loved that team. I will always have a soft spot in my heart for Ebbets Field."

And Irving Rudd, the kind of man Damon Runyan would have liked, remembers the players: "Great guys, all of them. As Swift would say, 'There wasn't a rotter in the bunch.'"

On April 24, 1940, Pee Wee Reese replaced Leo Durocher as the shortstop of the Dodgers. "I really did not want to be a member of that team," he says. "I didn't know too much about them, but what I did know was that it had not been too successful an organization. I had the image of two or three guys winding up on the same base."

The assessment Reese had was based on fact. In 1890, 1899, 1900, 1916, and 1920, the Brooklyn National League entry had won pennants, but it had not done very much since. During much of the 1930s, the team, under control of a bank that went under the name of the Brooklyn Trust Company, was entrusted to the skills of cast-off and over-the-hill players. "Daffiness Boys" was their nickname. Reese's image of two or three players winding up on the same base actually did take place. In the days of Manager Wilbert Robinson ("Uncle Robby"), three players wound up on third base. "Leave them alone," Robinson bellowed. "That's the first time they've been together all year." The rotund Dodger manager helped contribute to the "loser" image of the team. He did not play personnel whose names he was unable to spell out on the lineup slip and there were those who said he left players out of the lineup for months because he just did not remember they were on the team.

Reese, judged too slight to play for the Boston Red Sox, was picked up by Larry MacPhail, who created a new image and new power for the Dodgers of Brooklyn.

MacPhail had left the Cincinnati Reds in 1936. Numerous verbal altercations with owner Powell Crosley and one well-publicized punch made his exit imperative. A large, red-haired man, MacPhail was recommended to Dodger owners George V. McLaughlin and Jim Mulvey by then Cardinal general manager Branch Rickey and National League Commissioner Ford Frick. Signed as Dodger general manager on January 19, 1938, MacPhail received an unlimited expense account, raises in salary based on home attendance, and full authority on all matters dealing with the team.

MacPhail brought in Red Barber from Cincinnati to broadcast Dodger games and give New York City its first continuous baseball radio coverage. He staged a footrace between the slim Barber and his three-hundred-pound broadcasting colleague, Al Helfer. MacPhail paid Olympic track star Jesse Owens $4,000 for a pregame sprinting demonstration. He gave Babe Ruth a job as a first base coach.

His flair for the unexpected and the unusual led him to spend $35,000 on paint and decoration for the old ball park. MacPhail brought in Gladys Gooding to play on the pipe organ he had installed at Ebbets Field. A standard joke of the time was: "Who played at first base for the Dodgers longer than anybody?" The answer was Gladys Gooding. Her box that housed the organ was located right at first base.

The master promoter literally lit up Ebbets Field. He installed the lights for night baseball. What happened at the first night game ever played in New York City underscored the cliché that "everything happens at Ebbets Field." On June 15, 1938, 38,748 sat through the tension of every pitch and contributed $100,000 in gate revenue as Johnny Vander Meer of Cincinnati pitched his second successive no-hitter.

The MacPhail Dodgers finished seventh in his first season, but MacPhail jacked up attendance from four hundred fifty thousand to seven hundred fifty thousand. He obtained Leo Durocher from St. Louis and made him player-manager in 1939. "MacPhail was half-madman, half-genius," Durocher was to observe later. MacPhail spent $50,000 for Dolph Camili of the Phillies, $90,000 for Billy Herman of the Cubs. Another $100,000 went to Philadelphia for Kirby Higbe, a portly pitcher. He made a trio of Brooklyn portly pitchers with the acquisition of Freddy Fitzsimmons from the Giants and minor-leaguer Hugh Casey for relief work.

The Brooklyn Trust Company, which had placed the Dodgers in care of MacPhail, groaned. More money was spent — some of it went to Detroit for Dixie Walker, some of it went to St. Louis for catcher Mickey Owen.

In 1941, the MacPhail Dodgers won their first National League pennant in two decades. They lost to the Yankees in the World Series, but Brooklyn fans were exultant. The Brooklyn Trust Company and executives George V. Mc-Laughlin and Jim Mulvey were enraged. MacPhail's spending had exceeded the profits the pennant-winning team had earned.

World War II intervened and Larry MacPhail went where there was action. He left the Dodgers, enlisted in the United States Army even though he was over fifty years old, assumed the rank of major, and plotted his next move with another New York City baseball team.

Branch Rickey took MacPhail's place. When the man they called "The Brain" and "The Mahatma" became general manager of the Dodgers on October 29, 1942, he brought with him one of the most brilliant of baseball records. Rickey had invented the farm system in 1919 and in twenty-seven years of guiding the St. Louis Cardinals had recorded six National League pennants and four world championships.

Both Rickey and MacPhail were shrewd and highly organized baseball men. Rickey's reputation as being a tough man with a dollar was a particularly appealing feature for the Brooklyn Trust Company, especially after MacPhail's lavish spending.

Preacher Roe was fond of telling a story about Rickey's frugality. A member of the Pirates in 1947, the skinny Arkansas southpaw won just four games and lost fifteen. Rickey, "who could look inside a guy's muscles and see what was going on," according to Stan Lomax, "who could spot things in a man's play, a man's run, a man's throw that nobody else could spot," saw something in Elwin Charles Roe. The Dodger general manager engineered a trade with Pittsburgh. Roe became a Dodger. "Dixie" Walker was one of the players sent to the Pirates. Over the next half dozen years, the Preacher won ninety games, against just thirty-three losses, but he always seemed to have trouble at contract time.

One winter Roe and Rickey had a few fruitless salary sessions. Rickey suggested that Roe go home and ponder what they had discussed. "I think I've made you a fair offer," said the man New York City newspapers called "El Cheapo." "By the way, I know how much you like hunting, Preacher. I've got two wonderful hunting dogs that I'd like you to have."

Roe went home and went hunting and thought about Rickey's salary offer. The hunting dogs turned out to be the best he ever had. "One day I got to thinkin' that Mr. Rickey couldn't be too bad a fella if he'd give me such good dogs. So I signed the contract and put it in the mail. A few hours later, those two dogs took off across the field and I haven't seen 'em since."

Rickey had learned quite a few things in his twenty-seven years with the St. Louis Cardinals. One of them was that hungry (and underpaid) ballplayers generally performed best. His dealing with Roe and other Dodgers was an application of one of his theories.

The highly motivated executive also drove himself and his staff at a dizzying pace. Those who worked with him at the Dodger offices at 215 Montague Street considered themselves lucky if they were able to get home for dinner even once a week. Rickey, who had a fondness for lighting and chewing Anthony and Cleopatra cigars, labored long hours building teams to last. He had learned that the best way to build a team for the future was to assemble a group of players of approximately the same age and plan for a decade or more of service from them. Campanella and Erskine joined the Dodgers in 1948. Robinson and Snider and Hodges had arrived the year before. Newcombe came in 1949 and Clem Labine and Billy Loes made the roster in 1950. Except for Robinson, who retired in 1956, all of these players — the virtual heart of the team — lasted up to and in some cases past 1957, the final year of the Dodgers of Brooklyn.

During the war years, nearly every major league organization retrenched its scouting and expenditures for the future. Rickey did the opposite. Thousands of letters went out to high school coaches asking for their recommendations for the best players available. Rickey also dispatched scouts to look at new sources of talent — blacks, Hispanics, college athletes. By 1946, the twenty-five minor league farm teams of the Dodgers were stocked with talent. From Montreal to Ponca City, from Abilene to Zanesville, talent was developing.

At Newport News in the Piedmont League, Jack Pitler managed a team that had fifteen players who were seventeen years old or younger. One of the players was Edwin "Duke" Snider.

They called him the "Dook of Flatbush" and the Brooklyn fans made him one of their favorites when he arrived as a twenty-year-old in 1947. A handsome, tempestuous left-handed power hitter, he would star in center field for each of the remaining eleven years of the Brooklyn Dodgers. Mantle and DiMaggio were reserved. Mays was a natural. Snider was like the people, the Dodger fans said. He had his highs and lows, he showed emotion, and he could slug the hell out of the ball. No Dodger ever hit more career home runs than Snider (389), recorded more extra base hits (814), more runs batted in (1,271). No Dodger aside from Zack Wheat ripped more doubles (343), recorded more total bases (3,669). The California-born "Dook" is also third on the all-time Dodger list of runs scored, fourth in hits, sixth in games played.

Players like Snider and an older, more polished performer at Montreal named Jackie Robinson prodded Rickey into declaring, "Two years after the war, we'll be fully developed. After that I envision pennants, pennants, pennants."

In 1946, one year after the war, the two teams of Rickey — the one he had built into the National League's most exciting and powerful team, the Cardinals, winners of pennants in 1942, 1943, 1944, and the team he was building, the Dodgers — met in the first National League play-off. "I owe it all to Rickey," was Cardinal manager Eddie Dyer's comment as the St. Louis team won the play-off.

"I was in charge of a banquet at the Hotel St. George for a World Series party after the play-off," recalls Lee Scott. "There were hundreds of writers invited. After we got beat, instead of them going to the St. George, they all took off for the World Series."

Rickey told Scott, "They won this time, but we'll be the power in the National League for years to come." Three quarters of the Dodger farm teams finished in the first division in 1947. The future was on the field.

Rickey was following in MacPhail's path on the baseball field and in his bank statements. The 1946 Dodgers drew 1,796,824 paying customers to lead the league in attendance. The club made a net profit of almost half a million dollars. Rickey's contract called for a share of the profits, and he padded these profits by selling $239,000 worth of surplus players to other teams.

On October 26, 1950, after a series of behind-closed-doors maneuvers at 215 Montague Street, much enmity, two pennants and one near-miss, the man they called "The Mahatma" was eased out as Dodger general manager and president by the man they called "The O'Malley."

Walter Francis O'Malley had first become involved with the Dodgers in the 1930s when he discovered it was good business practice to take clients to Ebbets Field. In 1932, he became a director of the team and purchased a block of stock. In 1943, O'Malley became the legal representative for the Dodgers. Then together with Rickey, he was part of a syndicate that purchased the team from Larry MacPhail.

O'Malley and Rickey contrasted sharply. "The Mahatma" and his Anthony and Cleopatra cigars versus "The O'Malley" and the twenty or so expensive cigars he smoked each day (one wit cracked that "O'Malley spends more on cigars than most people spend on food") symbolized just part of their differences. In the last year of a five-year contract, Rickey's $50,000 per annum salary plus bonuses based on attendance provided him with a great deal of money. O'Malley thought that perhaps it was too much money.

At a press conference at the Hotel Bossert, the atmosphere was relaxed. All the fighting had apparently been concluded behind closed doors.

"Comest thou here," Rickey began addressing reporters, "to see the reed driven in the wind?" Then he resigned and explained that it was his "duty and privilege to introduce the new president of the Dodgers, a man of youth [O'Malley was forty-seven], courage, enterprise and desire . . . Walter O'Malley."

The new Dodger president and 60-percent stockholder was equally gracious. "I would like to say that for the past seven years that I have been associated with Mr. Rickey, I have developed the warmest possible feelings for him as a man. I do not know of anyone who can approach Mr. Rickey in the realm of executive baseball ability. I am terribly sorry and hurt personally that we will now have to face his resignation."

"The whole thing was a matter of finances and ego," said Stan Lomax. "O'Malley and Rickey were two dynamic people in one organization. You can only have one. And it had to be O'Malley."

The last general manager the Dodgers ever had, Rickey moved on to Pittsburgh, attempting to build a third National League power. With his departure the title of general

manager ceased to exist in the Dodger organization. Buzzie
Bavasi, general manager at Montreal from 1948 to 1950,
joined the Dodgers in 1951, inheriting Rickey's role but not
his title. Bavasi was listed as executive vice president. The
sagacious Bavasi and his Montreal teams had been the
supplier of much Dodger talent. In 1948 all twenty-one
Montreal players were promoted to the major leagues. Duke
Snider, Carl Erskine and Don Newcombe were three of the
players.

MacPhail had changed the Dodger image. Rickey had
enhanced it. O'Malley embellished it, and Bavasi extended it.

The organization prided itself on "home-grown talent."
Most of the players on the Dodgers were products of the
farm system that Rickey had developed. The 1955 world
championship team was assembled over the years for a total
cash outlay of $118,388 in bonuses, drafts, and purchases.
Only Pee Wee Reese and substitutes Rube Walker, Russ
Meyer, and Frank Kellert were obtained in trades. The rest
of the roster came through the farm system.

Johnny Podres, Roger Craig, and Clem Labine were
responsible for all the Dodger wins in the 1955 World Series.
The trio was acquired for a total expenditure of $10,500.
The largest sum paid for any Dodger was $42,500 — for Pee
Wee Reese. Billy Loes cost $21,000.

"Back in 1940, the owner of the Reading Club in the Inter-
State League got fed up and offered to sell out to Larry
MacPhail for five thousand dollars," recalled Fresco Thomp-
son, who headed the Dodger farm system and survived
Rickey's purge of MacPhail's personnel and O'Malley's purge
of Rickey's personnel. "That was dirt cheap for a franchise —
twenty players and two full sets of uniforms — but the thing
that intrigued MacPhail was the new bus which the team
used on road trips. This was a year before Pearl Harbor and
most automobile production was earmarked for the armed
forces.

"MacPhail figured the bus was worth twenty-five hundred
dollars and forty uniforms cost at least ten bucks apiece . . .
that meant Brooklyn was getting twenty players for twenty-

one hundred dollars or one hundred five dollars apiece." One of the players was a solidly built, scatter-armed pitcher named Carl Furillo.

While he never made it as a pitcher, Furillo's arm became a Dodger trademark. Dubbed "The Reading Rifle," because of his uncanny ability to play the caroms off the right field wall, he had what Brooklyn fans were fond of calling "da best arm in da biznez." The eccentricities of right field at Ebbets Field frustrated most outfielders. For Furillo, it was a challenge and a joy. "I loved the game," he says, "I wanted to be there in right field. It was my job like someone goes to an office every day. It was my job to take care of right field and I tried to do my job with all the ability I had." The right field wall was uneven. Part of it included the scoreboard. Atop the scoreboard was a twenty-foot screen that stopped many balls from landing on Bedford Avenue, which was behind the scoreboard and the screen. The lower portion of the wall was padded with foam rubber. "They put it in," Furillo recalls, "all over the outfield after Pete Reiser screwed himself up by banging into a wall." There was a sharp corner in right field created by the connection of the scoreboard to the wall. Balls batted against the wall, the screen, the scoreboard rebounded unpredictably. But predictably, Furillo, who knew at least seventeen different angles at which the ball could rebound off the eccentric contours, made the plays. "Right field was my home; I was comfortable there." The powerfully built Dodger was more than just an outfielder with homing pigeon instincts and a bazooka for an arm. He could also hit. Eight times he batted .295 or better. Six times he drove in more than ninety runs. In 1953 he won the National League batting title.

The black stars on the Dodgers, like those on other teams, were acquired for incredibly low prices. The grand total of $4,700 made Robinson and Campanella Dodgers. Newcombe was acquired for $1,500. Brooklyn records list the cost of obtaining Junior Gilliam and Joe Black at $6,666. And even that price was exaggerated. In 1951, the Dodgers were interested in obtaining pitcher Leroy Farrell of the Baltimore

Elite Giants. The asking price for Farrell, who was in the Army, was $10,000. Thompson balked at the price, which he thought was too high, but he wanted to make the deal and suggested that the Elite Giants toss in a couple of other players. The deal was made. Farrell never become a Brooklyn Dodger. He came out of the service overweight and never regained his previous form. The couple of other players were Joe Black and Junior Gilliam. Cost-conscious Dodger accountants divide the $10,000 purchase price into three. The cost for Gilliam and Black was $6,666.

Sandy Amoros cost the Dodgers $1,300; George Shuba was picked up for $150. Pitcher Clem Labine was acquired for $500. The "Dook of Flatbush" (Edwin Snider) was signed for $800.

Strong, steady Gil Hodges, the heartthrob of so many Brooklyn teenage girls in that era, cost the Dodgers $1,500. Indiana-born Hodges adopted the Borough of Churches as his home just as the Borough of Churches adopted him. A powerful right-handed batter, from 1949 to 1955 Hodges recorded one hundred or more RBIs a season and more than thirty-two home runs each year.

Hodges was unable to "buy" a hit in twenty-one at-bats in the 1952 World Series. The strange slump, in the view of many Dodger fans, was the reason for the Bums' loss to the Yankees. When the 1953 season started, Hodges still was afflicted with a case of batting anemia. In his first seventy-five official plate appearances in 1953, the man they called "Gillie" had managed to hit but thirteen singles and one home run. On May 16, Hodges was benched for the first time in his career. At St. Francis Xavier Church in Brooklyn, the May 17 10:00 A.M. mass was concluded with these words by Father Herbert Redmond: "Go home, keep the Commandments, and say a prayer for Gil Hodges to help him out of his slump." Soon after Hodges snapped out of his slump. There were those in Brooklyn who truly believed in the power of prayer. A few skeptics, though (it was always suspected they were closet Giant fans), claimed the whole Hodges situation was rigged.

"Nothing was ever rigged with Gil Hodges," insists Irving Rudd. "That came spontaneously from the church. Gil got a lot of publicity and a lot of sympathy, and he could have capitalized on it. I had two speaking engagements at seven hundred fifty dollars each for Gil. 'I'm not a public speaker,' Gil told me. 'I don't go in for those things.' I really wanted him to do it. I think I was down for one hundred fifty bucks to introduce him. But he turned the whole thing down. Gil was a very, very honorable man. Every bit as clean and decent as everybody said he was."

Sandy Koufax won only nine games for the Brooklyn Dodgers. And there were those who said that the $14,000 he was given in bonus money in 1954 was a waste of money. Sandy Koufax didn't do too much to distinguish himself as a Brooklyn Dodger, for his days of glory came after 1957 — as a member of the Dodgers of Los Angeles.

A product of Lafayette High School (he wrote in that Bensonhurst school's yearbook that his ambition was to "be successful and make my parents proud of me"), Koufax was signed off the campus of the University of Cincinnati. He had gone to the midwestern college on a basketball scholarship, and was talked into pitching for the baseball team after the basketball season ended. He struck out fifty-eight men in thirty-eight innings. Back in Brooklyn with his freshman year concluded, he joined the sandlot team, Nathan's Famous, a club sponsored by the Coney Island frankfurter institution. *Brooklyn Eagle* school sports writer Jimmy Murphy watched the intense left-hander pitch and was impressed. Scout Al Campanis of the Dodgers was tipped off and was impressed; Koufax became a Dodger. Signed as a 'bonus baby,' the major league rules of the time mandated that he stay with the Dodgers for two years and that he could not be sent to the minors.

"He couldn't hit the side of a barn door at sixty feet," recalls Tom Lasorda, who was sent down to the minors to make room on the Dodger roster for Koufax. "But he had that burning desire to whip control problems."

Lee Scott recalls, "The catcher in the bull pen wore all

the equipment to catch Sandy, he was so wild in those early Brooklyn years; he was so bad, so out of control in one stretch, that there was a lot of talk about trading him."

A 6-foot 2-inch, 210-pound southpaw, born on December 30, 1935, the sensitive Koufax was embarrassed by his control problems but determined to succeed. "He used to work out behind the Vero Beach playing field barracks," said Scott. "He didn't want anyone to see him."

Duke Snider in those early years was one player who didn't even want to bat against Koufax. "It was like playing a game of Russian roulette," said Snider. "And most of the time the choices were he'd strike you out or come close to killing you."

In his second major league start on August 27, 1955, Koufax pitched a fourteen-strikeout two-hitter against the Cincinnati Reds. The outing and a few others in his three years as a Brooklyn Dodger revealed the potential of the shy man who retired from baseball after a dozen seasons at age thirty-one.

"Koufax got so good," says Tom Lasorda, "that there were games when he was pitching to just half the plate, busting off the dropping curve and rising fast ball." Five times he led the league in ERA. Four times he pitched no-hitters. Three times he struck out three hundred or more batters in a season. He posted a 97–27 record his last four years and a fifteen strikeout victory over the Yankees in the World Series. Old Dodger fans groused. Not only did they lose their team to L.A., they also lost one of their native sons and perhaps the greatest Dodger pitcher ever.

Like Sandy Koufax, Don Drysdale's years of pitching greatness were with the Dodgers of Los Angeles. A six-foot six-inch sidearming fastballer, "Big D" was given sage advice from Sal Maglie when he arrived at the Brooklyn Dodger spring training camp as a nineteen-year-old in 1956.

"Every time a batter gets a hit off you," The Barber told him, "it's like he picked your pocket for a dollar." Drysdale remembered. Astride the mound, he was an intimidating figure who resented any batter who attempted to crowd the plate or "pick his pocket."

Six times he struck out two hundred or more batters in a fourteen-year career that saw him win, lose, and start more games; strike out more batters; shut out more teams, than any other pitcher in Dodger history.

When the bargain basement route of the farm system or the "bonus baby" still left a gap on the Dodgers, a major trade filled the gap. After the 1947 season the only missing link in what was to be an all-star infield was at third base. Rickey shipped Dixie Walker, Hal Gregg, and Vic Lombardi to Pittsburgh. Preacher Roe and Billy Cox became Dodgers.

"Billy was a sad man," recalls Irving Rudd, "a dear person. He looked like a plucked chicken when he stripped down . . . it always amazed everyone how he could go into the hole and get all that power into his throws." Cox was listed at 5 feet 10 inches, 150 pounds. There were those who said most of his weight was all heart. A Dodger from 1948 to 1954, he played third base with a magnet in his glove and a catapult in his arm.

Throughout the era, Dodger fans experienced moments of extreme frustration. The "Brooks" inability to beat the Yankees in the World Series caused depression in the heart of Flatbush. Even worse, for some, were catastrophic last-minute pennant losses in 1950 and 1951.

Cal Abrams remembers 1950 and the Phillies. "We could've won it in the eighth inning of the last game. I was on second base. There was a hit to short center field. Catcher Stan Lopata had called for a pitch out and Robin Roberts had taken something off the pitch. The third base coach Milt Stock had one hand waving me in and the other in his mouth — he was biting his nails. Richie Ashburn probably had the worst arm in baseball; it was a short throw and I was out at the plate."

In the ninth inning, Philadelphia's Dick Sisler hit a three-run homer to win the game and the pennant for the Phillies. "I won't ever forget that moment in my life," said Sisler. "We had to win it or else we would've gone into a play-off. I don't think we woulda won the play-off. Our pitching was shot. I just happened to be up at the right time. Newcombe tried to

get me to go for a bad ball with two strikes on me. The next
pitch was a high fast ball — away. I put the wood to it. I
didn't know it was gone until I rounded first base."

Duke Snider recalls, "I was chasing the ball that Sisler hit
and just ran out of baseball field. I was groping at the wall
wishing I could move it back. I kid Dick all the time when I
see him. I tell him it was a windblown home run. He says it
may have been windblown but that the only way I could have
caught the ball was to have bought a ticket and been in the
stands to catch the ball. It is more or less our hello whenever
we meet — our moment in history."

Throughout the era, the only unsettled position in the
Brooklyn lineup was left field. Pete Reiser played there in
1947, Marv Rackley in 1948; Gene Hermanski was the
"other outfielder" along with Snider and Furillo in 1949 and
1950. At the trading deadline in 1951, Buzzie Bavasi moved
to fill the left field spot. Eddie Miksis, Joe Hatten, and
Hermanski were shipped to the Cubs. The Dodgers received
catcher Rube Walker, infielder Wayne Terwilliger, pitcher
Johnny Schmitz, and outfielder Andy Pafko. Dubbed "Handy
Andy," the native of Boyceville, Wisconsin, helped the
Dodgers in 1951, and his nineteen homers and eighty-five
RBIs contributed some fire-power to the 1952 pennant-
winning Brooks. By 1953, Pafko was gone. "Shotgun" George
Shuba alternated with Jackie Robinson in left field. During the next three years Sandy Amoros played there most
of the time. Gino Cimoli was the 1957 regular left fielder
for the Dodgers. The position may have been unsettled, but
the players who came and went had such varying images
and personalities that Brooklyn fans had a ready-made topic
of conversation.

Some took a fancy to the part-time (1949–1952) streakhit-
ting Cal Abrams, Brooklyn born and Jewish. Others sighed
about what could have been had handsome "Pistol Pete"
Reiser stayed healthy. Pafko, the veteran, was solid and
reliable. Shuba had the alternative nickname and a fine arm,
but he lacked power as a batter. Amoros could not speak
English but he could run, run, run. His slight size and World

Series catch were endearing qualities. Gino Cimoli, a native of San Francisco, was hailed by some Brooklyn rooters as the second coming of Joe DiMaggio when he joined the Dodgers in 1956. Brooklyn fans saw him at his batting best. In 1957 he batted .293 but then he, like the team, went west.

The team was blueprinted for Ebbets Field. A collection of powerful right-handed sluggers plus southpaw Duke Snider, it seemed at times cramped in the small confines of the little ball park. Nineteen times in the years from 1947 to 1957, a Dodger recorded one hundred RBIs. The awesome scoring power of the Dodgers erupted time after time.

On August 31, 1950, sparking a 19–3 romp over Boston, Hodges slashed four home runs and a single, driving in nine of the nineteen runs.

On August 31, 1952, the Dodgers scored fifteen runs against the Cincinnati Reds in the first inning:

Billy Cox grounded out. Reese walked. Snider cracked a home run to right field. Jackie Robinson doubled. Andy Pafko walked. George Shuba singled. Robinson scored. Pafko wound up on second base. Bud Byerly replaced Cincinnati pitcher Ewell Blackwell. The Reds got the second out when Pafko was thrown out attempting to steal. Shuba took second base. And then the Dodgers really began to hit. Hodges walked. Shuba was singled home by Rube Walker. Dodger pitcher Chris Van Cuyk singled Hodges home. Cox drove in Walker with a single. Reese's single brought Van Cuyk in and made the score 7–0. Herman Wehmeier became the third pitcher for the Reds. He walked Snider, loading the bases. Robinson was hit by a pitch. Cox scored. Pafko singled home Reese and Snider. The score was 10–0. Frank Smith replaced Wehmeier. Smith walked Shuba, loading the bases once again. Hodges walked. Robinson was forced in with another run. Walker singled, bringing home Pafko and Shuba. Van Cuyk singled. Hodges scored the fourteenth run. The bases were loaded again when Cox was hit by a pitch. The fifteenth run came in when Reese walked, scoring Walker. Snider made the final out — lunging at a pitch and striking out. The Dodgers collected fifteen runs, ten hits, seven walks, and had three batters hit by pitches. The batting fireworks resulted in the following records: most runs in an inning, most runs scored with two outs (twelve), most batters to reach base safely in a row (nineteen), most batters to come up and hit in one inning (twenty-one).

On June 25, 1953, they pounded five home runs in a 12–3 shelling of the Reds. On July 10, 1953, a Dodger homered for the twenty-fourth straight game. Especially pleasing for Brooklyn fans was the fact that the Dodger homer was blasted by Campanella off Sal Maglie.

On August 20, 1953, Carl Erskine shut out the Giants, 10–0, for the thirteenth consecutive Brooklyn win.

On August 30, 1953, they slaughtered the St. Louis Cardinals, 20–4. In the seventh inning a dozen Dodgers scored.

On June 16, 1956, Snider stroked four home runs as the Dodgers won their sixth straight.

The pulverizing power, their crushing of the opposition, their come-from-behind victories just seemed to whet their fans' appetites. The Dodgers had pride in what they were doing. Their fans were uncontrolled in their bragging, rooting passion for the team. Adolescents filled brown paper bags with water and threw them out of apartment house windows, joyous after a Dodger romp. Adults on the job or the subway the day after a win cheered and congratulated each other. "That was some game we won . . . How did you like what Robbie did? . . . Ain't Newk somethin'? . . . That Cox is magic . . . What a glove . . . What an arm . . ." If one were a Dodger fan, and his or her co-worker were a Giant fan, so much the better. "Didja hear what the Bums did yesterday? . . . What'd you think of their pitching last night? . . . Why don't you give up on the Jints and root for a real ball club? . . . Wait'll we get at the Yanks in the series this year . . . We're ready this time, we are."

Power, speed, daring, drive, verve, clutch performance, bigger-than-life personalities, all shaped the Dodgers. As each new component fitted itself onto the team throughout that era, as each new season brought victories and pennants, the pride of the players increased. "We had such talent," said Pee Wee Reese, who once had balked at joining the Dodgers because of their "loser" image, "that it was tough for anyone to break into the starting lineup, to make the team."

"They were all-stars, the Dodgers, at every position," said Jerry Coleman, who envied them from inside his Yankee uniform. "With a couple of more starting pitchers — they would have been completely unbeatable."

Year after year, Reese would bring the lineup card out to home plate, would raise the right arm and lead the Dodgers out onto the playing field. "Being captain of the Dodgers was much more than those things," said Reese. "It meant representing an organization committed to winning and trying to keep it going. We could have won every year if the breaks went right."

All the moments of the Brooklyn Dodgers now belong to history. "We knew we were good," muses Carl Furillo. "Our fans knew we were good. You couldn't do anything wrong for the Brooklyn fans. They were hungry for baseball, and we were hungry to win for them."

Peter Golenbock

From *Bums: An Oral History of the Brooklyn Dodgers*

The Exodus

It began as a trickle right after the war. Before, the Jews who had come to Brooklyn had been content to settle in Brooklyn and remain. Many of them had been Eastern Europeans with simple peasant values and peasant tastes. Brooklyn had been good to them, and they saw no reason to move, except to go from apartment to apartment from year to year to save rent money. These Jews were devoted to their children, revered education, and their supreme goal in life was that their children would have better, happier, wealthier lives than they had. They wanted their children to grow up American, with American values and American goals.

When these children grew up, Brooklyn — with its concrete barrenness in winter and heat brutal enough to fry eggs in summer — was no longer acceptable. The sights of these new Americans were set on something better: the verdant, quiet suburbs of Long Island, Staten Island, and New Jersey.

MARTY GLICKMAN: "I moved out of Brooklyn because even before I got married, I aspired to have a house in the country like I had heard or read about. The house in the suburbs was the dream of every young man, a house with a two-car garage.

"After all, riding the subway to go to work every day was a chore. You were packed in like sardines, it was hot as blazes in the summer, and on a wet day it was particularly miserable. And back home, in the summer months, you sat out on the stoops. We didn't have air conditioning. So you thought about the country, you thought about the grass and the leaves and the trees. I remember as a little boy, my father with his Essex automobile would drive out into the country and we'd have picnics and fresh air and sunshine. It was a big deal. It was the desire to get away from the crowds, to get away from the cement, and to get out in the open and raise a family in the country."

In the early 1950s, Marty Glickman moved to Scarsdale.

That was the first wave of Brooklyn emigrants. The second wave grew to tidal force by the end of the 1950s. As the young Jews were getting mortgages and moving into the suburbs during the post–World War II economic boom, their parents were taking smaller apartments. Moving into their old places were lower-middle-class black families. These were working people, as their Jewish predecessors had been, blacks who found they could afford to live in the solid, comfortable homes and apartments left behind by the Jewish land rush. And when these black families began to move in, a curious thing happened. Many of the Jews who remained behind, often the same people who had championed the cause of Jackie Robinson, Paul Robeson, and the civil rights movement, began to move out.

JACK NEWFIELD: "It's one of the historic contradictions. Liberals, who were all for Martin Luther King when he was in Selma or Montgomery, had an entirely different outlook when it was their kids being bussed in Chicago or New York.

"My father died when I was four years old. I was an only child. We lived in a house with a bunch of relatives. We didn't have the wealth to give us mobility, and we were stuck. And I saw friends, whose fathers were doing well, who had two parents, and one by one they began to move out of the neighborhood, some to Sheepshead Bay and Flatbush, more to Queens, some to Long Island, some to Jersey. They had upward mobility. But we were stuck there. And with the blacks moving in came a great fear. There was blockbusting. There was panic selling. There were real estate speculators, the parasites and vultures who circle any changing or transitional neighborhood."

Herb Ross was born in the Brownsville section of Brooklyn in 1938. He lived off Eastern Parkway on Howard Avenue. On the block were two small apartment houses and eight two-family private homes. Doctors owned or lived in more than half the dwellings. In 1950, when Herb was twelve, black families had begun to move in, and the Rosses decided it was time to leave.

HERB ROSS: "The first black family I remember in Brownsville was the superintendent of the building, who lived in an apartment house next door to ours. I would play with his kid, and my parents didn't like that. My parents were very much against that, and I remember saying, 'What's the big deal?' But I was told these were not the kinds of kids they wanted me to play with. I remember one time I was going to Hebrew school on the other side of Eastern Parkway, and I had met a black kid, and he was shining shoes to make some money, and I asked my dad if I could get a shoe box, and oh, I never heard the end of it! I was a kid. I said, 'Why not?' 'This is not for you. It's not for you.' They didn't want me to be friends with the kid either. I used to say, 'What's the problem? His skin is different from ours, that's all.' They didn't want me to be friends with him. 'Not for you. Not your kind.'

"My father was an optometrist. His office was within walking distance from the house, about two blocks. The whole area was starting to change. Meanwhile my grandmother owned a two-family house on Montgomery Street, and her tenant moved out. I don't know whether she forced the tenant out because my mother and dad intended on moving, but during the summer of '50, the place was vacant, and we did move in.

"My parents didn't tell me until the very end, because they knew I did not want to move. And when the move came, I was told I had to go, although I was very, very unhappy.

"I don't know what it was about the blacks that was so frightening. Maybe they felt that . . . you used to be able to walk Pitkin Avenue on a Sunday afternoon. Some of the best clothing stores. Abe Stark of the 'Hit sign, win suit' had a store there. I guess little by little, people were afraid of getting mugged.

"The new neighborhood was a predominantly white, Jewish neighborhood. The Crown Heights section. Quite a few two-family houses. You also had apartment houses, with a lot of doctors living on a street called President Street, three blocks from where I was. A stable area, for want of better words. Meaning no blacks. I was five blocks from Ebbets Field."

The Rosses had fled deeper into the heart of Brooklyn, but slowly, block by block, by the mid-'50s the changes caught up with them.

HERB ROSS: "The same thing as what was happening in my old neighborhood. I remember when the houses started to sell. Everyone tried to hold on in the beginning. Then one or two would go, and a couple of people would panic, and everybody was worried about real estate values, and the Jews left. We all left."

The Rosses fled again, to the Flatbush section, near Brooklyn College.

By 1957 Brooklyn was no longer the same as it had been just ten years earlier.

BILL REDDY: "There were a lot more blacks and Puerto Rican people in Brooklyn, and certain sections of neighborhoods that had been German, Irish, Jewish, were now Hispanic and Jewish. And it changed the complexion of whole neighborhoods.

"Blacks brought change. They brought a whole new lan-

guage. Not a foreign language but a slanguage. Different
words for different things. All of a sudden, you had 'motherfucker,' which we had never heard before, that was brought
into the language and which is in common use today. And
new ways of doing things: the dancing styles changed, the
music changed. People began to appreciate black musicians.

"The Puerto Ricans also brought change. When before you
were hanging out at the corner candy store, now everyone
was at the local bodega and going for, as they called it, a
bag of beer. And also the graffiti artists started to appear,
which to me was really a bad day when they took over. They
ruined some of the nicest buildings. Even Kennedy's statue
in Prospect Park, for God sake.

"The language changed, the customs changed. Groups
began to take over that hadn't been there before. There was
an influx of black people from Jamaica and Aruba and Trinidad,
and they all talked in that singsong dialect and were all
different in their regular daily living than we were. Food
stores began to display different types of vegetables and
fruits. Brooklyn was changing slowly from the solid Italian,
German, Irish, Jewish that it had been to a tropical flavor.
Who the hell ever heard of frying green bananas?

"Many of the Jews moved away and gave in to the pressure
of the blockbusters and the people trying to get the neighborhood away from them. In '57 everyone who could was running to Long Island. Long Island, Staten Island, and New
Jersey, but mostly Long Island, which built up very, very
quickly.

"A lot of things changed. Coney Island wasn't Coney Island
anymore. The Steeplechase closed. There was no more Luna
Park. The midway section, the rides section, got so small it
really became insignificant. And the scratching for a quarter
to enjoy yourself. You give a kid a quarter in '58, what could
he do with it?

"The kids began to look for big money. A kid had to have
twelve or fifteen dollars in 1957 to buy a pair of slacks.
Where's he going to get it if he didn't steal? And everybody
had to be as well-dressed as his peers. The first time I can

remember young kids sixteen and seventeen years old becoming clothes conscious, becoming experts on how to dress and what to wear. And a simple night out, such as my wife and I enjoyed before we were married, a movie and go to Horn and Hardart, this wouldn't do anymore. Now you had to have folding money in your pocket.

"Tastes were changing. And sex. In my day sex before marriage was unheard of. Girls were virgins. If a girl wasn't a virgin and anyone found out about it, immediately she got a reputation of being an easy lay. And until right after World War II, girls carried their virginity like a banner. I know many a guy never had any sexual doings at all until he was twenty-one or twenty-two years old. This was not unusual. In '57 things had changed, because young Johnny was allowed to do what he pleased when he brought his friends up, and of course, the girls had to go along with them, and they had girls' clubs too that formed up in alliance with the boys. As a matter of fact, they used to carry the weapons when the gang fights would start.

"So little by little, not only Brooklyn, but the world, changed."

Rumblings

One insidious change was the shifting of baseball franchises. As white customers began to flee the inner cities, team owners searched for new markets they wouldn't have to share with another team. Since 1903 the two leagues had been stable. In the American League, there were the Boston Red Sox, Chicago White Sox, Cleveland Indians, Detroit Tigers, New York Yankees, Philadelphia Athletics, St. Louis Browns, and Washington Senators. In the National the lineup showed the Boston Braves, Brooklyn Dodgers, Cincinnati Redlegs, Chicago Cubs, New York Giants, Pittsburgh Pirates, Philadelphia Phillies, and St. Louis Cardinals.

In 1953 there was movement. The Boston Braves bolted to Milwaukee. The Braves had always played second fiddle to the Red Sox and owner Lou Perini wanted his own turf. Wisconsin beckoned. The next year the St. Louis Browns moved to Baltimore, and in 1955 the Philadelphia A's moved to Kansas City. Multiteam towns were growing scarce.

The change that gave Walter O'Malley pause was the Braves. Milwaukee's new County Stadium sat 43,000, and it had parking for 10,000 cars. Said O'Malley, "How long can we continue to compete on an equal basis with a team that can outdraw us two to one and outpark us almost fifteen to one, which pays its park at a token figure, and pays no city or real estate tax? If they take in twice as many dollars, they'll eventually be able to buy better talent. Then they'll be the winners, not us."

By 1956, though the Dodgers were still the second-best draw in the league, O'Malley was stepping up the pressure to get the city of New York to subsidize him. He demanded that city hall build a new ballpark, or he would move the team out of Brooklyn. Where, he wasn't saying, but to demonstrate that he wasn't kidding, he sold Ebbets Field to a housing developer, taking only a three-year lease.

O'Malley had talked about a new park even before he took over as president in 1950. Over in the Bronx, the Yankees were able to pack in 75,000 fans, and at the Polo Grounds, there were seats for 56,000. Ebbets Field sat 33,000 tops, and since its peak in 1947, attendance had been dropping.

In a conversation with reporter Dan Daniel, O'Malley blasted the Dodger fans for not flocking to the ballpark as in days of old. He specifically refused to blame the advent of television or the cold days of spring, and he boasted of the $350,000 he was getting paid by WOR for the seventy-seven home games. He was making a specific point: Decrepit Ebbets Field was at fault. The Dodgers needed a new, 55,000-seat stadium to reverse the trend.

Give me a bigger and newer stadium, he was saying. Give me. Not build me. Give me.

Between 1950 and 1957, attendance remained constant. It was never higher than 1,280,000 (1951) and never lower than 1,020,000 (1954), but O'Malley insisted the Dodgers were not making enough money. The attendance issue was the reddest of herrings. No team in all of baseball was more profitable.

IRVING RUDD: "The Brooklyn ballclub was the richest club in baseball. It was far richer than the Yankees. It made more money than the Yankees even with only 750 parking spaces! O'Malley was making more money than anybody! He talked about a bandbox ballpark, but the bandbox didn't do too badly by him. O'Malley kept saying he needed 1,200,000 to break even, but that was just O'Malley. If he had been drawing 1,800,000, he would have said he needed 1,800,000 to break even."

There was another aspect to the Ebbets Field crowd besides its small size that disturbed O'Malley. He didn't like its racial makeup. It wasn't the same going to see a game at Ebbets Field anymore. The white Brooklyn fan was not driving in from his new home in the suburbs.

JOHN BELSON: "By the time Hilda Chester had returned around 1955, Ebbets Field was no longer the same. It was very ersatz. The bloom was well off the rose by the mid-'50s. Willard Mullin may have been still drawing his cartoons, but the fandom was a whole different thing. In the '40s the crowds had been all white, but by the mid-'50s, after Jackie Robinson had been there a while, you go to a Sunday doubleheader, and the dominant smell in the ballpark was bagged fried chicken. Between games out came the brown paper bags with the fried chicken in it. You had a different crowd. It was no longer a unified crowd. It was more subdued, because you weren't as apt to jump up and scream across the aisle at someone because neither the white fans nor the black fans were comfortable with each other. The black fans certainly were not dancing to the Dodger Symphony. The spontaneity in the stands was lost. And the white fans were not responding as ardently to the Symphony or to Hilda either. Hilda Chester did not lead claques of blacks in snake dances down the aisles in Ebbets Field, as she once led the whites. It was a feeling-each-other-out situation. To recapture some of that excitement, you would have had to have two pipers, and there certainly were no black pipers. So the game moved back onto the field."

HERB ROSS: "Interestingly it was the Dodgers bringing in Jackie Robinson and other blacks to the ballpark, who changed the whole element of the crowd. And when they added Newcombe and Campanella and Black and Gilliam before many teams had any blacks at all, they in turn were filling up the park with blacks.

"When the blacks started coming to the game, a lot of whites stopped coming. And the black allegiance was only to Robinson and the black ballplayers. They didn't care about the Symphony or Hilda Chester or even the white players. They didn't have the history we had. The allegiance of the blacks was not to institutions. The allegiance was to Robinson.

"I guess O'Malley was like everyone else in Brooklyn: As long as you're not my neighbor, as long as they went home at night to wherever they lived, it was okay. But once they started to live in the neighborhood, then the neighborhood started to 'change'; it was time to move out."

BILL REDDY: "After we did the big job in '55 the talk of the Dodgers moving was rampant all over the borough. Nobody wanted to believe it, but deep in your heart you knew it was true. The white families were moving out of Brooklyn, and they were the backbone to Ebbets Field. We didn't have enough blacks to replace them. We had a lot of Jamaicans and West Indians coming in who didn't appreciate baseball as we did. They were cricket players. And until the Hispanics could find jobs and get enough money to go out to Ebbets Field, they didn't have hard-core baseball fans. They would hang out at the Parade Grounds, where they could see free baseball. Attendance did fall.

"But I think O'Malley planned it that way. He didn't push for attendance like MacPhail and Rickey, where Red Barber would be talking on the radio, 'Hey, we're close to a million.' And everybody in Brooklyn was running out to go again to make sure they made it.

"O'Malley wasn't pushing for the big attendance. He didn't want it. He wanted to justify his move to California. And I think he had that in the works long, long before the first inkling was let out to the public."

Beginning during the 1955 season, O'Malley began dropping hints that if he didn't get his new stadium, he was going to leave Brooklyn. Despite a record 22–2 beginning in '55, the fans were remaining at their television sets, and O'Malley caused ripples of panic throughout the borough by announcing at midseason that the Dodgers would play seven of their seventy-seven home games in 1956 at Roosevelt Stadium in Jersey City. He wanted a new stadium, and soon.

JOEL OPPENHEIMER: "The press was constantly full of theories as to exactly what the Dodgers were going to do, and when they announced some of the games would be played in Jersey City, I put my best face on it. 'Okay, that's okay if they play a few games in Jersey City. Why not play a couple of games there?' I assumed that would keep O'Malley happy. It never occurred to me that the Dodgers would go away. Brooklyn leave? That was crazy."

HAROLD ROSENTHAL: "Had you been alert to it, you could have picked up all the signs that the Dodgers were going to leave. The first sign was when O'Malley started to talk to sympathetic newspaper people about the problems he was having. The people who were buying season tickets, the furniture companies in Jamaica, Queens, and the manufacturers of Long Island couldn't give their tickets away to customers because it was too difficult to get there. 'Why do we want to go to Ebbets Field?' the customers would ask. 'We gotta drive.' So it was 'No thanks, we don't want the tickets.'

"And then the talk began that the area around Ebbets Field was a 'bad neighborhood,' and that after a night game you better get the hell out of there fast.

"There was an idea of building a new stadium over the Long Island Railroad tracks in downtown Brooklyn, but again there was the problem of bad parking. Then O'Malley got into an argument with Robert Moses. Moses wanted it built in Flushing, where Shea Stadium is now. O'Malley didn't want it there. Flushing wasn't in Brooklyn."

BILL REDDY: "We had the feeling that they were going to go, but I would go to bed at night hoping that the mayor would mysteriously erect a gorgeous new ballpark somewhere in Brooklyn, and they would stay. But when I read that Hollywood was giving half of L.A. to O'Malley without charge, plus all the concessions and parking, you knew it was a foregone conclusion."

In Search of Judas O'Malley

Much as it would have pained O'Malley to hear, he in many ways strongly resembled his proclaimed nemesis, Branch Rickey. Both were jowly and smoked long cigars. Both were men of presence. Both were tightfisted when it came to spending money. Both were expert at bestowing praise on employees when a raise would have been better. And both were brilliant orators who knew how to use words to get their way. In short, con artists. Blarney masters. With deep, resonant, hypnotic voices.

One of O'Malley's most valuable employees was a slight man of boundless energy by the name of Irving Rudd. Rudd had the title of Dodger promotions director, and he used his considerable skill to help O'Malley make a great deal of money, especially during the exhibition seasons and at Jersey City, where Rudd ran that operation the two years the Dodgers played seven games a season there. Rudd worked closely with O'Malley and got to watch the man up close.

IRVING RUDD: "I came to the ballclub in February 1951. O'Malley had just taken over from Rickey. He hired me to run the Brooklyn Amateur Baseball Foundation, which provided sandlot equipment for the kids in Brooklyn, Queens, and Staten Island. The Yankees took care of the Bronx, Manhattan, and Westchester. I knew Rickey would be a tight man, that he could talk you out of your pants, but this guy was just as good a bullshitter as Rickey when he wanted to be. He could turn on that charm.

"One time two American Legionnaires came to the Dodger offices. They were wearing their legion uniforms, and they wanted to see O'Malley about getting a bigger cut of the Brooklyn Amateur Baseball Foundation. They wanted more balls and bats, and when they finished O'Malley began telling them how tough it was to run a ballclub, explaining what he was up against. Honest to God, when they left, these guys were going to write him a check! He was marvelous. He was a very subtle, clever man, one of the most brilliant men I've ever met as far as hard business. I've often said that if he was up against Khrushchev in those crucial years, the Soviet Union would be a Dodger farm club today.

"Like Rickey he was a great storyteller. I remember a funny story O'Malley once told. There was a guy named Matt Burns, an arrogant Irish straw boss for O'Malley. Ever read *The Last Hurrah*? This guy was Knocko Monahan. Very much a Catholic, almost a professional Catholic. A lot of priests and nuns and rosaries and crosses. And evidently he had suffered trench foot during World War II, 'cause he always reminded you that if it wasn't for him, the fucking Nazis would be sitting at your desk.

"So one day at a meeting, there was a diplomatic task that had to be done, and someone said, 'Why don't we send Matt Burns to handle that?'

"O'Malley said, 'I'll tell you a story why we're not going to use Matt.' He said, 'Two guys were playing poker, and one of them, Jim Kelly, toppled over and dropped dead of a heart attack. A good pot of money on the table belonged to him, and now it was decided that one Frank O'Doud was to deliver the money and the news to this poor woman. And O'Doud came to the house and rang the bell, and when she answered he said, "Is this the widow Kelly's home?"'

"Everybody was laughing and O'Malley said, 'That's why we're not going to send Matt Burns.'

"I have to say that O'Malley was one of the brightest,

shrewdest of men. I'm in the office one day, and Lou Perini of Boston is on the phone. I hear O'Malley purr, 'Looouuuuu, that is why you are so brave and brilliant. That is why you are a pioneer.' This was 1953. Perini is moving his team to Milwaukee and O'Malley's showing his support. He's lining up a vote. Thinking ahead. Always thinking.

"I started at $5,200 a year and was being paid by the Brooklyn Amateur Baseball Foundation. It wasn't costing the Brooklyn Dodgers a nickel. I got paid from the proceeds of the annual Mayor's Trophy Game, which was my job to run. When the game was over, I had fulfilled my duties, but O'Malley soft-soaped me into pitching in and helping Frank Graham in the Dodgers public relations department. And so I became ex-officio promotions director. Even though the Dodgers didn't pay me for that aspect of the job.

"O'Malley, I found out, could snow you beautifully. He could make you feel twelve feet high, but he never backed it. The next year Graham was publicity director, Harold Parrott was business manager, Lee Scott was road secretary, and I became promotions director. I promoted the Dodger exhibition games, and I helped jump attendance from 4,200 a game to 7,600, with the help of some pretty good stats, of course.

"I was in Vero Beach having breakfast, and across from me was Bobby Bragan, the Ft. Worth Cats manager. I'm slurping down my oatmeal, and suddenly two vicelike hands are holding me right down into the plate, and Bobby is laughing like hell.

"I hear this gravelly voice, 'I will never forget this glorious, wonderful job that you did. It was outstanding. You are destined to become, dum da dum da dum . . .' It was O'Malley. God himself was speaking. Visions of sugar plums are dancing in my head. I'm saying to myself, 'Gertrude,' thinking of my dear bride, 'should we get the Cadillac Seville or do we move into the home with the Bigelow on the floor?' Recovering, I said, 'Thank you, Mr. O'Malley.' Not bad hearing from this guy, right? I figured I was in for a hefty raise, right?

"And after that I didn't get a chance to speak with him for two months. I could never get the guy alone. Talk about Benny Leonard in his prime or Sugar Ray Robinson. Forget it. He was beautiful. The guy was an expert. I never laid a glove on him. Forget the raise.

"That year Frank Graham and I were preparing for the next Mayor's Trophy Game, and to kick off the publicity, between games of a doubleheader there was a little home plate ceremony. The mayor was Robert Wagner, a nice man, and Frank Graham and Irving Rudd are called to home plate and presented with Dodger service rings by the mayor of the city of New York. In front of a packed house. That took care of one year's raise. After all, it isn't every time that you get called up in front of a crowd and are thanked by the mayor of New York. This was the sort of reward you got working for the Dodgers.

"By 1956 I was asking myself, 'Where's the money?' I had one conversation with him. He said, 'Irving, you don't seem to understand. The players get it all. There's hardly anything left for anybody else.' And if you looked at the player payroll, you knew it wasn't going to the players. The players didn't get it all. O'Malley got it all.

"I had started at $5,200 in 1951, and five years later I was making $5,800. Not exactly a living wage for a man with a family. During the winter of 1956, I sent O'Malley a memo asking for a $1,500 raise, and I would have settled for $750. Had I gotten the $750, I would have been with the Dodgers today. Maybe.

"In January 1957, on a snowy winter's night, I held a free rally for the Dodgers at the armory in Jersey City. I got Phil Foster, a comic, a very, very nice guy, to come for free. I had the Dodger Symphony there. Governor Meyner of New Jersey came down. And it was a smash. A smash. Twenty thousand people on a snow-filled night, and the next morning I'm lying in bed like a lox, and I hear the phone ring.

"'Yes, Mr. O'Malley.'

"'Irving, I have to compliment you on one of the most marvelous shows, productions, presentations.'

"I said, 'Thank you, Mr. O'Malley. Oh, by the way. Mr. O'Malley, did you get my memo?'

"'Memo, what memo is that?'

"'The one where I asked for a raise, Mr. O'Malley.'

"He said, 'I don't like to be pushed, Irving.'

"And I realized the point there was that I would have to start looking for a new job. I quit the Dodgers in 1957.

"Happy Felton got off a great line. We were riding down Atlantic Avenue one afternoon in a cab, and it was a poor, rundown area, near the Williamsburg Bridge on the way to Ebbets Field, and there was a neon cross in the window that said, 'Jesus saves.' And Happy said, 'They never heard of O'Malley.' Meaning that O'Malley even outsaves Jesus.

"When we won the World Series in '55, we were all going to get World Series rings. But I got wind that to get it, you had to give them back your Dodger service ring. What were they doing with them? At the office I saw they were buffing and polishing turned-in rings. They were to go to the scout in Pascagoula, Mississippi. 'Dear Peter, for your faithful service, please accept this Dodger ring. Buh buh buh boom.' My Dodger ring was what he was going to get! Frank Graham's Dodger ring was what they were going to get!

"O'Malley could be brutal. Frankie Graham tells the story of one Dodger employee who either quits or gets fired, and O'Malley says to him, 'Oh, by the way, on the way out take this out and mail it, will you?'

"When there was trouble in the ticket department in 1951, O'Malley asked Harold Parrott, the road secretary, to take over the job. Harold loved being road secretary. It was perks, fun, and a World Series share, which was significant money. The ticket manager didn't get any of that. O'Malley said, 'Harold, you'll never be sorry. I'll make it up to you in many ways.' A year or two goes by, and finally Harold braces him one day. 'Mr. O'Malley, gee whiz, you told me when I took this job that . . .' O'Malley cut him short. 'Harold, look out the window at Montague Street. You see that crowd going to work down there?' Harold says, 'Yes, Mr. O'Malley.' 'How old are you, Harold?' 'I'm forty-six, Mr. O'Malley.' O'Malley says, 'A lot of forty-six-year-old guys down there wouldn't mind having your job.' End of question. End of raise.

"And then there was Harry Hickey, an old-time director and a longtime pal of O'Malley's who was ailing. Hickey wanted very badly to go to Japan with the Dodgers after the '56 season, and O'Malley is giving him the stonewall and ducking him, and finally Harold Parrott, who ran the Japanese tour, went to O'Malley to ask him about Hickey. O'Malley said, 'Did you ever stop to consider what it would cost to ship a body back from Tokyo?' O'Malley wasn't joking. He had it all figured out. Four thousand eight hundred dollars for the casket. 'What if the guy dies over there? Hell, let him stay home.'

"Sentiment meant nothing. Everything was business. It was a winter's night, and I was alone with him in his office, and I don't know why, but he let his hair down with me. I was confiding in him that I was having trouble with a man who had once done me a big favor. But lately he had become a real pain, and though I didn't want to seem ungrateful, I really didn't want to have anything to do with him anymore.

"'Irving,' O'Malley says, 'sometimes you have to cut the past.' He continued, 'I had a similar thing happen to me. There's a friend of mine, a very wealthy banker, and after a while, Irving, you do outgrow certain people.' Why he suddenly confided in me I don't know, because it was very unusual for him. He was trying to teach me a lesson in life.

"He continued, 'George McLaughlin is a great guy and a great friend of mine, and in many ways he was an advisor and patron. Yes, McLaughlin did bring me into the picture. Yes, McLaughlin was responsible,' and he as much as said that without him he wouldn't have become president of the Dodgers.

"'So in the future, Irving, you'll find that it's great to have loyal friendships from the past, but sometimes you have to cut the cord to seek new horizons, and you can't be tied down by the past.'

"And he did feel badly about it, and yet, fuck it, on to Los Angeles, if you know what I mean."

The Betrayal

IRVING RUDD: "Whatever anyone wants to say, New York Mayor Robert Wagner and Parks Commissioner Robert Moses were right. If they had given O'Malley what he wanted, they should have gone to jail. If you remember, the talk was about a superdome in downtown Brooklyn, where the Long Island Railroad is, with stores, apartments. And who do you think would have owned all of this? O'Malley. He was offered the use of the Flushing Meadow site, à la Shea, and his answer was, 'You build a ballpark and give it to me.' Moses said, 'Fuck you.'"

Was O'Malley boxed in? Only under the guidelines he had set up — give me a new stadium or I'm leaving. Could he have built himself a modern edifice? In owning a property as valuable as the Brooklyn Dodgers and in being incestuous with the Brooklyn Trust Company, O'Malley could have condemned land and built a new park just about anyplace he would have chosen — if he had so desired. But Brooklyn was no longer middle class. Poor people drove out rich people, were nothing but trouble, and didn't spend money. O'Malley wanted to leave.

During the World Series of 1956, one of O'Malley's guests was Kenneth Hahn, a member of the Los Angeles Board of Supervisors. Hahn was serving his first term when the County of Los Angeles sent him to the World Series with all expenses paid to bring back a major league baseball team. Any team.

The World Series was being hosted by the Yankees and by Walter O'Malley and the Dodgers. Perhaps if another National League team had been playing, O'Malley would not have made his L.A. connection. Perhaps it would have been the L.A. Senators or perhaps the L.A. White Sox. Or maybe O'Malley would have merely picked up and moved his team to another panting city, such as Dallas, Houston, Atlanta, Minneapolis, or Oakland. But at the 1956 World Series, Hahn and O'Malley met, and the fate of the Brooklyn Dodgers was sealed.

The following is testimony that Hahn delivered at a hearing during a recent lawsuit between the Los Angeles Raider football team and the NFL. The most interesting excerpt is Hahn's admission that it was O'Malley who contacted Hahn, not the other way around. Hahn makes it clear that O'Malley was actively seeking to move out of Brooklyn. Sure O'Malley had a scale model of a new domed Brooklyn stadium sitting on his desk, but if the city of New York wasn't going to give it to him, he was going to find a city that would.

KENNETH HAHN: "To make Los Angeles great we had to have a major team. There were a lot of people that said we were not ready for it, we are not ready for a major team, but I went, and I first attempted to see Calvin Griffith, the owner of the [Washington] Senators, because they were at the bottom of the league.

"When I was attending the game at Ebbets Field, Walter O'Malley sent me a note and said he is interested in coming to Los Angeles. He won the world championship [in 1955]. I never dreamt we could get a world champion.

"Then he came here, and his team, on his way to Japan. He had some play in Tokyo. I met him at the Hilton Hotel — it was called the Statler Hilton then — on Columbus Day. I remember the date because it was a legal holiday, and I didn't have to go to work, but I came down to meet him.

"He said, 'I will come down here, but I will deny it to the press' because he had another season to play at Ebbets Field. He said the Dodger fans are rough fans. Literally would kill him, he said.

"I took Walter O'Malley in a helicopter by the Sheriff's Department and circled Los Angeles to find the best spot, and that was an abandoned housing project, and he said this is where he wanted to go.

"If you want to know the truth, and Mr. O'Malley is dead and nobody knows about it but me, but I had more faith than Walter O'Malley that the Dodgers would be a success. When he came to the Coliseum he wanted a three-year lease with an option for the next three years, because he said to me one day, 'If the people don't support major league baseball, I want to transfer my team to Phoenix or Tucson or some other place.'

"I said, 'Walter, they are going to really love you, you will be glad you moved from New York.'

"Later on my prophecy turned out to be absolutely correct. The Dodgers are the most profitable and the most liked team in the nation."

When O'Malley told Hahn he would entertain an offer from the city of Los Angeles, the town fathers did not equivocate. They made O'Malley an offer so incredible there was no way in the world he was going to turn it down. They gave him his stadium and much, much more.

IRVING RUDD: "Norris Poulson, the mayor of Los Angeles, showed up in Vero Beach one day, and he presented O'Malley with a laundry list — here's what I'll give you if you come to Los Angeles, including, 'You can sleep with my wife once a week.'

"Forget the emotion. O'Malley is a businessman. They say, 'This is what I'm giving you. The condominium is yours for life.' You say, 'But I got this contract.' They say, 'Two dancing girls and Jacqueline Bisset on weekends.' You say, 'Fuck the contract!' How many guys would say no? So what did Poulson give him? He condemned the land for him. They gave him the oil rights in case they discovered oil. They built him a stadium. Who needs Fort Knox to print money? That's why he went. Bye Bye Brooklyn."

But before he could accept Los Angeles's offer and go, O'Malley still had to pull two swindles.

First, he had to buy the rights to the Los Angeles area, then owned by the Chicago Cubs, who had a minor league team playing there. And once he did that, he had to talk another team owner into moving out to the Coast with him. With two teams on the Coast, it would be much more economical in terms of scheduling. To fly to the Coast to play but one team would be too expensive.

As it turned out, O'Malley had no trouble either buying the rights to Los Angeles or getting another team to go with him.

HAROLD PARROTT: "Walter O'Malley had been lucky enough to run into Phil Wrigley just when the chewing gum king was very angry at the whole city: Los Angeles. His team trained on Catalina Island, and the grounds were not in shape for spring training one year. Wrigley vowed he would never bring his team back. 'A bush town,' Wrigley called it, and swore he'd never have anything to do with the place again, as soon as he could get rid of his minor league franchise, the Pacific Coast League Angels.

"O'Malley was drooling but trying hard to hide his interest.

"All O'Malley did was con Wrigley into taking, in a straight swap — lock, stock, and ballpark and the L.A. franchise for Fort Worth in the Texas League. Branch Rickey had picked up the Fort Worth package ten years before for a mere $75,000.

"What the Irishman got, in addition to the franchise, was a square city block in Los Angeles."

In searching for a partner to flee west with him, O'Malley didn't have to look any farther than across the Harlem River.

HORACE STONEHAM: "I had intended to move the Giants out of New York even before I knew Mr. O'Malley was intending to move. I was unhappy playing in the Polo Grounds. The ballpark was old, and it was darn near impossible to finance one in that area. I had intended to go to Minneapolis. We had a ballclub there, so I had the rights to the area, and it's a big city in itself. Also, Minneapolis was well within transportation range of the league. Aviation at that time had been accepted by everyone.

"And then Walter called me up and asked me if I was going

to move. I said, 'I think so. I think the league will give me permission.' He said, 'Why don't we both move and go to the Far West together?' So we thought about it, and that's what we finally decided to do. When he asked me about moving west, I told him that I liked the San Francisco area, that I had worked there when I was a young fellow. I didn't even know he was intending to move. But when he saw I was, he saw we could make a rivalry on the Pacific Coast."

And so the Brooklyn Dodgers became the Los Angeles Dodgers, and the New York Giants became the San Francisco Giants. In Los Angeles O'Malley had gotten a deal better than that offered Cortez by the Aztec Indians. And like Cortez, once O'Malley moved west, he discovered other imaginative ways to cheat the natives out of their gold.

CHARLEY EINSTEIN: "This story could be apocryphal, only because it's hard to imagine anyone could be so dumb, but the story has been told that when O'Malley went out there, the L.A. politicians said, 'What do you want in the way of compensation from concessions?' He said, 'Well, we play a 154-game schedule, and back in Brooklyn we got all the concessions. I want to show you my heart's in the right place. I only want concessions for half the games.' They said, 'That's more than we expected. That's great.' So the Dodgers kept the concession money for the seventy-seven games they played in the Coliseum. The other seventy-seven were on the road. It never crossed their minds what O'Malley was telling them!

"He was devious, but he built the most beautiful ballpark in baseball. The story is that O'Malley asked the Giants to send him the plans for Candlestick Park, because Candlestick Park was the first of the postwar baseball stadiums. O'Malley said to his architect, 'Study these and learn what not to do.'

"And O'Malley built the most magnificent ballpark with a great sense of what to do with all the cars driving into the park. What he did was put all the cars in one place, and he provided for fans to enter the park on different levels. It was a short walk from the car, no matter where in the park you were seated. Easy in. Easy out. A superb job of design.

"O'Malley only made one mistake. If he had wanted L.A. all to himself, he should have also bought the Hollywood franchise, which the California Angels ultimately bought. But O'Malley could not possibly have been that farsighted. He wasn't thinking of competition. He didn't know for sure that he was going to succeed."

In fact, even after all O'Malley's planning and scheming, at the eleventh hour, he came within a whisker of losing it all.

IRVING RUDD: "There were a few people in L.A. who didn't have orange juice for brains. The Dodgers were in the Coliseum, and they were about to take over Chavez Ravine, and people started to scream and holler, 'Hey, wait a minute. We're being gulled. We're being had.' And so there was a referendum to vote whether or not to give O'Malley all this land. The people were catching on to what he was doing, and a campaign was growing to stop him. It was on the books for a vote, yes or no Dodgers. And if it's no, O'Malley's dead.

"On the Sunday before the vote, he ran a telethon, and ironically he ran it on Gene Autry's station — and did Walter give Autry a hosing when later he tried to get into baseball! — but he got all the great and glamorous stars saying: 'Vote yes for the Dodgers.' And not one of those stars came from Los Angeles. They all came from Beverly Hills, Hollywood, Santa Monica, Santa Barbara. And as it was, it just did pass — barely. But had O'Malley not done that, gotten a last blast on the Sunday before the election, it might not have happened. And O'Malley would have been up the creek without a paddle. A ballclub with no place to play."

In the end, of course, what O'Malley wanted, O'Malley got, and the Los Angeles franchise became the most profitable team of them all.

The Last Supper

The 1957 season was funereal. The team was old. Ebbets Field was old. And depressed by the knowledge that the Dodgers were leaving, the fans were feeling old.

Newk's career was ending in the bottle. Ersk's right arm pained him too much to pitch more than once a week, and Campy's catching skills began to erode after a careless doctor had cut a nerve in his right hand while performing an operation. The Duke needed knee surgery. Pee Wee was pushing forty and had stopped hitting, and Furillo's knees were beginning to pain him. Only the stout pitching of the six-foot-six right-hander Don Drysdale, winner of seventeen games, saved Brooklyn from the second division.

Ebbets Field, which O'Malley let go to seed, was dingy. Everything seemed so somber inside, as though a loved one were about to die. The crowds were thin, the cheering hollow, and when the dreary season came to a close, the demoralized Dodgers trailed the ebullient Milwaukee Braves by eleven games.

By the season finale, the arrangements for the Dodger funeral had been completed. The official word had been issued: The Dodgers were leaving Brooklyn for the Coast. The final game at Ebbets Field this year was really the final game.

It was scheduled for September 24, 1957, before 6,702 heartsick, nostalgic fans. At the start of the game, the Brooklyn Dodger theme song was played on the loudspeaker:

> Oh, follow the Dodgers
> Follow the Dodgers around
> The infield, the outfield,
> The catcher and that fellow on the mound
>
> Oh, the fans will come a running
> When the Dodgers go a gunning
> For the pennant that we're fighting for today.
>
> The Dodgers keep swinging
> And the fans will keep singing
> Follow the Dodgers, hooray.

> There's a ball club in Brooklyn
> The team they call "Dem Bums,"
> But keep your eyes right on them
> and watch for hits and runs . . .

Pee Wee Reese took his customary station at the top of the dugout, and when the record had ended, with the same motion he had employed since becoming captain, for the final time in Brooklyn he signaled the starters to run onto the field. During the playing of the national anthem there were brave tears.

The game went two hours and three minutes, as the Dodgers beat the Pirates 3–0. When it was over, announcer Tex Rickard made the pro forma announcement, as he had done since the '30s, "Please do not go on the playing field at the end of the game. Use any exit that leads to the street." He was completely ignored.

After the final out, as the throng of souvenir hunters ravaged the infield, grabbing clumps of dirt or blades of grass, Gladys Gooding began to play "May the Good Lord Bless You and Keep You." Before she was done, the recording of the Dodger theme song once again sounded, and when it was over, she played "Auld Lang Syne." It was like when the orchestra played the hymn "Nearer My God to Thee" as the *Titanic* was sinking. Only this time it wasn't an ocean liner but a way of life going down.

The Mourners

BILL FARRELL, JR.: "My childhood revolved around the Dodgers. Going to Ebbets Field was a family affair. It was part of growing up. I always said I was baptized a Catholic and a Dodger fan.

"We lived in Bensonhurst. My father, my uncle, and my cousins would pile into our Hudson, stop by Prospect Park in the morning, play some ball, and then walk to Ebbets Field for a two o'clock game.

"I can remember the vendor outside Ebbets Field selling steamed peanuts. I can still hear the whistle. And Ebbets Field smelled like no other ballpark I've ever been in. The thing I remember best was the smell. An unmistakable aroma of Ebbets Field. I visited several ballparks around the country, trying to see if maybe it was an old ballpark smell, but it's not. It was unique. An oily smell? Inky? Paint? Didn't smell like paint. It was pleasant. It used to smell like the *Coloroto* magazine in the *Daily News*. I heard they painted the grass. Maybe that's what it was. But no ballpark smelled like Ebbets Field.

"The game I remember best is the last Dodger game I ever went to. It was against the Philadelphia Phillies on the last home stand, 1957. The Pirates came in next to finish out the season. My uncle, my cousin Richie, and I went, and my cousin teased me all the way out there, saying the Dodgers were leaving, that they were going to Mexico. Richie was four years older than I was, and though he was teasing me, he was really teasing himself too. No one really believed the rumors. Kids don't believe it. The Dodgers were ours. How could they leave us? Richie said, 'If they win this game, they'll stay in Brooklyn, but if they lose, they're going to Mexico.' And needless to say, the Dodgers lost that game, and I cried all the way home.

"My cousin wanted to stay after the game, to wait for the Dodger players. My uncle said, 'No, they're leaving town. Why should we wait for them?'

"And that was the last time I was at Ebbets Field. But that woke me up to the reality of life, waking up to discover there is no Santa Claus in December, no Dodgers come the spring. It all happened at once. Instant maturity. It was such a disappointment, because I so looked forward to the baseball season. They were such happy hours, happy times.

"After the Dodgers left, I used to drive past there occasionally. I hated to look. For years my father had said, 'You'll be able to ride your bicycle to Ebbets Field one day and go see the games by yourself.' But by the time I got my bicycle and was old enough to ride, they were long gone."

CHARLEY STEINER: "The first time I listened to a Dodger game I was about six years old. It was listening to the play-by-play that first got me interested in radio. My childhood dream, I can tell you without equivocation, was to be the play-by-play announcer for the Brooklyn Dodgers. What I would have given to join Vin Scully, Al Helfer, and Jerry Doggett in the booth! Those were the last three broadcasters for the Dodgers, of course, before they moved out. Do you realize what it's like to have your childhood dream smashed at the age of eight? Years of therapy. My childhood dream was absolutely smashed, dashed, and folded, spindled, and mutilated. It was a devastating loss for me.

"I was eight years old in 1957. Eight years old. I loved Furillo. I loved Snider. And Gil Hodges, of course. And Campy. And Gilliam and the rest of them. I can run down the '57 Dodgers even now. I have yet to vote in a presidential election, and it was perhaps the only time I exerted a political preference. I registered my vote. I called Walter O'Malley. I picked up the telephone and got through to the secretary and said, 'You can't do this.'

"I was crying and babbling like an idiot. I said to her, 'How can you do this to me? This is my baseball team.' She said, 'Mr. O'Malley is out right now,' and she listened to me for about ten minutes. I said, 'You just can't do this to me.' And she said, 'We've had similar calls. This is something beyond my control. Let me take your phone number, and Mr. O'Malley will get back to you.'

"I'm still waiting for the call."

BOBBY MCCARTHY: "I never believed the Dodgers would ever leave Brooklyn. I don't think a lot of people did. I didn't think O'Malley would take them to L.A.

"The day it was announced, if you were in Behan's Bar and Grill, you'd have thought it was a wake. This was like seceding from the Union. It was hard to believe that one of your own kind, O'Malley, could do this. Tommy Corrigan, Timmy Murray, Willie Crane were there. Willie was a sick Dodger fan. He was almost a degenerate Dodger fan, and Willie wanted to go find Walter O'Malley and kill him. He wanted to kidnap him. He wanted to go get him and shoot him. He figured if he shot him, the Dodgers wouldn't move.

"We said, 'There will be another Brooklyn team. Whoever

thought they'd go out to L.A. and keep the name Dodgers? Whoever thought California should have a baseball team? That's where all the movie actors are. Baseball didn't belong in California. It belonged in Philadelphia or Boston or New York or Brooklyn. We figured we would always have the Brooklyn Dodgers, even after they said they were moving. But it didn't happen.

"And when they tore down Ebbets Field, that was like tearing away part of your heart. It was hard to believe. What do you do without Ebbets Field? I live in Staten Island now. Maybe if Ebbets Field was still there, I never would have left Brooklyn. I don't know. But after they tore it down, everything was different."

RON GREEN: "After all those years of heartbreak, to have it end like that — I never forgave the National League. I have never gone to a National League game since. To take the Dodgers and Giants out of New York, to leave New York without a National League team, was the crime of the century. How could they do that? Take both teams out of New York? And when they gave them to Mets, I thought they were selling them a bill of goods. I've never been back. Never even went to Shea Stadium."

JOEL OPPENHEIMER: "Most Dodger fans didn't take out their hatred on the players. After all it wasn't their fault the Dodgers had deserted them, so that when Koufax and Drysdale were having great seasons or when Willie Davis was running wild, they were still our boys, and you had to root for them. But then, slowly, the Brooklyn players dropped away, retired, and instead of continuing to follow the team, the Brooklyn fans either stopped following baseball or rooted for the Mets.

"By 1963, when the Yankees were playing the Dodgers in the World Series, most Brooklyn fans had no one to root for. I went only because I had tickets, and because my kid, who desperately wanted to see the game, unfortunately is a Yankee fan."

BILL REDDY: "O'Malley did nobody, including himself, any favors when he left. He may have gained a lot of money. But if it's true that there's a hereafter, every Dodger fan knows exactly where he is right now. I'll tell you something else. As old as I am now, and as much sense as I have, I was not unhappy when he died, and I don't think there were too many Dodger fans who were. He did a terrible thing to the people of Brooklyn, because he took away part of the cohesiveness that used to hold the borough together. Even if there was racial tension, at least they had something in common, something they could talk about. And whether they were Dodger fans or Giant fans, it really didn't matter. And O'Malley took away the Polo Grounds as surely as he took away Ebbets Field, and for no good reason. Stoneham was a sucker. It was the biggest mistake of his life. He never made a nickel.

"And I know, deep in my heart, that if it hadn't been for O'Malley, the team would have never moved. They would have found a way to build a stadium. Greed was the whole thing. O'Malley feathered his nest. They gave him half of Los Angeles for nothing, and the bum, he got the money, but what did he do to us?"

JOE FLAHERTY: "I think Hemingway said it, that if you live long enough, everything you love will be sullied, and it was O'Malley who was the first one to really put the shit into the game, the one who showed everyone that loyalty means nothing. O'Malley is the one who brought home the message that baseball wasn't a game, it was a business. Besides what he did — take the team away — he put the sour in. Sure, a team had to meet expenses, but he removed any illusion that he was in it for the pastime.

"Baseball always was an extension of innocence, the innocence of childhood, the innocence of America, and here was O'Malley saying, 'We're not what we think we are.' It was a terrible psychic blow. And Ebbets Field was replaced by a housing project. How could a father tell his son where Duke Snider used to hit one? Point out apartment 5Q?

"The Dodgers at the time were the best franchise. The Dodgers accounted for something like forty percent of the revenue of the National League, and you're talking about a ballpark that only had 32,000 seats. I mean, you could make a case for Stoneham leaving. His attendance was bad, and he was having a hard time making it at the Polo Grounds. But the Dodgers? O'Malley deserted Brooklyn just so he could be making more.

"When the Dodgers left, it was not only a loss of a team, it was the disruption of a social pattern. There was no more sense of waiting up for the *Daily News.* The life went out of the street corners. What were you going to stand there and talk about? Conversations in bars stopped. Except for everyone agreeing that O'Malley was a son of a bitch.

"Maybe Brooklyn was a minor borough compared to Manhattan, but Brooklyn had the Dodgers. In *Guadalcanal Diary,* William Bendix talked about the Dodgers while he was fighting the Japs. With the Dodgers you could swagger. It was like being in an elite unit, like being part of the Lafayette Escadrille, and when the Dodgers left, the feeling died.

"It wasn't just a franchise shift. It was a total destruction of a culture."

JACK NEWFIELD: "Once Pete Hamill and I were having dinner, and we began to joke about collaborating on an article called 'The Ten Worst Human Beings Who Ever Lived.' And I said to Pete, 'Let's try an experiment. You write on your napkin the names of the three worst human beings who ever lived, and I will write the three worst, and we'll compare.

"Each of us wrote down the same three names and in the same order: Hitler, Stalin, Walter O'Malley."

BILL REDDY: "O'Malley was the man who took the heart out of us. He took the Dodgers away. O'Malley had it all schemed out from the beginning. He was after the almighty buck, and how could he lose? Look what they gave him out there. We could have given him the world, and he wouldn't have stayed here. Had they built a stadium and put it in the middle of Flatbush Avenue and Fulton Street, he wouldn't have stayed. And they could have given him parking for 50,000 cars, and he wouldn't have stayed. My wife always chided me about it, but one of the best pieces of news I ever received was when I found out he was dead. That's the way I and thousands of others felt. I've never heard an old Dodger fan bless O'Malley. Not a single one of us have ever said a prayer for him."

The Ashes

GUS ENGLEMAN: "In 1957, which was the Dodgers' last season playing in Ebbets Field, I was at the army language school in San Francisco, and after I finished I went to Berlin and didn't return to the United States until March 1960. When I came back, I spent three days at Fort Hamilton, got discharged, and went back to live with my mother in Benson-hurst. You know the first thing I wanted to do? Go to Ebbets Field.

"In Germany, whenever the guys from the New York area got together, we would say, 'What's the first thing you want to do when you finally get home?' One guy would say, 'I can't wait to see the lights of Broadway.' 'I want to see Times Square again.' 'I want to go to Coney Island.' I said, 'I want to go to see for myself whether it was true, otherwise I'll never believe the Dodgers are no longer in Ebbets Field.'

"And so, when I came home, I spent the night with my mother to get reacquainted. I took the subway the way I used to, West End to Coney Island, taking the Brighton, getting off at Prospect Park. I wanted to walk, because I wanted to relive those memories as a kid when you got off at Prospect Park Botanical Gardens Station and you walked up the block and saw that big sign, Ebbets Field, 'cause when you were a kid it was a thrilling sight. It was marvelous to see that wonderful stadium with the crowds streaming towards it.

"And when I got upstairs that last time, I saw the big sign that said simply, 'Ebbets Field Apartments.' Only then did I finally accept that it did happen. And it had a tremendous effect on me. I choked up, and maybe it was then that I realized my boyhood was gone, that my great love affair was over, and most important, that you can't go home again. Thomas Wolfe had said it, and I guess he was right. It would never be the same. The Dodgers were no longer in Brooklyn."

BILL REDDY: "After the Dodgers left, I went to Ebbets Field only once. One of my kids wanted to see this thrill circus, a demolition derby, where drivers were riding automobiles backwards into each other. They had a ramp erected behind the pitcher's mound almost all the way to home plate, and one of the drivers was going to drive a car up the ramp and hurtle into open space.

"We walked into Ebbets Field, and I looked around, and I can't describe the feeling I had when I saw left field, center field, right field, just as they always had been, except for the ramp. The drivers came out in these Dodger automobiles, and they drove all the way across the outfield, where guys like Snider, Musial, Reiser, Willie Mays, Furillo, DiMaggio, Dixie Walker, oh God, had played. And as I sat there watching, as the outfield grass was being torn up by the cars, tears were streaming down my face, and I didn't even realize it. My son turned to me and said, 'Daddy, you're crying.' I was."

After the Dodgers left and the *Brooklyn Eagle* folded, newspaperman Tommy Holmes said, "Brooklyn is the only city of two million people that doesn't have an airport, a newspaper, and a ballclub."

And that's still true today.

The heart had gone out of Brooklyn. The soul had fled. It's a place to live now, that's all. It's a place to hang one's hat. It's just across the river, a place where people sleep. You don't hear Brooklyn stories or Brooklyn jokes anymore. Brooklyn lives only in loving memory, alongside Jackie, Gil, Campy, Big Newk, Clem, Oisk, Skoonj, Pee Wee, the Duke, and every other man who ever wore the Ivory Snow–white uniform with the Dodger-blue numbers and the lettering on the front that spelled out Brooklyn.

Neil J. Sullivan

Was the Move Justified?

The Dodgers Move West

On April 10, 1962, more than a decade after Walter O'Malley initiated his pursuit of a new ballpark, Dodger Stadium opened in Los Angeles. In that setting, 3-million attendance seasons have become routine; in season ticket sales alone, the Dodgers draw two million per year, exceeding their total yearly sales in Ebbets Field. During its tenure in Los Angeles, the team has won eight National League pennants, compared to nine during their almost seven decades in Brooklyn; and four world championship flags have flown in Los Angeles compared to the lone banner in Ebbets Field. By all measures, the Dodgers have been a spectacular success in Los Angeles, but a question continues to plague the franchise: was the move justified?

For Roger Kahn, Peter Golenbock, and others who followed the team in Brooklyn during its final years, the move represents the unforgivable abandonment of a community that had supported the team for sixty-seven years. Kahn maintains that a stronger commissioner would have blocked the move, and Bowie Kuhn, the former baseball commissioner, doubts he would have allowed the transfer if it had been attempted during his tenure. For Dodgers' supporters in Los Angeles, however, the move helped make baseball a truly national sport, and Los Angeles can justly claim that it has surpassed any city in the consistent backing it has given its team over thirty years.

The dispute about the propriety of the Dodgers' move persists not only because of the intensely conflicting emotions of the fans in Brooklyn and Los Angeles, but also because several distinct aspects of franchise relocation have become muddled. By treating these issues separately, each from its own perspective, we can gain a clearer understanding not only of the Dodgers' case but also of subsequent moves.

The first perspective is that of *business,* in which the Dodgers must be seen as an enterprise in an economic market. Almost every franchise has abandoned stadiums constructed at the time of Ebbets Field was built, and the few that haven't — the Red Sox, Tigers, and Cubs — are facing strong incentives to move to more modern facilities. The Dodgers could not have remained in Ebbets Field indefinitely, even if Walter O'Malley had wanted to. The only alternative for the Dodgers, if they wanted to stay in New York, was to accept the kind of arrangements the Mets have secured: tenancy in a public stadium in Queens. Robert Moses's objections to a privately financed stadium and the futility of the Brooklyn Sports Center Authority precluded the use of the Atlantic-Flatbush site; no other location in Brooklyn was feasible. Thus at some point in the 1960s, the Brooklyn Dodgers would have ceased to exist, even though they might have remained in New York. The most optimistic speculation about their future in New York pales beside the success they have enjoyed in Los Angeles. From the perspective of a firm seeking to maximize its return on an investment, the Dodgers made the correct decision when they moved to Los Angeles.

The players' two-day strike in 1985 made it possible to examine the finances of major league teams because the owners released statements to back their claim that under the combined effects of arbitration and free agency most clubs were losing sums so substantial that they threatened the entire financial structure of the game. In response, the Major League Baseball Players Association hired economist Roger Noll of Stanford University to evaluate the statements of the twenty-six major league teams. Noll found that the statements tended to distort the data because almost all the teams are part of large corporations, such as broadcasting or shipping firms, which can obscure the actual dollars involved in baseball operations.

The Dodgers, the only major league team whose ownership is involved in no business except baseball, declared that their net revenues were over $6 million. But Noll believes that "these profits, richly deserved as they are for the best managed team in sports, vastly understate the value of the Dodgers to the owners." Noll concludes that the Dodgers "are probably the most successful sports franchise that has ever been fielded." And in a trenchant summary that evaluates each of the major league teams, the Dodgers are described succinctly as "baseball's answer to the Denver mint."

The Dodgers would have remained substantially the same organization even if they had remained in New York, but undoubtedly a critical component of their prosperity is their stadium, which is not only the best in the game but also the only modern structure owned free and clear by the team. When Walter O'Malley died on August 9, 1979, ownership of the team was bequeathed to his son, Peter, and his daughter, Terry. Peter O'Malley has continued his father's style of management, which treats the Dodgers as a business that stands or falls on the skill and attention the executives and employees bring to their jobs. The O'Malleys have treated the baseball team as an enterprise that must be promoted through sensible investment and constrained through fiscal prudence. An article in *Forbes* in 1982 considered the ingredients, other than fielding quality teams, which contributed to the Dodgers' commercial success. "The Dodgers are the best-run franchise in all of baseball because of a lot of other things they do right. Compare Dodger Stadium, for example, to another entertainment success of the West Coast — Disneyland. Dodger Stadium is squeaky clean, beautifully landscaped and rests in a striking setting. As at Disneyland, Dodger Stadium attendants — even in the parking lot — are civil. The bathrooms are clean and safe."

"Do people go to Dodger Stadium to behold flowers?" asked Roger Kahn, commenting on their presence at Dodger Stadium. "Not primarily, but people have stayed away from other ball parks because of ambient filth." The organization has been likened to IBM, but a more apt analogy is a small family business that thrives because of its attention to detail and its awareness that shifts in the market, if not addressed, can become fatal. Since 1939, under MacPhail, Rickey and the O'Malleys, the Dodger organization has kept pace with social and economic changes that affect baseball, and this has been a vital element in the club's financial success.

Two changes that confront the Dodgers presently are the escalation of players' salaries and the related matter of dilettantish ownership committed to a win-at-any-cost strategy. Peter O'Malley is troubled by both developments, but he focuses on "the system" of free agency, which he believes is responsible, in combination with arbitration, for perilously increasing labor costs. The desire of owners to limit free agency and arbitration has led to confrontations with the players' union that resulted in the extended strike of 1981 and the two-day strike of 1985. O'Malley expresses confidence that his family-owned franchise can prevail against corporate competitors, but he is clearly alarmed by what he considers threats to the long-term financial health of the game resulting from wildly escalated salaries. Since he must generate the revenues to pay these salaries, O'Malley is understandably concerned, but he underrates another more fundamental point. Salaries are ultimately determined by owners in response to market demands. If their decisions are irresponsible the fault hardly lies with the players, their union, or even with an amorphous "system." Inescapably, one must conclude that the owners' problems are self-inflicted. The Dodgers have been comparatively restrained in their personnel decisions, though they are inevitably affected by arbitrators' decisions that reflect, in part, the salary choices of other teams.

The Dodgers' model of family ownership has become

increasingly rare in baseball. In recent years, the Stone-
hams, Griffiths, Carpenters, Galbreaths, and Wrigleys have
sold their teams to new owners without long-standing com-
mitments to baseball. Certainly these sales have been influenced by the difficulty family owners have keeping pace with
the increased costs of operating a baseball franchise. The
argument can be made that this change in ownership has
benefited the game by infusing more money into it, and that
as long as those who run ball clubs exercise sound judgment
the new style of ownership serves a useful purpose. Bowie
Kuhn points to the Chicago Cubs as a franchise that has
prospered under corporate ownership, and Peter O'Malley
notes that corporate ownership may reduce the extremely
idiosyncratic behavior sometimes exhibited by individual
owners.

The key point is that increased revenues have not made
baseball financially more secure. The greater sums are
proper targets for the players and their agents, and as the
sources of even higher salaries. Teams in smaller markets
like Pittsburgh and Seattle eventually will face even greater
strains because of the higher level at which equilibrium is
pursued. Financial security will be reached only when costs
and revenues achieve a reasonable balance. As long as some
teams are run as hobbies or diversions, prudent business
decisions will be virtually impossible, and every club will
eventually feel the pressure. The Dodgers have been run as
a serious business since the time of Larry MacPhail. Their
subsequent prosperity is no coincidence.

The second perspective from which to evaluate the move to
Los Angeles is the *romantic* attachment of the fans. From
this perspective the move can never be justified to the
Brooklyn Dodgers' fans. Revenues, tax advantages, mythical
mineral rights, demographic shifts, and other market forces
are utterly irrelevant. What counts, as Roger Kahn has
demonstrated so well, are the bonds developed over generations. The memories shared among friends and families
who exchange stories of "Uncle Robbie," Zack Wheat, Casey

Stengel, Babe Herman, Leo Durocher, Gil Hodges, Carl Erskine, and Jackie Robinson don't compute on a balance sheet. These memories not only remain a vital part of Brooklyn itself; they extend to communities where former Brooklyn residents themselves have moved, and have become part of baseball folklore.

Describing the frustrations of the Dodgers trying to wrest a world championship from the Yankees in the 1950s, Roger Kahn has written, "You may glory in a team triumphant, but you fall in love with a team in defeat. Losing after great striving is the story of man, who was born to sorrow, whose sweetest songs tell of saddest thoughts and who, if he is a hero, does nothing in life as becomingly as leaving it. . . . A whole country was stirred by the high deeds and thwarted longings of The Duke, Preacher, Pee Wee, Skoonj and the rest. The team was awesomely good and yet defeated. Their skills lifted everyman's spirit and their defeat joined them with everyman's existence, a national team, with a country in thrall, irresistible and unable to beat the Yankees."

The reaction in Brooklyn to the Dodgers' move is understandably bitter. Among the more moderate reflections recorded by Peter Golenbock from the abandoned fans of Brooklyn is this one: "The day it was announced, if you were in Behan's Bar and Grill, you'd have thought it was a wake. This was like seceding from the Union." "After all those years of heartbreak," said another fan, "to have it end like that — I never forgave the National League. I have never gone to a National League game since." And another: "When the Dodgers left, it was not only a loss of a team, it was the disruption of a social pattern. There was no more sense of waiting up for the *Daily News*. The life went out of the street corners. What were you going to stand there and talk about?"

The most vitriolic remarks focus, of course, on Walter O'Malley, whose unbridled greed, it is asserted, was the principal cause of the Dodgers' move. Golenbock summarizes O'Malley's petitions to Robert Moses and other city officials in New York as, "Give me a bigger and newer stadium. . . . Give me. Not build me. Give me."

In this interpretation, passion has overwhelmed the facts. O'Malley was always emphatic about constructing the new stadium with private funds, as indicated by his remarks at the time he announced the Jersey City move:

> To clear up any misconceptions, I would like to make it plain that we are not going into this thing with our hats in our hands.
>
> We are — and have been for some time — ready, willing and able to purchase the land and pay the costs of building a new stadium for the Dodgers. We have $6,000,000 available for this purpose if an adequate site can be made available.
>
> In fact, I feel rather proud to be associated with this evidence that the days of individual enterprise have not ended. This effort by the Brooklyn club is the first by any baseball club in more than fifteen years to build a new plant. . . .
>
> I believe the Dodgers should own their own ball park.

O'Malley's motives for wanting a private stadium were clear in his first public remarks about a new stadium for Brooklyn. In December 1953, announcing his plans for a replacement for Ebbets Field, he said, "The new park will not be a municipal stadium. That would mean a political landlord, which isn't desirable." For O'Malley, saving money in the construction of a new stadium mattered less than gaining control over the new park. The record in these pages establishes persistent efforts by O'Malley to build his own stadium in New York. The Dodger owner may be a convenient target for the emotions of Brooklyn fans, but the real causes of the Dodgers' move were far more complex than those put forward by the O'Malley Devil Theory.

For all the pathos that attends the recollections about the Dodgers in Brooklyn, the borough does not have a monopoly on the romantic perspective. In spite of popular impressions of Southern California, the Dodgers have established roots and traditions in Los Angeles similar to those recorded so poetically by Kahn. For thirty years, the Dodgers have continued to play a special brand of baseball unaltered by their new surroundings and by players not even born when the team moved West. The essence of the Dodgers' particular style of play may be that, whereas Yankee fans always expect their team to win and Red Sox fans fear that ultimately their team will lose, Dodger fans know that no matter how their club is doing at the moment, it is capable of reversing fortune to pull out either victory or defeat.

This pattern that so characterized the team's final years in Brooklyn continued in the Coliseum and still is in evidence in Dodger Stadium, enthralling millions of fans. The roller coaster began immediately in Los Angeles as the Dodgers rebounded from nearly a last place finish in 1958 to a world championship in 1959.

In 1960, the team slipped to fourth place as it continued to assemble the pieces of the one great Dodgers team that has appeared in Los Angeles. Tommy Davis and Frank Howard joined Wally Moon in the outfield, while Norm Larker took over for Gil Hodges at first base. Ron Fairly served a year in the army. And the pitching staff posted unremarkable numbers. Maury Wills emerged as a star of the 1960 team, batting .295 and stealing fifty bases to lead the league. Howard's twenty-three home runs won him the league's Rookie of the Year award. Davis's .276 average gave evidence of skills that would lead to two batting titles in the 1960s.

Another link with Brooklyn was cut in 1960 when Carl Furillo, the hero of the playoffs against the Braves, was released to make room for Howard, the rookie sensation. Furillo left bitterly, contending he was being let go because of injuries and that the Dodgers were trying to renege on his salary. Those claims were eventually sustained, and he was awarded his pay, but the matter compounded the awkward, indecorous ways in which the Dodgers tended to sever their Brooklyn associations.

In 1961, the club rebounded to a second-place finish, four games behind the pennant-winning Reds. Wills again led the league with thirty-five stolen bases, while hitting .282. Walt Alston platooned the few remaining Brooklyn stars with the many new players competing for permanent spots in the lineup. Ron Fairly returned from the army to share outfield duty with Snider, Tommy Davis, Wally Moon, Frank Howard, and a new "phenom," Willie Davis. Sandy Koufax broke through to win a career-high eighteen games, a total matched by Johnny Podres. Don Drysdale finished at 13–10, while Stan Williams was 15–12. Larry Sherry compiled a 4–4 record with a 3.90 ERA, but Ron Perranoski emerged from the bullpen in his rookie year to post a 7–5 record with an ERA of 2.65.

The inexorable transition continued as Gil Hodges played his final games for the Dodgers before being claimed in the expansion draft for the 1962 season by the newborn New York Mets. In sixteen years, Hodges hit 361 home runs for the Dodgers, batted over .270, and was impeccable with the glove. His brilliant knowledge of the game was confirmed in 1969 when he managed the Mets to a world championship after the club had set standards of futility unmatched since the days of the St. Louis Browns. By 1962, the pieces were in place for five spectacular years of triumph and frustration as keen as any known in Brooklyn. At last freed from the bizarre confines of the Coliseum, the club found Dodger Stadium an ideal home for their exceptional pitching, speed, and timely hitting — qualities that characterize the great team of the 1960s. The stadium opened on April 10, 1962, to a capacity crowd as enthusiastic about the park as those thousands of fans in Brooklyn had been when Ebbets Field opened in 1913. The stadium was "not just any baseball park but the Taj Mahal, the Parthenon, and Westminster Abbey of baseball," wrote Jim Murray in the *Times*. Wally Post's home run marred the inaugural and won the game for the Cincinnati Reds, but many of the honored guests correctly identified the opening of baseball's first modern stadium as the harbinger of a new era.

The organization's continued ability to field competitive teams is all the more remarkable when one notes the fundamental changes in baseball during the past decade, particularly free agency, which has made it possible for teams to pursue championships through free spending on salaries subsidized by other corporate assets. Unlike other teams, the Dodgers' revenues for player development, salaries, and free agency must be generated by baseball earnings rather than through shipping, hamburgers, or broadcasting. The Dodgers' principal venture into free agency left them with staggering contracts for two pitchers unable to perform up to expectation. Since then, the organization has withdrawn from the competition for free agents, and relies almost exclusively on its farm system.

The new realities of the contemporary era have been joined by the darker problems plaguing baseball, most noto- riously drug use. A dramatic case involved Steve Howe, who had been the league's Rookie of the Year in 1980. After he won a game against the Yankees in the 1981 World Series and saved the final game, Howe appeared to be in line to succeed Sherry and Perranoski in the tradition of star relief pitchers. But recurrent cocaine use changed Howe into an erratic figure who became too unreliable for any team, despite his estimable gifts. On the other hand, Bob Welch has set a courageous example in controlling the alcoholism that threatened his career. Throughout the history of base- ball, an adolescent part of the game's romance has included the exploits of players who performed through the haze of alcohol or after all-night amorous adventures. Drugs depart from that tradition because they involve players in illegal activities, perhaps in organized crime. The prospect of a player incurring obligations to people who might profit from fixing games threatens to return the sport to its seamy early decades when the integrity of the game was in question. Since the Black Sox scandal was dealt with in 1920, baseball has been free of pervasive suspicion about the legiti- macy of the sport itself. Now baseball finds it must confirm its integrity once again.

Any discussion of the close ties between Dodgers and their fans in Los Angeles must mention the team's principal announcer, Vin Scully. In recent years, Scully has become familiar nationally through his network broadcasts of baseball, football, and golf. In addition to those responsibilities, Scully continues to broadcast the Dodgers' home games. Despite his youthful appearance, Scully represents another link to the Brooklyn franchise. He began to announce Dodger games after graduating from Fordham in 1950. He thus has the perspective of someone close to the team when Walter O'Malley wrested control from Branch Rickey, when Jackie Robinson was in the early part of his career, when the unknown Walter Alston was tapped for the manager's job, when Bobby Thomson hit the famous home run, when Johnny Podres pitched the Dodgers to their first world championship, and when the Dodgers played their final season in Brooklyn.

Perhaps more than any player, Scully contributed to the Dodgers' appeal in Los Angeles. He tempers his enthusiasm to give an honest account of the action before him, and he never loses his awareness that in the end he is describing a little boy's game. The development of transistor radios in the late 1950s enabled fans to bring radios to the game so that they could continue to enjoy Scully's presentation, a practice not always understood by writers. The explanation is simple, however: prior to 1958 the technology did not exist, and since then few other announcers have been worth listening to. Scully himself says that the phenomenon of transistor radios in the ballpark originated in the days of the Coliseum, where fans sat so far from the field that they brought radios to help them follow the action. When Dodger Stadium opened, the habit had become ingrained, and continued. Not only is the transistor used more prevalently in Dodger Stadium than in the other parks Scully visits in his network broadcasts; he reports that their use in Los Angeles occasionally causes technical feedback problems through the crowd microphone. Scully's popularity affords him the opportunity to influence the way fans perceive the game, especially in its larger economic and social contexts. His upbeat but realistic approach emphasizes positive aspects of the game and of the players and he avoids any temptation to preach about their ills.

From the romantic perspective of baseball, Los Angeles has developed a rich tradition. The years in the West have included thrilling victories and championships as well as heart-breaking defeats. The Dodgers have fielded a few players of Hall of Fame caliber and other, minor stars who have endeared themselves to fans despite brief or statistically unimpressive careers. Al Ferrara, Jay Johnstone, Wes Parker, Manny Mota, Jim Brewer, Art Fowler, Dick Nen, and Bill Singer are among the players who have generated excitement for the millions who have followed the team since 1958.

In diverse ways, the Dodgers have developed ties in Los Angeles. Personnel decisions in response to free agency have triggered passionate reactions from the many fans of Steve Garvey, Andy Messersmith, and Tommy John. The decision to go with young players has led popular players such as Dusty Baker, Bill Buckner, and Ron Cey to be traded. The Hispanic community in Los Angeles has been gratified by the emergence of stars like Valenzuela, Guerrero, Alejandro Peña, and Mariano Duncan. Families who have struggled with the tragedy of drug abuse have seen that wealth and fame are not barriers to that lamentable illness. The heroic struggles of Tommy John and Sandy Koufax against serious injuries have set another kind of example. Finally, the game itself, the duel of pitcher and hitter, the strategic maneuvers of competing managers, the brilliant feats of world-class athletes, as well as the dropped fly balls, have enthralled the community. As the *Times* had anticipated, a diverse and parochial group has from time to time cohered around a common interest in the fate of a baseball team.

The history of the Dodgers in both Brooklyn and Los Angeles demonstrates that the romance of baseball is universal. The emotional attachments a community may feel for a team are insufficient to ensure that the franchise will remain where it is beloved. Major league teams will always be a scarce commodity, and cities will inevitably compete for a limited number of teams. Disappointment and even bitterness will accompany the allocation of franchises.

*   *   *

The business and romantic perspectives provide compelling, albeit conflicting, answers to whether the Dodgers should have moved to Los Angeles. A final perspective remains more significant, in part because it is created by the clash of the first two and also because this *civic* perspective is the arena in which public choice resolves the competing claims about franchises and their communities. This perspective is especially important for other cities facing issues similar to those raised by the Dodgers in the 1950s.

The Dodgers were not the first baseball team to change cities, but they were the first to do so with great controversy. They have not been the last. Seattle, Milwaukee, and Washington, D.C., have all lost baseball franchises amid allegations that legal and moral bonds to the community were improperly severed. Denver, New Orleans and Phoenix have debated the propriety of spending public money to attract a franchise that would enhance the status of the town as well as stimulate local business. Chicago is currently struggling to keep both the White Sox and Cubs.

In the Dodgers' move, the civic perspective remains controversial but the dimensions of the argument at least are clear. They are also instructive. Rather than consider franchise relocation and new stadiums on an ad hoc basis, other cities should develop a framework for analyzing issues and making use of the lessons learned in previous cases. This framework should identify three basic models local governments can employ when a team alleges a need for a new stadium and threatens relocation if the need is not met.

The first of these models is the classic free market economy, which states that government has no role to play beyond the protection of private property, and that no aid should be extended to any business in its efforts to secure land and facilities. The concept of the free market has always claimed a powerful hold on American culture, but from our nation's inception government has actively promoted certain businesses through tariffs, land grants, the awarding of monopolies, municipal bonds, and other measures. This history of market intervention shouldn't obscure the point that government aid to baseball teams is not essential and should occur only when various community representatives have determined that the public interest is served by such action.

A second basic model in this civic perspective considers sports franchises and stadiums as a public interest to which the government should extend some limited support. From this viewpoint, the free market does not cover the wide range of public interests; highways, schools, and police departments, for example, can only be secured through the collective action of a community. A free-market model requires that a baseball franchise purchase from each current owner the land needed for a new stadium, and then build its own facility. But even in the early part of the century, when the section of Brooklyn that he pursued was relatively underdeveloped, Charles Ebbets had trouble employing that technique. In the modern age, no team could contemplate purchasing land in such a manner. The individual parcels would steadily increase in value until the final one potentially cost as much as all the preceding plots combined, as nearly happened with the final twelve plots that the Dodgers purchased in Chavez Ravine. A public-interest model would recognize a role for the state in assembling the land for sale to the team through a device like the Federal Housing Act or through eminent domain. The public-interest model is intended to adapt the market to the social and economic conditions that have developed since Adam Smith proposed free market theory in 1776. A good illustration of this model is Los Angeles's response to the Dodgers' interest in a stadium. Dodger Stadium was privately built and operated, but the participation of government was indispensable in providing the opportunity for that private venture.

The third model in this civic perspective has characterized the construction of virtually every modern sports stadium, except for Dodger Stadium and a few other facilities. The model, is, in a word, socialism, with the government constructing the facility as a public venture financed through municipal bonds or tax money. While socialism remains

abhorrent to most Americans, many of our public en-
terprises — transportation, recreation, and utilities — are
owned by the public, operated by government agencies, and
thus obey the principles of socialism. Critics point to the
postal system and Amtrak as examples of the inefficiencies
of such structures, but they forget government's role in
directing the interstate highway program, the national
parks, and the Apollo space program.

The socialist option was exercised by New York when it
faced losing the Yankees, the third case of an established
New York team playing in a decaying stadium in a deteriorating neighborhood. During the administrations of Mayor John
Lindsay from 1965 to 1973, the Yankees voiced the same
complaints expressed by Walter O'Malley and Horace Stoneham a decade earlier. Threatened with losing the team
that had brought so much fame to New York, and keeping in
mind the city's experience with the Dodgers and Giants, the
Lindsay administration intervened more directly than had
the Wagner administration. More than $100 million was
committed to renovation of Yankee Stadium bringing the
aging park up to modern standards of comfort and conven-
ience. Title to the stadium was transferred back to the city,
which then leased the stadium back to the Yankees. The
team, of course, remained in the South Bronx, and rebounded to glory by capturing two world championships in
the 1970s, both against the Dodgers.

Given the realities of modern sports, the free market
option is not a serious one. Business and romantic attachments to major league franchises both compel some kind of
public effort to accommodate the demands of a team in need
of a modern stadium. The major issues are determining the
degree to which government should be involved, deciding
who should bear the financial burdens, and assessing the
impact of new construction on established businesses and
residents. Controversy arises, in other words, between the
public interest and the socialist models.

Several points should be considered in comparing these
options. First, because sports enterprise remains a frivo-

lous undertaking — children's games for spectators' amusement — one can argue that the state should be minimally involved in keeping the team, even if the community favors retention. Schools and hospitals should not be forced to compete with private entertainment firms for claims to the public treasury, no matter what financial benefits are returned to the community by its teams. Public investment should be as limited as possible, and government revenues should come in the form of taxes rather than rent.

Comparing these models raises a second point: franchise relocation. A community that adheres to limited support for a franchise faces the possibility that owners of a cherished team may opt for a more commodious setting. But this prospect is more remote than is often realized — no baseball team has moved since 1972, when the expansion Washington Senators shifted to Arlington, Texas. The possibility of further moves can't be dismissed; weak ownership and demographic changes will always threaten marginal franchises. How communities can responsibly retain a hold on their teams remains a vital issue.

In recent years, while baseball has enjoyed some calm, other professional team sports have seen a number of franchises relocate, to the extent that the business structures of football, basketball, and hockey have been challenged. For now baseball's continued exemption from antitrust regulations gives its leagues more control over individual clubs, but that privilege is a basic defect that at some future point will be redressed, and the leagues as well as the affected communities ought to have a policy in place to deal with the changed situation. For now the issue has been restricted to the federal level: Congress has considered legislation restricting the movement of clubs. This legislation is problematic because it is based on the dubious antitrust exemption, and because it simply perpetuates the delusion that federal, rather than local, government is the appropriate place to halt the movement of franchises.

Since franchises relocate for financial reasons, a device that addresses this issue directly is a more effective solution to unwarranted shifts than legislation that simply forbids them. One solution is for communities not to construct municipal stadiums, thereby forcing club owners to finance them privately. A number of devices exist to provide such financing, including venture capitalism, equity offerings, and limited partnerships. If the financing is structured in a way that gives the investors part-ownership in the franchise, the expenditure for the stadium will tie the team to the community more effectively than a law restricting franchise movement. Owners who wanted to move their franchises would have to sell the stadium, which would be of interest to only another ball club. Dissatisfied owners would probably sell the team rather than move it.

An incidental benefit of private financing is that investors might prefer stadiums that are smaller and less costly. Modern ballparks resembling Wrigley Field or Fenway Park could replace multipurpose monstrosities like Minneapolis's Metrodome. In smaller settings, baseball could recover its more appropriate function as entertainment, and its financial base could be strengthened by owners who are serious about the game and disciplined by market forces.

If practiced in only a few cities or suburbs, this public good model has profound limitations. Rather than submit to it, owners may well prefer to move their teams to cities where the socialist option is available. The check on this activity lies in the prudent exercise of citizenship: municipal bonds for the purpose of stadium construction must be rejected. The recent tax law may prove to limit the attractiveness of municipal bonds and prevent their use as subsidies for lucrative businesses. When thoughtful observers such as Howard Cosell argue that franchise relocation may arguably be legal but clearly is immoral, they are focusing on a secondary issue. If modern stadiums and arenas were privately financed, the team would be tied to the community in a way that would preclude frivolous shifts from city to city. What is immoral is not the casual transfer of sports teams but the expenditure of hundreds of millions of public dollars for private entertainment businesses. The argument that the community benefits from stadium rental ignores the obvious source of revenues available through taxation on a privately owned stadium.

In the past cities have preyed on one another by luring existing franchises to replace a departing team. This unseemly and irresponsible use of resources often subordinates the public good to the narrow interests of large corporations for which the team may be a mere marketing trinket. The several congressional hearings on franchise relocation in the 1980s and the litigation that followed the Oakland Raiders' move to Los Angeles may well be obviated by more responsible behavior at the local level. The municipal stadium is a most pernicious form of welfare awarded to millionaire sports owners. Perhaps now that a sufficient number of cities have been burned by franchise relocation, they will discover that a saner public policy is to tell teams they are welcome only if they build their own stadiums.

City officials in New York, commonly seen as falling short of Walter O'Malley's demands, actually went too far. By declining to assemble the land at Atlantic and Flatbush, which O'Malley could have purchased, New York bypassed an appropriate government response. By proposing instead a public stadium in either Brooklyn or Flushing, the city went overboard in committing public resources to private entertainment. A report from New York City's Office of the Comptroller on the impact of professional sports in the local economy began with this statement: "Increasingly, owners of sports franchises demonstrate their portability. This has impelled the City to commit millions to keeping or attracting professional sports teams in and to New York." This bureaucratic syntax conceals a remarkably wrongheaded idea, that the great cities of the country must dance to a tune played by a handful of wealthy owners who unabashedly pursue welfare in amounts exceeding $100 million during a time of widespread fiscal austerity.

In Los Angeles, the electorate was indisposed to use public funds for a stadium, and even scrutinized the private purchase of Chavez Ravine with extraordinary care. The city and county governments played the limited role of extending for sale to the Dodgers the land which the city had owned at Chavez Ravine. Since then the public treasury has received tens of millions of tax dollars from the Dodgers while limiting public investment to grading and road construction.

In both New York and Los Angeles, public officials appear to have acted in good faith, promoting what they believed were the best interests of their constituents. Brooklyn was disadvantaged because its voice was lost in the federated Board of Estimate, where each borough enjoys equal power, an arrangement recently repudiated as unconstitutional for denying equal representation to the residents of the more populous boroughs, such as Brooklyn. Los Angeles, even more dispersed geographically, has a governmental structure that represents the interest of local communities less rigidly. In a sense Los Angeles made less of a commitment to the Dodgers than New York was prepared to do, but the nature of the commitment was more appropriate to Walter O'Malley's interests. The perception that O'Malley played New York and Los Angeles against each other is at odds with the facts; the two cities were motivated by internal concerns rather than by a competitive desire to outbid one another for the prize of the Dodgers.

O'Malley was unquestionably a shrewd businessman unaffected by sentiment in his operation of the Dodgers, but in the end he lacked the influence in New York to exert his will. In Los Angeles, O'Malley found that his interests fitted those of the city, which desired a major league baseball team and wanted to dispose of the land at Chavez Ravine. O'Malley's business skills deserted him in his estimation of the risks awaiting him in Los Angeles, but his luck prevailed as the electorate rejected Proposition B and the state supreme court reversed Judge Praeger's repudiation of the Chavez Ravine contract.

From the civic perspective, the Dodgers had received no special benefits from New York as of 1957. They left neither a stadium whose site had been assembled by government action, nor a municipal stadium constructed at public expense. Ebbets Field had been privately financed and operated for over forty years. The free market model was in operation, and, according to it, O'Malley had as much license to move his business as did any other entrepreneur. The perception of Walter O'Malley as a villain not only evades the real causes of the Dodgers' move; it also obscures the achievements of the franchise in Los Angeles for which O'Malley merits inclusion in the Hall of Fame, joining his predecessors, MacPhail and Rickey.

The fact that the Dodgers' move can be justified from the civic perspective is, of course, no consolation to the fans in Brooklyn. The lesson for cities with similar emotional bonds to a franchise is that those feelings must be translated into commercial or financial ties that can't be broken so easily.

In the years after the Dodgers' move, Brooklyn and New York City encountered some of the grimmest times in their history. Race riots produced the worst violence in the city since the Irish rebelled against military conscription during the Civil War. Cohesion and civility ceased to govern the institutions of the city during the 1960s as unions, universities, banks, corporations, and politicians singled one another out as scapegoats for New York's vast social and economic problems. The city that thought itself wealthy enough to build Shea Stadium and renovate Yankee Stadium was too poor a few years later to pay its teachers.

During this time, Brooklyn's suffering was particularly acute. Once the borough had proudly argued that it had the best team in the country; now it was reduced to bitter debate about whether it contained the nation's worst slum, Bedford-Stuyvesant. To the biblical plagues of hunger, disease, and ignorance were added new scourges, such as drug addiction. Recently, the city has turned around somewhat. The solution had nothing to do with baseball; the Mets' miracle was confined to the diamond, and the Yankees remained the only visible success in the South Bronx. The reversal was achieved, rather, through responsible decisions made by those with authority in the government, finance, labor, and other vital institutions; and while many thousands still are disadvantaged, the city can justly point to improved conditions for millions of people and businesses.

Brooklyn has also begun to recover and reassert its own unique culture. The Atlantic-Flatbush neighborhood, which so easily could have been the Dodgers' new home, is at last the object of a redevelopment project. The Dodgers were turned down, but new opportunities are being given to others to develop businesses and provide jobs in a crucial part of the borough. The residential neighborhoods of Brooklyn occasionally are featured in the *New York Times* real estate section, which calls attention to and promotes the gentrification of old neighborhoods. The new class of wealthy young inhabitants introduces different challenges, but they are certainly preferable to the old blights of neglect and decay.

A final sign of Brooklyn's return is the effort to restore professional baseball to the borough. The fanciful appeals to the Dodgers to return have been replaced by realistic attempts to locate a Triple A franchise near Coney Island. For the moment these efforts are stalled because the New York teams may invoke a territorial prerogative forestalling the potential competition. If that shortsighted maneuver is reversed, Brooklyn may again develop baseball as a vital part of its culture. A top minor league team is a long way from the Boys of Summer, but it is also a stride forward to a realistic and productive future and away from the mire of a bitterly nostalgic past.

During its years as home to the Dodgers, Los Angeles has faced many of the same problems confronting all great American metropolitan areas. The 1960s outbreak of race riots began in Watts in the summer of 1964. Gang wars have introduced to some barrios a measure of terror that grips Beirut. Drugs and illiteracy thrive alongside fashion and wealth.

At the same time the city boasts achievements that would make any community proud. In 1973 Los Angeles became the first city in the country with a minority black population to elect a black mayor. Tom Bradley has been reelected three times, and narrowly missed winning the governorship in 1982. Faced with the challenge that New York met a century ago — that of being our major urban center of assimilation and opportunity as immigrants have flooded the United States from Central and South America and from Asia — Los Angeles has performed the role with remarkable success, providing children from utterly diverse backgrounds with the tools for economic and social advancement.

In 1984 the city mingled Hollywood glitter, administrative efficiency, and fiscal prudence in hosting the Summer Olympic Games. Officials were financially restrained by the same public scrutiny that so earnestly reviewed the Dodgers' case. Few major facilities were constructed for the games — the Coliseum was upgraded to function as an Olympic stadium, just as it had been in 1932. The growth of Los Angeles sports since 1958 was evident in the availability of other sites for contests, such as the publicly owned and little-used Sports Arena and the Forum in Inglewood, the home of basketball's Lakers and hockey's Kings. Los Angeles even introduced baseball to the Olympics as a demonstration sport. Those games were held, fittingly, in Dodger Stadium, returning the favor owed since 1958, when the Olympic Stadium had accommodated the Dodgers upon their arrival from Brooklyn.

Demographic projections indicate that by the turn of the century Los Angeles will have replaced New York as the most populous city in the United States. The reversal of status will introduce new challenges to both communities. For New York the era of cheap labor migrating from Europe, which helped sustain the industrial age, will have passed and the city will have to find new ways to serve its citizens. Los Angeles will have to meet new demands for services in a city even more diffuse and varied that it is today. To that end, the role of baseball is unmistakably minor. From time to time, however, the diverse population that constitutes the nation's largest city will set aside its immediate and pressing concerns and become lost for a moment in the adventures of

the Los Angeles Dodgers. Few will consider the anomaly of
the name "Dodgers" in a city where automotive courtesy is
prized among the highest civic virtues, perhaps fewer still
will reflect on a place once known as Pigtown, where the
team had its birth. They will simply be drawn to the
excitement of a child's game being played in a magnificent
stadium, and they will enjoy, at least temporarily, a sense of
community.

Maryann Hudson

Take Them Out of
the Ballgame

Los Angeles Times, 1991

From the canyon parking lot hideaway at Dodger Stadium —
known to the less romantic as Lot 39 — the 48,804 fans
attending a recent game appear motionless. Only an occasional roar of the crowd, a rotating ball atop the resident gas
station and that incessant voice on the radio break the
stillness that surrounds the 14,000 cars, trucks and buses.

But then, it's only the fourth inning, much too early for
Dodger fans to be leaving. Some have just arrived.

Then the game reaches the seventh inning, and a frenzy
begins to take hold. Stadium exits suddenly look like the
start of a race-walking event. Soon, the parking lot looks
like an anthill.

By the middle of the eighth inning, half the crowd is in the
lot. By the end of the game about a quarter of the crowd
remains.

This lemminglike phenomenon is indigenous to Los Angeles and happens to some degree at every game, regardless
of the team on the field, or the score.

Fans in other cities are baffled by it; visiting television
broadcasters make fun of it, showing diehard fans back home
a sea of taillights that provokes sarcastic play-by-play banter.

One of those cars may even belong to Dodger President
Peter O'Malley, who has said that he occasionally leaves

early, not because he does not care about the outcome of the game but because he has to be back so early the next morning. When O'Malley leaves, he can easily say good night to former Brooklyn Dodger great Roy Campanella, who sits in his wheelchair in the season seat area outside of O'Malley's private box on the club level. Along with his wife, Roxie, Campanella stays until the final out of every game that his health allows him to attend.

Rarely, though, do fans stay past the game to savor a victory or mourn a defeat. When Jack Clark hit a home run off Tom Niedenfuer in the top of the ninth to put St. Louis in the World Series in 1985, it may have stunned the crowd, but not enough to keep them from bolting for the exits even before Clark's ball hit the ground.

"I was sitting there thinking this is a sad moment. How can these people be thinking about traffic?" said Ruth Ann Taylor, a fan who attended the game.

Now there is renewed interest in this bizarre Dodger fan syndrome, even outrage. During a recent Dodger series against the Montreal Expos, thousands of fans left early during two magnificent pitching performances by the Montreal Expos — Dennis Martinez's perfect game and a nine-inning no-hitter by Mark Gardner that he lost in the 10th.

In baseball, it does not get any better.

The Panic Theory

On the surface, the reason Los Angeles fans leave early is to beat the traffic. But befitting a metropolis that keeps so many psychotherapists employed, it is really more complex.

It is a psychological problem. Wherever Angelenos go, they think about getting out before the next person, says Jack Woody, a book publisher who splits his residence between Pasadena and Santa Fe, N.M.

"The game is completely secondary. People start to panic in the fifth inning and they just crack in the seventh," he says. "Others are sitting there composed, thinking about what a great game it is, a possible no-hitter, and how they are going to try to make it till the end. But when they see these other people break and run, it breaks their concentration, and they go, too."

Among supporters of the "panic theory" is Todd Collins, who runs a Dodger souvenir stand. He listens to fans as they leave and hears them talk about beating the traffic, even when there isn't any.

"About the sixth inning tonight," Collins said, "a man said to his son who stopped to look at the merchandise, 'C'mon we're going to get caught in the traffic.' So I peeked out to look at the lot, and there weren't even any cars out there yet."

The traffic excuse is reserved for those who depart after the fifth inning. Those who leave earlier often come up with something more creative.

"Slow, dull, boring game," said one man taking flight at the close of the fifth inning, after Darryl Strawberry had singled in the go-ahead run for the Dodgers. At that point, there had been 15 hits in the game, including a home run by Strawberry.

There are plenty of other reasons for early departures: long commutes, long days, long games, early morning alarm clocks. All of which were seemingly without validity for the thousands who left early during Martinez's perfect performance.

That game, played on a Sunday afternoon, started at 1:05 and lasted only 2 hours and 14 minutes. It was only the 15th perfect game in the history of major-league baseball.

The question of those who left, wrote Donald H. Camph of Culver City in a letter to *The Times,* is: "Are these people too stupid to know or too ignorant to care what is transpiring in front of them?

"Did it occur to any of these folks . . . that an alternative [to traffic] would be to remain to the end, and then some, to savor the beauty of the game or just to enjoy being out on a sunny afternoon?"

Camph has a suggestion for the Dodgers: time-sharing.

"Betty and Sid could occupy space from the second

through fourth innings and Ethel and Fred could use the same space from the sixth to the eighth.

"The fifth inning, while the grounds crew tidies up the infield, would be the time of transition. Since the wave generally occurs in the sixth inning, there might be a surcharge for Ethel and Fred."

The Entertainment Theory

Dodger Manager Tom Lasorda knows the fans have things to do. But it sure would be nice if they stuck it out until the end. "We like to have them there, pulling for us," he said.

Lasorda says fans in other stadiums may trickle out early, but it is nothing compared to the numbers leaving early at Dodger Stadium.

In fact, sportswriters and baseball personnel who travel to stadiums all over the country agree that it just does not happen anyplace else. Even at Anaheim Stadium, where fans complain about traffic after the game, the early departure of fans is not as pronounced.

Dodger catcher Mike Scioscia is forgiving. "We have a unique situation here — where else do they sell that many season tickets? . . . In L.A. we have almost 30,000 season ticket holders who come to the games day in and day out, and they have their own lives to lead. Some of them may have to leave; maybe they have to be at work early the next day."

Scioscia, who says he does not really notice when fans are leaving early, has a good sense of which ones do. Season ticket holders are the majority of those who depart, according to parking lot officials. Reserved parking areas, which are for season ticket holders only, empty out earliest.

The Dodger season ticket base is 27,000, the largest in baseball. Toronto is next with 26,000. The Mets are also high on the list, at 23,000.

But in Toronto and New York, fans can use public transportation — trains, subways and buses — to get to the stadium. Not prey to the kind of traffic fears common in Los Angeles, rarely do Toronto fans — who are on a pace to set a new attendance record in baseball this season — leave before the end of the game. Met fans who leave early are usually just those who park far from the stadium and do not want a late-night walk.

Some Los Angeles fans "come out to an event and after a couple of hours, they go home," theorized Phil Ianniciello, the Mets' director of ticket operations. "They look at it more as a night out — looking to be entertained — than they do as a game, where the result is secondary."

Many of the Dodger season tickets are held by corporations, which give away tickets to employees, some of whom are not baseball fans and do not care to stick around for hours. The majority of seats occupied at the end are those sold on an individual game basis, primarily in the upper decks and outfield pavilion areas.

Dodger officials often boast that their games offer the best entertainment in town. Todd Siegle and Dave Sterling take it a step further. Both 18, they left a Mets-Dodgers game that was tied in the fifth inning — to go bowling.

To these two, a Dodger game is mostly a party.

"We come to the game, we have some beer or vodka, get smashed, then eat massive quantities of food, like hamburgers and fries, and go home," said Siegle, who said he has only stayed to the end once.

The Vin Scully Theory

Los Angeles Times columnist Allan Malamud, who has covered sports in Los Angeles for 25 years, traces the early departure phenomenon back to when the Dodgers moved to Los Angeles in 1958 and played at the Coliseum. That is when Vin Scully began earning the trust of Dodger fans with brilliant imagery and storytelling in his play-by-play radio broadcasts.

"Fans started to realize that they could listen to Scully on their transistor radios, hear the game all the way home and still beat the traffic," Malamud said. "And they never stopped doing it."

Dodger pitcher Jay Howell has heard that fans leave early

because the radio broadcast is so good. Listening to the Dodger broadcast is just "part of the package," Howell said.

Scully counts it his good fortune that fans listen to him, but says he does not think for a minute that fans leave early for that reason. He says Dodger fans who leave early get a "bad rap."

"People tend to forget that a majority of these people have a considerable distance to drive to get to the stadium," Scully said. "Someone may say, 'Well I live right outside West Covina.' And you say, 'Oh, that's' nice.' But try it sometime. When you get on that San Bernardino Freeway and hit traffic after a long day, it isn't fun.

"I guess I have a strong defense for the people in Los Angeles, rather than the Eastern attitude of, well, those people in La-La Land, they don't know what they are doing."

Scully says Dodger fans began listening to the radio immediately when the team moved here from Brooklyn. Pocket transistor radios, with corresponding earplugs, were tuned to the Dodger broadcast and could be spotted everywhere at the Coliseum, where the team played from 1958–61.

In New York, Brooklyn Dodger fans would bring larger portable radios to the games and hold them up to their ear, Scully says, but they were not listening to him or his mentor, Red Barber.

"In New York there were three baseball teams, so the fans would bring radios to hear the scores from the other games, the Yankees and the Giants," Scully said. "But in Los Angeles, the Dodgers were playing in a football stadium, so a number of the fans sat far away from the game and listened to the broadcast to hear what was going on. Also, I think Southern California fans knew the superstars, like Willie Mays and the older established Dodgers, but they didn't know the rank and file players, so they brought their radios to the games to learn and it became a habit.

"It just happened to be my good fortune to arrive at the same time."

Now those transistors have been replaced by fancy Walkmans and radio headsets, although there are not as many.

Perhaps the decrease is because the Dodgers broadcast the radio play by play over speakers in the hallways behind the seats and show the games on television monitors at concession stands. Perhaps it is because fewer fans are interested in the game.

Or as Scully suggests, Los Angeles is "now a baseball city; we have won pennants, World Series, lost heartbreakers. We are now a mature baseball city.

"I really don't think people leave the games because of Vin Scully and the radio. Maybe they will say, 'Well, we'll get a jump on the traffic and listen to the rest of the game on the radio.'

"But when I am dead and buried they will probably do the same thing. They'll say, let's leave and listen to John Brown."

Tips for Getting Out

Fans may leave other sporting events early, but not as early or as regularly as Dodger fans. Only Laker fans are on a par, leaving games in the fourth quarter.

But early leavers have something to say in their defense.

"I just got a letter from a guy defending himself for leaving early," Malamud says. "He says too many people park where they aren't supposed to, blocking the passageways, and it makes it murder if you wait until the end of the game to leave."

It takes about 45 minutes to an hour to empty the stadium after an average crowd of 42,000, according to Bob Smith, the Dodgers' director of stadium operations. Of course, that's if everybody stayed — which they only do at playoff and World Series games.

Many people believe that Dodger Stadium's parking lot is poorly designed, leading to congestion at the end of games. But Dodger officials say most fans use only a couple of the marked exits.

There are ways fans can get out faster.

There is parking for 16,000 cars in 21 lots, with five marked exits. What few know, however, is that there are two lots that have their own unmarked exits — Lot 33 and Lot 39. Both are unreserved.

"The exit gates in both these lots are open after every game," Smith said. "Both exits dump out on Academy Road. You take a right to get to the Pasadena Freeway and a left to get to the Golden State."

Another reason it takes so long to get out is that most fans use only two exits: "C" behind left field between lots 29 and 33 and marked as the exit to Golden State Freeway, and "E" behind right field and marked for College Street and the Pasadena Freeway, south and north. Of these two exits, C — which exits on Academy Road and is closest to the Golden State Freeway — is the most congested. Parking supervisors say that after all the other exits have cleared, this exit is still backed up.

Drivers can get to the Golden State Freeway by taking the marked exit before it, Exit D, or the private exits out of lots 33 and 39.

In addition to the Pasadena and Golden State freeways, nearby roads provide access to the Glendale and Hollywood freeways.

At the Dodgers most recent home game, Frank Torrez, traffic supervisor, was making the rounds in the parking lot, dropping the chains on the exit gates that stay closed until about 90 minutes after the game begins.

Blocking the exit at Lot 39 was a large van. It was only the fifth inning, but Torrez knew he had to get the van towed away quickly. At any time, even those who park in this little hideaway may return for a quick exit.

"They come in the third inning and leave in the seventh," Torrez said matter-of-factly.

"That's the way it is."

DEFINING
MOMENTS

Claudell Washington broke for the ball like a man answering a phone at 4 in the morning.

That may not be an exact quote, but that's the essence of a line Peter Gammons, the sage of ESPN, wrote when he was nothing more than a humble beat writer covering the Red Sox for the *Boston Globe* in 1975. The line didn't appear in a column or a collection of essays days or months after the game. That was how he described it in his report the next morning on a Sox-A's playoff game. I saw that play myself, but my visual memory of it pales beside Gammons's description of it, and I was reminded of the vividness of the line when my research for this book led me to some of the early writings of Dick Young and Red Smith.

My own firsthand reading of Young was in his later years, primarily as a columnist in the *Sporting News* when his reactionary voice was aimed at every progressive impulse in sports and every individual who threatened his fossilized view of the world. His column was called "Young Ideas" and there was abundant irony in that. However, youthfulness, zest, vibrancy, exhilaration, fun — the sheer joy of watching a game — fairly jump off the page in Young's description of Bill Bevens's near no-hitter against the Dodgers in 1947, which leads off this section.

There's no less a sense of playfulness and wonder in the piece that follows — the legendary Red Smith's reportage on the famous Bobby Thomson home run for the Giants against the Dodgers in 1951.

Like Gammons's description of that '75 playoff game, these pieces were written when sportswriters were still covering the game rather than the locker room, when their job was still to make the play come alive in the morning sports pages rather than record generally banal answers to equally banal questions:

Was this win more or less satisfying than your last win, Lefty?

Ah, no, they're all about the same, I guess.

It's no wonder the relationship between athletes and sportswriters is steadily deteriorating. Each finds in the other a jaundiced witness to his unique talents. Ball players are special because they can go deep into the hole at short, throw 97-mile-an-hour strikes, and hit curveballs 450 feet. Sportswriters are special because they can paint word pictures that make plays and games resonate through the years. If sportswriters can stop covering ball players like politicians, placing more weight on what they say than what they do, they may both be happier for it.

Enough pontificating. Back to the ballpark. Back to October 1955, to be exact. Talk about defining moments! The Dodgers finally get the monkey off their back. They beat the Yankees in the World Series and Brooklyn goes wild. Here to tell us about it is Mr. One Year at a Time himself — Walt Alston, who managed the Dodgers that year and twenty-two others without ever laying eyes on a multiyear contract.

The beat writers of the nation's sports pages can be excused for envying the likes of Jim Murray. He's one of baseball's literary elite, picking and choosing his assignments, dodging the daily drudgery of postgame interviews, writing for a largely literate audience with a taste for irony, alliteration, and metaphor. Freed from the need to compete with game highlights on "Baseball Tonight," he's able to luxuriate in the game's pastoral pace and provide us with insightful and delightful metaphors that help us understand why we ever thought to call it our national pastime in the first place. Here this Pulitzer Prize winner compares Kirk Gibson's memorable ninth-inning home run against the A's in the '88 World Series to a scene from a Hollywood movie.

Now what's wrong with this picture? Or what's wrong with that pitcher? In other words, what's Juan Marichal doing here? Well, it's not because he's a great sportswriter, that's for sure. But this wasn't really supposed to be a dissertation on modern sportswriting. This is actually a section on notable games in Dodger history, and surely one of the most notable was the Marichal-Roseboro affair when the great Dodger-Giant rivalry really drew some blood. So why do we offer up Giant Marichal's version, rather than Dodger Roseboro's? Sheer perversity, that's all.

Dick Young

1947: Brooklyn Dodgers 3, New York Yankees 2

New York Daily News

Out of the mockery and ridicule of "the worst World Series in history," the greatest baseball game ever played was born yesterday. They'll talk about it forever, those 33,443 fans who saw it. They'll say: "I was there. I saw Bill Bevens come within one out of the only series no-hitter; I saw the winning run purposely put on base by the Yankees. I saw Cookie Lavagetto send that winning run across a moment later with a pinch-hit double off the right-field wall — the only hit, but big enough to give the Brooks the 3–2 victory that put them even-up at two games apiece."

And maybe they'll talk about the mad minute that followed — the most frenzied scene ever erupted in this legendary spot called Ebbets Field: How some of the Faithful hugged each other in the stands; how others ran out to the center of the diamond and buried Lavagetto in their caresses; how Cookie's mates pushed the public off because they themselves wanted the right to swarm all over him; how Cookie, the man who had to plead for his job this spring, finally fought his way down the dugout steps — laughing and crying at the same time in the first stages of joyous hysteria.

Elsewhere in the park, another man was so emotionally shaken he sought solitude. That was Branch Rickey, the supposedly cold, calloused businessman, the man who has seen thousands and thousands of ball games and should therefore be expected to take anything in stride. But Rickey had to be alone. He left his family, sat down in a quiet little room just off the press box, and posted a guard outside the door.

After ten minutes of nerve-soothing ceiling-staring, Rickey was asked if he'd see a writer. He would. Now he was calm and wanted to talk. He wanted to talk about the ninth-inning finish — but he started a little earlier than that.

He flashed back to the top half of the frame, when Hughie Casey had come in with the bases loaded and one out, and got Tommy Henrich to hit a DP ball right back at him on the first serve. "Just one pitch, and he's the winning pitcher of a World Series game," Branch chuckled. "That's wonderful."

Rickey then turned to his favorite subject. "It was speed that won it," he said. This tickled Rickey because it had been the speed of Al Gionfriddo which saved the game. They had laughed at Gionfriddo when he came to the Brooks back in June in that $300,000 deal with the Pirates. They had said: "What did Rickey get that little squirt for; to carry the money in a satchel from Pittsburgh?" And they had added, "He'll be in Montreal in a couple of weeks."

But, here it was World Series time, and "little Gi" was still around. Suddenly he was useful. Furillo was on first with two out. Carl had got there just as eight Brooks before him had — by walking. For a prospective no-hit pitcher, Bevens had been under constant pressure because of control trouble. A couple of these passes had led to the Brooks' run in the fifth, and had cut New York's lead down to 2–1.

That's the way it still was when Gionfriddo went in to run for Furillo, and Pete Reiser was sent up to swing for Casey. Only now Bevens was just one out away from having his bronze image placed among the all-time greats in Coopers-town. Already, at the conclusion of the eighth frame, the chubby Yank righty had pitched the longest string of no-hit ball in series history — topping Red Ruffing's 7⅔ innings against the Cards in '42.

Now Bill was out for the jackpot. He got the first out in the ninth on a gasp provoker, a long drive by Edwards which forced Lindell up against the left wall for the stretching grab. Furillo walked and Jorgensen fouled meekly to McQuinn, who was white as a sheet as he made the catch.

One out to go — and then came the first of several switches that were destined to make a genius of Burt Shotton and an eternal second-guess target of Bucky Harris.

"Reiser batting for Casey," boomed the loudspeaker, "and Gionfriddo running for Furillo."

Soon the count was 2–1 on Pete. Down came the next pitch — and up went a feverish screech. Gionfriddo had broken for second. Berra's peg flew down to second — high, just high enough to enable Gi to slide head first under Rizzuto's descending tag. For the briefest moment, all mouths snapped shut and all eyes stared at umpire Babe Pinelli. Down went the umpire's palms, signaling that the Brooks had stolen base No. 7 on the weak-winged Yankee backstop corps.

The pitch on which Gionfriddo went down had been high, making the count on Reiser 3-and-1. Then came the maneuver that makes Bucky Harris the most second-guessed man in baseball. The Yankee pilot signaled Berra to step out and take an intentional fourth ball from Bevens.

The cardinal principle of baseball had been disdained by Harris. The "winning run" had been put on — and Miksis replaced the sore-ankled Reiser on first.

It was possible for Reiser to hurt more than Stanky in such a situation — and the Brooks had run out of lefty pinch hitters. But a good right-side swinger, a clutch money player like Lavagetto, who batted for Muggsy, didn't get to be a fourteen-year man by being able to hit only one kind of chucking.

On the first pitch, Harris' guess still looked like a good one. Cookie swung at a fast ball and missed. Then another fast one, slightly high and toward the outside. Again Lavagetto swung. The ball soared toward the right corner — a territory seldom patronized by Cookie.

Because of that, Tommy Henrich had been swung over toward right-center. Frantically, Tommy took off after the drive, racing toward the line. He got there and leaped, but it was a hopeless leap. The ball flew some six feet over his glove and banged against the wooden wall. Gionfriddo was tearing around third and over with the tying run.

The ball caromed under Henrich's legs as Tommy struggled to put the brakes on his dash. On the second grab, Henrich clutched it and, still off balance, hurried a peg to McQuinn at the edge of the infield. The first-sacker whirled desperately and heaved home — but even as he loosed the ball, speedy young Miksis was plowing over the plate with a sitting slide. A big grin on his puss, Eddie, just turned 21 last week, sat right on home plate like an elated kid. He was home with the winning run, and he didn't want to get up. For what seemed like much more than the actual three or four seconds, Miksis just sat there, looked up at his mates gathered around the plate and laughed insanely.

That's when God's Little Green Acre became a bedlam. The clock read 3:51, Brooklyn Standard Time — the most emotional minute of the lives of thousands of Faithful. There was Lavagetto being mobbed — and off to the side, there was Bevens, head bowed low, walking dejectedly through the swarming crowd, and completely ignored by it. Just a few seconds earlier, he was the one everybody was planning to pat on the back. He was the one who would have been carried off the field — the only pitcher ever to toss a no-hitter in a series.

Now he was just another loser. It didn't matter that his one-hitter had matched the other classic performances of two Cub pitchers — Ed Reulbach against the Chisox in '06 and Passeau against Detroit in '45. The third one-hitter in series annals — but Bevens was still nothing more than a loser.

Bev felt bluer than Harry Taylor had at the start of this memorable struggle. In the first five minutes, Taylor had been a momentous failure. Unable to get his sore-elbowed arm to do what his mind demanded of it, the rookie righty had thrown his team into a seemingly hopeless hole before a Yankee had been retired.

Stirnweiss had singled. So had Henrich. And then Reese had dropped Robinson's peg of Berra's bouncer, loading the bases. Then Harry walked DiMaggio on four straight serves, forcing in a run. Still nobody out, still bases full. Taylor was through; he had been a losing gamble. In one inning, the Yanks were about to blow the game wide open and clamp a 3–1 lock on the series.

But, just as has happened so often this year, the shabby Brook pitching staff delivered a clutch performer. This time it was Hal Gregg, who had looked so mediocre in relief against the Yanks two days before. Gregg got McQuinn to pop up and then made Johnson bang a DP ball right at Reese.

Only one run out of all that mess. The Faithful regained hope. This optimism grew as DiMag was cut down at the plate attempting to score from first when Edwards threw McQuinn's dumpy third-frame single into short right. But, in the next stanza, as the Yanks did their only real teeing off on Gregg, the Brook hopes drooped. Johnson poled a tremendous triple to the center-field gate and Lindell followed with a booming two-bagger high off the scoreboard in right.

There was some hope, based on Bevens' own wildness. The Brooks couldn't buy a hit, and they had men aboard in almost every inning, sometimes two. Altogether, Bev was to go on to issue ten passes, just topping the undesirable series record set by Jack Coombs of the A's in the 1910 grapple with the Cubs.

Finally, in the fifth, Bill's wildness cost him a run. He walked Jorgensen and Gregg to open the stanza. Stanky bunted them along, and Jorgy scored while Gregg was being nailed at third on Reese's grounder to Rizzuto. Pee Wee then stole second for his third swipe of the series, and continued on to third as Berra's peg flew into center. But Robinson left him there with a whiff.

Thus, before they had hit, the Brooks had a run. And right about now, the crowd was starting to grow no-hit conscious. A fine catch by DiMaggio, on which Joe twisted his left ankle slightly, had deprived Hermanski of a long hit in the fourth, and Henrich's leaping stab of another Hermanski clout in front of the scoreboard for the final out in the eighth again saved Bill's blossoming epic.

Then the Yanks threatened to sew up the decision in the ninth. Behrman had taken over chucking an inning earlier as a result of Gregg's being lifted for a pinch swinger and Hank got into a bases-bulging jam that wasn't exactly his responsibility. Lindell's lead-off hit through the left side was legit enough, but after Rizzuto forced Johnny, Bevens' bunt was heaved tardily to second by Bruce Edwards. Stirnweiss then looped a fist-hit into right center. Hugh Casey was rushed in.

Hugh threw one pitch, his million-dollar serve which had forced DiMag to hit into a key DP the day before. This time the low-and-away curve was jammed into the dirt by Henrich. Casey's glove flew out for a quick stab . . . the throw home . . . the relay to first . . . and Hughie was set up to become the first pitcher credited with World Series victories on successive days.

Tough luck cost Hughie two series defeats against these same Yanks in '41. Things are evened up a bit now.

Red Smith

1951: New York Giants 5, Brooklyn Dodgers 4

New York Herald Tribune

Now it is done. Now the story ends. And there is no way to tell it. The art of fiction is dead. Reality has strangled invention. Only the utterly impossible, the inexpressibly fantastic, can ever be plausible again.

Down on the green and white and earth-brown geometry of the playing field, a drunk tries to break through the ranks of ushers marshaled along the foul lines to keep profane feet off the diamond. The ushers thrust him back and he lunges at them, struggling in the clutch of two or three men. He breaks free, and four or five tackle him. He shakes them off, bursts through the line, runs head-on into a special park cop, who brings him down with a flying tackle.

Here comes a whole platoon of ushers. They lift the man and haul him, twisting and kicking, back across the first-base line. Again he shakes loose and crashes the line. He is through. He is away, weaving out toward center field, where cheering thousands are jammed beneath the windows of the Giants' clubhouse.

At heart, our man is a Giant, too. He never gave up.

From center field comes burst upon bursts of cheering. Pennants are waving, uplifted fists are brandished, hats are flying. Again and again the dark clubhouse windows blaze with the light of photographers' flash bulbs. Here comes that same drunk out of the mob, back across the green turf to the infield. Coattails flying, he runs the bases, slides into third. Nobody bothers him now.

And the story remains to be told, the story of how the Giants won the 1951 pennant in the National League. The tale of their barreling run through August and September and into October. . . . Of the final day of the season, when they won the championship and started home with it from Boston, to hear on the train how the dead, defeated Dodgers had risen from the ashes in the Philadelphia twilight. . . . Of the three-game play-off in which they won, and lost, and were losing again with one out in the ninth inning yesterday when — Oh, why bother?

Maybe this is the way to tell it: Bobby Thomson, a young Scot from Staten Island, delivered a timely hit yesterday in the ninth inning of an enjoyable game of baseball before 34,320 witnesses in the Polo Grounds. . . . Or perhaps this is better:

"Well!" said Whitey Lockman, standing on second base in the second inning of yesterday's play-off game between the Giants and Dodgers.

"Ah, there," said Bobby Thomson, pulling into the same station after hitting a ball to left field. "How've you been?"

"Fancy," Lockman said, "meeting you here!"

"Ooops!" Thomson said. "Sorry."

And the Giants' first chance for a big inning against Don Newcombe disappeared as they tagged Thomson out. Up in the press section, the voice of Willie Goodrich came over the amplifiers announcing a macabre statistic: "Thomson has now hit safely in fifteen consecutive games." Just then the floodlights were turned on, enabling the Giants to see and count their runners on each base.

It wasn't funny, though, because it seemed for so long that the Giants weren't going to get another chance like the one Thomson squandered by trying to take second base with a playmate already there. They couldn't hit Newcombe, and the Dodgers couldn't do anything wrong. Sal Maglie's most splendrous pitching would avail nothing unless New York could match the run Brooklyn had scored in the first inning.

The story was winding up, and it wasn't the happy ending

that such a tale demands. Poetic justice was a phrase without meaning.

Now it was the seventh inning and Thomson was up, with runners on first and third base, none out. Pitching a shutout in Philadelphia last Saturday night, pitching again in Philadelphia on Sunday, holding the Giants scoreless this far, Newcombe had now gone twenty-one innings without allowing a run.

He threw four strikes to Thomson. Two were fouled off out of play. Then he threw a fifth. Thomson's fly scored Monte Irvin. The score was tied. It was a new ball game.

Wait a minute, though. Here's Pee Wee Reese hitting safely in the eighth. Here's Duke Snider singling Reese to third. Here's Maglie wild-pitching a run home. Here's Andy Pafko slashing a hit through Thomson for another score. Here's Billy Cox batting still another home. Where does his hit go? Where else? Through Thomson at third.

So it was the Dodgers' ball game, 4 to 1, and the Dodgers' pennant. So all right. Better get started and beat the crowd home. That stuff in the ninth inning? That didn't mean anything.

A single by Al Dark. A single by Don Mueller. Irvin's pop-up, Lockman's one-run double. Now the corniest possible sort of Hollywood schmaltz — stretcher-bearers plodding away with an injured Mueller between them, symbolic of the Giants themselves.

There went Newcombe and here came Ralph Branca. Who's at bat? Thomson again? He beat Branca with a home run the other day. Would Charlie Dressen order him walked, putting the winning run on base, to pitch to the dead-end kids at the bottom of the batting order? No, Branca's first pitch was a called strike.

The second pitch — well, when Thomson reached first base he turned and looked toward the left-field stands. Then he started jumping straight up in the air, again and again. Then he trotted around the bases, taking his time.

Ralph Branca turned and started for the clubhouse. The number on his uniform looked huge. Thirteen.

Walter Alston

From *A Year at a Time*

Those months between the close of my first year as manager of the Brooklyn Dodgers and the opening of spring training at Vero Beach in 1955 flew by. Winters had always been pretty peaceful for me but I discovered being a big league manager also carried some demands I hadn't had to meet before.

I had a lot of requests to speak around Ohio. I'm not the most eloquent speaker now and I sure wasn't then. But speak I did. I also had to attend my first major league winter meeting. I didn't know whether I was going to enjoy sitting around a hotel for a week in meetings, but I've got to the point where I kind of look forward to them. It's about the only time you can sit down and just shoot the breeze with the other managers without worrying about the next pitch or who's coming up next. You get to know the men as men rather than as rival managers.

But I was eager to get back to Vero Beach for spring training despite some of the grumblings and criticism I had read in the winter. A rookie manager is always subject to second guessing, and when we didn't win in 1954 there was probably more than usual. But I learned long ago that all I could do was my best and hope the players could do their best and between the two put together a winner.

Now some of the veteran writers who covered the Dodgers and were critical of my performance in 1954 carried that attitude over into spring training. This was in a time when a club's readiness for the season was measured by the number of pitchers going nine innings.

As I recall, the only pitcher who had gone nine for us in Florida was Carl Erskine, and that was considered rather reckless. But I was convinced our starters were ready and so was our new pitching coach, Joe Becker. We also had some pretty good bullpen specialists, like Clem Labine and Don Bessent, who came up in midseason.

There was a little bit of fuel added on during the spring since we didn't have too good a won and lost record. I wasn't the least concerned. I felt we were in good shape. Don Newcombe, who struggled so long in 1954, was back to the Newcombe I'd remembered before his two-year tour of service when he had a league-leading 164 strikeouts.

I didn't hear any objections from Buzzie Bavasi or Mr. O'Malley, and all my coaches felt our progress was right on schedule for the season opener.

A day or two before we opened the season, one newspaper carried the story saying that I made it one year as Dodger manager and now I would probably make it a second year, but there was trouble ahead.

I've never been one to be concerned about what I read or hear. I went to Vero that year with no contract. One day Buzzie reminded me that we hadn't signed a contract, so after the workout we sat down and put one together. I got a little raise, as I recall, but I was never one to push for a contract. I just let them come along one year at a time. But the way some of the writers felt I might have signed my last in 1955.

Joe Becker, who was in his first year in the Dodger organization, had replaced Ted Lyons as pitching coach. He had caught a couple of years with Cleveland in the mid-thirties. We had managed against one another in the Western League when I was at Pueblo and he was at Sioux City. Then Buzzie knew Joe and we decided he'd be a good coach.

We'll never know if it was a coincidence or what but we started off the 1955 season in unreal fashion. We set a

National League record, as I recall, by winning our first ten games. The first six were won by six different pitchers, which was remarkable. Carl Erskine, Don Newcombe, Billy Loes, Russ Meyer, Johnny Podres and Clem Labine recorded those victories.

The streak was snapped when Marv Grissom, who later became quite a pitching coach, beat Podres for the New York Giants, 5–4. Then we started off another string, winning eleven more before losing.

It was probably one of the hottest starts in baseball history. We won 25 out of our first 29 games and had a 9½-game lead. We were the talk of baseball and Brooklyn was beside itself talking World Series and championship. And we hadn't even run into warm weather.

One thing that streak did was silence all my critics. I never really objected to criticism and I still don't. But I've always felt every fellow should have a chance. We lost four in a row early on and finally settled down into a solid groove. We seemed to be on a steady incline with very few valleys and no giant peaks.

By July 4 we were 12½ games in front and winging. We clinched the pennant in 1955 on September 8 — then the earliest on record in the National League.

Even that created a little controversy. There was a lot of wondering going on if perhaps we hadn't clinched things too soon. Would we lose our edge? Would it have been better to have won it by four or five with a week or so to play?

Now baseball folk can argue that point forever. I didn't know the answer in 1955 and I don't know it now. I think there's a certain advantage to clinching the title with four or five days to go so you can rotate your pitchers around the way you want and get things set for the Series. I also think there is an advantage in playing in a tight pennant race, finally winning it with only a game or two to go and coming in with momentum on your side.

Which is the most important?

Over the years I've had a little of each, but I don't think there is any real edge to having to wait around a long while.

And when you win by 13½ games as we finally did that might allow a bit of complacency to settle in.

It was rather ironic that Brooklyn hadn't been picked to win the pennant in 1955. The *Sporting News* poll in preseason favored Milwaukee, with the Giants and Dodgers figured to fight things out for second. They had the three clubs right, but the order was reversed as we won, with the Braves second by 13½ and the Giants back in third by 18½.

It was a historic season in Brooklyn, and pretty hysterical, as we went into the World Series against Casey Stengel and the New York Yankees.

For me it was unforgettable. I'd seen only one Series and that was the year before when the Giants swept Cleveland in four. Now it was mine to win or lose. Literally everything ceased in the borough of Brooklyn. I don't think I've ever seen more baseball mania.

Brooklyn — the city, that is — was convinced this was the Dodger year. Winning so early by such a large margin had convinced the fans of that. True, we were a solid ball club and things had gone our way almost all year. But New York was solid as well, and Stengel and the Yankees had been winning World Series a long while.

A lot of Brooklyn came tumbling down and I was right along with them when we lost our first two games in Yankee Stadium. Newcombe was bombed out in the sixth inning as we lost, 6–5. Then the Yanks jumped Billy Loes early, getting four runs in the fourth on their way to a 4–2 triumph.

It was Stengel's sixth Series in seven seasons at New York. History and a lot of baseball experts were against our coming back to win. No club had ever come back to win the Series after losing the first two.

Brooklyn had been in eight World Series. The previous seven had all been failures. It was my first, and as we moved back to Ebbets Field for three games we were determined to beat history and win.

Johnny Podres was our selection to start the third game. The call fell on his twenty-third birthday. John gave us all a reason to celebrate, going the distance, allowing the Yanks only seven hits, and winning 8–3. The skeptics still pointed out that no club had ever come back from losing the first two games in all the years since the Series began back in 1903.

We evened things up the next day even though Carl Erskine, our sore-armed starter, was driven out in the fourth. The actual victory went to young Clem Labine, who went the final four and one-third innings. A truly strange incident occurred in this game. Don Larsen, the Yankee right-hander, ripped a pretty good foul ball back into the stands in the lower box seats. It bounced off the head of Del Webb, then a co-owner of the Yankees.

Things were all starting anew on Sunday, but we couldn't afford to lose and go back to Yankee Stadium down a game with two to play. There was a lot of public debate over our pitching selection, but within the club there wasn't.

We went with a rookie, Roger Craig, who had joined the club along about the middle of the season from Montreal. Roger had done real well for us, appearing in 21 games and starting 10. His 5 and 3 record wasn't overly impressive but his earned run average of 2.78 was excellent.

Our lineup was pretty well set for the Series. Roy Campanella did the catching, Gil Hodges was on first, Pee Wee Reese at short, Jackie Robinson at third, Duke Snider in centerfield and Carl Furillo in right. I platooned second base and left field. Jim Gilliam was in left, Don Zimmer was at second base. When Gilliam was at second, Sandy Amoros was in left.

Sandy gave Craig a big lift with a two-run home run off Bob Grim in the second inning. Roger did exceptionally well for a young guy in his first Series, going six innings officially before giving way to Labine. Labine, by the way, came out of the bull pen four times in the Series to establish himself as a fine relief pitcher.

That 5–3 win gave us a big lift.

For game six at Yankee Stadium, a lot of people expected that I might go with Don Newcombe. Even though he had lost the opener, he had been our big gun all year. But I decided to go with Karl Spooner, who might have a better chance in a park that favors left-handed pitchers.

The only problem was that another left-hander named

Whitey Ford had one of his great days, throwing a four hitter and bringing everything down to game seven by beating us, 5–1. Later on I learned that this was the first time in history that a club started six different pitchers in the first six games of the Series.

Now we were down to one. There was no tomorrow, only today. Brooklyn needed a win for its first pennant. A Yankee victory would add another to their string and Casey's.

There was no doubt who I was going with. Podres. Johnny loved pressure. Really thrived on it. To me he was at his best with the most at stake. And on this Tuesday in New York he was in the cooker down there in the fire. But he wasn't alone. Every man on each club faced the same challenge.

Podres had completed only five games in twenty-four starts in the regular season but two of the five were shutouts. Ironically, none of his complete games came after June 12, which left some room for conjecture when he got my call to start game seven. His big problem was a bad foot.

Hodges worked Byrne around to where he singled to score Campy to give us a 1–0 lead.

Now one run isn't much against the Yanks, and in the sixth we added another with a hand from Lady Luck. Pee Wee Reese singled to bring up Duke Snider. He was bunting for a sacrifice, but when he brushed past first baseman Bill Skowron's glove tag trying to reach the bag, Duke knocked the ball away and we had runners on first and second.

Campy moved both of them along with a sacrifice. Stengel elected to walk Carl Furillo intentionally to fill the bases but it also brought Hodges up. Stengel decided to remove Byrne and replace him with Bob Grim. Then Hodges lifted a deep fly to left center that scored Reese and gave Gil his second run batted in for the day.

Up 2–0 now, I still wasn't comfortable against the Yankees with that lead. When Grim made a wild pitch to Hoak, Yogi Berra blocked the ball but couldn't find it rolling around near his feet. Furillo took second while Yogi was scrambling around. Then Grim walked Hoak.

Don Zimmer, who was playing second, was up next. I decided to go for a long ball and sent George (Shotgun) Shuba, who hadn't been in the Series before, to bat for him.

While my immediate strategy failed, Shuba for Zimmer required me to make an adjustment in the field. I brought Gilliam in from left field to replace Zimmer at second base and sent Sandy Amoros into left.

Billy Martin started the Yanks off in their half of the sixth with a walk. Gil McDougald beat out a surprise bunt single. With batters on first and second, Berra came to the plate. In such a situation Yogi was even more dangerous than normal. He thrived on competition but he was up there against Podres, who was equal to almost any challenge.

Berra tied into one of John's high pitches and sliced a sinking fly ball into the right field corner. Sandy, playing a little bit toward left center for Berra, had a long, long way to come. I really couldn't see the ball too well from our dugout. All I knew when the stadium roar went up was that it was either a hit or a catch.

I could see our players set up for a throw so I knew it was caught. Both Martin and McDougald had taken off, figuring there was no way Amoros would catch the ball. Martin managed to scramble back to second in time, but Sandy's throw to Reese and the relay to Hodges was one of the finest double plays on McDougald I ever saw. Hank Bauer then grounded out to end the inning and for all intents and purposes the Series.

Now there was good fortune in my having Shuba hit for Zimmer. If Gilliam had still been in left, from what the guys told me, it would probably have been impossible for Jim to get it. Since Gilliam is right-handed, his glove would have been on his left hand. Amoros, a left-hander, had his glove on his right hand and had just the few inches edge to make the catch.

I remember looking at the clock when Podres retired the final batter. It was 3:44 P.M. At that moment every place in Brooklyn must have come apart. Thirty years of waiting was over with John's 2–0 shutout.

It was the Dodgers' first World Championship. It was my first World Series win. It stopped a Yankee streak of seven world championships without a defeat and it ended Casey Stengel's string of never having managed a losing team in a World Series.

It was really Johnny Podres's hour. He'd won a big one for us on Sunday, to take us back to Yankee Stadium. Now with three days' rest he had come back to shackle some of the great bats in baseball and win the big one. Twice I had gone out to the mound to talk with him but neither time was I close to taking him out. I had Clem Labine up ready to go in the eight inning, but when John got Berra I decided to leave him in.

There was great joy in our clubhouse. A lot of champagne and beer was spilled. Far more went on the floor than down the throats of our screaming guys.

From Walter O'Malley on down, everyone in the Dodgers organization was thrilled beyond comprehension. It was a great win. A great hour for a bunch of guys who had an unbelievable year.

The celebration was really big in Brooklyn, as we found out when we tried to get home that night after the game. I'm sure no one went to bed until the wee hours.

And back in Darrtown Dad created a little celebration of his own. He told me he never left the TV set throughout the Series, but as soon as Elston Howard grounded to Pee Wee Reese and the ball hit Hodges's glove for the last out he let out a war whoop and ran out of the house.

He jumped into his pickup truck and drove down Main Street blowing the horn. A lot of the folks raised the American flag in their yards and before the sun had set someone had painted a WELCOME HOME SMOKEY sign in anticipation of our return.

My friend Earl F. (Red) Huber, who ran Darrtown's only tavern at the time, The Hitching Post, did a roaring business. Friends and folks came in from Oxford and Hamilton and when I got back they threw a big party at the Knights of Pythias Hall for the hometown boy who'd made it big as a major league manager.

I'd been interviewed and reinterviewed at the Stadium, in Brooklyn the next day and literally every second before I had a chance to sit down at home and read what all the writers said.

There weren't many knocks about Walter Alston and quite a lot of praise. It was great, especially for Brooklyn. Five times — 1941, 1947, 1949, 1952 and 1953 — they'd made the World Series only to lose. Now we'd won and we'd won against one of the best.

Of all the comments I recall from that first win in the World Series one stands out, and for the life of me I can't tell you who wrote it. Whoever it was compared Brooklyn's reaction to that win to the warning cry of one of the citizens of Hades who was exhorting the townspeople to flee.

"Get out. The Dodgers just won the World Series. All hell is freezing over."

Wonderful news. And it was going to make for an even more wonderful winter.

Juan Marichal and Charles Einstein

From *A Pitcher's Story*

It is possible that the events leading up to the Roseboro episode began in the Friday night game of that Giant-Dodger series. In the top of the fifth, Maury Wills was given the right to go to first base because umpire Forman, behind home plate, ruled that Tom Haller, our catcher, had "tipped" Wills' bat with his glove, thus interfering with Wills' swing. The Giants protested unsuccessfully that Wills had deliberately stuck his bat back to cause the contact with Haller's glove.

Now, leading off the bottom of the fifth for us, Matty Alou touched Roseboro's glove with his bat — or vice versa, but this time Forman did not send the hitter to first base. Our dugout started yelling at Forman, and Roseboro got mad.

"Haller didn't get mad at Wills!" I called to Roseboro.

When Matty came back to the bench, he said Roseboro had told him "Somebody told you to tip my glove with your bat. If somebody hurts me, I'm going to get one of you guys." And when I yelled from the bench, Matty said that Roseboro had said: "If Marichal doesn't shut his big mouth, he'll get a ball right behind the ear."

Later, Cepeda told me Roseboro said the same thing to him in the clubhouse runway after the game.

But I tended to shrug it off. In fact, just the day before, Roseboro and I had talked pleasantly for three or four minutes, out by the bullpen bench in right field, as the Dodgers came on to the field to take pregame batting practice.

In Sunday's game, Wills opened by bunting my first pitch and beating it out for a single. Fairly got a double, and the Dodgers were off to a 1–0 lead.

Then in the second, a double by Parker and a single by Roseboro made it 2–0. Then Wills came up again, and we certainly didn't want him bunting this time. So I threw high and inside, and he went down. I wasn't trying to hit him.

Koufax "retaliated" for them by throwing a "courtesy pitch" over Mays' head when Willie batted in the second inning for us. He wasn't trying to hit Mays, either — just letting us know the Dodgers didn't appreciate Wills going down.

In the top of the third, Fairly went down too, but the pitch to him wasn't close to him.

Then I led off the third. I didn't know if Koufax would throw at me or not, but he didn't throw at people, and maybe he realized the pitch to Fairly hadn't been that close. Nothing was said. He put a curve across the plate for a strike, then a ball low and inside. Roseboro dropped it — on purpose, I believe, and I do not think this was the first time a catcher, or Roseboro himself, ever did that. He dropped it in a way that brought him directly behind me, but the first thing I realized was the ball ticking my right ear as he threw it back to Koufax.

That was when I said what I said and he said what he said, and the next thing I knew he was coming at me.

I am quoted in the following extract from an article in the June 1966 issue of *Sport* magazine, written by Harry Jupiter of the *San Francisco Examiner*:

"Now I knew Koufax wasn't throwing at me. I never dreamed it would come from behind.

"I was looking at Koufax. Then I felt the ball tick my right ear. If I had turned my head it would have hit me in the face. Nobody has to throw a ball that close and that hard. Now I remember what Matty and Orlando had told me after the Friday night game. I looked back. I asked him, 'Why did you

do that?' He moved two steps toward me and he said '———
you.'

"I had the bat on my shoulder. If he didn't do it on purpose
he didn't have to give me that kind of answer. He's got
everything on. He's got the mask, the chest protector. I don't
think I can fight with a guy like that. I know from the way he
came toward me he was coming to fight. I only hit him one
time — the first time."

Jupiter's article then continues:

Roseboro's head was gashed open and there was blood but
Roseboro kept moving after Marichal. Juan still recalls his
thoughts during the riot that followed. "I know I didn't want
them to take the bat away from me," he says. "I know if they
take the bat away then everybody will hit me. They (the
Dodgers) were a lot closer than the guys on my team. The
Dodgers were in the field and close by."

Marichal was hauled away from the center of the fight but
it didn't die quickly. Lou Johnson and Dodger coach Danny
Ozark were fighting to get at Marichal. Roseboro kept trying
to get at Marichal, too.

"I went into the clubhouse with a policeman," said Marichal.
"After a few minutes, four or six guys came to see how I was.
I had scratches on my chest but I wasn't hurt. I was lucky not
to get hurt. I sat at the desk in Eddie Logan's little office in
the clubhouse and I listened to the game on the radio. I was
sorry about what happened. I was sorry I was out of the
game. I don't like to fight but I don't like anybody to hit me,
either."

There is a corridor between the two clubhouses at Candlestick Park. With the door open you can see the corridor from
Logan's desk in the Giant clubhouse. "I saw Willie [Mays] go
into the Dodger clubhouse three or four times between
innings," says Marichal.

"Since the umpires threw me out, I figured it was an
automatic fine. I figured it would be a fine for Roseboro too.
Then Herman [Franks] came in and he said I should go to the
airport in a cab with some policemen. There were just a few
people outside the clubhouse when I left, and they were
quiet," he says.

The Giants flew to Pittsburgh that night. "I didn't talk much on the plane to Pittsburgh," says Marichal. "I slept some. It was a long day."

That was August 22, 1965, the day that Juan Marichal became a villain in most people's minds. They booed him after that. Wherever they booed, there were cheers too, but Juan heard the boos. "When I heard the boos, I was sorry," says Marichal, "but there was nothing I could do. It was the first time they did that to me. If the people know what happened, then I don't think they would boo me."

There were aftermaths, and I will try to enumerate them:

1. I have already said the 1965 Giants had a "short" roster because they had to carry two bonus rookies. As a result, the pitching was thin. Ordinarily, a man can play any position on the field, but in order to pitch he must be listed as a pitcher. This rule is there so that teams far ahead or far behind in the standings or the score do not make a joke out of the game, in front of paying customers, by sending anybody in to pitch. In our case, however, manager Franks won approval from league president Giles to use other players as pitchers during my suspension. We went from San Francisco to Pittsburgh, where we had a four-game series. We lost the first two, then were leading in the third game, only it started to rain and the umpires finally called it — a 3–3 tie — even though we had scored in the top of the tenth. The Pittsburgh groundskeepers found that their automatic tarpaulin equipment didn't work, meaning they couldn't cover the infield. It's amazing how often the home team can't cover the field when the visiting team has scored in the top half of the inning; for now the score had to revert to the end of the previous inning, meaning a tie and a doubleheader the next day.

And then and there, Herman Franks simply ran out of pitchers. We were so badly behind in the second game that he brought in Matty Alou. All Matty had was a nickel curve and desire, but he struck out Willie Stargell twice, and they say it was one of the funniest sights anybody ever saw on a ball field.

2. I have already made something of the fact that my suspension was for eight *playing* days. Actually, that meant

nine days, because we had an off day on the eastern swing. That ninth day, when I still wasn't permitted to pitch, was the day of a scheduled twi-night doubleheader at Philadelphia, which meant not one but two extra games in which the Giant pitching still was shorthanded. Even timing a full nine-day suspension from the moment of the Roseboro episode to the equivalent moment nine days later would have made me eligible to work at Philadelphia in that twi-nighter. But that was not to be.

The *San Francisco Chronicle* was interested in this — and started to do some questioning. They came up with some intriguing answers.

My suspension had been timed, they concluded, so that I would have two pitching starts — one at Philadelphia, another at Chicago — before the Giants went to Los Angeles for the final series of the year between the two teams, a two-game set Labor Day September 6 and again the night of September 7.

In other words, the league did not want me pitching in Los Angeles! Why? Because of the recency of the Watts riots. Though there was nothing racial in the Roseboro episode itself, to pack fifty-six thousand people together in so small an area as a ball park, with feelings running high anyway, was not something they wanted to complicate by having me appear on the field there.

Some people did not think this story was true when the *Chronicle* printed it, but it was proved true when it turned out I was not even permitted to make the trip to Los Angeles, let alone pitch there.

In effect, therefore, my suspension was for eight playing days, meaning nine actual days, becoming eleven days on account of my being barred from L.A.

Since it was not my turn to pitch in Los Angeles, the loss may seem slight. And so, apparently, the league reasoned in timing my suspension. But they did not think of the possibility of rain-outs in Philadelphia and Chicago. When this was called to their attention, I think, from what I have heard, that they wanted to give it a second consideration. But in the meantime, as we flew from San Francisco to Pittsburgh, the

Dodgers had flown from San Francisco to New York. New York is the headquarters for the television news and the baseball press. With the Dodgers getting first crack at these people — in other words, their side of the story — I suppose it would have looked bad if the league had announced it was shortening my suspension by one day. And so, even though I think they realized they hadn't thought about the possibility of rain and so wanted to give it some reconsideration, the league had to stay with its announced penalty.

And it did rain. In Philadelphia. I worked there on September 5, 1965 and lost, and ordinarily now I would not work again till Monday. But Monday was Labor Day in Los Angeles. So manager Franks did the only thing he could do. He worked me on short rest Sunday in Chicago. We won the game, 4–2.

3. About the booing. I heard it in Philadelphia. And in Chicago. But the next time I pitched was at home, at Candlestick Park. Here I did not get boos. I got cheers. And I will never forget a play made behind me, in the fifth inning of that game, which was against Houston. This was my tenth shutout game of the season, and into the fifth inning no one had reached base against me. Then one of their hitters put a ground ball up the middle, and Dick Schofield, playing shortstop for us, went back of second and got it. He had no play at first. Off balance, he shoveled the ball to Maxie Lanier, the second baseman, and Maxie wheeled and threw blindly to first base. Too late. The hitter had crossed first with the first hit against me. But that crazy play those guys made behind me — an utterly foolhardy and impossible try to get the ball to first — gave me one of the warmest feelings I have ever had in my pitching career. It showed they were behind me. And you should have heard the applause from the crowd!

4. As I have said, the August 22 game was the last time I was to see the Dodgers in 1965. For the next meeting with Roseboro, I will quote again from Harry Jupiter's article in *Sport*:

The new ballpark in Phoenix was packed. Almost 8000 people were in the seats, hundreds more stood behind the right-field screen, at least a thousand on the embankment beyond the left field fence and another 200 or so stood on the high mound across the street.

The Giants and Dodgers were playing each other in the Phoenix park this Sunday, April 3, and they pack ballparks everywhere. But it was more than a Giant-Dodger game that had brought many people out in the blaze of a high Arizona sun and 96 stifling, gnat-filled degrees of desert temperature. This was the first meeting of Juan Marichal and John Roseboro since their bloody battle at Candlestick Park on August 22, 1965. The air was heavy with anticipation. Nobody really knew what to expect. It was like the crowd that packs the Indianapolis Speedway every Memorial Day. Nobody wants to see anybody get hurt or killed, but if it's going to happen . . .

Marichal was in the Giant clubhouse, trying to doctor a cold. "It's not really bad," he said, "but it's annoying."

Roseboro was moving around during the Dodgers' batting practice. Now, he was at third base, fielding grounders with his big catching mitt. One sharp bouncer took a wicked hop. Roseboro got his mitt up just in time to prevent being struck in the face. "Better be ready out there, Gabby," came a shout from the Giant dugout. Roseboro didn't turn around.

There had been talk earlier of efforts to get Marichal and Roseboro to shake hands at home plate. Neither would make the first move. Nothing happened.

"If he says hello to me, I'll say hello to him," said Roseboro. "But I won't pose for pictures. Nobody would be asking us to pose for pictures if it wasn't for the fight."

Marichal didn't show any enthusiasm for saying hello, or shaking hands, so the matter was dropped quickly. Walter Alston and Herman Franks, the managers of the teams, took the attitude that the beef was all part of another season. They were all for forgetting about it.

But the air of anticipation still was heavy as the Giants took the field. Marichal stood on the mound, facing the flag beyond the center-field fence, as an old Kate Smith recording of "The Star-Spangled Banner" scratched to a conclusion .

The fans sat down, then grumpily arose again. The man running the public address system was fouled up and the national anthem ran again. It went halfway through for the second time before anybody figured out how to shut it off.

Marichal needed only nine pitches to dispose of Maury Wills, Wes Parker, and Willie Davis in the first inning. Claude Osteen wiped out Tito Fuentes, Jesus Alou, and Willie Mc-Covey just as promptly.

Ron Fairly singled into center on Marichal's second pitch in the second inning. Tommy Davis flied out, Jim Lefebvre singled, and now it was Roseboro, stepping into the batter's box. The crowd cheered. There they were, finally, face to face.

The first pitch to Roseboro was outside, the next high. The 2–0 pitch was a called strike and then John fouled one off. The 2–2 pitch was a belt-high slider and Roseboro lined it cleanly to right field.

Jesus Alou, who is Marichal's roommate, came in fast, hoping to make a quick throw. The ball took a high hop — over Alou's head.

Fairly scored and Lefebvre scored. Roseboro scored too, standing up, with an inside-the-park home run. It was a ludicrous home run, really, on a crazy bounce, and it became even more ludicrous a second later as Roseboro tripped over a television cameraman's power cord and fell flat on his face.

"I saw the wire," Roseboro said later, "but I couldn't stop myself."

The game wound up 8–4, with the Dodgers winning. Marichal worked five innings, allowing seven hits and five of the Los Angeles runs. Roseboro flied out in his other at bat against Marichal. There were no words, no incidents, nothing expressed between Roseboro and Marichal.

"I didn't feel any tension," said Roseboro. "It was just another game as far as I was concerned."

Marichal had nothing to say about Roseboro after the game. He spoke as if it had been a very ordinary exhibition game. "I feel real loose," Marichal said. "I don't have any control yet and can't hit spots the way I'd like to. I didn't think I'd pitch as long as five innings this time, but I think I should be able to go seven innings by next time."

5. In my first appearance of the 1966 season at Los Angeles, I was booed tremendously when my name was first announced and when I first came to bat. But as the game wore on, a strange thing began to happen. Don Drysdale, my pitching opponent, was booed, by his own fans, worse than I

was. I think this was a combination of two things. He had thrown inside to Mays. And he was off to a slow start after his celebrated and extended spring holdout, along with Koufax, and I think the fans were a little down on him for that. It was ironic in a way, because I had had practically no spring training either — I too was a holdout in '66 — yet I won my first ten games of the season.

6. Did the Roseboro episode affect my pitching? For some time, it did. I have already told the story, at the beginning of this book, of Mays being angry at me because I would not throw inside to Ernie Banks. The truth was, I would not throw inside to anybody, for the remainder of the '65 season and into '66.

Tom Sheehan came to me, finally, and said, "You're pitching one way." I am glad he said this, because a lot of it was subconscious — I did not want to make a mistake and hit a batter, with the Roseboro thing so recent in people's minds — so I was not going for the inside. It took somebody to come to me and say it outright, and Sheehan was the one who took it upon himself to do it.

It is bad for a pitcher not to use the inside part of the hitter's area, but doubly bad for a *control* pitcher not to do it. And primarily I am supposed to be a control pitcher.

Gradually, I was able to correct that "overcorrection," and now it is no longer a problem.

7. Speaking of the tension that arises in Dodger-Giant games, it certainly can lead to fights. In our final series of the year at Los Angeles, in September of 1966, we looked over at the Dodger dugout and saw Tommy Davis and Maury Wills beating the socks off each other.

It seems the Dodgers had a system, where with two out the shortstop (Wills) would hold up two fingers, to show there were two out, and the left fielder (Davis) would also hold up two fingers, to show that he had read the signal loud and clear and understood. Only with two out in our half of that inning, Wills had held up those two fingers, but Davis didn't respond.

When they came to the dugout, Wills is supposed to have

asked Davis "Why didn't you respond to my signal?" and Davis is supposed to have asked Wills "Why don't you something-or-other?" And the next thing you know, there was a full-fledged battle royal going on in their dugout. I bring this up here because it is another piece of evidence of the tension that I suppose does exist when Giant meets Dodger.

8. That *Sport* article by Harry Jupiter carried the headline: JUAN MARICHAL'S HARD FIGHT TO REDEEM HIMSELF. Underneath, there was what they called a "subhead." It said:

"Only Roseboro's side of the story was emphasized," says Juan. "I don't think my side was considered." He tells his side here.

Jim Murray

It Could Happen Only in Hollywood

Los Angeles Times, October 16, 1988

Well, you can believe that if you want to.

As for me, I know a Warner Bros. movie when I see one. I've been around this town long enough to spot a hokey movie script.

I mean, this is "Rambo IV," right? That was Sylvester Stallone that came out of the dugout in the ninth inning of Game 1 of the 1988 World Series. That wasn't a real player?

Believe this one and you'll think "Superman" is a documentary.

The country is never going to buy it. This is the thing Hollywood does best. But it never happens in real life. In an Italian movie, he dies. He doesn't hit a last-minute home run with 2 outs and 2 strikes and the best relief pitcher in baseball throwing. This is John Wayne saving the fort stuff. Errol Flynn taking the Burma Road.

A guy who can hardly walk hits a ball where he doesn't have to. A few minutes before, he's sitting in a tub of ice like a broken-down racehorse.

Kirk Gibson is the biggest bargain since Alaska. He should be on crutches — or at least a cane. He wasn't even introduced to the World Series crowd in the pre-game ceremonies. He wasn't even in the dugout till the game got dramatic. Some people were surprised he was in uniform. Some were surprised he was upright.

The odds against his hitting a home run in the situation were about the odds of winning a lottery. The manager was just milking the situation, trying to keep the crowd from walking out early. No one seriously expected a guy with two unhinged knees to get a hit, never mind *the* hit.

Here was the situation: The Oakland Athletics, who are less a team than a packet of mastodons, baseball's answer to a massed artillery attack, had the game all but won, ahead by 1 with 2 out, 1 on.

Somehow, a quartet of Dodger pitchers had held this mass of muscle to 4 measly runs. The Dodgers had somehow pasted together 3. They got 2 of them when Mickey (Himself) Hatcher, who may be himself a figment of the sound stages, hit his second home run of the year.

Oakland got back 4 when Jose Canseco hit his 46th homer of the year.

So, the score was 4–3, favor of Oakland. Two were out, the crowds were streaming out, the traffic jam was starting, when pinch-hitter Mike Davis drew a walk.

Out of the dugout came our hero. Tom Mix, Frank Merriwell, the Gipper never had a better part.

The wonder was, they didn't have to carry him up there. There should have been a star in the East or lightning playing around his forehead the way this postseason has been going for Kirk Gibson. He had posted the most devastating .154 average in the history of playoffs (his slugging average is .800) this fall. Every hit he gets wins a game. Three out of three of them have been home runs.

A World Series crowd doesn't know much about baseball. But a Hollywood crowd knows all about happy endings. They know an MGM finish when they scent one, too. They began to holler and scream.

You wanted to say, "OK, nice touch," to the manager, Tommy Lasorda, but you wanted to tell the crowd, "Grow up! This isn't Disneyland."

On the mound, Oakland pitcher Dennis Eckersley didn't believe in fairy tales or Horatio Alger Jr. dime novel plots, either. Nor did Oakland Manager Tony La Russa.

If they did, they would have walked Kirk Gibson. Even

when the count went to 3 and 2, they were putting their money on logic, reason, percentages.

Hah!

Eckersley threw a here-hit-this! pitch.

If you saw "Sands of Iwo Jima," "Rio Hondo" or even "Singing in the Rain," you know what happened. When last seen the ball was headed to the moon.

Fadeout. Up the music. Roll the credits. The guys in the white hats win again. The big bad rustlers from Oakland, the hit men, the seat-breakers, had to stand there helplessly while the good guys won again.

It had everything but a schoolmarm and a dog. Or Gibson riding slowly off into the sunset.

You knew it would happen. A movie is 9 reels of disaster and calamity befalling the star. But the last act finds him getting fanned into consciousness by his horse and led by Rin Tin Tin to where the outlaw has his fiancee and he rescues her in the nick of time, the ninth inning, so to speak.

It's the way we do things here in Hollywood. You have to figure that's what happened. Somewhere out there, the screenwriter in the sky brought in this ending where the hero takes a called Strike 3 while everybody cries. Or he pops up to the pitcher. But somewhere out there, C.B. or L.B. takes a disgusted look and says, "You call this a picture! What's this dreck! Take it back and write me something for Doug Fairbanks or Mary Pickford, something that'll sell in Dubuque. When I want a 3-handkerchief picture I'll remake Camille."

Well, look at it this way: You got a better explanation for what happened at Dodger Stadium Saturday night? You believe it, do you?!

Nah!!

A CAST OF
CHARACTERS

Jimmy Cannon, who covered the Dodgers in the East, and Jim Murray, who covers them in the West, are generally regarded as two of sportswriting's greats. Tom Boswell is fast approaching them in stature, and the very funny Mike Downey may one day move into that upper echelon himself if he doesn't trip over his punch lines on the way. In this section the four of them assay four notable Dodgers — Jackie Robinson, Orel Hershiser, Sandy Koufax, and Fernando Valenzuela, respectively.

Fred C. Harris and Brendan C. Boyd are not sportswriters; they're just a couple of guys who once upon a time sat down with just about every baseball card they could get their hands on and wrote down the first things that came into their heads about boys who were lucky enough to grow up and get their faces packaged with bubblegum. The result was *The Great American Baseball Card Flipping, Trading and Bubble Gum Book,* from which we've extracted the Dodgers cards for your amusement.

Harris and Boyd aren't the only nonsportswriters here. When we started out with this series of books, we had the idea that each would be filled with the "best" writing done on any of these ball clubs. For the sake of providing a well-rounded perspective, however, we soon found we'd widened the strike zone to accommodate a full roster of athlete authors. We thought the Yankees led the majors in this category, but now we're sure it's the Dodgers. Even the unfortunate Mr. Roseboro, whose only claim to fame was having the temperamental Mr. Marichal whack him on the side of the head with a bat, put a book out.

If we lived in a litocracy, jocks would not be allowed to write (nor would movie stars or criminals for that matter) but we don't and they do. Sometimes it works; most times it doesn't. If a jock approaching his life story ever wants to get an idea of how bad he's going to look writing it, he ought to try to imagine Roger Angell or Tom Boswell wielding a forty-two-ounce bat against a Nolan Ryan fastball. Still, nothing's as appealing to the sales team of a New York publishing conglomerate than the life story of last year's twenty-three-year-old phenom. And if he's got a drug problem or wets the bed, all the better. So there's always going to be enough money around to lure almost anyone into foolishly exposing himself.

The very first chapter of Maury Wills's autobiography offers up the sordid details of his discovery that his girlfriend Judy was having an affair with Bump, his son, under Wills's own roof. Curious that. Here's a guy who can rightly be called the father of modern base stealing, a former MVP, a guy who was the key everyday player behind the great Dodger pitching staffs of the '60s, and the first thing he feels he has to tell us about is how he got cuckolded by his own kid. Like bad air, embarrassing celebrity confession has become a sign of our times.

The Dodger Reader passes over that chapter in Wills's life story in favor of Chapter 2, wherein Wills offers some truly unique insights on base stealing, a talent that he raised to an art form and that, in the end, is the only thing that really compels us to want to read about the life of Maury Wills.

Maybe the same wise editorial judgment should have prevailed over our choices here to include chapters on Steve Garvey's failing marriage and Bob Welch's climactic battle with alcoholism from their respective autobiographies. But it didn't. In Garvey's case, we found his plaintive retelling of how he and his former wife were sandbagged by *Inside Sport* magazine instructive in helping us understand why more and more athletes refuse to talk to the media. And in Welch's case, his insider's view on the debasing and debilitating effect of abusing oneself with alcohol is a cautionary tale worth repeating.

In addition to Wills, Welch, and Garvey, in this section you'll find excerpts from books by Don Drysdale, Leo Durocher, and Tommy Lasorda. For a Dodger story, Drysdale's is unusually full of braggadocio, almost Yankee-like. In surveying the Dodger lives that fill our bookshelves we've been struck by what a wounded bunch these Dodgers are — car crashes, arthritis, drug addiction, alcoholism, you name it. Yet no career- or attitude-altering miseries for Big D. He even manages to brush a high, hard one by revered former teammate Sandy Koufax. Leo the Lip may be more famous as a Cardinal or even a Cub than a Dodger, but we have a chapter here on Branch Rickey from Durocher's *Nice Guys Finish Last,* and although Rickey is truly one of the giants of the game, it was refreshing to find something on him that fell a little short of hagiography.

Our last entry is from Tommy Lasorda's book, *The Artful Dodger,* which comes damn close to being overlong. But Tommy gets the space for a number of reasons. First, it's pure Lasorda — the hype, the sentiment, the rah-rah. If you live in one of those cities where the ball club is managed by someone the sports pages tend to describe as taciturn, this reading will show you what you're missing. Second, if modern managing is 10 percent strategy and 90 percent therapy, then Lasorda is the master and this chapter shows why. A lot of rinky-dink teams have caught lightning in a bottle and won a world championship — like the '88 Dodgers. But no one has kept as many rinky-dink teams as competitive for as many years as Tommy Lasorda has.

Finally, the Dodger organization/family takes quite a few knocks in this book. It wasn't planned that way. It's just that the Dodgers, like the country they seem so perfectly to represent, have sold themselves so hard and high to the world that their shortcomings provide an irresistible target. Anyway, no club ever had a better spokesman than Tommy Lasorda, the preeminent company man of his time, so in our final pages we give the ball to the little lefty and leave it to him to single-handedly balance the scales. Go get 'em, Tommy.

Jimmy Cannon

Jackie Robinson's Precious Gift

Nobody Asked Me, But . . . : The World of Jimmy Cannon

There is no one I respect more in sports than Jackie Robinson. This was the loneliest man I've ever seen during his first season with the Dodgers. He will tell you how many people helped get him to the Hall of Fame. But this was a journey Robinson made all by himself.

The circumstances of his accomplishment created the bitter solitude. He was the first Negro to come into organized baseball and was unwanted by most of those connected with the game. It is for this that Robinson goes to Cooperstown tomorrow. He was a great player and belongs with the elite of the sport.

He is gray now and portly. But he moved with the old heavy-bodied agility as he walked around the desk of his office at the coffee firm where he is vice president. He has it all.

He has been honored by his sport; he holds a responsible and lucrative job with the Chock Full O'Nuts Corp.; his fame lasts; his marriage is a good one. He worked for all he has. But he is troubled by a sense of regret.

"I don't like my relationship with the Dodgers," said Robinson. "It all boils down to I'm a very good Branch Rickey man, and always will be. I never could figure it out, this animosity. I'll be truthful. I dig Walter O'Malley any chance I get. O'Malley doesn't like Mr. Rickey. He does it to me too. But he's too smart a man to do it publicly. This man has such charm and grace. I've had my difficulties with Walter Alston, but they were all ironed out."

He always thought he would finish at Brooklyn where he started.

"The last thing Alston told me was to keep in shape," Robinson said. "He needed me. Then I was sold to the Giants. I tell you how bad it is. The Dodger organization keeps no news of Jackie Robinson in the files. The Hall of Fame people told me not to blame them but they asked the Dodgers for some pictures of me to distribute and were told by the Dodgers they have none."

He would have played for the Giants except for a remark uttered by Buzzie Bavasi who runs the Dodgers.

"I was as close to Buzzie as a ballplayer can get to a general manager," Robinson said. "Basically, he's a fine man. But he hurt me very badly. I had made up my mind to quit and take this job after I was traded to the Giants.

"But the people here told me it would be all right with them if I played with the Giants. They said the public relations would be worth a lot. I wanted to play. Then Buzzie said something about my integrity.

"I forget exactly what it was. But it was something like: 'You'll find out Jackie's different than you pictured him.'

"In other words I hadn't meant it when I announced my retirement. I was only doing it to get money from the Giants. That's what I thought Buzzie meant. When I heard that, I decided not to play with the Giants. He kept me from playing ball another year. I didn't want to play into his hands."

There were many good days and a few bad ones. The best, Robinson believes, was the afternoon he testified before the House Un-American Activities Committee and eloquently discussed the Negro and Communism. The worst one was the evening in Milwaukee when his flung bat struck a spectator sitting above the Dodger dugout.

"It was raining," remembered Robinson. "The Braves had a four-run lead. I feigned anger. I was stalling. I wanted to get the game called. The bat was slippery. I held it too long. I wasn't trying to throw it into the stands but some people make it out that way."

In modern times there has never been a more passionate competitor than Robinson. He made every play as if it were a crucial one and ran just as hard on a ball hit back to the pitcher as he did on one that bounced off the fence.

"The greatest competitor in a clutch — Yogi Berra," Robinson said. "When it meant something Yogi always came through. He showed me something in 1955 when we beat the Yankees in the World Series. It was just as if he hadn't lost when he came into our clubhouse . . . laughing and joking.

"I remember going into the Giants' clubhouse when they beat us in the playoff. I really didn't feel it. But it was tradition. But Berra . . . he meant it."

"Who is the greatest player you've ever seen?" I asked.

"Joe DiMaggio," Robinson replied. "I once thought Willie Mays was going to be. The best pitcher? Ewell Blackwell. After that, Allie Reynolds. I didn't take a third strike often. I took three of them in one World Series when he was pitching.

"In my opinion, Charlie Dressen was the best manager. He was the same guy, win, lose or draw. Leo Durocher? He wasn't quite the same with a losing club. But give him a team a game and a half out of it . . . and he got the most out of them. But Dressen . . . he was great with any kind of a club."

The player whose friendship Robinson values the most is Pee Wee Reese.

"What a decent human Pee Wee is," Robinson said. "How much he helped me. But he refuses to take the credit."

The secretary said Jackie, Jr., was outside. He came in, rangy and shy. He plays first base in the Babe Ruth League.

"What do you hit?" I asked.

"Four hundred," he replied, slightly embarrassed.

"He can play," said Robinson, and not without pride.

Only the skills will count if Jackie Robinson, Jr., decides to be a ballplayer. No father ever gave a son a more precious gift. We are a better country because of it.

Leo Durocher with Ed Linn

Mr. Rickey

Nice Guys Finish Last

I wasn't exactly worried about losing my job when Branch Rickey replaced MacPhail. To my way of thinking, Mr. Rickey had sent me to Brooklyn from St. Louis so that I could become their manager, and so when I heard that he was coming over too, I thought to myself, "Oh boy, I'm in." My only concern, really, was whether I would be able to get as large a raise out of Rickey as I had expected to get from MacPhail. Mr. Rickey, as a lay preacher, was a virtuous man, and he rated thrift among the greater virtues.

I was still living in St. Louis. Mr. Rickey had a magnificent estate, Country Life Acres, just outside the city. He phoned me at four in the morning, something I was going to become used to, to invite me over for breakfast. Mr. Rickey was a ridiculously early riser, and he saw no reason why his manager shouldn't be up and working alongside him. Always it would be the same. The phone would ring, and his low, rumbling voice would be in my ear. "Hello. What are you doing?"

Invariably I'd say, "What do you think I'm doing? I'm bowling! I'm snowshoeing down the Alps. *I'm trying to sleep,* Mr. Rickey! It's still dark outside."

I had breakfast with the entire family and then accompanied the Old Man on a four-hour tour of his estate. We returned to the house, had lunch, and still not a word was spoken about baseball in general or my contract in particular.

And, I tell you, the more we didn't talk about it the more I began to worry. It was mid-afternoon before he got into baseball and then he told me bluntly that Charlie Dressen was not going to be rehired as a coach. "He's a gambler," Mr. Rickey said. "He's a horse player. He spends all his time out at the racetrack."

Well, I came out of that chair about three feet. "Hold it right there, Mr. Rickey," I said. "Why, you're taking my right arm away from me. Invaluable this man is to me."

Invaluable. Charlie Dressen was the best coach in the business. His sense of timing was so perfect that we had been able to develop a system of absolutely undetectable signs. Billy Herman and Pee Wee Reese, two of the smartest ballplayers who ever lived, once sat right in front of me, within touching distance, and told me they were going to catch them.

"Anything on?" I asked them within a minute.

"No," they said.

"Well," I said. "It happens that I just put the hit-and-run on."

They both threw up their hands and gave up.

All I had done was move my head a fraction of an inch to the right and let my eyes drift in the same direction. If I had moved my head to the left it would have been another sign; down, still another.

So I said to Mr. Rickey, "Every manager needs help and I'm no different. I need this man."

Mr. Rickey looked me right in the eye and said, "Who said you were the manager?"

I collapsed right back into the chair. *So long, Charlie.* Now, I was fighting for my own life.

Rickey had heard there was a great deal of gambling in our clubhouse and on the trains, that bookmakers and other undesirables had free access to the dressing room, and that I was not above sitting in on a friendly little poker game with the boys myself.

He asked me, straight out, whether his information was correct, and if I had lied I'm sure I would have been gone right there. We did have some lively games on the club. "Yes sir, Mr. Rickey." Lively enough so that you could win or lose a couple of hundred dollars without straining yourself. Of course, we'd had even livelier poker games on Rickey's own Gas House Gang when I was there. And I could name a few clubs today where the manager sets a sociable limit and the stakes go sky high as soon as his back is turned. Much of the glamorous life of a ballplayer is spent just killing time, and cards are as good a way as any to kill it.

I couldn't say that it had been done behind my back, though. I admitted quite readily that I could have held the stakes down and, just as readily, that I should have.

Nor could I deny that there might well have been some objectionable characters around the clubhouse. Ebbets Field was a small, intimate park with the special flavor of Brooklyn about it. Anybody could come into the clubhouse. The supposition was that you wouldn't be there unless you had good reason.

I promised Mr. Rickey the card games would come to an end — completely and absolutely — and that anybody he found objectionable would be barred from the clubhouse.

"Then you do want to manage this ball club?" he asked. Finally.

"Well, of course I do, Mr. Rickey. You know I do."

"The first thing I'm going to do," he said, "is cut your salary to twenty thousand dollars."

I was stunned. I had come looking for a raise and instead he was going to cut me fifteen grand. "For what?" I said. I reminded him forcefully that I had just completed two very successful seasons, winning the pennant and then finishing a very close second. Finishing second, we had won 104 games, enough to have won the pennant in all but a handful of previous years.

"You didn't let me finish," he said. "I am also going to put you in the position to make more money than any other manager in the history of the game."

The $20,000 was to be only the base salary. "If you draw half a million people, you'll get twenty-five thousand," he said. And slowly, mouthing the figures lovingly, he went right up the line, lifting my potential salary another $5,000 for every 100,000 additional people. "And if you draw one person over a million," he said to finish it off, "you will get fifty thousand dollars."

I tell you, my wheels were spinning: *Is it possible he's forgotten he's not in St. Louis anymore? Doesn't he know we've been drawing over a million in Brooklyn every year?*

To make certain there were no loopholes stuck in there anywhere, I made him repeat the offer all over again. Then I said, "Put it in writing." After it was down in black and white, I said, "Sign it."

That was my deal with Mr. Rickey. I made $50,000 every year I was with him. After the first two years we didn't even bother with the attendance clause.

I wasn't sure at first whether he had lost his mind, whether he thought that, with the war on, attendance had to drop, or whether he felt I needed some kind of special incentive to keep me in line. Like a piece of the action.

Before I left the farm that night, I had my answer. While we were discussing our personnel, Mr. Rickey paused over the name of one of our minor-league pitchers who had a reputation for being a real night rider. I didn't want any part of the guy. Rickey began to defend him, though, and suddenly he was saying: "Luke. Chapter Fifteen, verse eleven: 'A certain man had two sons . . .'" And, as I sat there, Mr. Rickey recited the parable of the Prodigal Son from beginning to end. Mr. Rickey, you must understand, was a biblical scholar. He could not only cite chapter and verse, he could tell you what page you could go to in your Bible.

I may not be a student of the Bible, but I didn't go to school just to eat my lunch either. I'd have had to be a fool not to know that he was talking about me, not some mediocre minor-league pitcher. Through our years together, Mr. Rickey recited the return of the Prodigal Son to me many, many times. Always in comment, ostensibly, about some other sinner or wastrel, but always at a time when I knew he looked on me as something less than the leading candidate for secretary of the YMCA.

But that was typical of Mr. Rickey, too. You had to know him to understand that he was a shy and, in certain ways, an indecisive man. Like most good men, he wanted other men to be better than they were. Unlike most good men, he found it unthinkable to intrude upon another man's private life. It would have been impossible for him, for instance, to come right out and say that he disapproved of sleeping with loose women on the Sabbath. Or even to allude to that kind of thing indirectly. Except for lecturing me about my debts and associations and exhorting me to become "more responsible," he never, in all our association, said one word to me *directly* about my other personal failings, which were, of course, enormous.

I knew he liked me. I knew he wanted the press and public to like me too; to see me not as brassy, opinionated and worthless, but as brassy, opinionated and worthwhile. If a majority of the press and public never quite came around to his way of thinking, I can't say that I blame them, because, frankly, I have never been able to understand what men like Rickey and Weil and Landis saw in me either. Or even why they put up with me.

Knowing as I did that it would take a major catastrophe to get me fired, I was able to take advantage of Branch in many ways.

There was, as an instance, the time I decided that there were better ways to spend a summer afternoon than going to Olean, a small town in upper New York, to play an exhibition game. At the last moment I told Dressen, who had been rehired a couple of months into the season, to take over the club. I said not a word to anybody else.

Now, I didn't *know* Branch was going to be there with his whole family. I found out later from Branch, Jr., that the Old Man fired me the moment he got into his car after the game and didn't rehire me again until he reached the approach to the George Washington Bridge.

The next day, Mr. Rickey dropped into my little office in the clubhouse. A little cubicle with a desk, a chair and a little two-seater divan. Rickey sat himself on the divan, I sat down on the step in front of the door. He just looked at me for a long time, the way he would, chewing on his cigar, to let me see that he was very disappointed in me again. As always, he started by way of Kansas City by delivering a lecture about responsibility, dependability and a few other essential qualities of a manager. At length he got down to the key question. "Where *were you* yesterday? *Why weren't you* at the exhibition game? *Where* did *you* go? *What did you* have to do that was so important?

Just as with Judge Landis, I was always afraid to lie to Branch Rickey because I was always sure he knew the answer before he asked the question. So I smiled my most winning smile and I said, "I went to the racetrack."

The words were hardly out of my mouth when he reached up with both hands, pulled his soft fedora down over his eyes and screamed, "*Judas Priest!*" With the hat still down over his eyes, he went barging right past me and out the door in a cloud of smoke. He didn't speak to me again for about two weeks.

No two men could have been more unlike than Larry Mac-Phail and Branch Rickey. Unlike MacPhail, who put a team together by patchwork, Rickey built his teams from the bottom up and built them to last. It was Rickey's Cardinals who had beaten us the previous season when his young team had jelled at mid-season, as Rickey teams had a way of doing, and won 37 out of their last 43 games. That was another hallmark of a Rickey team; they came on like gangbusters at the end.

The quality of his mind can best be demonstrated by the way he cornered the young talent after the United States got into World War II. Everybody else stopped signing kids. "They'll be going into the army," they said, "and who knows which ones will come back?" Rickey signed twice as many. "*Some* of them will be coming back," he said, "and we'll have them." The next year he was in Brooklyn doing the same thing. In 1946, the first postwar year, Brooklyn and St. Louis, the two teams he had built, battled each other into the first playoff series in baseball history. Unfortunately his old team beat his new one.

When it came to "putting a dollar sign on a muscle," as he liked to say, nobody could come close to him. When it came to trading his players "when they turned to money," as he also liked to say, he was in a class by himself. As a student of technique, he was simply unchallenged.

Our first training camp was at Sanford, Florida, and for one hour every morning Mr. Rickey would lecture on baseball fundamentals. How to field each position, the correct techniques for fingering a baseball and throwing it, for getting a lead off base, sliding. What it took to be a great hitter. Every phase of the game. On the second morning I hired a male stenographer, sat him down and told him not to miss a word. Other people gave instruction. Mr. Rickey *knew.*

The word was always out around St. Louis that Branch Rickey could have been governor if he had wanted to. For myself, I'd have felt perfectly safe if he had been running the country. He could have been a leader in politics, industry, anything; and he didn't care to involve himself in anything except baseball.

He didn't even care how he looked. Oh, every once in a while he'd come over to me at a banquet or something and ask where I had bought my suit. "That's beautiful," he'd sigh. "Just beautiful. Now why can't I look like that?"

"Forget it, Mr. Rickey," I'd tell him. "You could pay a thousand dollars for a suit and in twenty minutes you'd look like you fell out of bed."

Wearing clothes is as much a matter of attitude as of tailoring. You have to feel that clothes are important. Half the time he'd be at the park in an old pair of khaki pants and some beat-up loafers. Which was just as well. I've seen him come in looking as if he had just stepped out of a bandbox, and if he saw a good-looking kid warming up, he'd take his coat off and throw it right down in the dirt. The kid was what he was interested in. Ten seconds later he'd shout, "Jane Anne!" and his secretary, little Jane Anne Jones, would come down from the stands with her notebook to take down his running commentary. The first thing he'd do was to take the boy's complete history. Age, mother, father, sisters, brothers. His whole background. He'd work with him for an hour, an hour and a half, and if the kid showed anything at all, he could give you back his whole history any time the kid's name came up.

And yet, it's funny. Here you had the most brilliant baseball man who ever lived, and before he let the kid go a silly look would come over his face, he'd call the catcher in about 30 feet and — while I was trying not to groan outwardly — he'd say, "All right, Jane Anne, now we're going to give him the aptitude test."

Worst aptitude test you ever saw in your life. Let me ask you something. How many fellows can take a baseball and hold it against their shoulder with the palm cupped inward and then throw it, with their arm coming straight out and over, so that it will go 30 feet? I've seen some of the great ones try it and on the first attempt the ball will always go straight up in the air. Also the second, third and fourth. I'd say to myself, "Poor kids, they want to do it so bad, and there's no way."

The idea seemed to be to see whether they could adapt themselves to a wholly unnatural way of pitching. To me, that made it an aptitude test in reverse. The worse they did, the better the pitcher they were sure to become. Every once in a while he would find someone who could do it and he'd say, "Ahhhh, got a good mind. Good mind. He's all right. He can pass the aptitude test, he's all right."

I'd write the kid off immediately, and Branch would never forget him. We'd be going over the Class D rosters a couple of years later and he'd pause over a name and say, "Got a good mind. Father's a pressman, mother used to teach school. Two older sisters and a younger brother. He passed the aptitude test, he'll be all right. All he has to do is find himself a girl and get married."

Yeah, he had passed the aptitude test, and he was in Class D with a record of 3–7. If he finds himself a girl, I'd be thinking, she'd better have a good job.

As a trader of ballplayers he was simply without peer. Over and over, when he was operating with that great St.

Louis farm system, he'd throw two men at the other club, "Take your pick," and have it set up so they'd take the wrong one. You can still hear how he gave Pittsburgh their choice between Enos Slaughter and Johnny Rizzo, and Chicago their choice between Marty Marion and Bobby Sturgeon, and in both cases they picked the wrong one. It wasn't quite that simple, though, because it doesn't give either Rickey or the man on the other side of the table enough credit. Believe me, Rickey wasn't taking that kind of a chance of losing such great players as Slaughter and Marion.

Slaughter had been the best minor-league prospect to come along in years. But he was a left-handed hitter, and the Pirates were so overstocked with left-handed hitters, like the Waner Brothers, Arky Vaughan and Gus Suhr, that they had been seeing every left-handed pitcher in the league for years. The one thing they needed was a big right-handed bomb like Rizzo in the middle of their lineup. By throwing Slaughter into the pot — "Take your pick" — the Old Man was able to set a much higher price, and even upgrade Rizzo in Pittsburgh's mind. He was not only making it seem as if Rizzo was as valuable as Slaughter, but, really, that he was angling to save Rizzo for himself.

The Marion-Sturgeon choice was entirely different. The Cubs' great second-base combination, Billy Jurges and Billy Herman, had begun to slow up, and the Cubs had decided to break them up. They sure weren't going to trade Herman, and that meant they were looking for a young shortstop. They wanted Marion. Rickey, who had absolutely no intention of giving Marion up, set an all but prohibitive price on him, something like $150,000, but let them know they could have his other Triple A shortstop, Sturgeon, for $85,000. In the course of the conversation he confided to Pants Rowland, the Cubs' general manager, that the thinking in the Cardinals system was that Marion had been able to get away with playing such an excessively deep shortstop only because of the speed and agility of his second-baseman, a young man named Maurice Sturdy. Perhaps, Rickey suggested, Sturdy could do the same for Billy Jurges if the Cubs should decide to go with the young second-baseman and an aging shortstop, instead of the other way around. "Here's what I'll do for you," he said at last. "You can have either one of them for eighty-five thousand dollars. Sturgeon or Sturdy, take your pick."

Marion, the man they wanted, had been whisked out of sight. The choice he was giving them was between two other players. Now, Sturgeon and Sturdy weren't worth $85,000 if you put them together and threw in the team bus. It was only in comparison to the figure he had put on Marty Marion that the price didn't seem quite so outrageous.

That was always a favorite tactic with Rickey. Watch out when he threw out a string and pulled it back. If he had come to sell you a catcher, he would start by explaining why a second-baseman was going to solve all your problems. He would then hand you a list, price tags attached, of just about every second-baseman in his system. Starting at $200,000 for his best Triple A prospect and working all the way down to a giveaway $50,000 for some kid in Class C. The catcher's name is never going to be mentioned until you bring it up yourself. As, sooner or later, you will, because the catcher is who you want. Why else would Rickey have been there? At the first mention of his name, Rickey will either dismiss him with a contemptuous wave of his hand — "Not ready" — or give you what seems to be a valid reason why he has to hold onto him himself. (When he said, "Not ready," or even better, "I'm afraid I can't help you there; we're counting on him to fill our own needs very shortly" — *that* was the guy I always knew he was there to sell.) You're going to have to overcome all his arguments. And happily pay the price he has set after you have beaten him down and trapped him.

In Brooklyn, I sat in on several meetings with him when he dealt players, and what an education it was. During the war years we had a big, tall first-baseman, Howie Schultz, whom Rickey had bought from the minors for $52,000. He was exactly that, a wartime player. He was awkward and ungainly, but he could hit one every now and then and the thinking had been that he had to be more athletic than he looked because he had been a basketball player in college.

Lou Perini wanted him up in Boston, where they were in dire need of a first-baseman. And I couldn't believe my ears. For three hours, Mr. Rickey undersold this boy to Perini and his general manager, John Quinn. I want to tell you, the tears were streaming down my eyes. It made you cry to listen to this man talk. He didn't want to stick Boston with him. The boy couldn't field, couldn't hit, couldn't get out of his own way. The more he ran Schultz down, the more Perini's tongue hung out. When finally he couldn't stand it any longer, he jumped up and said, "Branch! Put a *price* on the man. I *want* him."

Mr. Rickey bit down on his cigar and said, "One hundred twenty-five thousand dollars."

Perini fell right back on the sofa. Ten minutes later they were out the door of the suite. Gone. I looked at Branch and I said, almost shocked, "Branch . . . how could you do that? I know you want to get rid of the fellow. You know you wanted to sell him. What are you doing, Branch?"

And he just bit down harder on his cigar and spat three words out: "They'll be back."

They were.

Howie was a wonderful kid, but he couldn't get all his coordination together.

It is well to keep the very special relationship between Mr. Rickey and myself in mind, as well as the man's genius for maneuvering, as background to the most critical period of my life: the eighteen-month period in which I was married to Laraine Day, suspended from baseball and transferred — through Rickey's sleight of hand — to our mortal enemies, the New York Giants.

Brendan C. Boyd and Fred C. Harris

From *The Great American Baseball Card Flipping, Trading and Bubble Gum Book*

Ralph Branca/Bobby Thomson

Is there anyone who doesn't know that Ralph Branca threw Bobby Thomson the home run ball that won the pennant for the Giants and lost it for the Dodgers in 1951? It is curious how a chance, two-minute encounter on a motley overgrown playing field in the hazy late September sun can wed two men more or less permanently in the collective consciousness of a nation. It is further curious that Thomson, a mediocre outfielder at best throughout his entire major league career, should emerge the hero of this encounter, and Branca, an excellent pitcher for the Dodgers for many years, the goat. But no matter what these two might have accomplished before or since, that is all anybody is ever going to remember them for. I have it on good authority, incidentally, that Branca, who took his misfortune particularly hard at the time — as who among us would not — is now rather happy that the whole thing transpired, as it affords him the opportunity to demand exorbitant speaking fees at numerous public functions in and around the greater New York area.

I doubt it.

John Roseboro

Some more funny-things-you-can-do-with-Louisville-sluggers department.

On August 22, 1965, Juan Marichal, the Giants' star pitcher, efficiently and unexpectedly cold-cocked John Roseboro, the Dodgers' star catcher, with his 36-ounce white ash Adirondack. For this "unprovoked and obnoxious" assault Marichal was fined $1,750, suspended for nine days, and made to write fifty times on the blackboard in Warren Giles' office, "I will never again attempt to rearrange a fellow player's hair style without first obtaining that player's permission." Roseboro, for his part, from that time forward wore the peculiarly eye-popping, air-sucking, and perpetually astonished expression he displays for you here in this photograph.

Whoooooooooooeeeeeeeeeeeeeeeeeee.

Billy Loes

Billy Loes never would have gotten into the majors at all if they could have found someone to sign papers on him. He is to my knowledge the only ballplayer in the history of the National League ever to have lost a ground ball in the sun. What, if anything, do you think is going through his mind in this picture? Never mind, never mind. I don't want to know.

PETE REISER

Harold Pete Reiser

"SANDY" KOUFAX   *pitcher* BROOKLYN DODGERS

Pete Reiser

Pete Reiser made a career out of being injured. By far his favorite way of hurting himself was to run headlong into a concrete outfield fence at full speed in a futile attempt to catch a hopelessly uncatchable fly ball. Of course if an opportunity to employ this particular gambit was not immediately forthcoming, he could easily make do with sliding into third base and breaking his ankle. I had heard it said, in fact, concerning his masochistic proclivities, that on days when there was no game scheduled for Pete's particular team of the moment he would cheerfully pass the time in his hotel room by dropping large objects from great heights onto his toes. There is a little bit of this in most major league outfielders — Jim Piersall, Elmer Valo, and Ken Berry, to name a few examples — but in Reiser's case these overt self-destructive tendencies very nearly constituted a mania. The hardcore Brooklyn Dodger fans were great appreciators of this kind of frolicsome morbidity, however, and Pistol Pete was a great favorite in Flatbush.

Break Da Bum Up!

Sandy Koufax

This is Sandy Koufax's Bar Mitzvah picture. The uniform was a present from his grandmother.

Depressing Statistics

The most depressing of many depressing statistics in the annals of baseball's lengthy history belongs to one James Thomas Garry, a right-handed pitcher from Great Barrington, Massachusetts, who in his lone appearance in a major league uniform in 1893 pitched one inning for the Boston Nationals, gave up 5 hits, 4 walks, 7 runs, and took the loss. For this singularly iniquitous transgression Mr. Garry took with him to his cold and lonely grave a major league ERA of 63.00.

63.00!

The second most depressing statistic in the history of the sport belongs to Doug Camilli, the son of the great National League first baseman Dolf Camilli and certainly one of the weakest hitting catchers ever to don the tools of ignorance, in this era or any other. In eight major league seasons, five with the Los Angeles Dodgers and three with the Washington Senators, the junior Camilli had a grand total of 18 home runs, 80 RBIs, and a corporate batting average of .199.

That's .199.

Not .200.

.199.

Think about that for a few minutes should you be trying to get yourself up for committing suicide.

Gino Cimoli
Gino Cimoli was the
Italian Ossie Chavarria.

Cal Abrams
Cal Abrams was the
Jewish Gino Cimoli.

Sandy Amoros

Sandy Amoros was a member of the second-to-last generation of excellent black ballplayers exported to the United
States from Cuba after the end of the Second World War. He
was a speedy, heady, solid outfielder, who helped anchor the
numerous Dodger pennant winners of the fifties and early
sixties. He made front-page headlines in 1955 when his
spectacular catch of a Yogi Berra line drive helped win the
World Series for Brooklyn and, again in 1970, when he was
discovered penniless and unemployed, applying for family
assistance in an upper Manhattan welfare office. This is an
indication of how far the mighty can fall in this country if
they are black, unskilled, not particularly thrifty, come from
Cuba, or have at one time or another worked for Walter
O'Malley.

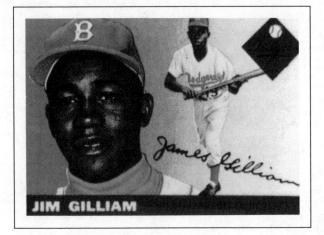

Jim Gilliam

Junior Gilliam stepped in at second base in his rookie season with the Brooklyn Dodgers, 1953, when that team was in its prime, or maybe just passing it. His exceptional speed turned doubles into triples, and he led the league in triples his first year. He was always among the stolen base leaders, and was agile and effective as an infielder over the course of a 14-year career.

I See the
Boys of Summer
in Their Ruin
Lay the
Golden Tithings
Barren

Roy Campanella

Billy Cox

I see the
boys of summer
in their ruin
lay the
golden tithings
barren.

Carl Furillo

Joe Black

Don Drysdale and Bob Verdi

Was I Mean? Well . . .

Once a Bum, Always a Dodger

When I was playing, I was forever hearing about what an ogre I was, forever reading remarks like the one from Pittsburgh's outstanding shortstop, Dick Groat: "Going to bat against Drysdale is like going to a dentist appointment."

And now that I'm damn near a senior citizen, I still hear it. Charlie Fox, a veteran baseball man, recently came up to my wife, Annie, and said with a big smile on his face, "Oooh, you should have seen your husband when he was in his prime . . . was he ever a mean bastard!"

That sort of talk still amazes me, not because I'm unaware of my reputation, but because I never thought much of it when I was earning it. I'm not trying to play dumb or naive here, because it's a fact. When I pitched, there were any number of guys who wouldn't think twice about knocking a batter on his ass. You want mean? Nobody was meaner than Bob Gibson of the Cardinals. Sam Jones was no prince, same with Larry Jackson and practically every guy on the great Milwaukee staff of the late fifties — Lew Burdette, Warren Spahn, and Bob Buhl. And Vern Law of the Pirates? The man they called "The Deacon"? He'd have gladly drilled you. It just depended on what mood he was in, or what the game situation was.

So, I didn't exactly feel like a lone wolf out there on the mound when I took the position that I didn't give a damn what happened, as long as I got the job done. There are two little categories in the box scores you see in the morning papers. One is "WP" for winning pitcher, the other "LP" for losing pitcher. There's a hell of a difference between the two and my attitude was, you do everything possible to get the win, everything possible to get that edge, everything legal. Sometimes, I even crossed that line and did a few things that weren't legal. No big deal.

I was called "intimidating," and I wasn't about to dispute that. I never talked about my reputation, but I was very much at peace having others talk about it. Baseball then was a game of intimidation, and if opposing batters figured you were going to throw the ball inside at 94 miles an hour on a day when you didn't feel like you could break a pane of glass, fine. Let 'em think that way. Perfect. I always believed that it was them or us, and nothing was going to stand in my way. Take no prisoners, and if you were going to lose, take down the son-of-a-bitch who beat you, too. Make him feel the cost of victory. That was the Sal Maglie philosophy, and it was good enough for me. I was making a good living playing baseball, more money than I ever thought possible. I liked what I was doing too much to let any guy with a bat in his hand take it away from me.

I wasn't one of those guys who woke up mad on the day I pitched. I wasn't a bear around the house or anything like that. I didn't wake up in a bad mood, growling at my wife. I think if you dwell on a game all day, you can become mentally whipped. I might have started thinking about it when I drove to the ballpark for a home game, and relaxed in the hotel on the road. But when I got to the ballpark, which was my office, and put that uniform on, I guess I worked myself into a frenzy. I had a pretty good temper — and still do on occasion — but I basically kept my red-ass personality at the ballpark. It all locked in when you saw that first batter staring out at you from the plate. Then, after the game, it was over. That's how I developed that "Jekyll-Hyde" label as a guy who was an SOB on the mound, but a pretty decent drinking companion afterward. As the old saw goes, I was the same guy who would "brush back his grandmother" to win a game one minute, and then sing songs at a baseball writers' banquet the next — as I did at the 1963 affair in Hollywood. My assignment was, "One Love," "Give Her Love," and "Secret Love." See that? All love and kisses.

Of course, I do have this record of leading all National League modern-day pitchers in hit batsmen, 154 in fourteen years. That mark is still alive. In 1959, I hit 18 batters, the most for one pitcher in the National League since 1915. Overall, though, Walter Johnson has me beat in the American League by a bunch. He had 206 in his career. But he pitched for a lot longer than I did, and during a different era. Yet, for all those batters I nailed, I can honestly say that I never tried to hurt any of them, never tried to hit any of them in the head — never tried to hit any of them, period. Of those 154 victims, I'd say I wanted to knock down only 15. To only 15 of them was I trying to deliver a little message.

Also, for all my reputation, I got into only one real fight — the brawl I mentioned earlier with Johnny Logan and the Braves in 1957 — and that happened because I dinged Logan with a pickoff throw at first base, not a pitch. I got suspended just once, after an incident involving Cincinnati's Frank Robinson in 1961 at the LA Coliseum. Frank was a great hitter, who actually changed his stance after his first year by moving up on the plate and closing his feet. On this particular day, I pitched him inside and he went down. Dusty Boggess, the plate umpire, came out to warn me.

"Shit, Dusty," I said. "What do you want me to do? Lay the ball right down the middle so he can beat my brains in?"

I came right back and threw another pitch inside, and down Frank went again. This time, the ball hit Robinson, and Boggess immediately threw me out of the game. I was suspended for five days by Warren Giles, the National League president, and fined $100. I wasn't too happy about it, and neither was Buzzie Bavasi, our general manager. But there was nothing we could do, except to try to point out how ridiculous it all was. I mean, pitchers all over baseball were hitting batters without being ejected or suspended, but I guess that might have been one case where my reputation hurt me instead of helped me.

So I owed the National League $100 and the next time we went into Cincinnati, I decided to pay my debt in person. I went to a bank and got $100 worth of pennies in those rolls, emptied them out, then put all the loose coins in a sack, and delivered them to Mr. Giles's office at the league headquarters in Carew Tower. I dumped the sack on his secretary's desk, she gave me this little smile, and I took off in a hurry. I was pretty proud of myself when I headed back to my hotel room, but I wasn't there too long before the phone rang. It was Mr. Giles's secretary.

"Mr. Giles would like to see you," she said.

I went back to the office and had a bit of a conversation with Mr. Giles. He told me to be careful about the way I was pitching, and I told him that I wasn't going to change my philosophy of keeping batters off the plate. It was all very amiable.

"And by the way," Mr. Giles added, "I want you to take those pennies of yours and roll them back up for me."

Fortunately, I had the paper rolls back in my room. I took the sack back to the hotel, and sat there for hours, putting the damn pennies in their containers, cursing all the way. Thank God I saved those containers or I would still be back in that Cincinnati hotel, rolling up $100 worth of pennies.

My first official warning had occurred a year earlier in San Francisco against the Giants. I came inside on Willie Mays, and he went down. That wasn't unusual for Willie. He went down often. He didn't do it to be a showboat. That was just his style. Some people pass another automobile on the highway by ten inches; other people want to be on the safe side, so they pass it by ten feet. Willie wanted to be on the safe side, although umpire Frank Secory came after me.

"Watch it," he said. "Don't be coming inside like that."

With that warning, I was automatically fined fifty dollars, according to the rules. I didn't care about the money.

"What the hell are you talking about?" I asked. "Jesus Christ, you're a former pitcher. Can't you tell when I'm throwing at somebody and when I'm not?"

"You're throwing at Mays and cut it out," he came back. "That'll be fifty bucks."

"Well, screw you," I said. "You better make it a hundred, because this next pitch is going in the same goddamn place."

I threw the next pitch inside — same spot — and Mays stepped back and fouled it off. That proved my point. I looked in at Secory and just raised my arms, as if to say, "Well, was I trying to hit him there?" I never did pay that fine.

Later that season, I had another episode with umpire Stan Landes. I threw a pitch that hit Joe Cunningham of the Cardinals in the right elbow. This was in the third inning of a game at the Coliseum; Cunningham, who was on a real tear at the time, had hit a home run off me in the first. When Cunningham went down, Solly Hemus, the St. Louis manager, came onto the field like he wanted to punch me out. I don't know if you remember Solly Hemus, but he was at least thirty pounds lighter and nine inches shorter than me.

Anyway, Landes came out and had a little discussion with me.

"You better look out where you're throwing that ball," he said. "That's a warning."

"Well, you can take that warning and stick it up your ass," I snapped. "You're standing there telling me what I was thinking, that I wanted to hit the batter. How do you know what he's thinking? Was he looking for a pitch outside and did he just step into a pitch that was inside? Cunningham's one of the toughest guys in the league to pitch to because he does that all the time. He steps into the plate. If you're so smart, find out what he was thinking. Did you ask him where he was looking for the pitch?"

"I don't have to ask anybody anything," Landes said.

"Well, I'll tell you what," I told him. "If you fine me, I'll get a lawyer and I'll sue your ass over this stupid rule and I'll sue the entire National League. How can you tell me what I was thinking, what my intent was?"

I was never fined there, either. I can only guess that Landes, like Secory, realized that I had a good argument.

In 1962, it was Drysdale against the Cardinals again in another controversy. In the sixth inning of a game at the Coliseum, I was the runner at first base. Maury Wills was up and he hit a chopper toward the third-base line. Kenny Boyer, their third baseman, was cheating in. He was a heck of a good fielder, mobile and quick, and he grabbed the ball and threw to Julian Javier at second base to force me. As I went into the bag, I made a pretty good hook slide and I flipped Javier. Nothing serious. I was within my rights. I was trying to break up a double play, fair and square. I wasn't trying to hurt Javier or spike him.

Well, as it turned out, the play was ruled a foul ball. Boyer had picked it up and made the throw, following his instincts as a player should. You continue the play and worry about whether it's fair or foul later.

I returned to first base, and on his next swing, Wills slapped a ground ball to shortstop Dal Maxvill, who tossed it to Javier, again for the force out on me. Javier had a lot more time this time, though, and after he wheeled to relay to first base, I could see that he had other things on his mind than the double play. He backed off the bag and aimed the ball directly at me. I was well on the outside of the basepath, knowing I was already out, and Javier's throw wound up hitting the auxiliary scoreboard in short right field — eighty feet from the bag, and in foul territory. He'd had no idea whatsoever of throwing to first base. He wanted to hit me in the head, and if I hadn't ducked, he would have. I said nothing to him. I got up and went to the dugout.

One inning later, it was my turn. Javier came to bat, and I threw a high, inside fastball right at his chin. He went down like he'd been shot by a cannon, his helmet flying one way, his glasses going up in the air. When he got up, it looked like he'd been in a flour sack. He was filthy. He'd had his shot, and I'd had mine. I just looked at Javier, waiting to see if he had any notion of coming after me with the bat.

Johnny Keane, the Cardinals' manager, was livid. He said afterward that I'd deliberately attempted to injure Javier on the play at second base, and then compounded my felony by deliberately throwing at Javier. At least Keane was right on one count — the latter. Keane went on to say that if I denied that I was guilty on both accusations, I was a liar. Then he issued a challenge, saying that the Cardinals would retaliate against me, sooner or later.

"If they do," I said, "they better make sure they take me out of the park on a stretcher. Because if they don't, if I'm just wounded, I'll take out every one of those sons-of-bitches."

There's one important point here. I didn't hit Javier, nor did I want to. That was part of my philosophy, and it evolved partly from discussions with Maglie years before. If you wanted to brush a batter back or knock a guy down, the place to throw the ball was at his head. A batter would always see the ball that way, and be able to duck. The ball came in at eye level, and it wasn't all that difficult to avoid getting hit. I speak from experience, because I was a batter, too, and with my reputation for being a mean bastard, I faced my share of skin-bracers from other pitchers. But I knew I wouldn't get hit in the head for the same reason — I knew I could see the ball and get out of the way in time. The rest of my body, I didn't really care about. The worst thing that could happen was that you'd suffer a broken bone somewhere. I was fortunate to have a pretty high tolerance for pain. I played with cracked ribs, I had the shingles and I pitched. I was an animal and I expected everybody else to be like me.

So that was one part of my pitching plan. If you really wanted to hit a guy, don't throw at his head. If you did want to hit him, the best place to throw was down and behind him. Whenever a batter sees a wild one coming his way, the natural instinct is to back up. If you throw the ball behind a guy, chances are he'll back right into it. That's just the way it was, and still is.

I also had the belief, as did Maglie, that for every one of my teammates who went down, two players from the other team would go down. Or, if two Dodgers were knocked down when I was pitching, four opponents would bite the dust. I thought that was a nice, orderly way of doing things. I never really talked to my teammates about this little arrangement of mine, but I suspect they appreciated it. When I was on the mound, the Dodgers knew that they were going to be protected. I got some terrific support from Dodger hitters through the years, and some great defensive plays behind me, and I have no doubt it had something to do with the fact that my teammates knew I was behind them until the end. You'd have to ask my teammates about their inner thoughts when I was on the mound. I did see a quote here and there that would lead me to believe they felt good about my presence.

Don't get me wrong. The Dodgers always put out hard for whoever was pitching, but I think they were dead sure I wasn't going to let any opposing pitcher take shots at them without a reply from me.

I didn't like to save my retaliation pitches for the lousy hitters, either. If I felt moved to knock down the opposing pitcher, I would. But that was only one. I still had another to go, and I preferred to hold that one for a big guy in the lineup. If I didn't use one brushback on the other pitcher, then I had two to play with. And if the other team wasn't aware of my addition, that would keep them on edge. Depending on what the situation was, I might wait or I might go right at them. It was like Russian roulette, but the general rule of thumb was, hit 'em where it hurts. Don't waste your time with a guy who isn't hitting his weight unless you really have a good reason.

I remember an exhibition game we played against the Pirates in the Bahamas. We were playing on a cricket field to a big crowd. The people there loved the Dodgers, not only because we were a good ballclub but because we had that history of having black players, starting with Jackie Robinson. On this particular day, though, the fans' loyalties were divided because the Pittsburgh pitcher was Alvin McBean, who was a native son. He was from the Bahamas, and I was pitching against him.

Well, damn if Bob Bailey didn't hit a home run for us just before I came up to bat. And damn if McBean didn't throw a pitch that hit me right in the butt. Now, I'd been thrown at a fair bit during my career, but in an exhibition game? I had trouble figuring it out, except that McBean obviously was pissed and probably embarrassed. There he was, having a tough afternoon in front of his countrymen. I didn't say anything. I tossed the bat aside and took first base.

What the hell is going on here? I thought to myself. Here we are in a nothing game, and this guy hits me in the ass. Well, if he wants to play by those rules, so will we.

The thought of a civil war or a riot never occurred to me. The only thing I went over in my mind while I was standing at first base was, Who's coming up for them in the next inning? Sure enough, McBean came up with a couple men on base. The Pirates sent him up there to bunt, and it's a good thing he got his bat on the ball, because if he hadn't managed to sacrifice successfully, the pitch would have hit him right between the eyes. I give him credit. I didn't bother throwing at another member of the Pirates to satisfy my quota of two that day because, after all, it was only an exhibition game. Regular season addition didn't apply.

I can't honestly say that the Pittsburgh incident was my only scrape in an exhibition game. There was another one in Vero Beach in 1961 against the Minnesota Twins. Zoilo Versalles hit a home run off me and on an 0–2 pitch to the next batter, I decked Lennie Green. I got a warning from umpire Nestor Chylak, who didn't even know me. He worked in the American League. There was no immediate trouble, but a couple innings later, we met again. I was at the plate waiting to make the tag, and Green was trying to score. I saw Green raise his leg as if to spike me.

"You cock that leg and I'll rip it off," I told him.

Green then had a few choice words for me, and we went at each other. In a matter of seconds, both benches emptied and we had a fine old time. Buzzie had a brief talk with me, and so did Alston. He told me that I was of more value to the club on the mound than I was in the clubhouse. He told me to watch my legendary temper because, the more of these things I got involved in, the greater the chances I had of getting hurt. I wasn't ejected from the game, but I was taken out by Walt himself. Just another shiny day in the Grapefruit League.

Now, let me get another point across here. Some of the best and most effective brushback pitches I ever threw were never intended to be brushbacks. They just happened. The way I threw, with that sidearm motion and the action on the ball, meant that my pitches just naturally ran in on right-handed batters. If you crossed the plate and I aimed a ball toward the inner half, chances are you were either going to have to bail out in a hurry or be hit. I'll never forget the time I hit Ernie Banks with a pitch in Wrigley Field. Doing that in Chicago was trouble, because Ernie was so popular. Hitting him with a pitch was worse than hitting the Pope. But Ernie never made a big thing about it.

"I was looking for a ball away, and his pitch came in on me," Ernie said. "Drysdale wasn't trying to hit me."

And that was that. Instances like that were inevitable. I must have plunked Carl Sawatski on the back of his left knee five times. Sawatski was a pretty good-hitting left-handed catcher. When one of my pitches came in on him, he had the habit of getting his right, or front, leg out of the way in time. But his left leg was planted, and bingo — he'd get nicked. Then there were batters who just froze when they saw a ball coming at them. Our own Carl Furillo was one, and so was Don Zimmer. For some reason, they just didn't react. I was petrified when I had to pitch to Zimmer after he was traded away from the Dodgers. Not only because he was my friend and because he had already been seriously beaned twice in his career. But because he just stood over the plate and stayed there, no matter where the ball was headed. That's probably why he was hit twice in the head, because he had the habit of freezing.

Not all of my brushback attempts were prompted by actions of opposing pitchers or players in the game. Every so often when I was on the mound, I heard guys from the other dugout yelling things at me. They might have figured they could remain anonymous, but I had a knack of sneaking a look to find out who was doing the yapping. Lots of times, it was a guy who wasn't in the game. I didn't think that was too brave and I didn't care for it, so every once in a while, I took it out on a guy who was in the game. That was the only way to stop the music. What was I going to do? Throw a high, hard one into the dugout?

Also, of course, there were occasions when I felt I had to take care of some personal business. In 1968, before the All-Star Game in the Houston Astrodome, Tom Haller, who was our catcher with the Dodgers, happened to be in the National League locker room when he caught Rusty Staub poking through my shaving kit. Staub was an All-Star from the Astros, a member of my own team that day. But there he was, messing with my shaving kit. I don't imagine that he was looking for a spare razor, either. He wanted to check on whether I was carrying any foreign substances around. I didn't appreciate Haller's report on the invasion of my privacy, but again, I had my chance to deliver a message later in the season.

In a game against the Astros, Staub came up to bat and I sent him sprawling.

"That's for looking through my goddamn shaving kit," I yelled at him. Rusty never said a word.

I never did have much fun pitching in the Astrodome to begin with. They had this huge electric scoreboard in the outfield, and whenever something big happened — like an Astro hitting a home run — this damn thing would show a long and loud cartoon with whistles and horns blowing and animals running across the screen. It you're a pitcher who's just given up a run, the last thing you want is to stand there and watch this crap with your ears ringing, but you had to wait until the damn thing was over. I don't remember the date or the individual, but I do recall taking out my anger one game on the Houston batter. Whoever it was just looked at me like I was crazy, and I explained myself from sixty feet, six inches away.

"Tell them to cut that friggin' cartoon short," I yelled.

I didn't have any great or novel theories about how to win games in the big leagues. I suppose I thought like most other pitchers. If you were going to get beat, get beat by the good hitters, not the .220 ones. Keep the Punch-and-Judy guys off the bases, so the Henry Aarons and Frank Robinsons and Willie Mayses wouldn't be able to hurt you too badly. You knew the great hitters would get their share of hits. Aaron hit 17 home runs off me, which sounds like a lot, but considering all the times I faced the Braves, it's not all that bad. Mays and I had some memorable confrontations. When he went down after one of my pitches in San Francisco, the place got up in arms. They booed me for hours. When I kept him off the plate in Los Angeles, naturally, I was cheered. I never worried too much about getting batters mad — about waking sleeping giants, so to speak — although if there was one guy who seemed to hit better when he was angry, I'd nominate Frank Robinson. He seemed to make better contact than the rest when he was boiling. On days when I wasn't going well, of course, it seemed like the good hitters were hitting out of order. It seemed like they were up there every third guy.

I don't see all the pitchers in the major leagues, but the only one I can think of offhand who reminds me of some of the guys like myself twenty years ago is Roger Clemens of the Boston Red Sox. He throws hard and he throws inside and if you happen to get in the way, well, your ass is on the ground. He's a hell of a competitor, Clemens is. I think he would fit right in during the fifties and sixties when so many of those games were like sparring matches.

In my current job as a broadcaster, I can pick out probably nine of ten times when a pitcher is trying to hit a batter or brush him back. You can just sense it. But there aren't that many occasions when it happens anymore. There are lots of games when you figure somebody has to go down, but nobody does. Pitchers just get themselves into jams and stand out there getting the living crap beat out of them. It's like banging your thumb with a hammer. It's amazing to me how some of these guys get tarred and feathered in broad daylight without even attempting to back hitters off the plate, but that's the way it is. Sooner or later, you have to declare yourself and say, it's my ball and half the plate is mine. That's the way I pitched, only I never let on which half of the plate I wanted. If I took the half of the plate that a batter was claiming, then there was a hell of a chance of a collision. That's why I've always said, show me a guy who doesn't want to pitch inside and I'll show you a loser.

I have to laugh at people who criticize Sandy Koufax for being too perfect, for never throwing inside with the Dodgers. Nothing could be further from the truth, and if you don't believe me, talk to Lou Brock. He'll tell you about the night he got a walk from Koufax, then stole second and third, and scored on a sacrifice fly. The Cardinals got a run without a hit and Sandy was irate. I was sitting in the dugout with Jim Lefebvre who had just come up to the ballclub.

"Frenchy," I said, "I feel sorry for that man about what he just did."

"Who?" he asked.

"Brock," I said. "Sandy doesn't appreciate that sort of thing. Sandy gets mad enough when you beat him with base hits. But when you score runs without hits, look out."

Sure enough, the next time Brock came up, Koufax drilled him in the back with a fastball. You could hear the thud all over the stadium. Brock went down like he was a deer who'd been shot. He got up and trotted toward first base, not rubbing, pretending he wasn't hurt. But he never made it. Brock just collapsed and they had to carry him off on a stretcher.

"Goddamn!" Lefebvre said. "How about that!!"

How about that! Way to go, Sandy.

I don't remember exactly when I got this label as a "headhunter." It might have been when a magazine writer from Santa Barbara did a story on me one day, took a few liberties, and they stuck a headline on the thing making me sound like a combination of Frankenstein and Dracula. Then there were those remarks from other ballclubs branding me as the "meanest pitcher in either league." I never paid much attention to all the ink, and I never, ever talked about it. I let other people have their say, and every once in a while, my reputation rose up and bit me. When I came out of a hotel or a stadium and a bunch of kids wanting autographs would ask me how many batters I'd hit that day or that season, I wasn't too thrilled about this neon sign I was carrying around on my back. But I knew I wasn't doing anything vicious. I didn't hate opposing batters. I just wanted to win, and brushing them back seemed to be the professional way to do it.

No doubt my physical stature helped me intimidate batters, if that indeed is what I did. I was tall and lanky and all arms. Also, the angle the ball came from was unusual. There weren't many pitchers delivering the ball by way of third base or left field. I'm sure that kept a few guys loose. I know this. The Braves had a guy, Gene Conley, who looked a lot like me. He was a basketball player with the Boston Celtics, so he had some real height on him. I liked to hit and I took pride in it, but I never thought of stepping in there against Conley as a day at the beach. He looked like an octopus out there. You didn't know where the ball was coming from or where it was going and Gene had a bit of an ornery streak in him, too.

But I was never such a villain that I ever attempted to maim an opposing batter. There's a big difference between brushing back a hitter and trying to hit him. There's all the difference in the world. And I wasn't interested in ending anybody's career. I just wanted to keep my own going. I wanted to win in the worst way; I did not want to ship the other guys off to a hospital. I'd prefer to think of myself as one of those players you love to have on your team but hate to have on the other team. And as much as I was blasted during the years, I would hope that opponents realized that I was nothing more and nothing less than a competitor trying to do his job. I think I was respected for being that and, hell, guys who ran into me off the field might even have learned to like me.

I'm sure a lot of critics were flabbergasted when they discovered that I'd applied to be a public relations man with the Meadow Gold Dairies during the off-season early in my career. My first interview was with W. A. (Bill) Hutchinson, who was general manager of the company.

"When I met you, Don," Hutchinson was quoted as saying,

"I couldn't help thinking how amazed I was to find you such a gentle, polite young man."

"What did you expect?" I asked. "A convict?"

All I wanted to do as a pitcher with the Dodgers was win, and everything worked out well. In fact, when I was voted into the baseball Hall of Fame in Cooperstown, New York, in 1984, I read the inscription engraved on my plaque. It stated all the particulars — how many games I'd won, how many shutouts I'd pitched, how many batters I'd struck out, and so forth.

But it also said that one of the reasons I'd survived was because I was "intimidating." I guess I was.

Thomas Boswell

Koufax: Passing the Art Along

How Life Imitates the World Series

None of the greats of baseball retired as young as Sandy Koufax, and perhaps none retired so well.

No one else in the Hall of Fame disappeared from the game so quickly. For thirteen years, he wandered from the coast of California to the coast of Maine, disappearing from public view for years at a time.

"I wasn't looking for anything . . . just looking for time," Koufax said. "It was a mindless period to do what I wanted to do and go where I wanted to go. I decided to take a few years for myself . . . I wanted to see how long I could stretch it."

After he had been out of the major leagues one year longer than the dozen seasons he was in them, Koufax quietly reappeared in a corner of the Los Angeles Dodgers clubhouse as a low-profile pitching coach, one of three such coaches in the Dodger organization.

Mr. K., the man who many say was, at his peak, the most overwhelming pitcher in the history of baseball, sits on a pedaling machine in the Dodgers' weight-lifting room. Cap tilted back, he looks as delighted as a bat boy to join in the big league banter.

Koufax has come home.

He wears the old number — 32 — and, if anything, is a

few pounds trimmer than his playing weight in 1966 when he shocked his entire profession by hanging up his spikes at age thirty. "That's right," he says, with a wry and enigmatic smile, "thirty."

Koufax's hair is a distinguished pepper and salt. He is tan and utterly at ease. Like Joe DiMaggio, he has, with age, gone from movie-star handsome to some higher plateau.

"Hey, Sandy," said Dodger Manager Tommy Lasorda, "you're gonna pitch for us coaches in the charity game against the media men today, right?"

"I guess I'll be there," said Koufax, just as he did before Walter Alston handed him the ball to start the World Series.

"I knew it," said Lasorda, glowing, his mousetrap all set. "That's why all them newspaper guys are lined up outside with bats."

Koufax is too delighted to be the butt of such a ridiculous joke to offer any retort. Everybody hits Sandy Koufax these days — the scrubs in batting practice, the paunchy L.A. reporters.

When Koufax stepped off the mound after the '66 Series, he had won 27 games with a 1.73 ERA. He had been baseball's Player of the Year for four consecutive years. He was not at the peak of his game: He was somewhere above it.

So, he will be remembered forever that way. "He could step on the mound and win today," said veteran Don Sutton.

Retirement is baseball's cruelest joke. What player has truly survived it without a sense of erosion? Willie Mays does not wear his bald spot well, nor Hank Aaron his spare tire. Mickey Mantle is a pulpy Oklahoma good ol' boy.

"Ted Williams, Joe DiMaggio, and Sandy," said Dodger Steve Garvey. "They're the only ones that seem to grow bigger with the years."

Perhaps Koufax does it best because he tries least. Williams and DiMaggio are both fiercely aloof. Koufax seems to tread an easy middle ground between pal and deity.

"This man was my idol," said young pitcher Robert Castillo, patting Koufax's embarrassed shoulder. "I snuck into every game he pitched."

At that, Koufax goes from eyes-down displeasure to mischief. "Well," said Koufax to Castillo, "where's the money? You can pay me now."

There is hardly a word strong enough for the way other players feel about Koufax; it almost goes beyond affection to a sort of total protectiveness for a man so gentle he seems misplaced in a jock shop.

"I played with Sandy in '66," said pitcher Don Sutton proudly. "It's like he's never been away. He's absolutely unchanged. He's the greatest, most sincere and humble . . ." Then Sutton stops, as if laying it on too thick might reflect badly on Koufax.

"He helped me as a rookie and he helps me now. If anybody ever deserved to be at the top of the ladder, it's him," said Sutton. "A lot of people look around to see how they can keep you from climbing up there with them. Sandy has always gone out of his way to pull everybody up there with him."

That desire to pull others up the ladder is part of Koufax's pleasure now. "Pitching is a branch of learning, no doubt of it," said the southpaw who struggled for six big league years as a 36–40 pitcher before suddenly learning control. "You're part of a chain that goes back for generations passing the art along."

For a man so reticent as to be a recluse by baseball's gregarious standards, Koufax is almost shockingly candid about the other reasons for his return.

"I need the money," he said. "I'm not destitute by any means, but I always knew I couldn't stay retired forever. I just wanted to stretch it as long as I could.

"It took me eight years (as a player) to get to twenty thousand dollars a season. Then I had only four more seasons, so you can figure that out. I did some TV announcing for NBC for five years [salary nearly $100,000 a year], but nothing since then.

"I'm like a lot of older people living on fixed incomes," said Koufax. "I need a regular supplemental income just to keep up with inflation."

Koufax has investments and real estate holdings, as well as a sports-medicine clinic in Eugene, Oregon.

"Sooner or later, you're going to say, 'That's enough of that.' You need to find something to do, another purpose," said Koufax.

"Also, it's hard to be away from possibly the only thing you ever did really well," he said, with an expression that looks more like hard insight than false modesty.

"Baseball is a way of life. It's pleasant to be in a large group with one pursuit — everyone working for the benefit of all. Other people find the same feelings in other ways. It's hardly unique to sports. It's like an orchestra making music together.

"Sometimes, on the right team, baseball can bring out a lot of the best in people. On the wrong team, I expect it can bring out a good deal of the worst."

Koufax, thanks to baseball, has always been able to lead a simple, untarnished, almost philosophical life.

"The game has a cleanness," he said. "If you do a good job, the numbers [statistics] say so. You don't have to ask anyone or play politics. You don't have to wait for reviews."

That pursuit of pure pitching performance remains an essentially untransmittable lesson. Like a Talmudic scholar, Koufax can pass on the letter but not the essential mystery of his pitching teachings.

"Success and confidence," he said. "Who can say which one comes first? It took me six years to get them, and I still don't know which led to the other or how they sort of fed on each other. It's like relaxation and concentration . . . they go together, but it's hard to learn.

"Pitching is a static situation. You initiate the action. That means you can develop a special depth of concentration."

None of that is altered by the years. "I feel perfectly at home," said Koufax, "because the game doesn't change. There's no proficiency without dedication.

"It's surprising that baseball hasn't had to update anything since Ty Cobb. On the ground ball in the hole, a fast man's still out by a step and a slow man by two steps."

That seems to please Koufax. He mulls it.

It is that silence and self-containment that have always set Koufax apart, made his psyche a parlor game for baseball psychiatrists. No man ever refused to pitch a Series game on Yom Kippur before Koufax. No man, for that matter, ever retired at his earnings and performance peak.

"My retirement was entirely a medical decision," Koufax says now, just as he said then.

That, of course, explains nothing. Hundreds of pitchers have had arm problems that turned arthritic, that threatened to become chronic and cause lifelong discomfort or minor deformity.

It is difficult to find a fan or athlete who truly has a feeling for how Koufax could walk away after a 27–9 season. Obviously, he still had a brilliant, if painful, pitching future ahead of him.

"I didn't believe it when I heard it," said Sutton, then a rookie.

"I called Sandy that day. He said, 'There are some things in life I might be jeopardizing, if I keep pitching with this elbow . . . you know, I might want to swing a golf club sometime during the rest of my life.'"

That brings us to the edge of Koufax, which may be as far as he will ever allow anyone to go. How is the great consuming public, avid for heroes, going to understand a man who forsakes fame simply because the idea of crippling himself, perhaps losing the feeling in his fingers, offends him deeply?

The pressure of the game did not drive him away. "Sometimes, you find that you like those extreme pressure situations," he said. "You like the responsibility. You know, sometimes the most terrified people do the best work."

The heat of the public spotlight burned him more than the heat of the mound. "You are part of an entertainment," he explained. "But you are not an entertainer. That is unnatural. But I enjoyed doing it . . . probably even more than the fans enjoyed watching. I thank them for enjoying it with me."

Even in that Southern California media whirl, Koufax maintained his privacy by refusing to do otherwise. "If you want your life to be private, it can be," he said. And that's that.

That wall of privacy is not topped with Ted Williams'

barbed-wire snarl but with a gentle, disquieting smile. Where was Koufax for seven years from 1972 to 1979? "Wherever I wanted to be . . ."

Koufax, in his blank-faced, enigmatic moments, can seem like a man protecting an enormous and simple secret that is more important to him than it could possibly be to anyone else. Like some adventurous introvert in a Joseph Conrad novel, he seems to have glimpsed a sobering heart of darkness either in himself or in the world.

When someone praises him too much, Koufax gives a weary, knowing look and says, "Who are we talking about? I don't think I know this person."

When a man says, in passing, "You know, Sandy, I think if I had to be interviewed as much as you, I'd crawl in that trunk."

"I'm tempted," says Koufax gently.

Yet, at other times, Koufax seems comfortably ordinary recycling the driest baseball cliché as though it were new. The clue, perhaps, is that Koufax has seen through the veil of his game. A sport can be extremely difficult without being extremely important. Baseball could fascinate him, but not control him.

"It is unfair to make comparisons. I don't want to be compared to anyone," he said, as though saying it one more time is unlikely to change anything. "I am just myself . . . the same person I have always been."

And who might that fellow be — that chap who retired at thirty, who has lived in blessed gossipless solitude with his wife since, and who has returned to baseball with such natural ease? That central inviolate self remains as untouchable as a Koufax fastball, as admirable as a Koufax curve.

Maury Wills and Mike Celizic

In Control

On the Run: The Never Dull and Often Shocking
Life of Maury Wills

I'm taking a lead off first base in the Los Angeles Coliseum. I have 92,000 people in the palm of my hand. I can make them go, "OOOOOOOH!" I can make them cheer. I can make them boo. I can make them kill the umpire.

They start chanting, "Go! Go! Go!" And, yes, I hear them.

I actually controlled people. I controlled ballgames. I always wanted that. I wanted things to be my way. I never wanted to consider anyone else if it interfered with my rhythm.

So I take my maximum lead off first, a lead big enough to make the crowd go, "OOOOOOOOOH!"

I build up to it. I know the pitcher is going to throw over. When I can get back standing up, that means I can take another step off the bag. When I have to dive head first to get back, that means I have my maximum lead.

Then I'd take another half step beyond that, so that when I dive back head first with my hands, I'm too far off to get back safely.

But I can take that extra half step and still be safe. I do it by taking my lead from the back edge of first base. I don't know how many ballplayers know this, but first base is 15 inches wide. If I take my lead from the back edge and the first baseman is standing at the front edge, that gives me an extra 15 inches to get back. That gives me the extra half step.

And I take that extra half step just so when I dive back the umpire has to get down on his knees — get down almost on his belly with both hands on the ground — to get down low enough to see if I'm safe. When I came up to the big leagues in 1959, the stolen base wasn't a big part of the game. Umpires stood with their hands on their knees a couple steps behind first base in a half-crouch. I got them so that they were right on my butt, right behind the bag and down on the ground. They got down like that in order to tell if the first baseman was just missing me by a fraction of an inch. That's the only way they could give me a fair shot. Otherwise, they had to guess.

And that just made the fans gasp.

There were times the play was so close that when the umpire got down to see it, he paused before he made his call. " ———— SAFE!" The margin between my hand hitting the base and the mitt tagging me couldn't have been more than one light block — you know, the time it takes for light to go one block.

Umpires like Ron Luciano loved it. Luciano was an American League umpire who got in on my act during the All-Star Game. He was a showman, too. I put him and the other umpires in the action and gave them a chance to be animated and on stage.

Now, when the throw comes and I dive back and the tag comes down, the umpire takes that little pause and you have 92,000 people not knowing whether he's going to call me safe or out. They catch their breath and then scream, "YAY!"

All I have to do is get too cocky and get picked off and maybe 92,000 people are going to feel like coming down out of the stands. They're going to boo that umpire something terrible. I mean, this is Little Maury Wills, the Darling of the Dodgers. This is the Coliseum. And I'm using all of that.

They're on the edge of their seats. The pitcher throws 10 straight times to first. Then, the first time he goes to the plate, BAM! I'm on second base.

And the crowd is cheering.

I stand up and dust myself off. The only thing that's dirty

is a little patch on my knee from my bent-leg slide. Today, players have to dust themselves off because when they slide head first they get dirt inside their clothes. They have to shake it off. But I slid feet first. I didn't have to take that kind of time. But I'm dusting my whole pants off. I'm walking off the base. It all takes time.

And the fans are cheering. They keep cheering until the pitcher is ready to pitch again, and he can't do that until I get done dusting myself off and get back on the base.

That's control.

I used to make things happen. Jim Gilliam, Wes Parker and John Roseboro were guys who didn't lose the game for us. They didn't make mistakes. They held the opposition and matched them. Then Maury Wills was supposed to do something to win the game. That's the way I saw my job. That's why I was always being innovative, trying to do something to win the ballgame because some Dodger teams I played for were not good enough to match the other team talent for talent and win in the conventional way. We had to do something different.

I remember a game that Warren Spahn pitched against us in the twilight of his career. He was old but he was still winning ballgames throwing what we call slop — a screwball here, take a little off there, bust a fastball in on your fists. It wasn't a real good fastball like he had early in his career, but it was fast enough when he had us leaning out over the plate looking for the slow stuff.

Spahn had us down, I think it was 1–0, and was throwing about a one-hitter in about the seventh inning. I went up and down the bench yelling, "C'mon guys! We're letting this old man beat us. He can't even move and here we are swinging from our heels because the ball looks big coming in. And we're walking back to the bench talking to ourselves.

"We got to bunt this guy," I said. "He can't field his position anymore. Let's bunt!"

I led off the inning with a bunt for a hit. Wes Parker came up. He laid down a bunt for another hit. Somebody else came up and laid down another bunt. Then somebody got a base hit and the next guy squeaked one through the infield somewhere. Before you knew it, we had about four runs, Spahn was out of there and we won the game.

Another time, we were playing the Giants at Dodger Stadium and Juan Marichal was pitching a 1–0 shutout going into the bottom of the ninth. It was late September, and we were fighting the Giants for the pennant. In the stands, the consensus was that every time a pitcher like Marichal, Sandy Koufax, Don Drysdale, Bob Gibson, Ferguson Jenkins, or Jim Bunning was ahead in the late innings, they were going to win the game.

The fans were booing us and getting up to leave. They were fighting, too. The Dodger fans were beating up on the Giants fans because they knew we'd lost.

I was 0-for-3 against Marichal and leading off the ninth. Jim Ray Hart, the Giants' third baseman, was playing way in to take away the bunt.

Marichal was a right-hander. He had this big motion and follow-through that took him toward the first base line. Normally, I didn't get into my bunting stance early, but this time I did. Hart saw it and came charging fast. Marichal was falling off the mound toward first. So instead of holding the bat loose to deaden the ball, I held it tight.

BAM! I bunted it hard right across the edge of the dirt past the charging Hart and to the third base side of the shortstop, Jose Pagan. I was on first.

People were coming back to their seats. The fighting in the stands stopped. There was something to watch on the field.

Jim Gilliam bunted me to second and somehow I got to third and scored on an infield out or a sacrifice fly and the score was tied, 1–1.

We finally won it in the 13th or 14th inning and I drove in the winning run. Marichal went all the way, but we beat him with that bunt.

Charlie Dressen and Leo Durocher used to say, "Hold 'em, guys, for eight innings while I think of something."

That was me. "Hold 'em, guys. I'll find a way to get us a run before it's over." A great many times I did. Those 92,000 people I had in the palm of my hand. All the cheers I heard in Dodger Stadium, the good memories. All the autographs I signed in the parking lot. They call that the big leagues. It's the highest level of baseball in the world.

For me, it was a tremendous feeling of power. It's what I always dreamed life should be. I was young enough to have the stamina and the strength. I was mature enough to have the knowledge, the wisdom and the courage.

I was in control.

And now, all of a sudden, came Judy and before I know it I'm an alcoholic and an addict. I could control 92,000 people and a ballgame, but I can't control myself.

Bob Welch and George Vecsey

Out of Control

Five O'Clock Comes Early

It all came to a head in San Francisco, my favorite city in the league. From the first time I visited the city, I felt as if I had discovered it myself, like Sir Francis Drake. I love the hills and the harbor and the food. Love going out and having a good time there.

I should have been in a good frame of mind going into San Francisco late in September because I had just combined with Joe Beckwith for a shutout earlier in the week, my first victory since May. But I was sulking about the season getting away from me, and I was out of control.

On Tuesday night, after our first game in San Francisco, I went to my favorite hangout — the Pierce Street Annex on Fillmore Street. I had discovered the place all by myself my first year in the majors. We stay at the Hilton downtown but I like some of the neighborhoods better. I hailed a taxi and told the guy I wanted a good local bar where you could hang out and listen to music. He took me to a section not too far from Fisherman's Wharf, to this bar with an open front and cartoons of some of the patrons hanging on the walls. Lots of guys, lots of pretty girls, lots of laughing and music. No sports motif at all. I don't think anybody cared about my being a ballplayer, although nowadays you might find a few of the guys in there when the Dodgers are in town. Even though I'm sober now, I still make a beeline for the Annex when I'm in San Francisco, to visit my friend Gary Ferrari, a big, tall guy with a beard who is one of the owners.

I closed the Annex both the Tuesday and Wednesday nights after our games in September of 1979, and on Thursday I flopped back there around noon, pretty well messed up from the night before. I had a few drinks at the Annex and then I joined Gary Ferrari and Mickey Hatcher, one of my teammates, for lunch. I love the seafood in San Francisco, can't get enough of it. Sole, crab, shrimps, calamari, you name it, man, and put some cocktail sauce on it. Gary took us over to Alioto's on the Wharf, where he knows the owners. We hung around the bar for a while and I drank six Seven-and-Sevens while we waited for a table. Just belted them down like water, with a couple of beers for chasers. Then we sat down and ate lunch and I must have put away a bottle of wine. I would have stayed there forever but Hatcher reminded me we had to pack and put our luggage on the team bus to the ball park because we would leave for the airport right after the game.

I had only thirty minutes to pack and catch the team bus but there was something I had to do that was even more urgent. I needed a drink. I called room service and persuaded them to send up a bottle of wine right away. As soon as the waiter was out of my room, I chugged down that bottle like a kid drinking water from a canteen on a long hike. Just glugged it down. Somehow I put my clothes in a suitcase and checked out of my room and stumbled to the team bus, carrying my overnight bag.

The bus was crowded because we had brought up a lot of younger guys from the minor leagues, so there was not much room. I had to stand in the aisle, holding my bag, and I couldn't manage to place it in the overhead rack. I was laughing and I was crying — out of my mind.

One of my friends, Gerald Hannahs, did not want me to get caught by Tom Lasorda, who always sits in the front seat, so Gerald got up and gave me his seat. When we got to Candlestick Park, somebody ran into the clubhouse and alerted Rick Sutcliffe that I was in bad shape. Rick had become my closest friend (I guess you'd say he was my protector) on the team. I had pulled Rick into my army, as they say at The Meadows, and now I was really going to make him serve me. Rick has since supplied me with most of the details for this ugly moment in my life, because I do not remember them on my own.

According to Rick, I was slobbering tobacco juice all over my suit, weeping out of control and saying, "I'm drunk, I'm drunk," which anybody could tell from looking at me. He hustled me into the bathroom and got me some hot coffee and tried to pour it down me. Although most people think this is a good way to treat a drunk, it is not very effective. Alcohol is one drug, one chemical, for which there is no antidote. There is nothing you can take to alleviate the effect of the drug alcohol. You have to wait until it passes through your system, doing whatever it will to your brain cells, your liver, whatever.

Rick somehow managed to get me dressed and he shoved me into the locker room and told me to take a short nap while the rest of the guys were out taking practice. I guess I slept a few minutes and then woke up again. The trainer gave me some more coffee but that only made me more hyper. I decided to go out and take practice.

The visiting dressing room at Candlestick is down a long runway from the rightfield corner. I stumbled down the runway and managed to push open the door and stagger onto the field. The Giants were taking batting practice and their guys were in the outfield shagging flies, but I decided to join them. I made one effort to catch a long fly ball and fell flat on my face. Couldn't take two steps. It was the way I had been in high school when I couldn't hit the back-boards with a lay-up during warm-ups. People in the stands must have laughed. Rick says I just keeled over, as if I were shot.

I didn't care. I wandered toward home plate, where some of the Giants were standing around, waiting their turn to bat. Rick had followed me, afraid I would do something dangerous, and his instincts were correct. I saw some of the Giants looking quizzically at me as I lurched toward the batting cage. I decided that one of them, Terry Whitfield, was making fun of me, which was probably not the case.

Nevertheless, I started cussing him out, in the worst language you can imagine.

Rick says Whitfield or anybody else would ordinarily start fighting at some of those words, but Whitfield apparently could tell I was not in my right mind. Rick says he shouted, "Terry, I'll explain later, don't think anything of it."

Whitfield did not go after me, although I understand I was challenging him to fight, shouting, "I want that man," like a regular Muhammad Ali. You have to understand, I did not even know Terry Whitfield. Had nothing against the man. Rick slapped me across the face five times before he could shove me into left field, away from Whitfield and the rest of the Giants.

Rick walked me around left field, where some of the guys were loosening up. I must have been a sorry sight, because some of our pitchers started staring at me. Burt Hooton called over, "Hey, Bobby, what's up?" which was all I needed. I cursed at Hooton, who came over to investigate, but Rick told Hooton, "Just leave him alone," which got Hooton annoyed at Rick. A few months later at The Meadows, Rick said he was still angry at me for getting him caught between me and Hooton, a friend of ours.

At the end of practice, Rick took me back to the clubhouse, where Lasorda was looking for me. He's got a few people on his staff who are supposed to keep him informed, and somebody had done the job.

Lasorda told me he had to file a report to Al Campanis because too many people had seen me drunk. Lasorda chewed out my ass for not taking better care of myself, which just made me madder.

"You don't give a shit for me as a person," I yelled at Lasorda. "You let me go to the bullpen and I hurt my arm and now everybody's down on me because I had a horseshit season. You wouldn't care if I got drunk if I could pitch. You just throw me out there to win for the team."

I had volunteered for the bullpen, but now I was making Lasorda the scapegoat, turning it all around. Because he had no way of knowing I am an alcoholic, he was trying to be reasonable with me, stressing the loyalty to Dodger Blue, urging me not to let my career go down the drain because of drinking. He kept saying he didn't want to hurt me but he had to tell Campanis because otherwise the front office would hear about it from some other source and get mad at him. In the meantime, Lasorda told me to stay in the clubhouse and sober up, which I did eventually.

The next afternoon, in Los Angeles, Al Campanis called me into his office, along with Lasorda and Red Adams, the pitching coach. Campanis said, "We've got information you're drinking on the plane. We warned you about bringing bottles in paper bags to your room" — which I never did — and he said he knew all the details of my drunken adventure in San Francisco the day before.

Lasorda said he was fining me five hundred dollars but that if I cut down on my drinking he would cut the fine in half by spring training. Campanis said, "I know what I would do if I were acting the way you are." His implication was that I should stop drinking altogether, that I just couldn't handle it.

The Dodgers also ordered me to see a liver specialist to determine if I had any malfunction or enlargement, since some people can ruin their health in a few months of drinking. The doctor did not find any damage but the Dodgers did implant in my mind the possibility of long-range physical harm from drinking. This scared me so much I got drunk during the final home games that weekend. Sneaked some more beers into the weight room.

By now everybody on the club knew about my behavior in San Francisco and were pretty much disgusted with me. Almost nobody talked to me that final weekend. I said to myself, "I'll show them," and I sneaked a few more beers and packed my gear and went home to Michigan, hardly saying good-bye to anybody.

When I got home, I could tell my parents were worried about me, too. They must have heard some of the stories, or maybe they just picked up on my actions. They didn't say much to me, however. I have come to realize this is a pattern in my family and in most families. Things go unsaid, even the most basic feelings. People think to themselves, "Well, they know how I feel." But it's much better to get it out, the way we later did at The Meadows.

My objective for that winter was to prove I did not have to get drunk all the time. I could tell that a lot of people were worried about me, and I wanted to stop. I worked out at Hamilton Place, a private club in Detroit, playing a lot of basketball. I even met a psychologist hanging around the club and thought about talking to him about my drinking. It hadn't dawned on me that I was an alcoholic, but I was beginning to realize I had some kind of drinking problem. I could go a few weeks without taking a drink, and then I'd have a beer or two and go out and get loaded. I could not stop, once I started.

Late in October, Dale McReynolds invited me to have lunch with him at the Rennaissance Center in Detroit. I think the Dodgers may have asked Mac to check up on me, and I agreed to have lunch because I really liked the man.

Mary and I drove into downtown Detroit, and over lunch Mac told me I was his No. 1 project for that winter. He said he was going to keep tabs on me, and he urged me to visit a hypnotist in Minneapolis who had worked with some other athletes' problems. I remember him saying, "Hell, it might even cure you of biting your nails."

I listened to Mac and agreed with everything he said, but I made that private reservation that I could drink with moderation. I was a little scared after fucking up in San Francisco and I wanted to stop for a while. Mac was telling me to cut down, but that wasn't enough for me.

In late November the Dodgers invited me to Toronto, where the baseball winter meetings were being held. Al Campanis asked me how I had done over Thanksgiving and I lied to him, saying I just had a glass of wine, when actually it was about forty beers, too. I was really trying, but there would always be a holiday or a family gathering I couldn't handle.

At Christmastime we visited my Aunt Lorraine and Uncle Art and I drank a whole fifth of C&C, got disgustingly drunk right in their house. I remember my father looking at me as if to say, "Son, there's a lot I'd like to tell you right now," but he didn't say it. I didn't give a damn, really. I was so badly drunk, yet I kept insisting I had to see my buddies at the Rainbow. I talked my father into driving out of his way to drop me off at the Rainbow, and later I passed out in Bryan's car and they just tossed me in the back doorway of my house.

Right after New Year's, Al Campanis called me again. He wanted to know how I had gotten through the holidays. Great, I told him. Just an occasional glass of wine with meals. He sounded skeptical on the phone and maybe a little unhappy I had been drinking at all. Maybe he knew more about my holiday drinking than I suspected. It's a possibility. The man did not discover Sandy Koufax and Roberto Clemente without having a few sources of information.

A few days later, Al's secretary, Marge, called me and said Al wanted to talk to me again. This time he said, "Bob, we'd like you to come to California and talk to somebody." I had just read an article in the *Sporting News* that the Dodgers had become the first club in sports to form an alcoholism program. I think I knew what they had in mind for me, but I really didn't ask. He said they had a plane reservation for me to come out and meet this person. I think they said he was a counselor.

I had been planning to go out to California toward the end of January because the Dodgers hold winter workouts in Dodger Stadium a month before spring training. It's a great time for baseball. While the rest of the country is freezing their ass off and watching pro basketball on television, the Dodgers get the jump on every other baseball team. You can tell it's time for baseball around the third week in January, right after the Super Bowl, because there's a picture of Steve Garvey wearing Dodger Blue, taking his first cuts of the season. I was ready for that.

But was I ready for what the Dodgers had in mind? If the Dodgers were going to start a program about alcohol abuse, maybe they were going to use me as a speaker, since I took a drink once in a while. This was my line of reasoning, at least outwardly, but I think deep down inside I knew they were going to do something about me and I was glad. I was out of control, I knew I had a problem, but I didn't know what to do about it.

Mary didn't have any idea what was going on. I took her to the train station to go back to Kalamazoo and told her I was going out to Los Angeles to take care of some business. She had expected me to stay in Michigan for a few more weeks, and she was sad that I was leaving. Her face was full of tears as I put her on the train, but I couldn't tell her what the Dodgers planned. I really didn't know.

The next day I was flying to Los Angeles to meet this counselor. My friends, Jeff McKinney and Janet Falendysz, were going to drive me to the airport. We stopped for a package of eight little Millers to tide us over on the way to the airport. On the way out, I was giving them this bullshit story about how the Dodgers wanted me to work with youngsters who had alcohol-abuse problems. As I described my future in the alcohol-abuse field, I belted down five of those beers in half an hour. Then I got on the plane and drank as much as the stewardess would serve me. When I got to Los Angeles to begin my new career as a counselor to wayward youth, I was halfway smashed.

From *Garvey*

It was in 1980 that I was contacted by *Inside Sports,* the magazine that had been started by *Newsweek* to compete with *Sports Illustrated.* A freelance writer named Pat Jordan wanted to interview me for an "in-depth story." Jordan had spent a brief time as a pitcher in the Braves organization and later wrote intelligently about the experience. I didn't give it any special thought; by then there had been many reporters and many articles. I said okay.

But when he arrived, he spent only a small amount of time with me, and considerably more interviewing Cyndy. It was a difficult time for Cyndy. The girls were now four and six years old, and she had been working in television in Los Angeles for about two years and doing very well.

That in itself caused some problems, though it was no different from the situation a lot of couples find themselves in today. Two people and two careers. I had my responsibilities as an athlete. She had her responsibilities as a television interviewer and co-host. And we had our responsibilities as partners in a marriage and as parents. Those conflicts had begun to pull us away from one another. And there were other problems, caused by baseball and the complex little world in which it exists.

Cyndy enjoyed the game. Growing up with two brothers who played baseball, and being married to me, she learned the game well. But even when we were first married and she'd make 85 to 90 percent of the home games, her interest was mainly in me. She'd watch the game, but she'd also bring a book. When I wasn't hitting, she would read.

After Krisha was born, Cyndy went to fewer games. And when Whitney came along — in the summer of 1976 — that number continued to drop. Once she started working, attending became even harder. She still made some games during the week, but mostly she came to home games on weekends. And whenever she did attend — in the early years alone, or later on with the girls — she drew a lot of attention. People had seen her on television, or in magazines and newspapers, and they recognized her. And the other players' children were naturally drawn to her; she is pretty, and very warm.

All of this helped separate her from the other wives. It was not so different from my own situation with many of the Dodgers. But while the players and I weren't close off the field, playing together gave the appearance of great friendship. The wives had only their off-field activities — socializing in the stands, or away from the park — and Cyndy was rarely a part of those.

Feathers were ruffled because of that, and I'm sorry. But she wasn't under contract to the Dodgers. Only I was. Still, she got dragged into everything. When the stories of my estrangement from some of my teammates implicated her, she took a lot of flack. As I said earlier, the argument with Don Sutton came to blows because he threw Cyndy into the mix.

It all put terrible pressure on her, especially when added to a series of horrendous incidents that included harassment and even death threats. Some came anonymously, made against me through the club, or were telephoned to the hotel where I stayed on the road. Some of the harassment was more direct.

One night, after a game at Dodger Stadium, a woman was waiting for me by my car. She was about twenty-five, wearing slacks, a blue windbreaker, and tennis shoes. She asked for an autograph, and I gave it to her. She said she wanted to talk. I told her I was late. She insisted; I apologized.

She was there the next night, and the next, and the next. She would stand in the way so I couldn't close the car door. The following night I had two plainclothes policemen go out with me, and she got violent. She scratched one of the policemen's face, drawing blood, and then turned on the other.

One day game later that season, Cyndy brought the girls. The woman saw them and almost knocked Krisha down the escalator. After the All-Star luncheon at the Biltmore Hotel in 1980, she was waiting by a side entrance, and when she saw us coming out, she elbowed Cyndy in the ribs, bruising her badly.

It got to the point where Cyndy couldn't show up at a game without being harassed by her — pushed and assaulted and threatened. I finally had to take out a restraining order, just so my wife could attend a game. Even after that, my mother-in-law saw her one morning walking on the street outside our house. She called the police, but the woman ran away.

These bizarre incidents added to the tensions that came along naturally with our own lives. I was in the midst of the consecutive game streak in 1980, and intensely involved with being the best ballplayer I could be. Cyndy, in addition to being a wife and mother, was making a name for herself in her own career, as Cyndy Garvey and not just Mrs. Steve Garvey.

At the same time she was living in another world, and there she was the wife of a professional baseball player and put under enormous pressure because of that. The pressure got in the way of everything she was trying to accomplish, and she felt great anxiety because of it.

That was the scene into which Pat Jordan stumbled. It never occurred to me that it would end up in the story; I thought the focus of the piece was baseball. When it came out, in the August issue of *Inside Sports,* I discovered baseball was not the subject.

The article, about nine thousand words long, was broken into seven sections of varying lengths, each bearing a short, almost accusatory headline: "THE WIFE," "THE JOB" (her job, not mine), "THE PROBLEM."

It all came under the title TROUBLE IN PARADISE.

Selected quotes from the *Inside Sports* article, along with the names of their respective sections:

The House

All the photographs were the same. Stylized. Posed. Perfect exposures without a blemish. . . .

All the mementos were the same. Unblemished. Disposable. There were no cheap objects purchased when the husband was struggling; no slightly more expensive objects purchased as the husband's fortunes improved slowly. There was no unused space. It was as if, for this family, all these expensive-looking objects were needed to fill in the gaps in their unformed natures.

The Wife

Cyndy Garvey is 30 years old. She is tall and thin. She has long blond hair. She is pretty in the manner of a Miss America contestant, a look she embellishes — bleached hair, heavy makeup — to give it distinction. It is a look thought glamorous in certain regions of this country, and despite her protestations ("I don't try to look this way. I just always was glamorous"), it is not a look acquired without effort. She claims her looks are a burden, which is not uncommon among women who have been pretty all their lives.

The Husband

Garvey hops up the dugout steps and breaks into a trot toward first base while his teammates are taking pregame batting practice. He moves precisely, almost in slow motion. He is conscious of the way he runs and of the fact that he is being watched. His pumping arms are properly bent into Ls at his sides, and held away from his body a bit, like wings, as if to keep his shirt from wrinkling. He resembles a man trotting to catch a bus in a new silk shirt on a hot day.

A fan in the stands calls out his name. Without breaking stride, Garvey glances back over his shoulder and smiles. It is an odd smile, both humble and smug. It is automatic, like someone who is used to smiling in public, even when the occasion does not demand it, just as a foreigner smiles too readily at things he does not understand.

There was much more, and very little of it pleasant. In describing me, in the midst of an interview with a sports-writer: "He looks down and flutters his eyelids as he speaks. It is meant to be a humbling gesture." Describing Cyndy in a restaurant: "It is the smile of a woman who thinks she is being sexy. It is merely a dessert filled with empty calories."

I read the piece over several times, and it was hard to know what angered me more — the quotes of Cyndy's words of frustration taken out of context, or the snide remarks. The agonizing thing is there was a real story he happened across, a story of people in transition, of a two-career family where both parties are highly visible, the pressure that creates; and mostly, the story of a woman finding her way in a world of shifting values.

Had he reported that story straight — let the people and the situation speak for themselves — he would have had something that said something important about our times. I might still have been upset to see it in print, but I couldn't have cried foul, and I would have had no legal recourse. But he didn't. By his nasty, condescending references to who we were and how we lived, his prejudice as a reporter distorted whatever merit the piece might have had.

I discussed the matter with Cyndy. Then we had a meeting with Alan Rothenberg, our lawyer. We talked about the legalities of the situation — what is malice, what is defamation. Then we discussed the chances of winning a lawsuit against *Inside Sports* and *Newsweek*. We decided to sue for libel.

In retrospect, it was probably a mistake. We ended up settling out of court. And while we pretty much broke even on expenses and legal fees, the enormous amount of aggravation is something you can't put a price on. The time, the anxiety, the strain, the trips to New York for taking depositions.

But we were so angry. We felt the whole thing had been so shabby, so immoral, that to accept it would be to compound the sin. What I wanted to do was to take the magazine by its corporate lapels and shake it. It wasn't just Pat Jordan. You don't have that kind of article, the length, laid out that way, with the juicy lines blown up as teasers, without an editorial decision saying, "Good, let's get 'em." What we probably should have done was to call a press conference, declare that the article was a collection of half-truths and quotes taken out of context, and walk away.

But it was getting more complicated by the minute. After the article appeared, the *Los Angeles Herald-Examiner* planned to publish a five-part series excerpted from it. *Inside Sports* and the *Herald-Examiner* are both owned by the Hearst Corporation.

We took out an injunction to stop them, at least till the libel suit was settled. The court issued a temporary restraining order, but in the meantime the *Los Angeles Times* printed pieces of the story, so we were surrounded by it.

Whatever strains existed between Cyndy and me because of the circus accompanying my life were magnified by the *Inside Sports* drama and the mass of publicity that it generated. Cyndy's difficulties with that circus were made the focus, so she received the bulk of the criticism. It was all very unfair, and it helped drive us apart.

The experience taught me something about the press that I had been slowly learning but did not want to confront. There are people in the business who enjoy discovering something and then building it up, and enjoy all the more tearing it down, destroying it in public.

Cyndy and I never introduced ourselves as the All-American couple. The press did. It's true that I enjoyed that image. I thought it was healthy and positive. And I did my best to live up to it. But I never said there were no flaws.

When flaws appeared in our marriage, the press jumped

all over us as if it were a personal offense to them, and began stomping on the image they had created.

It's all part of being a public figure, another lesson I was slow in learning. Though it would take me several more years to come to the decision, I finally concluded that the personal aspects of my life — such as with whom I am sharing my most private moments — are better left out of the news. I think my candor cost me in the past. I regret that I must be less open today.

Jim Murray

They Won't Call Him Dr. Zero for Nothing

The Los Angeles Times, September 28, 1988

Norman Rockwell would have loved Orel Hershiser. The prevailing opinion is, he wasn't drafted, he just came walking off a *Saturday Evening Post* cover one day with a pitcher's glove, a cap 2 sizes too big and a big balloon of bubble gum coming out of his mouth.

You figure his name has to be Ichabod. I wouldn't say he's skinny but when he turns sideways, he disappears. If it weren't for his Adam's apple, he wouldn't cast a shadow.

He's paler than Greta Garbo. He's so white you can read through him. If you held him up to the light you could see his heart.

He says things like, "Golly gee!" and "Oh, my goodness!" If he gets really upset, you might figure he would go to, "Oh, fudge!"

He can't really see without glasses and when he puts them on, people either think he's a sportswriter or a guy doing his thesis on major league baseball as a metaphor for the society we live in.

It should come as no surprise to anyone that he has a Roman numeral after his name. He is descended from the Hessian troops George Washington crossed the Delaware to defeat at Trenton.

He is about as far from the public perception of a major

league pitcher as it is possible to get. If you wanted to picture a big league pitcher, a guy like Burleigh Grimes would come to mind.

Some guys pitch out of a sidearm motion, others from a crouch, Grimes pitched out of a scowl. He had this big chaw of tobacco and a blue-black beard that could sand furniture, and the batter had 2 strikes on him stepping in.

Or you might prefer Big D, Don Drysdale. He pitched out of a towering rage.

Every batter was Hitler to Drysdale, or a guy who'd stolen his girlfriend. He threw the ball as if it were a grenade, or he hoped that it were. Big D didn't much care whether he knocked the bat off you or you off the bat. He hit 154 batsmen in his time — 155 if you count Dick Dietz in the ninth inning of a spring game in 1968.

If anyone told you Orel Hershiser is on the verge of breaking one of the most unassailable pitching records in the books, Don Drysdale's 58 scoreless innings, that this scholarly-appearing right-hander is almost certain to win this year's Cy Young Award, you might be pardoned for asking, "With what?"

Orel Leonard Hershiser IV does not intimidate the batter, although his 9 hit batsmen last year indicated it's not entirely a good idea to lean over the plate looking to get at the curveball when he's on the mound.

Hershiser throws ground balls. This is not to say his curve bounces but that his "out" pitch is a roller to shortstop. He throws a sinker, or what we kids in the old neighborhood used to call the drop. This is a pitch you hit on the top and it does exactly what a golf ball hit on the top does — it rolls along the ground till it hits something, usually an infielder's glove.

Hershiser also throws a heavy ball — as did Drysdale. That's a ball that comes up to the plate like a 16-pound shot. It can break your bat — and your wrist along with it — if you meet it squarely. Which you seldom do.

These are Hershiser's stock-in-trade pitches and he can put them pretty much where he wants them, but he cut such a less-than-commanding figure when he first came into the game that the brain trusters thought he was a relief pitcher. He pitched in 49 games 1 year and worked only 109 innings. He started only 4 games. But he finished 1.

One year, he pitched in 49 games, started only 10 but finished 6. Somehow the message began to seep through that this guy had better than 2-inning stuff and, when he came up to the Dodgers, he appeared in 45 games, started 20 and finished 8. Eight complete games is star billing in today's baseball, particularly for someone who spent more than half the season in the bullpen.

It's not that Orel Hershiser is your basic ragpicker or junk dealer. His fastball is a 90-m.p.h. horror that struck out 190 last year. Still no one calls him Dr. K or the Big Train. They might begin calling him Mister O, or Dr. Zero if he puts up 9 more innings of shutout ball. Dr. Zero has put up 49 in a row so far. Only two pitchers have logged more — Drysdale, 58, and Walter Johnson, 55⅔.

The record was once widely believed as unattainable as Joe DiMaggio's 56-game hitting streak.

Five shutouts in a season is Cy Young stuff. Five shutouts in a row is Hall of Fame stuff. Drysdale holds the record with 6 in a row in the National League, and you have to go all the way back to 1904 to find a pitcher with 5 in a row in the American League. (Walter Johnson set his scoreless-inning record with a lot of relief appearances.)

Drysdale's scoreless-inning progression was saved at Inning 45 in 1968 when, with the bases loaded, he apparently hit batter Dick Dietz. Umpire Harry Wendelstedt ruled that Dietz stepped into the pitch. Drysdale's argument was even stronger, "How can you hit a guy with a strike?" he wanted to know.

Hershiser's saver was an interference call on a base-running assault that broke up a double play and apparently let a run score. Umpire Paul Runge ruled that the baserunner neglected baserunning and would have gotten 15 yards in football for what he did to the pivot man in the double play. Runge called the runner out, which disallowed the run.

It's important to remember that Drysdale had to get 3 outs with the bases loaded after his incident in 1968. And Hershiser still had to get the next 9 outs in 1988.

Dr. Zero needs a 10-inning shutout to pass Drysdale. If he gets it, he may celebrate with a hot chocolate.

If he misses it, he'll say, "Oh, heck!"

Mike Downey

Joker, Ace of Hearts
Is Released

The Los Angeles Times, March 29, 1991

Very funny, go ahead and pull our other leg now. Monday is April Fools' Day, not today. The Dodgers released Fernando Valenzuela. Ha, ha. Sure they did. That is a hot one. And they traded Eddie Murray for Eddie Murphy. And they replaced Vin Scully with Vic the Brick. And they dumped Tom Lasorda and gave his job to Pete Rose. And they burned their blue caps because Peter O'Malley prefers pink. And O'Malley is moving the team to Brooklyn. No, Bakersfield. No, Tokyo.

Drop Fernando. Yeah. Get real.

What???

Oh, come on. You made the whole thing up.

Chavez Ravine without Fernando Valenzuela is like a deck of cards with no ace of hearts.

Freddie is everything you ever wanted from a Dodger. He is El Dodger. He belongs on that mound of dirt, tugging on that cap, tucking in that gut, rolling those eyeballs, hurling those screwballs. What more artful Dodger has ever there been?

Chalk up another loss for Los Angeles. First, Bo Jackson. Then, Mickey Hatcher. Now, 'nando. Is this spring cleaning or what? Like hey, don't take away our favorite athletes or anything. Next thing you'll be telling us, the Lakers will unload Michael Cooper and he'll have to go off to Italy or something.

Wasn't it only yesterday that Fernando's face was on a box of corn flakes? Didn't we see him on billboards from Echo Park to MacArthur Park? Wouldn't we hear about him in Johnny Carson or Bob Hope monologues? Weren't we just discussing last season's no-hitter or this spring's triumphant return to the land of his birth?

When was the last time any Mexican or Mexican-American in this country had been so immortalized, so respected, so adored? Who among his people — not Cuban, not Dominican, not Puerto Rican but Mexican — had ever represented an entire nation in American baseball more nobly?

Valenzuela was better known to the Spanish-speaking public than Venezuela. He was bigger than big. He was big in every way, from his paunches to his pitches. Those chubby cheeks gave him one of the most famous faces in the game, a one-of-a-kind mug, as readily identifiable as the angular jaw of Sandy Koufax or the handlebarred lip of Rollie Fingers.

Fernando wasn't some superhuman physical specimen. He was overweight and wore eyeglasses. He wasn't built like Bo Jackson. He was built like Keith Jackson. But he was as popular as Michael Jackson. And he meant as much to baseball as Reggie or Shoeless Joe. His body didn't make him what he was. His heart did. His soul did.

We don't mean to speak about him as though he died. But a little life did just ooze from the Dodgers.

It doesn't take a doctor of philosophy to understand the reasons behind the rise and fall of Fernando Valenzuela. This is nothing more than a management-labor thing, same way it was back when Fernando had the leverage, back when he was in control. He is an employee, not a dependent. He supports himself.

There was a time when he toured this country like a carnival. They called it Fernandomania and mobbed him like a Beatle. Thousands more bought tickets whenever he performed. News conferences were organized for a man whose every response at the time began: *"Bueno."* Little League lefties wondered how to throw the pitch that broke backward.

He never shot off his mouth in any language. He became a clubhouse comic, roping the calves of teammates with a little lasso. One day, when he wasn't looking, somebody handcuffed Fernando in the dugout. He sat there inning after inning, twisting his wrists, trying to wriggle free. It was about the only jam he couldn't get out of.

Valenzuela was valiant in victory and gallant in defeat. He contributed to his own causes by swinging a sweet bat, to the point that Lasorda often let him pinch-hit. If Roy Hobbs of "The Natural" could return to baseball as a hitter once his pitching days were over, why not Fernando? He can outhit half the Atlanta Braves as it is.

It seemed practically an umbilical cord that connected Valenzuela to the Dodgers. He seemed to have grown up with them. Corny old Lasorda couldn't help roasting him with one-liners like: "I knew Fernando when his alarm clock was a rooster." Lasorda loved this guy, loved conversing with him on the hilltop in Spanish, loved bumping bellies with him during we-win bearhugs. Letting him go like this, well, you can bet Tommy took it harder than Fernando did. A man got cut Thursday, but it was another man who bled.

So here comes the ultimate left-handed compliment.

Fernando Valenzuela, a Dodger forever.

Somebody handcuff him so he can't get away.

Tommy Lasorda and David Fisher

My Blue Heaven

The Artful Dodger

". . . join the Dodgers coaching staff." Danny Ozark was leaving to manage the Philadelphia Phillies and Roy Hartsfield was joining the Atlanta Braves as a coach, and they wanted me to fill one of the vacancies.

After four years of sending people up to the big leagues, my time had come. I just wasn't sure I wanted to go. "I don't know," I said. "Al was absolutely right, I really do enjoy managing. I'm not sure I want to give it up."

"You want to manage in the big leagues someday, don't you?" Peter asked.

"Sure. Course."

"Okay, well then, believe me, the easiest way to get a job is from the coaching ranks . . ."

I wasn't sure that was true. "Who gets to be President first, a senator or a congressman? There's a lot of guys who got major league jobs directly from the minor leagues. You know, you can get forgotten pretty quickly as a coach."

Peter paused. He knew me very well. "Tommy," he pointed out, "I'm confident you won't let anybody forget about you."

I knew I had no real choice. I'd spent too many years being loyal to the Dodger organization to refuse. If they wanted me to coach, I intended to be the best coach in major league baseball. The only thing that concerned me were the feelings of manager Walter Alston. I knew that the moment my promotion was announced people would begin asking if I was after his job. Well, I was after his job — but only when he was ready to give it up. "How does Walter feel about this?" I asked.

"He's all for it. He'll be glad to have you."

So, after a seventeen-year absence, I was back in the big leagues. I really was reluctant to give up the minor league managing job, I loved running my own team my own way and I loved working with the kids, but I'd been selling Los Angeles Dodgers baseball for so long I couldn't help but be tremendously excited.

Walt was extremely supportive. He told me I would be his third-base coach. And I told him how pleased I was to be working for him. "I'll try to be the same kind of coach for you that I would want working for me," I said.

I really was the obvious choice for the job. Seventeen players on the Dodgers' twenty-five-man major league squad had been with me in the minor leagues, and I'd worked with most of the others in spring training. My job was to supervise the pre-game workout, coach third base during games, do whatever additional chores Walt needed done, and help create a positive, winning atmosphere.

Walt Alston was a quiet, private, serious man. I was exactly the opposite. But it was a mix that worked very well. I had played for him in Montreal, I had worked with him while scouting, I had spent many years assisting him in spring training, and I ended up coaching for him in the major leagues for four seasons. Never once did he ask me to change or tone down my enthusiasm, and never, ever, did he appear threatened by my close relationships to the Dodger players. He knew that I was loyal to him, and the Dodgers, and he pretty much let me do whatever I wanted to do.

One year in spring training, for example, I established the 111 Percent Club for the nonroster players I was supervising. George Allen, then coaching the Los Angeles Rams, was quoted as saying his players gave 110 percent. I told my people I wanted even more than that. So each day John Carey, Del Crandall, Jim Muhe, and I selected a group of players who had hustled most that day, then the players voted for the winner. Naturally, we awarded outstanding prizes. Our first winner received a guided tour of the major league locker room, during which he had his photograph taken, in color, sitting in the locker of his favorite major league player while eating a major league ham and cheese sandwich. On another day the winner was allowed to use my personal electric heater. One of our most desirable prizes was the privilege of assisting the chief of clubhouse sanitation in feeding the ducks in the pond adjoining Holman Stadium. Still another winner had the honor of riding in the backseat of the car that drove to Melbourne, Florida, to pick up Don Drysdale. And our grand prize winner was invited to lunch with Walter O'Malley and *twice* during the meal was permitted to say, "Please pass the salt, Walter." You think there wasn't a lot of hustle in that camp? I'll tell you one thing, they never had an incentive program like that when I was playing.

On another spring training occasion, I thought I'd liven things up by putting a ringer into an exhibition game between our Bakersfield and Albuquerque farm clubs. Fred Claire, then a sportswriter for a Long Beach, California, newspaper, but now the Dodgers' executive vice-president, had told me he had played some baseball in school and asked permission to work out with one of our farm clubs. So I put him in uniform and sent him into the game to replace Dukes short- stop Bobby Valentine.

Bobby always disliked being taken out of games, but I told him Claire was a prospect we really wanted to look at.

Fred Claire distinguished himself in the field; he didn't get hurt.

When he came to bat for the first time I was sitting next to National League umpire Billy Williams. "Watch this kid, Billy," I said. "He's just out of college and we gave him a $100,000 bonus. He could be a great one."

Fred struck out on three straight fastballs. He didn't even foul tip a pitch.

Billy didn't know what to say. He hesitated a moment, then said softly, "I think maybe you paid $999,999 too much, Tommy."

As I promised Walter Alston, I did as good a job for him as

I would expect my coaches to do for me. Before games I'd pitch batting practice if the team we were playing was starting a left-handed pitcher, and I'd punctuate each pitch with a comment. "Hitting is the toughest thing to do in sports, Garvey," I'd scream. "If I throw ten pitches to the greatest professional golfer in the world, he wouldn't hit one, yet I could hit that golf ball nine out of ten swings!" After batting practice I'd hit hundreds of grounders and fly balls to fielders, using the long, slender fungo bat. I made those players work, warning them, "It's called a fungo bat because when I pick it up the fun goes out of the game," but I also tried to make it enjoyable, challenging them to catch a certain number in a row or trying to bang one off some part of their body.

When the game began I took my position in the third base coach's box. Not exactly in the box, but in the general vicinity of the box. I liked to move around, diving on the ground if I wanted my players to slide. I was an aggressive, gambling coach, and, like any gambler, sometimes I'd win and other times . . . Probably my worst moment came during our stretch drive in September 1974. We were tied with the Phillies in the ninth inning, two outs, Manny Mota on first base. Ken McMullen drove a line shot off the left-field wall. Greg Luzinski was playing left for the Phillies and I decided Manny could score easily. I waved him around third just as Luzinski made a perfect throw to shortstop Larry Bowa, who then made a perfect throw to catcher Bob Boone. Manny was out by fifteen feet. I wanted to dig a hole, crawl in, pull the dirt over me, and then plant it with sod so no one would know where I had been. I felt awful, terrible, and helpless, but there was nothing I could do about it. Fortunately, we won the game in the twelfth inning.

Walter never said a word to me about it.

But I continued to believe that aggressive baseball causes the defense to make mistakes. In a similar situation, we were tied with Montreal in the bottom of the ninth, one out, Joe Ferguson our runner on third base. Now once, when I was managing and coaching third base in the Dominican, Ferguson had been my runner on second base when Tom

Paciorek bounced a single past the shortstop into left field. Somehow, the outfielder picked up the ball and threw Ferguson out at *second base*. I couldn't believe it. I started screaming and yelling at Ferguson. He screamed and yelled right back, "Hey, Skip," he shouted, "what are you yelling about? That could've happened to anybody!" Happened to anybody? I had been in baseball twenty-five years and I had never seen a runner who started at second base get thrown out at second base on a hit.

So this time Ferguson, the potential winning run, was on third. The batter hit a routine fly ball to the Expos' Kenny Singleton. I knew Singleton had an outstanding throwing arm. I knew Ferguson had no speed. I remembered what had happened in the Dominican. But I decided to take a chance and send Ferguson to the plate. I don't know why.

Singleton's one-bounce throw had Ferguson beaten by twenty feet. But when it bounced, it hit a rock and sailed over catcher Barry Foote's head. Ferguson scored the winning run. Which again demonstrated to me that aggressive baseball — and a well-placed rock — can win ball games.

The thing I did best for Walter was help create a loose, happy ball club. I've always believed in laughter, because a team that is laughing is happy, a happy team is a relaxed team, a relaxed team is a confident team, a confident team is a winning team. Laughter is food for the soul, and I wanted any team I was with to be as well fed as I was. And Walt Alston let me have fun. We'd be on the Dodger plane, the Kay-O II, named after Walter O'Malley's beautiful wife, Kay, and I'd be walking up and down the aisle screaming "Remember this, gentlemen of the fourth estate. Remember this, Allan Malamud of the *Herald-Examiner*. Mark my words, Mr. Bud Furillo of KABC radio. Listen closely, John Hall of the *Register*. I hereby predict Bill Russell will hit .300 soon. He is capable of hitting .300 because he has extraordinary talents . . ."

Walter would be sitting in the front seat, listening, smiling, enjoying my performance.

". . . Bill Russell can run like a deer. He can throw like a rifle shoots a bullet. He can swing like a major league player. Most important, he wears the Dodger Blue. There is no better trademark. It stands for speed, strong bodies, .300 hitters . . ."

Russell would be shaking his head, his cheeks turning red, and smiling.

". . . There is no player on this team with blond or black hair. Russell's isn't red. Everything is blue. They say blue is supposed to mean sadness, but don't you believe it. I'm here to tell you right now blue is happiness. That's why blue is for boys. Boys are always happy in blue, especially Dodger Blue. That's why they called that painting a long time ago *Blue Boy*. That's why they called that song 'My Blue Heaven.' Look at Russell. He's an exact replica of that painting *Blue Boy*. Look at that smile. Would you call that sad . . ."

Writers Mel Durslag of the *Herald-Examiner* and Jim Murray of the *Los Angeles Times* would be desperately turning up the volume on their headsets. But I didn't care, I continued to tell my message to the world.

". . . I'll tell you what, Bill Russell. See this watch? It's expensive. It has everything on it. Instead of waiting until I die to will it to you, I'm gonna promise you here and now it's yours when you hit .300. And you're gonna do it, mark my words.

"You're gonna do it just as surely as the members of the fourth estate will finish their stories aboard this plane. Look at that Gordy Verrell type. Look at that Bob Hunter typing away. That's what you call dedication to Dodger Blue. That's why we took over first place in the National League today. We wanted to make their stories better. We did it for you, Gorden Edes, of the *Los Angeles Times,* and you Ken Gurnick of the *Examiner.*

"These great journalists deserve it! Look, all but one of them typing on a blue typewriter. Don't give that guy any answers when he asks you questions . . .

". . . We are going to fly over blue mountains. We are going to fly over the blue desert. We are going to fly over the blue chips of Las Vegas. We are going to fly over the blue pools of Palm Springs. We are going to land in the blue smog of Los Angeles International Airport. I love the smog as much as I love rain. Rain isn't really bigger than baseball. I don't see why we have rainouts. Anyone in Dodger Blue should love to play in any kind of weather.

"Look at you, Ron Cey, the Penguin. I named you the Penguin because you are a cold weather man. But I have supreme confidence that you're a special kind of penguin. You will make an effort to acclimate yourself to hot weather. You'll open up a whole new world for all those other penguins who are afraid to get out of the cold.

"We'll have penguins at Catalina. We'll have penguins at Dodger Stadium. We'll have blue penguins instead of black and white. I love penguins. That's why you, Penguin, are going to be the best third baseman in the history of the game. You don't want to let me down."

Fortunately, it was not difficult for me to carry on a monologue like this for an entire plane trip, or for four seasons.

I wasn't the only one on the team who told the jokes, or played the jokes. Sometimes, in fact, the jokes were played on me. I became the outlet, the target, the member of management on whom employees, or management, could play jokes that everyone would enjoy.

Once, for example, during my first season with the Dodgers, I found a letter from Peter O'Malley waiting for me when the team arrived in Houston. When I opened the envelope, I discovered that the first page was missing. But the second page read, "and very serious consequences involved, I'm sure you will agree, Tom, that I had no alternative but to give them the information they requested. I certainly hope that this will in no way affect our friendship. Peter."

Serious consequences? No alternative? Them? What "information"? I had no idea what this letter was about, but I was extremely concerned. I immediately called Peter's office. He wasn't there and was not expected. I called his home. He wasn't there either and no one knew when he would be back. I went to the ball park, but I couldn't concentrate. I was really worried. I couldn't even guess what this was about. I must have said a hundred prayers at third base that night, and none of them were for the team.

The one thing that never occurred to me was that this was a practical joke. I was so used to playing jokes on other people, I didn't expect them to play them on me. This, of course, was unlike the Attack of the Green Phantom, which I knew was a joke. Or at least I think I knew it was a joke.

The Green Phantom first appeared in spring training. One of my real peeves was players who spent too much time in the trainer's room. "When I was pitching," I'd complain, "the only thing our trainer had was one bottle of rubbing alcohol, and before the game was over he'd drink it." Consequently, I rarely used the whirlpool or other devices in the trainer's room. One day, though, my arm stiffened up and I decided to give it a whirlpool treatment. Since I didn't want the players to know about this, I enlisted John Carey as a guard. "I want you to warn me if any players are coming in the locker room while I'm in the whirlpool," I said.

"Here, Tom," he said, handing me a straw, "if anyone comes in, take this straw, duck under the water, and breathe through it."

A few minutes after I got into the whirlpool, John warned me that someone was coming and I ducked under the water, breathing through the straw. Unfortunately, someone twisted the end of the straw protruding out of the water. I almost drowned.

When I went into the clubhouse the next day someone, or something, had painted across the whirlpool "U.S.S. Lasorda" and signed it "The Green Phantom."

A few days later I found a can of ant spray and a can of weed killer in my locker, with labels pasted on them reading "Lasorda's Shaving Lotion" and "Lasorda's Deodorant." Both were signed . . . "The Green Phantom."

Naturally, the entire squad was as concerned as I was about finding out the identity of this perpetrator. "I can now deduce that this Phantom has a college degree," I told the team when I found those labels, "because he spelled the word 'deodorant' correctly. That immediately eliminates half the people in this room."

The next night the Phantom removed all the furniture, including my bed, from my room, leaving a baseball, painted green, and a clue. The clue led to an abandoned storage room in which I found my furniture. The day after that the Phantom painted everything in my locker green — my shoes, gloves, shorts, my uniform, everything was green. "You have to pay the price," I said, "and I'm paying for it."

Throughout the entire spring the Green Phantom plagued me. He had me called out of the Dodgertown movie theater to receive a telegram that had no message — but for which I had to tip the delivery boy a dollar. He wrote me threatening poems and he challenged me to uncover his identity. Of course, I knew who it was the entire time. I figured it out right away. But everyone in the camp was enjoying this duel of wits so much I didn't want to spoil their fun. Really, I did know. Honestly. The Green Phantom was . . .

I can't. I would like to reveal his identity, but I believe there are some things better left inside the clubhouse, and this is one of them.

The one thing Al Campanis and Peter O'Malley both requested when I joined the Dodgers was that I please, please do not get into any fights. They pointed out that my temper might prevent me from getting a big league managing job. I knew they were right, and I told them they would not have to worry about me getting into fights anymore, those days were over, done, finished. It was different when I was an active player, or an active scout, or a minor league manager, then I was practically required to fight. "I've hung up my fists," I said.

And I kept that promise too, at least for the next five months.

In August, we were in San Francisco for a weekend series with the hated Giants. The hated Giants were managed by Charlie Fox. I'd managed against him in the minor leagues, so we knew each other. In the seventh inning of the Friday night game, Giants relief pitcher Elias Sosa decked our pitcher, Andy Messersmith. Both benches emptied, but no punches were thrown. I knew Sosa from the Dominican, and we had had problems down there, so I really let him know how I felt about him. I hit him with a barrage of threats, calling him every unpleasant name I could think of, some of them more than twice.

On Saturday morning, I was standing near the batting cage when Charlie Fox came over to me and said, "Don't be getting on my pitchers no more."

"I will if I want to, Charlie," I told him, "because that guy's a ——— no-good ———. He was throwing at our players all winter and he's doing it again."

"Yeah? Then why don't you say it to me? You do and I'll kick your ———. How come you didn't look for me in that fight last night?"

The players around the cage waiting to hit thought we were kidding. I didn't know about Fox, but I knew I was serious. "'Cause you're too old," I told him, "but if you want me, the only thing between us is daylight." That was it. He came right at me and I took a couple of shots at him. He swung at me, but missed. Then, just as I was getting warmed up, my own catcher, Chris Cannizzaro, and Giants coach John McNamara grabbed Fox, while Giants coach Joey Amalfitano held me.

"That's enough," Chris was screaming, "that's not necessary, 'specially before a game. During the game is different." And when Fox refused to calm down, Chris added, "Come on, Charlie, don't you realize you're being restrained by two guys who were signed by the same scout?"

Other than that, though, my fighting days were about over.

Ironically, Sosa was one of my better relief pitchers when I took over the Dodgers, and Amalfitano became my coach.

As I knew would happen when I accepted the coaching job, sportswriters and fans immediately began speculating that I was in line for Alston's job. Every time a writer needed a story, he wrote some version of "Is Tom Lasorda the next Dodger manager?" I began to think my name was "heir-apparent Tom Lasorda." No matter where I went, no matter what group I spoke to, I would always be asked, "Are you going to be the next Dodger manager?" It was tough. It was hard. The Dodgers already had a manager, and he was my friend. I always responded the same way. "Of course it's everybody's ambition, including mine, to manage the Dodgers, if and when the time comes. I just hope Alson lasts a long time. I played for him six years. He's a great man to play for and work for.

"I've never been told the job will be mine when Walt steps down, but I know that when that happens the O'Malleys and Al Campanis are going to find the best man they can for the job. I just hope and pray that my contributions and dedication will warrant my selection."

I was being truthful, the Dodgers had made no promises to me. When Walter O'Malley was asked if I would succeed Walt, he said, "When Walter Alston leaves, Tommy certainly would be high on our list of candidates. He knows baseball, he knows our organization, he knows our personnel. He was a big winner as a minor league manager and he is great at teaching young men how to play this game. He also gets along well with veteran players and this is important. But he'd have to go through a screening process with a lot of other people. And if we did pick him, it would be for a variety of reasons and not just one."

I was certainly not the only candidate mentioned. For a while, Gene Mauch was supposed to succeed Walt. Then there was speculation that Jim Gilliam, who had played for Walt, managed in the Winter Leagues, and was with me on the coaching staff, might get the job. There was nothing any of us could do but wait, wait until Walt decided to retire.

To make my situation even more difficult, writers began naming me as a candidate for every managerial vacancy. At various times I was supposedly offered jobs in Atlanta, Montreal, Pittsburgh, and Kansas City. I tried to be honest with the writers when they asked me if I'd be interested in these jobs. "I've been in the Dodger organization for twenty five (or twenty-six or twenty-seven or . . .) years and I don't want to leave. But all of these players I brought up aren't getting any younger and I'd like to manage them in the majors before they get much older. If I was offered another job I'd first have to talk it over with Peter O'Malley. If he told me to stay, I would, because I want to stay with the Dodgers as long as they want me. But I would ask him how long I'll have to wait to manage here. If it was a long time, I would have to consider other offers."

And there were other offers. I met with John McHale, general manager of the Montreal Expos, for three hours in a conference room at Denver airport. If I was not going to manage in Los Angeles, Montreal would be very attractive to me. It's an outstanding city and I have many wonderful friends there. At the conclusion of the meeting John McHale told me I'd be hearing from him in a few days.

I really hoped he would not offer me the job, it was a decision I preferred not to have to make. But a few days later I was at Dodger Stadium, preparing to leave for the Dominican to manage the Licey club, when McHale called. Peter O'Malley knew what the call was about and suggested I take it in his office. "Tommy," John McHale said, "we'd like to offer you a three-year contract to manage the Montreal team. I know you're leaving for Santo Domingo, and there'll be a ticket for you there to fly to Montreal to meet our reporters . . ."

There it was. I finally had to make a choice. Take the offer and become a major league manager at a salary almost twice what the Dodgers were paying me, or wait, with no guarantee I would get the job when Alston stepped down.

I just couldn't see myself telling people about the Big Expo in the Sky. "John," I said, "you're one of the finest people I've ever met in baseball and I truly appreciate your considering me. I'm extremely honored, but I'm afraid I'm going to have to turn down the job."

"You know," he said pleasantly, "I had a feeling you were going to say that."

"Lemme tell you this though. If I ever left the Dodgers, it would have to be for a man like you. But I'm just not ready to go yet." When I walked out of the office, Peter looked at me questioningly. "I turned it down," I said.

"Good," he said, and that was all he said.

Later, when I told Al Campanis I had decided to stay in that third base coach's box, he said, "Tommy, wouldn't it have been terrible if you took another job and then saw another man named manager of the Dodgers?"

He was right, it would have been terrible. And so I waited.

But there were moments during the 1976 season that, as I was standing in the vicinity of the third base coach's box, I thought to myself, Can you believe you turned down a job that would have doubled your salary? That you could have been managing your own club? And when we played the Expos, I did find myself staring into their dugout and wondering what it would have been like to be sitting there.

I just couldn't do it. Jo and I both agreed, we had too much love for the O'Malleys and the Campanises and all the people with whom we'd spent so much of our lives to leave the Dodgers. Now, with no guarantee, I had proven my loyalty. It was just a matter of time until I found out if the Dodger organization felt that same loyalty toward me. Deep inside, I believed that it did.

I didn't exactly wait quietly, that wouldn't have been me. Los Angeles is the entertainment capital of the world and, because I was not exactly the average seen-but-not-heard third base coach, I began receiving some attention. A lot of attention, actually.

My television career had begun in Kansas City in 1956, when I appeared on the action-packed show "Bowlin' with Dolan," and won a banlon shirt. After that, I often appeared on the local sports shows in Pocatello, Ogden, Spokane, and Albuquerque. I was a household name in Ogden, Utah. In 1972, when I was managing Albuquerque, a local station did a half-hour documentary about me. And my first national appearance came on my friend Joe Garagiola's "World of Baseball."

Joe and I had known each other for years, and once I had taken him to a party at Joe Ferguson's house. As we drove there, I told him, "Joe, I'm gonna show you something today you have never seen in your entire career in baseball."

He laughed. "I've been in baseball a long time, Tommy."

I laughed too. I knew what I was going to show him.

At Ferguson's, after I'd introduced Garagiola to everyone there, I said loudly, "Paciorek, come over here." He did. "Tell me something."

Wimpy dropped to his knees, lifted his head to the heavens, and screamed, "I *LOVVVE* the Dodgers."

"And the Dodgers love you, son," I said. Then I yelled, "Charlie Hough, get over here." Charlie came right over. "Charlie Hough, tell me something."

Charlie dropped to his knees, lifted his head to the heavens and screamed, "I *LOVVVE* the Dodgers."

Garagiola's mouth was open and no words were coming out. I knew this was something he had never seen before. "And the Dodgers love you, too, son." Lopes. Crawford. Ferguson. Russell and everyone else there followed. And it was not a case of me showing off what these players would do for me, it was all of us showing what we could do together. And having a good time doing it. It was the beginning of an outstanding party.

The following winter Garagiola invited me to lunch. Any time anyone wants to see me they can guarantee I'll show up by inviting me for a meal. "I've been thinking about this for a long time," Joe said. "That thing you showed me at Ferguson's party, can you get those guys to do it on television?"

"Joe," I replied, "I can get those guys to do it on Fifth Avenue in New York City during the Christmas rush hour!" Garagiola showed up in spring training with a camera crew and we taped an entire show.

By 1974, Garagiola was announcing NBC's "Game of the Week," and he was trying to do some things that had never been done before. In order to give the fans a taste of what it was really like to be down on the field, he asked me if I would wear a microphone while coaching third base. Me? Talk? I would've paid for the microphone.

With the permission of baseball commissioner Bowie Kuhn, the Dodgers, and Walt Alston, I was miked during a Dodgers–Chicago Cubs game. My mike would be activated when the Dodgers were batting in the second and fifth innings. While my mike was on, the announcers would not say a word. It was just me and the entire United States of America.

Was I nervous? Did I feel any pressure? Pressure, I believe, is what you put on yourself by worrying about failure. When you know you are going to succeed there is no pressure. I knew I'd be fine, it was the players I was worried about. To make things interesting for the viewers, the players had to provide some action. When nothing's going on, third base can really be a wilderness outpost.

Nothing happened in the second inning. I did my best to fill the silence, talking about getting signs from Alston and relaying to the batter. When Billy Buckner smashed a line shot through the infield I said, "Gee, the way we're hitting the ball, they better get those married people off the infield or somebody's gonna get killed."

If the fifth inning wasn't more exciting, I realized, my show was going to close on opening night. As we came to bat in the fifth inning I could see that Cubs pitcher Ken Frailing was starting to get tired. "Put the camera on Frailing's face," I said. "Get a good look at him. There is a man who did not sleep well last night. He was awake all night, tossing and turning, worrying about facing this great Dodger ball club."

We got a couple of hits and Penguin came to bat. I knew he was going to save me. "Ron Cey, the Penguin, is at bat," I said, "and if Frailing tries to get a low fastball by him, he's going to hit it up in the seats." On the next pitch, the very next pitch, Frailing tried to throw a fastball past Cey and the Penguin hit it up in the seats. Talk about a star being born on one pitch. Penguin hit the home run, but I got the credit for it. As he was rounding the bases, I was whooping it up for him, and as he ran by me, I said softly, so that only America could hear, "Thanks, Penguin, for making me a hero."

Garagiola's producers liked it so much they gave me the greatest possible reward: They turned on my mike for another half-inning.

The success of that appearance led to others. A contestant on "Truth or Consequences," for example, was told he would be dressed in a Dodger uniform and brought to Dodger Stadium, where I would instruct him how to catch flies batted by Tommy John.

That's exactly what happened. Tommy John knocked some insect-type flies out of a glass jar and the contestant tried to catch them with a butterfly net as I shouted, "Keep your eyes on the flies, don't take your eyes off the flies."

That was a considerable advancement from "Bowlin' with Dolan," but nothing like what happened after I'd managed the Dodgers to the 1977 pennant. Then I was invited to appear on some of television's most popular programs, including "Today," "Tonight," and "Tomorrow," as well as "Dance Fever."

Los Angeles is a city of celebrities, and it is impossible to work for the Dodgers without meeting many of them. Movie and television stars are baseball fans just like everyone else. Once, for example, Jo and I were at Robert Wagner's birthday party when we were introduced to Bette Davis. In Ogden, the biggest celebrity we'd met was the owner of the big used car lot, so we were both in awe at meeting Bette Davis. "Miss Davis," I said, "it's a tremendous thrill to meet you. I've always considered you to be the Sandy Koufax of the film industry."

That was my way of saying I thought she was the very best, but I wasn't sure she understood what I was talking about until she responded, "I felt so sorry for the Dodgers last week when Joe Morgan hit that hanging curve for a home run." Bette Davis, I discovered, was almost as big a Dodger fan as I was.

The only celebrity outside of baseball we knew when we moved to California was Chuck Connors — and we knew him from baseball. But gradually we began to meet some of the people who had given us so much pleasure over the years, among them comedian Pat Henry, who was Frank Sinatra's opening act.

In 1976 the Dodgers were in Chicago and I was with Al Campanis and one of my closest friends in the world, Eddie Minasian. When Eddie mentioned that Pat Henry was also in town, we left a message at his hotel telling him where we were. About 10 o'clock that night Pat called and said, "Come over here right away. I told Frank you called and he'd like to meet you."

I didn't have to ask who Frank was anymore than I would've had to ask who Babe was. There was only one Babe, and there is only one Frank. We went right over to the hotel, and Pat brought us in to meet Frank Sinatra.

For me, this was like meeting Babe Ruth, or the President of the United States. When I was growing up in Norristown I idolized Frank Sinatra. I was so proud of him, an Italian boy like me, the son of immigrants like me, from a poor family like me, growing up to be cheered by millions and millions of people.

Frank Sinatra, I found out, had been an outstanding Dodger fan since Leo Durocher had been one of Walt Alston's coaches. So we talked baseball for a while, and then he said to me, "You should be managing the Dodgers."

That was always a tough spot for me to be in. I didn't want anyone to believe I had anything but the utmost respect for my boss, so I gave him the stock answer, "If the Lord's willing, I will be someday."

"I'll tell you what," he said, "when you become manager of the Dodgers, I'll come out and sing the National Anthem for you."

I knew he was kidding, but I appreciated it. I've done some exaggerating in my time, but even I wouldn't tell too many people about this. They might have believed me when I said Gabby Hartnett had been an outfielder, they might have believed me when I told them about the man who drowned four yards offshore, they even might have believed that the greatest team in sports history had lost nine games in a row. But Frank Sinatra singing the National Anthem at

Dodger Stadium for me? There are some things even I don't believe.

As it turned out, I didn't have much longer to wait. I was sitting in the locker room after a game on September 28, 1976, when someone came in, I don't remember who it was, and said, "Walt's just announced his retirement."

I took a deep breath. This was it, this was the moment I'd been waiting for. Alston's announcement took me completely by surprise, he hadn't said a thing about his plans to anybody. I just sat there. I don't know what I expected to happen. I didn't know if Peter O'Malley and Al Campanis were going to announce that someone else had been hired to manage the Dodgers. I was caught halfway between my dream and reality. So, not knowing what else to do, I continued doing what I had been doing after thirty years of baseball games, getting dressed to go home.

Before I left Dodger Stadium that night Peter O'Malley found me and told me point-blank that I was the leading candidate to replace Walter Alston, but that no final decision had been made. He promised he would call me the following morning at 9 o'clock.

Normally, in our home in Fullerton, the telephone rings every minute, twice a minute. I usually let Jo answer it, in case the caller is someone I don't want to talk to, although, as Jo points out, we've been married more than three decades and there still hasn't been anybody who has called that I didn't want to talk to. But that morning I guarded the phone. I didn't let Jo or either of the kids use it. I just sat there, waiting. Fortunately, our phone is in the kitchen, which made the waiting slightly easier. I knew Peter's call was going to change my life. I was either going to be the manager of the Los Angeles Dodgers or a soon-to-be former Dodger coach. If the Dodgers didn't want me, I knew some team would.

I waited. Have you ever seen a telephone grow? This one did. As it got closer to 9 o'clock that telephone got bigger and bigger.

I was confident I was going to get the job.

On the other hand, Jim Gilliam was a tremendous man, no one could criticize his selection. Maybe I was a little too flamboyant. Maybe I yelled a little too much. Why hadn't Peter said something more positive the night before?

At 9 o'clock, exactly, the phone did not ring. A year later, at 9:02, Peter called and asked me to come to his office.

That was the longest twenty-five miles I have ever driven. They've got to offer me the job, I kept thinking, I know they're going to. But maybe they aren't going to offer me the job and Peter wants to explain why not in person. I tried to concentrate on keeping my car on the freeway.

I sat down in Peter's office and crossed my hands in my lap. "Tommy," he said, "we'd like to make you manager of the Dodgers . . ."

I breathed for the first time in hours. I had hoped, I had prayed, many people told me I was going to get the job, but until Peter said those words, there were always doubts in my mind. "Peter," I said, making one of the greatest understatements of my life, "I accept. This is the greatest thing that has ever happened to me . . ." I felt so good, so proud; my love for the Dodgers, my loyalty, had been repaid. Only in America could the son of an Italian immigrant, a runny-nosed little left-handed pitcher with a decent curveball, a player good enough only to be the third-string pitcher on his high school baseball team . . . grow up to become the manager of the greatest team in baseball.

I immediately called Jo. "I got the job," I said.

"I knew you would. I'm so proud . . ."

"I got the job."

"You deserve it, too. You worked so hard . . ."

"I got the job."

Sports reporters were waiting in the stadium club for the announcement of the new Dodger manager. Most of them believed the official announcement was only a formality, assuming I had the job locked up. But as they waited, and waited, one writer said loudly, "Anybody see [Dodger coach] Jeff Torborg here yet?"

Finally, I walked in with Peter, Al, and Walt Alson to meet

the reporters for the first time as Dodger manager. "To be named manager of the Dodgers," I began, "to replace the greatest manager in baseball . . . well, it's like inheriting the Hope Diamond.

"I believe managing is like holding a dove in your hand," I continued, "if you hold it too tightly, you kill it, but if you hold it too loosely, you lose it."

A reporter asked the question I would be asked all winter, would I continue to socialize with my players. "That depends," I admitted, "on who's paying the check. Look, I happen to believe I can be close to my players and still command their respect. I love my son, Spunky, but I discipline him when he needs it. I'll do the same thing with my players."

Another reporter asked if I hoped to match Walt Alston's twenty-three seasons as manager of the Dodgers. "All I want to do is live twenty-three more years," I answered. "I'm forty-nine now and that would put me at seventy-two and that ain't bad!"

After the press conference, I did my first interview as manager of the Los Angeles Dodgers. My friend, baseball's greatest announcer, Vin Scully, asked, "You're replacing a legend, don't you feel that puts a lot of pressure on you?"

Walter Alston had managed the Dodgers in Brooklyn and Los Angeles for twenty-three years. The only two men in baseball history to manage one team longer than that were Connie Mack, who owned his team, and the New York Giants' John McGraw. Walter won more than 2,000 ball games, he won seven pennants and four World Series. He was a certain Hall-of-Famer. Did I feel any pressure in replacing him?

"Vin," I answered honestly, "I'm worried about the guy who's gonna replace me. That's the guy who's gonna have it tough."

Walter Alston and I both had bittersweet feelings. I knew he was happy for me, but sad to be leaving the field. I was thrilled for me, but also sad to see my friend taking off the uniform for the last time. He asked me to take over the team for the final four games of the season. "But bear down," he warned me, "because these four games count on my record."

In a vaguely similar situation when I was an active player, Walt selected Karl Spooner to pitch instead of me. This time, he gave me the decision. The Dodgers won my first game as manager, beating the Houston Astros 1–0.

The telephone rang continuously for months as reporters called from all over the country. "I have a wait problem," I told them, "I can't wait for the next season to get started because the Dodgers will be champions in 1977." They asked about the length of my contract. Alston had signed twenty-three one-year pacts. "I signed a multimonth contract," I said. How much? "I told Peter O'Malley he wasn't a very good businessman. If he had waited a little longer I would've agreed to pay him more." Seriously, how much? "I never looked at the figure. Let other people hold out, I'm just thrilled to be holding on."

But the one question I was asked repeatedly, on the day I was named manager, throughout the winter, and every day in spring training, was: How could I expect to remain close to my players and still command their respect? No manager in baseball history had socialized with his players the way I did, and certainly no manager had ever gone around hugging them. A number of sportswriters predicted the "Dodger Love Boat" would spring a leak the first time we lost four or five games in a row. Other people said knowingly that I had been able to get away with that kind of behavior as a coach because I didn't have to discipline the players, but I would not be able to act the same way as a manager. It was as if I were introducing something dangerous to baseball, rather than mutual respect between me and my players. It was the same criticism I had heard in Pocatello and Ogden and Spokane and Albuquerque, and I had my answer down pretty good.

"When I was growing up," I explained, "my father would put on his blue sports jacket with a pair of green pants. 'Pop,' my brothers and I would tell him, 'you can't wear that coat with those pants. They don't match.' And he would say,

'Yeah? Who wrote that rule? You show me a law in the United States of America that says I can't wear this coat with these pants!'

"I don't believe there's a law that says a manager can't be friendly with his players and still command their respect. There's no rule prohibiting me from telling my players that I think they're great, because I do think they're great. Let me ask you, if I'm invited with four of my players to speak at the Lions Club, where do I sit? Am I going to sit with my players? Of course. So what's the difference if we don't get invited to the Lions Club and just go out to eat together?"

Among the first calls I received after being named manager was from Frank Sinatra's secretary, Dorothy, asking me when I'd like Frank Sinatra to sing the National Anthem at Dodger Stadium. He had remembered, he had been serious. "Well, I think it would be great for him to sing it on opening day next season," I said, "because that's when I officially start. We can start out together."

I hadn't been kidding reporters when I told them about my "wait" problem, I really couldn't wait for the 1977 season to begin. I wasn't just taking over a team, I was taking over the team of players I'd grown up with in the minor leagues. Steve Garvey, seven years in the big leagues and still looking as if he'd just stepped off the Michigan State campus, was my first baseman. Davey Lopes, who I'd heard before I'd seen one day in Vero Beach, was my second baseman. Billy Russell, the red-headed kid who had worried about being cut from my Pioneer League team, was my shortstop. And the great Penguin, a man who failed to beat me in pool for an entire season in Albuquerque, was my third baseman. Rich Rhoden and Doug Rau, who I'd had at Triple A, and Happy Hooton, who I yelled into losing weight in the Caribbean, were three of my five starting pitchers. Charlie Hough, the former infielder who I stuck on the pitcher's mound and convinced to learn the knuckleball, was my leading reliever. And my pitchers were going to be caught by Steve Yeager and Joe Ferguson, who caught them in Albuquerque. In all, eighteen players on the roster had been with me in the minor leagues or Winter Leagues. So I wasn't just taking over a team, this was my family.

A few people were missing. Valentine broke his leg crashing into a wall for the Angels and his career was in jeopardy. Wimpy Paciorek had been traded to the Braves in 1976. And, just after I had been named manager, Mad Dog Buckner was traded to the Cubs. Trades are made by general managers, not managers, and we needed a centerfielder who could run. I came home one afternoon and found Jo sitting there crying. "What's the matter?" I said, fearful that something had happened to one of our kids.

In a sense, I was right. She had just heard on the radio that Billy Buckner had been traded. These kids were hers as much as mine, and it just broke her heart every time one of them left. My explanation that we needed a centerfielder really did not make her feel better. The centerfielder we got, ironically, was Rick Monday, who had played for me on the Dodger Rookie team I'd managed during my scouting career, and who almost signed with me. Well, I had finally gotten him.

The Dodgers had finished 10 games behind Cincinnati in 1976, the second consecutive year we'd trailed the Reds. In both seasons we'd been out in front and in both seasons we let the Reds catch us. My job in 1977 was to find eleven games.

I had no doubts we would do it, and told anyone who asked every time they asked. I knew my players were better than the Reds' players, I just had to get a little more out of them. My philosophy of managing had always been basic: If I put on a hit-and-run play, or Sparky Anderson puts on a hit-and-run play, or Chuck Tanner puts on a hit-and-run play, the success of that play does not depend on me, Anderson, or Tanner. The best we could do is get the right player up at bat at the right time. So I concentrated on getting the maximum ability out of each player.

I started by writing a letter to every player on the team. "Dear Steve," I'd write, "it is a privilege and honor to have been selected your manager. We have the nucleus of a very fine ball club. Each player is gifted with talent and will play a major role in the success of the Dodgers, but there is only one way we can win a pennant and that is for twenty-five players, the coaches, and manager to pull and work together. We have to be totally involved and totally prepared . . ."

Then I visited or spoke to every player. I told them exactly what their role on the team would be and what I expected from them. I called Billy Russell in Oklahoma, for example, and asked, "Is there a wall by the phone?" There was. "Well, write on that wall 35–45. Got that? Write 35–45."

"I got it," he said, "but what does it mean?

"That's how many bases you're going to steal this year," I told him.

I told Garvey we needed home run power from him. "You had 200 hits in '75 and '76," I pointed out, "and look where we finished. You hit 13 home runs last year and I know you're capable of doing better than that. When you come to bat in the late innings with men on base, I don't want you thinking base hit, I want you trying to jack that ball out of the park."

"Every time you open a game by getting on base," I told our leadoff hitter, Davey Lopes, "you're going to be stealing. I want you running with reckless abandon, but I want to see more discipline from you at the plate. If you can get 100 walks, combined with your 150 hits, you can be the best base-stealer in baseball."

We'd gotten Dusty Baker from the Braves in 1976 to provide the power we'd desperately needed, and he'd hit a very disappointing four home runs for us. A lot of people were saying the trade had been a mistake, and that we needed an outfielder to take his place. "You haven't heard that from me, though," I told him, "and you won't because you're gonna be my left fielder from the first day of spring training to the final game of the World Series. I've seen the way you run, throw, hit for power, and hit for average when you're healthy, and I know you can do it again." I told reporters that Dusty had been a great player and "we weren't guessing when we traded for him," and that I was confident he would be a great player for the Dodgers.

Right fielder Reggie Smith had acquired a reputation as a malcontent while playing for Boston and St. Louis. "Reggie,"

I said, "I've been watching you play for three years. I know how good you are, and I'm relying on you to demonstrate your superstar talent. I need you. I really and truly need you, and I want you to help me."

Reggie looked at me and said, "You know, nobody's ever told me that before." I knew at that moment that Reggie Smith was going to have some kind of season in 1977.

I spoke to everybody, not just the starters. I didn't want any player on the club trying to guess what his role would be. I told my reserves they were like understudies in a Broadway show. They had to understand how important their jobs were and they had to be ready to play if anything happened to one of our starters. Baseball is a team game played over a long season, I reminded them, and the best *team*, not just the best collection of players, wins.

Once everyone knew what I expected of them, I made some changes in our batting order. I moved Russell from eighth to second to take advantage of his speed and his ability to make contact and hit behind the runners. I dropped Garvey from third to fifth, moved up Reggie Smith to third, and Cey to the cleanup spot, so pitchers, knowing Garvey was following them, couldn't afford to walk them and would have to give them good pitches to hit.

On the first day of spring training or "refinement of capabilities camp," as I prefer to call it, I said, "I'm tired of watching someone else in the World Series. What we're striving for is to win the World Series. That is our supreme objective. If you players believe as much as I believe, then I have the utmost confidence we'll do it.

"Unity, hard work, confidence, and ability to execute, coupled with the fact you guys are outstanding players, will enable us to reach our goal if we're willing to pay the price. It's not always the strongest who wins the fight, nor the swiftest who wins the race, nor the best team who finishes first, but the one who wants victory the most."

From the first workout of spring I kept my eight starters together. Yeager, Garvey, Lopes, Russell, Cey, Smith, Mondy, and Baker practiced as a group, played in games as a group, and got taken out of games as a group. Before the exhibition season opened, I kept them together on their own practice field, away from everyone else, like a heavyweight champion preparing for a title bout. During exhibition games, when one played they all played and when one rested they all rested. "They're the Octopus," I told reporters, "because if you're lucky enough to hold down one tentacle, another one will rise up and get you."

This had never been done before and, naturally, a lot of people knew it wouldn't work. I had them running in the outfield as a group before a game with the Reds, and my former teammate, Cincinnati manager Sparky Anderson, predicted, "By September they'll all be running in different directions."

"Sparky's right," I said, "they're going to be running in eight different directions — to get to eight different banks to deposit the money they receive for winning the world's championship."

We had an outstanding spring, winning 17 of 24 exhibition games, the best record in baseball, as well as leading the league in reporters, photographers, and autograph seekers. I tried to answer every question, I know I signed every piece of paper put in front of me, and I tried to heed the sage advice once given to me by Stan Musial. "Always stand in the middle when you're having a group picture taken," Stan the Man told me, "because that way they can't cut you out of it."

The first thing I did when we got back to Los Angeles to open the season was move the manager's office. Walt had operated out of a tiny space barely large enough for him and one coach leaning in the door. He was happy there. I took a large trainer's room, moved the whirlpools to another empty space, and installed a desk, some chairs, a couch, a television set, a refrigerator, and a beer tap. I made arrangements to have food, I mean real food, delivered to my office after every game. I wanted that office to be a place that my players felt comfortable walking in and out of, where they could sit down and have something to eat, watch television, even use my telephone — for local calls. I wanted to create a relaxed, enjoyable atmosphere.

I hung a lovely photograph of Jo, Laura, and Spunky on the cement wall. Then I was ready to start the season.

How could any baseball season that begins with Frank Sinatra singing the National Anthem turn out to be anything but sensational? There were a lot of people watching the Dodgers carefully to see how the team reacted to me. If we had gotten off to a poor start, the critics would have been all over me. I suspect that more than one person would have said that I had been proven wrong, you just couldn't treat ball players like people.

On the first very pitch of the very first game of my very first season as Dodger manager, the hated Giants' Gary Thomasson hit Don Sutton's fastball for a home run. Some way to start a season, or a career. After that, however, the rest of the game, and the season, was tremendous. We won that first game 5–1. Then we won 21 of our next 25, giving us the third best season-opening record in baseball history. We won 10 of 11 on our first road trip. By May 13, we were 11 games in front of the second place Reds, the largest lead any Los Angeles Dodger team had ever enjoyed. Penguin, getting better pitches to swing at because Garvey was batting behind him, hit .429 with 9 home runs and a record-setting 29 runs batted in for the month of April.

"You're doing pretty good now," read a telegram from comedian Don Rickles, who had become a close friend, "but if you start losing, don't tell anybody you know me. P.S. Do you really know Sinatra?"

Not everybody was impressed, of course. Now that I had proven I could manage a major league ball club while it was winning, people wanted to know how I would react when the team suffered its first, inevitable, losing streak.

"I never even thought about it," I told a Philadelphia reporter who asked.

"You must have," he insisted. "You've sat and watched this team lose for the past two years. You must have thought about how you would handle a losing streak."

"I haven't. I don't know why you even ask that. Why think about losing?"

"Because it's inevitable," he answered.

"Tell me something," I countered, "are you gonna pay your taxes next year?"

"Sure."

"Have you thought about it?"

"No."

I smiled. "See?"

Sparky Anderson wasn't impressed either. "We've given them a good lead," he said. "It doesn't bother us. They always come back to us in July. Don't ask me why, but they always come back to us."

"Sparky's entitled to his opinion," I responded. "Opinions are like rear ends. Everybody's got one."

Sparky responded to that by calling me "Walking Eagle," claiming "He's so full of it he can't fly."

Still, we kept winning. It was a season in which I tasted the fruits of victory, and then tasted some more of the fruits of victory, and then a little more. The fruits of victory, I learned, are not low calorie. Reporters began calling me "a heavyweight among managers" as I gained thirty-five pounds. And Steve Garvey, my friend Steve Garvey, noted, "The only thing Lasorda hasn't handled this season is his weight."

Once, I remember, I was sitting in my office before a game, enjoying a plate of linguini, getting ready to throw some batting practice, when Al Campanis walked in. "Gee," he said, "Earl Weaver looks at computers before a game, my manager eats linguini."

"It's for my health, Al," I explained. "It's like a heart stress test. Let me ask you, where does Sears test its Die-Hard batteries, Malibu, California, or Anchorage, Alaska? They take 'em to Alaska and bury them in ice. Then, if they can start a car, they can start a car anywhere, right? Now if I go out there and throw 300 pitches after eating a big plate of linguini and my heart holds up, it'll hold up under any circumstances. So I'm really eating this for the good of the Dodger organization."

As I had hoped, my office became a gathering place for my players, their friends, friends of their friends, people waiting for a bus, reporters, and, naturally in the entertainment capital of the world, entertainers. On a typical night during the season it was possible there'd be more celebrities in my office than at the Beverly Hills Hotel Polo Lounge. Milton Berle, Jack Carter, Walter Matthau, Robert Wagner, Norm Crosby, Tony Orlando, Ron Masak, Vic Damone, Jerry Vale, Harvey Korman, Ernie Banks, or Gregory Peck might just walk in. It was incredible to me that these people would wander into the office of the son of an Italian immigrant, a runny-nosed little left-handed pitcher with a decent curveball, a player . . . There were nights that we had more people in my office than some clubs had in their ball park. So I began to fix up the place a little. Put some wood paneling on the walls. Threw an outstanding Dodger Blue rug with the Dodger emblem on the floor. And I began hanging up a few photographs of some of my players, some celebrities, then a few more photographs, and just a few more, maybe a couple on the far wall, two over the door, and eventually most of the four walls were covered. I did, however, restrict the wall opposite my desk to photographs of my friend Frank Sinatra.

Sinatra earned that space. Not just by attending Dodger games or singing the National Anthem, but by being there when I needed him. After my mother suffered a stroke, and was in very poor health, Sinatra found time to go to Norristown and spend an afternoon with her. I had done a lot of things in my lifetime to make my mother and father proud of me, I had married an outstanding woman and had two wonderful children, I had become manager of the Los Angeles Dodgers, I had helped people whenever I could, and I earned a good living. But the day Frank Sinatra showed up at my house in Norristown, I was made.

A few days after his visit, he had a limousine pick up my mother and, accompanied by a doctor and a nurse, she was his guest at a concert. He gave her flowers, he took her around to meet everyone, and gave her one of the last great evenings of her life.

A few months later her health got much worse, and the family gathered in Norristown. I remember sitting alone with her, talking about my father, their life together, my four brothers and the very successful restaurant they had opened in Exton, Pennsylvania (in which they raised the price of a Tommy Lasorda Special from $3.50 to $12.50 the day we won the pennant). I told her I believed I had been the luckiest man in the world that my father had lived long enough to see his sons happy and successful, that I was proud of her and I hoped she was proud of me. Later, when my brother Joe was with her, she asked, "How much does Tommy get for making a speech?"

"Twenty-five hundred dollars," he said, shaking his head. No one in my family could believe people would actually pay to listen to me.

"Give him the whole twenty-five hundred," my mother told Joe, "'cause he just made the best speech I ever heard."

One of the people I became close with that season was Don Rickles. Although he seems hard and tough on the outside, on the inside he really has a heart of lead. Because I didn't want his feelings to be hurt when I gave Sinatra an entire wall, I gave Rickles his own corner. And, after we'd clinched the pennant, I put him in uniform one day and let him work as a ballboy. I told him I could only pay him $15 for the game, but promised him top billing over the other ballboys. That was enough for him. The primary job of a ballboy during the game is to run from the dugout to the home plate umpire to give the umpire new baseballs when he needs them. Rickles did an excellent job throughout the game; he didn't drop one ball and he didn't get lost.

From opening day to the final day of the 1977 season, we were never out of first place although we did falter a bit after the All-Star Game. In late August I felt the team was starting to coast on its 9½-game lead and called a clubhouse meeting. The meeting lasted fourteen minutes and I told them exactly what I thought of the way they had been playing ball. After the meeting Don Sutton handed me a note. "Congratulations," it read, "you have just set the all-time record using a certain four-letter word 124 times, by precise count, in fourteen minutes." We then went out and beat the Cubs.

To make the season even sweeter, we clinched the Western Division championship against the hated San Francisco Giants. I remember sitting in the dugout, watching the final out of that game, feeling so elated, so proud. These really were the kids I'd grown up with in baseball. I'd taught Russell how to hit a curveball, I'd moved Lopes to second base, and here they were dethroning the world champion Cincinnati Reds. It was a feeling of culmination. We had finished ten games behind the Reds in '76, and beat them by ten in 1977, an incredible twenty-game turnaround. We had proven that ballplayers could be hugged and still play winning baseball.

I'd yelled, I'd screamed, I'd argued with my players. I don't keep anger inside me very well. And when we did fight I reminded them that the reason a jockey in the Kentucky Derby carries a whip is because even the greatest racehorses have to be reminded to do what they know how to do from time to time.

Every player contributed to the victory. Garvey hit 33 home runs and knocked in 115, 35 more than in 1976. Russell hit .278, the best he had ever done. Yeager lifted his average 42 points while hitting a career-high 16 home runs. Reggie Smith had the best year of his career, batting .307 with 32 home runs and 104 RBIs. Dusty Baker had a tremendous season, .291 with 30 home runs. The Penguin had career highs of 30 home runs and 110 RBIs. Davey Lopes hit .283, 42 points higher than '76, and knocked in 33 more runs. For the first time in Tommy John's outstanding career he won 20 games, while losing only 7. Burt Hooton won 12, lost 7, and had the lowest earned run average of his career to that point. Rick Rhoden had a career-high 16 wins against 10 losses. Doug Rau was 14–8, and Charlie Hough led the relief corps with 22 saves.

Not one player set a baseball record, no one led the National League in any significant category, and all we ever did was win the pennant. The team set two records, however. Never before in major league history had four players on the same team each hit 30 or more home runs in a season. On the last day of the season, Garvey, Cey, and Smith had their 30, Baker had . . . 29. It came down to his last at bat. Houston's J. R. Richard was on the mound. Every player on our bench was on the top step, screaming for Dusty. And when he hit the home run to set the record the dugout exploded. It was as if we had . . . the pennant.

Our other record was really set by our fans. We shattered a fifteen-year-old attendance mark by drawing 2,955,087 true blue Dodger fans to Dodger Stadium, or what I had started to call "My Blue Heaven on Earth."

The Philadelphia Phillies had won the Eastern Division title, and we met them for the right to represent the National League in the Fall Classic. The Phillies won the opener of the best-of-five series, 7–5. I was disappointed, but encouraged by the fact that we had fought back from a 5–1 deficit to score four times off Steve Carlton. Still, we had a difficult task ahead of us, we had to win three of four games, and three of them were to be played in Philadelphia.

I wanted to give the team a lift the next day, so for one of the few times in my career, I brought a guest motivator into the clubhouse before the game, our former ballboy, Don Rickles. "Look at Lasorda," he began, "look at that stomach. You think he's worried about you? No way. If you guys lose he's gonna tie a cord around his neck and get work as a balloon."

Rickles had kind words for everyone. Tommy John, for example, was sitting in front of his locker wearing long johns. "Look at him," Rickles said, "he makes a million dollars a year and he's wearing trick-or-treat underwear.

"Lee Lacy, what're you laughing at? You're the only one on this team *owing* points on your batting average."

Rickles looked at Dusty Baker and threw both his arms straight into the air. "It's okay, Dusty, I'm clean. I'll give you everything, the house, the wife, just don't get mad . . .

"Oh, Davey Lopes, I want to tell you, it's okay. I spoke to my neighbors. You can move in Friday . . ."

We beat the Phillies three straight games, proving some team will do anything not to have to listen to another lecture from Don Rickles.

The fourth and final game was played in a rainstorm. The

Phillies' Veterans Stadium had an artificial surface, and many people thought I was making a mistake starting sinkerball pitcher Tommy John. John depended on his sinker causing batters to hit groundballs, and groundballs shot through that plastic infield. I didn't even think about not starting Tommy John. I remembered what Walt Alston told me as I led cheers from the Brooklyn Dodger bench in 1954, you go with the people who got you there. Tommy John was an outstanding pitcher who would've started that fourth game for me if we were playing on ice. He pitched a tremendous game, giving up only seven hits in winning, 4–1.

After the game, some Philadelphia reporters complained that the game never should have been played under those terrible conditions. "Conditions?" I screamed. "Are you kidding me? This is the most beautiful night of my life."

We drank champagne that night and the fruits of victory never tasted sweeter. "Tell Peter O'Malley he'd better get a vineyard," I shouted, "because we ain't gonna stop winning. We have tasted the fruits of victory, and we love it."

I had come a long way with these players, from squirting shaving cream at each other to celebrate winning the Pioneer League pennant to champagne as National League champions. "There's nobody in the world who can knock a tear out of me," I admitted, "but tonight there are tears in my eyes."

I spent half the celebration dousing people with champagne and the other half reminding my players, "Four more yards! Four more yards to shore!" We'd won the pennant, but now we had the World Series, the Fall Classic, in front of us.

It was a tremendous matchup. For the first time since 1963, the Dodgers were to meet the New York Yankees for the championship of the world. Me managing against Billy Martin, with every seat in the ball park filled and every television set in the country turned on to watch us. I was returning to Yankee Stadium, the ball park of my dreams, the place where I'd marched out of the bullpen in a meaningless exhibition game to get out Yogi Berra, the place where I'd fought Billy Martin, and Hank Bauer, and I was returning as manager of the National League champions. It was fall, and the thrill was in the air. I was going back in style.

I've been in a lot of ball games in my career. I've seen a lot of batters get a lot of important hits. I've seen almost anything that can happen on a ball field happen. Certain moments are unforgettable, of course. Reggie Jackson's three home runs on three swings in the final game of the '77 Series. Rick Monday's two-out home run in the ninth inning of the '81 playoffs off Steve Rogers to give us a 2–1 victory and the pennant. The historic confrontation between Bob Welch and Reggie Jackson in the ninth inning of the second game of the '78 World Series. The controversial play in the fourth game of the same Series when Reggie deflected Russell's throw to first base with his hip, turning the game, and the Series, around. The determination of young Fernando Valenzuela in the third game of the '81 Series when he gave up nine hits and seven walks, but staggered to a 5–4 victory. I can remember each one of those as if they took place yesterday, but don't ask me if Hooton pitched the second or the third game of the '77 or '78 World Series. After more than three decades of baseball, the details begin to blend together into a lovely Dodger Blue. Did Sutton pitch a particular game in the '77 or '78 World Series? Did that play take place during the '72 season or was it '75? Who made that catch? Monday? Guerrero? Did Fernando pitch the fourth game or the fifth game?

I do remember what Reggie Jackson did to us in 1977, though, I remember it very well. He killed us. In six games he hit 5 home runs, knocked in 8, scored 10, and hit .450. It had started out to be a tremendous Classic. In the first game we scored in the ninth to tie the score 3–3, but lost in twelve innings, 4–3. We had had some opportunities to win, but couldn't pull the trigger. In the second game, Burt Hooton pitched the biggest game of his life, holding the Yankees to five hits and beating them 6–1. So we had split a pair of games in New York, and we were going home to our stadium and our fans for the next three games. I was confident we were going to be the 1977 world champions.

It did not happen precisely as I had planned. Mike Torrez beat us 5–3 in the third game. Doug Rau started the fourth game for us and the Yankees started banging him around in the second inning. I went out to the mound to bring in a relief pitcher — and Dougie didn't want to come out. We had an argument on the pitcher's mound in Dodger Stadium in the fourth game of the World Series. "There's a left-handed hitter coming up," the left-handed throwing Rau said. "I can strike this guy out!"

"Yeah?" I replied, but not precisely in these words. "Then how come the three runners on base are all left-handed hitters?" Rick Rhoden relieved and pitched seven solid innings, but it was too late. We lost game four, 4–2.

We were down three games to one, and two of the remaining three games were scheduled to be played in New York City. I called a clubhouse meeting before the fifth game. If we lost it, the Series was over. I didn't scream, I didn't blame anybody, I just told my team exactly what I thought of them. "You beat one helluva club this year in Cincinnati," I said. "Then came the playoffs and everybody thought Philadelphia was going to wipe you off the face of the earth. We split two games with them here in Los Angeles and nobody gave us any chance when we had to go back to Philadelphia. But we beat them there.

"Now we're two down with the Yankees and we've got to win the next three. I know you can do it. The odds against winning three games in a row are very high, but if we win today, then we only have to win two in a row, and those odds are much lower. In my heart I honestly feel we have the better ball club. I honestly feel if we win today, we're gonna win all the rest of the games. But whether we do or not, I want you to hold your heads up high. Regardless of what happens out there today, I want you all to know how proud of you I am, and I want to thank you for everything you did this year."

Davey Lopes led off the game with a triple. Russell singled him home, and we beat the Yankees 10–4.

In the sixth game, the last game as it turned out, Reggie Jackson put on one of the greatest displays of power in baseball history, hitting three home runs on the only three swings he took in the ball game, to lead the Yankees to an

8–4 victory. He hit the first one off Hooton, the second off Sosa, and the last shot, a titanic shot, off Charlie Hough's knuckleball. I knew I was watching history being made, but that didn't make me enjoy it. Charlie told me that after Reggie hit the third home run and was trotting around the bases, he was watching him and thinking, What a season that guy has had tonight.

"Don't feel bad, Charlie," I said, "that guy's hit a lot of them before tonight."

But Charlie pointed out few of them had gone quite as far as that last one.

In the second game of the Series, a foul ball had bounced off the ground and hit my catcher, Steve Yeager, in the groin. He was in tremendous pain, balancing himself on his hands and knees, trying to get his breath back. I put my arm around his shoulder and said softly, "It'll only hurt for a little while."

That's the way I felt about losing the 1977 World Series. As I told my team, next to winning the World Series, the best thing that could happen to a team was losing the World Series, that there were twenty-four other teams who would have loved to have been right where we were. I just didn't want that loss to spoil an otherwise perfect season.

I flew home to Los Angeles, and I was sick to my stomach for a week — and I had a lot of stomach to be sick to. But once the depression had worn off, I was able to appreciate the season. The United Press International voted me Manager of the Year, which I knew really meant team of the year. The "Love Boat" hadn't sunk. We'd shown our detractors that a manager and players who liked each other could win, win often, and win big.

Naturally, a few weeks after the World Series, reporters began writing that my love-'em-and-hug-'em philosophy had worked one season because it was new and because the team had gotten off to such a tremendous start we never faced adversity. That glow would wear off, they predicted. And how would I react when we didn't win the pennant?

"I hope I never find out," I said.